AN EVIL WIND

AN EVIL WIND

MICHAEL FRASE

Dedication —

For Bill & Rioko...
wonderful people too far away.

&

For Anita...
the best person I know.

"American blood is the best, and we will taste it soon. We will raise our flag over the White House and put our foot on the neck of your President."

ISIS

PROLOGUE

Saturday, 15 August—Termez, Republic of Uzbekistan,
six miles north of the Afghanistan border

THE SHORTEST OF THE five hooded men slumped slowly forward, exhausted beyond measure and unable to keep his eyes open another minute. There would be no escaping for now.

He understood this clearly in his mind, but his spirit, though weary to the bone and nearly broken by fear, refused to bow to the certain death that slithered nearby like a viper waiting patiently to claim him.

To claim them all.

Salty droplets of sweat stung his eyes and seeped into his ears. Hot breath, coming in anxious, shallow stabs, filled what scant space remained within the tightly drawn hood, like an oven whose door had been slammed shut. Every breath he exhaled felt as if it were cooking his flesh.

He was certain he would go completely mad before they finally ended his life, and yet apparently indifferent to his approaching insanity, the relentless siren of sleep intoned her sweet song of repose over and over and over again. If he could just rest for a few hours, even a few minutes, he could continue to resist, perhaps even manage to free himself somehow.

He only needed to sleep, to pull the warm blanket of oblivion over a body that was dog tired and racked with pain.

He was a stocky man in his late forties with thinning black hair and broad, rounded shoulders. He appeared more suited to an office than this hostile land in which he had fought for—how long had it been now? He could not recall exactly.

Too damn long, this much he knew.

Fading steadily with each passing second, he felt himself surrendering to the hypnotic melody of nothingness. The inner voice of resistance was now less than a whisper. It was like the memory of a whisper; a gossamer web loosed from its anchorage and floating as vapor itself on a distant breeze.

His chin now met his chest, the slow, steady descent as sure as night following day. Suddenly, a resounding rap to the side of his head from the wooden butt stock of an AK-47 slammed him back to reality.

"Stay awake, you dog!" his assailant ordered in Pashto. "You can sleep in hell after you're dead."

A lightning bolt of pain shot through the stocky man's skull as he ground his teeth together hard enough to erode the enamel. He felt a small stream of blood mingling with the ceaseless flow of sweat that had now completely blocked his left ear.

As his head began to clear from this latest assault, his mind returned to the moment the nightmare had begun, when he and his team had been taken to this godforsaken place by the thugs who now had them bound like pigs for slaughter.

But where had they been taken? he wondered, though he dared not speak a syllable out loud. The man with the AK-47 was still nearby, and he was not alone. The stocky man could smell at least three guards even when he couldn't place their exact whereabouts by their footsteps or whispered conversations. This vile enemy had a hated, repugnant odor to it that would have been, on its own, reason enough to want the earth rid of it once and for all.

He forced his mind to bring forth some sense of clarity, any memory at all that could help him comprehend their capture. There hadn't been so much as a struggle, not the first shot fired, and yet they were here, in this place with no name. In less time than it takes to inhale and expel a single breath, he and his team had been overpowered without a syllable of protestation. It was incomprehensible. They were all hardened fighters, men of action, men of war. He could not begin to count the number of lives they had taken, and yet not one fist had been clenched in defiance. Not a single weapon raised in defense.

As each lay silently where he fell, as limp as the dead itself, a lightweight, opaque Kevlar bag had been pulled over each man's head and cinched tightly around the neck. Though entirely unnecessary while Shiva still held absolute sway over her five captives—though she would keep them in her loving embrace for only forty minutes or so—their hands had also been bound behind their backs with a pair of heavy nylon restraints. These were overlapped at right angles to ensure any attempt at freedom would prove nothing more than a fruitless torture of wrist flesh and sinew. The last possibility of flight evaporated when their ankles had been similarly shackled.

The totally conscious but virtually lifeless men had been dragged from their tiny apartment like sacks of trash and had endured more than an hour's ride face down on the filthy wooden floor of a small delivery truck. Its heavy leaf springs cushioned the brutal and frequent shocks of the pockmarked roads as effectively as if the steel chassis had been bolted directly to wheels of stone. To make matters worse, the stinking amalgam of rotten meat, old vegetables, sweat, and sulfurous diesel had permeated the interior of the small trailer to such a degree that two of his men had vomited repeatedly during the arduous drive, the remnants of their last meal still contained within the hoods that blanketed their heads.

Shiva—the drug that had rendered his entire team immobile—was named for the ancient Greek goddess of sleep. It had been delivered in aerosol form beneath their door, from a container no larger than a can of spray paint. Odorless, silent and transparent, it could more quickly render an enemy defenseless than a platoon of Marines. Once inhaled, it induced complete physical immobility for up to forty minutes rather than producing a state of unconsciousness. Automated functions like heartbeat and breathing remained unaffected, but the ability to lift even single finger in defense vanished in that single breath.

With his head pounding, the stocky man prayed again for rescue, for God to intercede on their behalf. He knew, of course, there would be no intervention, divine or otherwise. Only a small handful of people had known of their presence in Afghanistan, and even fewer of their specific mission, and none of these would be sending help in any form.

Deniability. Wasn't that the word his superiors had used?

What the hell, the stocky man thought. *We all die eventually.*

When the truck finally came to a stop, the doors had been flung open and the men had been yanked to their feet only to be pushed to the ground, a fall equal to the height of a man's shoulders. The sand upon which each had landed cushioned his fall to a degree, though not without exacting its toll of wrenched sockets and tortured muscles.

The one man who had somehow managed to land on his feet had been swiftly knocked to the ground. Then, each had been dragged by his ankles through a narrow doorway, across a wide stone floor, and down two flights of stone stairs. Since that time, the five had remained in the same upright kneeling position, scarcely moving a muscle. Not a word had been spoken between themselves or to their captors for the last three and a half hours.

He knew they had been betrayed, sold out, given over to the enemy. Probably for the value of a single week's groceries, perhaps even for food itself. In a country where knowledge of one's enemies always brought death or reward, a secret's life could be measured in minutes, hours at most. It was the only plausible explanation for their location having been discovered so quickly; for their perimeter guards having not fired so much as a warning shot. They had been in the tiny apartment a mere four hours and had been scheduled to leave in less than ninety minutes, and yet they had been found and taken.

As his mind fought to connect the pieces, the loathsome stink of stale vomit from the man to his left nearly brought up the stocky man's stomach. He struggled to keep it down.

It was then that he heard a significant change in the building's sounds for the first time since their arrival: footsteps descending from the floors above, falling heavily and quickly on the same stone steps that had banged and chaffed his arms, back, and shoulders hours before. He listened intently, angling his head slightly as a deer in the forest might when trying to locate and identify an approaching predator.

Two sets of heavy footfalls. Boots.

They belonged to soldiers he decided quickly.

Whatever was going to happen now, the waiting was over.

The two men from the stairs entered the small dungeon of a room and took turns walking slowly and methodically around their captives.

Three of the hooded men continuously shifted their body weight on knees that felt as raw as burned flesh. One nervously twitched his head back and forth within his hood, as though a bumble bee shared that confined space, then began to pray in a low whisper. The stocky man chose to remain as still as a statue, despite perspiration running in torrents from beneath the Kevlar hood, soaking his back and chest.

"Our ticket out of this shit hole is two clicks away, gentlemen," one of the new arrivals stated succinctly. "Like us, our little band of mujahideens here has a date with destiny." The words had been said in English that rode on a thick south Boston accent. The man had spoken enough Pashto during his previous eighteen months in hell to last three lifetimes. He was ready to go home, back to the States, as were all his men.

He turned to the only man in the group senior to him. "Sir, you want us to walk them out or carry them out?"

The man with the bee in his hood now elevated his frantic praying to the point that it drowned out all other sounds in the room. Like his four confederates, he understood English as well as the average American, though he had learned it as a tool of carnage, to help him become a more effective soldier of death, not as a dialect he ever intended to speak socially or among friends. He hated the language just as he hated everything about the evil empire called America.

"Enough of that," the senior officer said in an even voice, indicating the praying man with a casual gesture of his left hand. The stock of an AK-47 was already on a path to the praying man's head. The assault to the hooded skull was more than enough to send him to the stone floor with a heavy organic thud.

Once there, he didn't move a muscle. To the immense satisfaction of those on their feet, neither did he pray.

The stocky man drew in a deep breath, trying to find his voice, then exhaled it noisily through clenched teeth. "You have no idea what you have done. You and your band of cowboys will not see tomorrow's sunset in this holy land. Already our friends are coming for us. And for you. By this time tomorrow, you will all be dead. I will see to it myself. We will then post videos of your beheadings on the Internet for all the world to see, for your families to see."

The senior officer smiled at the man's words, finding them both amusing and predictable. He'd heard it all before.

"My band of cowboys and I, as you so colorfully put it, will be long gone before your associates even know you've been taken. And you, my pudgy friend, along with your four highly-sought-after playmates, will be joining us for an all-expense-paid trip to the good old U.S. of A. Now doesn't that sound like the adventure of a lifetime?"

He spoke with a sarcastic snicker he made no attempt to hide. His words had obviously not been well received by the stocky man and his three associates who were still conscious, as each renewed his efforts to break free of his restraints while trying to stand on legs that refused to respond after hours of numbing immobility.

The general swiped a single finger beneath his throat and the stocky man immediately joined his unconscious associate on the stone floor, quickly followed by the others.

"Sorry about that, Jim. It seems you're going to have to carry them out."

"It's all good, General. This way, at least, we won't have to listen to the sons of bitches." He snapped his fingers once and a dozen men rapidly descended the stairs toward the confined room. "Get them onboard the choppers the second they touch down, Nate," he said to the man who now stood on his immediate left. "I want to be out of here in five ticks without so much as a sweat bead left behind."

"Consider it done, Colonel," sergeant major Nathaniel Fisher answered smartly. The distant sound of rotor blades approaching grew steadily louder.

"I'll be leaving you once we reach the east coast, Jim," the senior officer said to his second in command. "I'll be a few days in D.C. tidying up some details but will join you and the boys at the ranch by week's end. See that our—" He seem to be searching for the right word.

"Martyrs," Colonel James Merkett offered respectfully.

With a broad smile and a nod, Lieutenant General Clayton Longmont finished his thought. "See that our soon-to-be *martyrs* are well fed and well rested, and get them whatever medical attention they need. We can't have them dying on us just yet. After all, Colonel, we must have them looking their 'Sunday best' when they bring America to her knees."

PART 1: DISCOVERY

"I pushed my soul into a deep dark hole
and then I followed it in."

Mickey Newbury
(1940-2002)

ONE

Saturday, 7 June—Utah (the present)

JASON PARKER HAD SEEN dead men before. And women. Even children. Had seen them countless times, thousands of bodies, the victims of every imaginable manner of dispatching life. He had killed more often than he could remember. It meant nothing to him. Less than nothing. Unfettered by conscience and immune to the suffering of his victims, he had been free to dispense destruction and carnage without emotion, without hesitation, and without regard to race, sex, age, guilt or innocence.

Jason proudly saw himself as an "equal opportunity" killer.

He was nothing less than the completely predictable byproduct of his world. Jason's parental avatars trod liquid crystal screens in jack-boots and RayBans, wading with abject indifference through seas of bodies whose vital essence pooled in communal tarns of crimson misery measured not in droplets but in barrels.

But none of the Wonder Bread years surrendered to sunless arcade abattoirs had prepared Jason for that which riveted his vision at this moment.

3

Before now, he could just press EXIT and walk away whenever the slightest suggestion of conscience or remorse tried to interject its unwanted presence into his private universe, pleasantly devoid of all human frailties and feelings.

Before now, that is.

Now Jason Parker stared in silent disbelief at a grisly object thrusting skyward from the snow-packed earth only inches from his face.

It was unmistakably the hand and forearm of an adult male—the left to be specific—and from its unearthly violet hue, belonged to a lost soul who had long ago released his fragile grip on life. Not in the celluloid or digitized context of the word was this man dead, but in the real world, flesh and blood, pain and suffering sense of the word.

The sight was not at all like the detached, soulless images he was used to seeing on an LED display. The frightening awareness of its human actuality brought with it an instant taste of nausea.

As bile began to sour his mouth, a portion of Jason's mind, still refusing to accept the image as genuine, tried its best to 'morph' the grotesque shape into a stick or a rock—*anything* other than what it was in fact. Steadfastly, the hand refused to alter its molecular identity merely to lessen Jason's discomfort.

Against the lips of his halfopen mouth, lacy flakes of snow melted quickly, leaving behind in their transformation a scent of fragrant mountain pine. Under different circumstances, on any day other than this, such simplistic natural wonders would have formed pleasant and lasting memories of the mountain trek with his best friend, one he might have painted in melancholy hues as the adventure was retold over a glass of port by the fire, a gaggle of grandchildren gathered at his feet.

It went unnoticed and unappreciated; only a tinge of vomit registered as it began to rise in his throat.

With a gloved hand, he brushed the icy slush from the cold, red skin of his face and squeezed his eyes tightly together, like a child trying to escape a moon shadow that mysteriously appeared, creeping slowly across a bedroom wall.

He reopened them quickly, hoping that it had all been nothing more than a brief nightmare; a moment of cosmic penance. The scene that confronted him sent a chill slowly along his spine, as if a slender serpent had just slithered down the collar of his shirt and had coiled tightly between his shoulder blades.

"Brad," he mouthed, creating only a hint of actual sound. His friend, fifty feet above and twice that distance behind Jason's position, had not heard his name pathetically whispered.

Jason Parker lay on his stomach at the base of a small slope, more than thirty yards west and well below the ridge trail, the result of a clumsy misstep moments before. The wintry air swept tufts of long black hair across his face; they remained untouched as he added volume and pitch to his mounting fear. "Brad! Get down here! Now!"

Brad Minick shook his head in amusement as he noted Jason's predicament. Just because his klutzy friend had tripped over his own two feet and had tobogganed headfirst down the hill instead of staying on the trail—as he had skillfully done—was no reason he had to come to the rescue. It would be a simple enough task for him to reach the trail again without assistance. He was certain Jason was unhurt—notwithstanding a severely bruised ego, of course.

Brad was, however, a bit puzzled by the odd—no, decidedly frightened—tone in Jason's voice. *Weird*, he thought, but quickly realized that word aptly described his best friend precisely.

He was about to respond to the increasingly emotional call for assistance when a vividly-remembered image of Jason plowing head-first through the half-melted snow—like a mole burrowing through soft garden soil—made him rethink his response. "Hey, dork," Brad roared from his dry vantage point high on the narrow trail. "Whining like a little girl isn't going to keep me from sharing this priceless moment with the entire BYU campus. Just wait until the guys hear about this. Cindy, too. Oh, man, she's absolutely gonna bust a gut. You're gonna be *Snapchat* dork of the month." He shook his head and lamented under his breath, "Shit, I knew I should have brought my cell phone." You Tube would just have to wait.

Tears of laughter coursed down the sides of Brad's face as the capricious wind, gusting in short, lively bursts across the mountain ridge, taunted his exposed skin.

It may have been June, but to Brad, it felt more like mid-March.

"You're such a dick, you know it, Brad," Jason grumbled, forcing his body backward in the snow and putting as much distance between himself and the purplish hand as possible.

The airborne flakes, kicked up by his frenetic movements, melted on contact as they encountered the warm tissue and hot air of his mouth and nostrils. Between heavy, anxious breaths, Jason petitioned his buddy one final time. "Now Brad, dammit!" Then, to add emphasis that was apparently needed if the taunting was going to cease, "There's a body down here, a man in the snow. He's dead." His last words had tapered off to a whisper again.

To Jason's disgust, though not his surprise, his mournful appeal earned him nothing but further ridicule.

"A dead man?" Brad roared. "Oh, my God, Jason, I don't believe it. You've found him at last, after all these years! You've really found him!"

Jason shot an immediate questioning stare toward the other boy, a year ahead of him at Brigham Young University. His wide, unblinking eyes demanding to know what the hell his friend was talking about.

"Elvis!" Brad yelled, timing the jeer perfectly. "You've found the King!" He stood and bellowed even louder toward the sky, pretending to hold a microphone in his right hand. "Ladies and gentlemen, Elvis has left the building. Excuse me, the *mountain!*"

Laughter echoed through the valley, though the boy still on his belly in the snow didn't add a single decibel to it.

When Jason hadn't so much as cracked a smile, not even the hint of one, and his eyes remained locked on a spot not three feet from his face, Brad sensed for the first time that his friend's words may not have been spoken in jest. The realization brought with it instant sobriety, like being pulled over by a cop when you had an open bottle in the car.

Brad quickly analyzed the situation, trying to decide if it all might still be an act. He was reticent to let such an excellent opportunity pass without additional well-deserved mockery, certain such a clumsy head plunge on *his* part would not have gone uncelebrated for an intolerable hour had the shoe been on the other foot.

No, Jason wasn't that good a liar, Brad reasoned. *He was*, he thought with pride, *but not Jason.* He yelled down the ridge, "Better not be lying to me, Parker. If I come all the way down there and don't find a body, I swear on your mama's eyes I'll bury *your* lying ass in the snow and walk away!"

Jason barely heard the innocuous threat, his stare fixed on the violet-colored hand, silently praying it wouldn't unexpectedly reanimate and seize him by the throat.

It *was* penance for all the hours wasted in the pursuit of ever more violent video games, he was certain of it now, though he forced the idea away as quickly as it formed.

The wind howled angrily for an instant, like the wailing of a thousand anguished souls, and then fell eerily silent just as quickly.

Brad shot a quick look over his shoulder as a feeling of absolute certainty that he was being watched washed over him.

Joining Jason, dead body or not, suddenly seemed like a splendid plan.

Redmon's Ridge, the trail on which the boys had been hiking, ran along the twisting crest of Dutch Mountain, in the Ashley National Forest. Its southern slope, bathed in the rich amber glow of a clear June morning, was virtually free of snow, while the opposite slope, the one on which Jason Parker now lay, remained in shade most of the day and still bore the pale reminder of winter's recent fury.

Brad Minick stepped carefully onto the slushcovered tundra and worked his way down a medium grade slope into everdeepening snow, his long walkingstick providing a needed measure of support.

Fifty feet below the ridge trail, at the point where the slope flattened out for the width of a twolane road before plunging out of sight, Jason waited impatiently for the older boy to join him. He'd somehow managed to stand, but despite having changed positions, his eyes had not wandered for a moment from the dark, grotesque form in the snow at his feet.

As he grew ever closer to his friend, Brad unexpectedly lost his footing in the slick underlying ice and landed squarely on his back.

When his own act of clumsiness was allowed to pass without a syllable of derision from the other boy—not even so much as a glance in his direction—Brad's head snapped involuntarily to the right. His eyes fought to make sense of the object that met his gaze. Though its color was no longer from the accepted pallet of human hues, it was nonetheless human; the left hand of an adult male knotted into a tight fist, to be specific. It was thrust skyward, perpendicular to the ground. The tattered fabric of a filthy white shirt and overlying charcoal gray suit jacket covered the forearm before disappearing into the snow. A heavy silver-colored watch hung loosely around the forearm, just below the wrist.

"SON OF A BITCH!" Brad squawked noisily as he quickly distanced himself from the horrid sight, scooting backward like a crab for several feet before springing to his feet. He now stood shoulder to shoulder with his friend, staring at the ground in shared amazement.

For a full minute, neither boy spoke.

Beneath a soft, white mound they could just make out the form of a body lying flat on its back, now no more than a few inches beneath the quickly receding blanket of snow which had covered it for... they had no idea how long.

Brad finally spoke, trying to make light of the moment, though his words came out scratchy and lacking their usual bravado. "Now there's something you don't see every day." Jason seemed unimpressed by the attempt at humor. Clearing his throat, Brad grew more serious. "Any idea who it is, Jase?"

Jason gave his friend a contorted "how the hell should I know" look but didn't otherwise respond. The air that kissed his bare skin was dry and cold and he had yet to realize he was soaked from head to toe in front.

With the initial shock of the corpse's actuality rapidly wearing off, Brad's natural audacity began to get the best of him. He crouched beside the mound and cocked his head slowly side to side—like a puppy before a squeaky toy—touching nothing but taking in everything.

He carefully studied the hand and forearm, pausing briefly at the trio of dark blue, elegantly formed, letters skillfully stitched into the cuff of the soiled silk sleeve.

To himself he whispered, "R–W–G?" He thought for a moment, trying to put a name to the initials but they meant nothing to him. He quickly turned his thoughts elsewhere.

Jason could not have cared less who the man was or what the initials stood for and would have said so had he been asked.

Brad then spied the man's watch. "Oh, my sweet Lord! You see this, Jase? The dude's sportin' nothing less than a Rolex Day-Date Special Edition in solid platinum. With diamonds. Shit, diamonds all over the friggin' thing. Talk about bling." He moved his face closer. "And not those crappy little chips you usually see on watches either, these are the big bastards. The real deal. Any one of them would make one hell of an engagement ring. God, this is the exact same watch I've wanted ever since I saw Brad Pitt with one. Or maybe it was Johnny Depp. Whatever. Anyway, you have any idea how much one of these sumbitches costs?"

Jason merely shrugged. His mind struggled to be elsewhere.

Brad would not be put off by his buddy's inapprehensible indifference. "They cost, well, a hell of a lot. At least a hundred thou. More. Maybe two." He took a deep breath, then punctuated his previous ramblings with, "This is sooooo damn cool!"

Brad's final words at last evaporated the fog that had clouded Jason's thoughts. As his repressed emotions burst forth, he said angrily, "Listen, I don't really give a shit what the guy's watch costs, Brad, he's fuckin' dead! Doesn't that seem just a bit more important to you right now than how rich he was? His money don't matter now and it sure as hell didn't save him. He's *dead!*"

With his eyes still riveted to the Rolex, Brad puzzled over Jason's question of morality versus money for less time than it would have taken him to answer the question of whether or not he would like to have unbridled sex with a Victoria's Secret model. "Nope. Sorry. Not really." He turned to his friend, his expression serious. "Listen, man, we don't know the guy, so his death is no real loss to either me or you. I mean, it's too bad he had to die and all that shit, but this whole thing is way too cool not to get excited about, even for a geek like you. Jesus, Jase, you gotta learn to lighten up. Who else at BYU is likely to find a dead guy over summer break? A stinking-rich dead guy at that. We'll be the two coolest brothers in Kappa Alpha next term. We'll be like, you know, campus super heroes."

Jason shook his head in stunned amazement—Brad's well-renowned lack of social propriety had reached a new low point. "I think we should just leave now and call the sheriff," he said in a voice that barely rose above the wind. Despite a burning desire to turn the whole scene over to the authorities and get back to the peace and quiet of his warm and dry dorm room, he couldn't help wondering who the man was and how he had come to die in this unlikely place. Had he been murdered? Had he starved to death or succumbed to the cold? Had he suffered? What was he doing here, on *this* mountain, in *this* spot? How long had he been here?

Did anyone know where he was? Were they looking for him? Did they even care?

The questions came so fast they made him lightheaded, as if he had just stood too quickly. Unfortunately, for now, all he would get would be question upon unanswered question. The lack of resolution tore at his soul. He needed to know why. The 'why' always mattered more than 'how.'

Jason was a sensitive boy, far more sensitive than anyone else in his fraternity. But then, as his father would have said had he not died when Jason was still in middle-school, he always had been like that.

Oh, sure, he could kill video villains as fast and furiously as anyone he knew, but he could never have taken a life in actuality, perhaps not even in self-defense. For reasons probably relating to his father's early passing, an act that is always inexplicable to a child, death haunted Jason. Now, with the death of this man—stranger or not—literally thrust in his face, it clutched at his very essence. This man was probably some child's father, as well, a father who would never be coming home again.

Brad's fertile, if indifferent mind, by contrast—stimulated by the sight of wealth he had only fantasized about before now—began to explore the infinite possibilities the situation presented a person of "vision." Jason had always been such a narrow thinker, when he bothered to think at all, as Brad was quick to point out. "Well, you should give a shit, dumbass," he continued. "This guy was obviously loaded, maybe even like dot-com rich. I'll bet there's a big fat reward for finding him." He looked up at his buddy again, a Cheshire-cat grin bisecting his face. "You just don't misplace an entire billionaire without a whole shit-pot-full of people caring a great deal and wanting him back. It simply isn't done."

"Reward?" Jason muttered with an interest that initially surprised him. The tantalizing word had involuntarily slipped past his lips. Before he could explain that he had no interest in profiting by this man's death, Brad's grin had become a full-fledged smile.

11

"Sure, you bet. Hell, you don't think a guy with a hundred-dollar manicure, a hand-made monogrammed silk shirt, and a Swiss watch with more bling than a Beverly Hills pimp could be missing without someone lookin' for his rich ass, do you?" Brad smiled at the thought. "It's probably a bundle, too. I sure as hell hope so. Man, I can really use the cash."

Jason was now fully in the moment, snatched from his deep introspection by his friend's crass irreverence and single-minded selfishness. What came out of his own mouth next surprised him even more than Brad's vulgarity had. "What do you mean '*you* can really use the cash?' *I* found him, remember." His fingers flew to his face but the words had already passed his lips.

Brad smirked but would not be deterred. "Yeah, by falling head-first off a mountain because you never learned to walk. That don't exactly make you Magnum P.I." He had never seen the show when it originally aired in the Eighties, of course, having been born after its last season, but such was the impact of a billion kids worldwide all suffering from some level of ADHD: everything old became new again as cable, satellite, and the Internet strained to fill three hundred HD channels and a dozen Wi-Fi streaming services with something other than a test pattern. Both he and Jason had become huge fans of the campy detective series, as had their entire fraternity.

"Oh, yeah! Well, I'll bet his family won't give a crap how I found him. Dumb luck is as important as skill any day."

"That's a good thing, because you've got the 'dumb' part down pat, my friend!"

They glared intensely at each other for an awkward moment, forgetting their long friendship as visions of instant cash by the car-load erased all memories, replacing them with the thick fog of greed.

"Well *I* still found him," Jason finally said, though this time with far less conviction.

"Fine. No problem," Brad said curtly. "He's your corpse, you dig him out. Find out who he is so you can tell the cops when you get back to the diner *alone*."

He had not been prepared for this turn of events. "What?" he stammered.

Brad put his nose an inch from Jason's. "*You* found him, dickhead. *You* want the reward, *you* dig him out. Me, since I'm not part of this equation anymore, am headed for trail's end." His expression was resolute as he turned up his collar and prepared to leave.

Jason threw a wideeyed glance around the side of Brad's head, fixating on the mound and its slowly thawing contents. The most graphically vile scenes from every horror movie he'd ever seen played sequentially in his mind, as if they'd been spliced together by Satan for this precise moment. There was no way on earth he could do what Brad had just suggested and Brad knew it. "I, uh..." he stuttered.

The older boy folded his arms across his chest, providing a small crevasse of breathing room between their bodies. His tone, however, remaining less than cordial. "I, uh, what? You're so anxious to inform the cops and collect all the reward *you're* entitled to, how else are you going to tell 'em who you found up here? Answer me that. In fact, I'll bet you fifty bucks you couldn't even find this exact spot again, couldn't get within a mile of it."

Jason knew Brad was right on that point; he had been known to misplace his own car in a mall parking lot while Brad seemed to have a natural, even uncanny, sense of direction. He looked again at the horrid purple fist, the life so obviously vacant from its tissue and bones. Sunlight had begun to thaw the exposed skin, creating small rivulets of water that coursed down the back of the hand dampening the silk cuff. There was no way he had the grit for any of this. In fact, he didn't even know why any of this conversation was occurring. He didn't care a thing about the money, not if it meant the loss of his only real friend. "Listen, Brad," he said apologetically, "if there *is* a reward, I'll split it with you, you know that. Fifty-fifty. That's totally fair, right?"

Brad patted his buddy on the shoulder with a nod of the head and a smirk that said, "Smart boy, I knew you'd come around to my way of thinking." He then knelt beside the mound, using his bare hands to scoop away the snow that still concealed the man's body and face.

When his fingers brushed the hard, cold form of the frozen face, he jerked them back as if they had just been scalded.

Jason jumped in concert. "Screw it, man, just leave him alone." He stepped back another foot. "We don't have to know who the bastard is. That's the sheriff's job, right. It'll be good enough that we found him." He backed up even more. "I'm getting the hell out of here." Despite his words, he did not turn to move.

Brad thought briefly about joining his friend, but something within him wouldn't allow it. With renewed resolve, he swept the glistening powder away from the head, trying not to touch the skin any more than necessary.

When the entire face had at last been wiped clean, he stood. Except for the eerie ashenblue color, the man could have simply been asleep; his expression was not anguished, but surprisingly peaceful. It was as if the torments of life had left the man with the exhalation of his final breath and only harmony and peace remained with their exodus.

The sight, not at all what he'd expected, made Jason shudder. He thought that such a death as this man has surely suffered would be accompanied by twisted facial features and wide, glaring eyes.

The wind howled mournfully again and in the western slopes, thunder proclaimed a sudden, rapidly approaching, change in the weather.

After a moment or two of careful study, Brad announced with his usual insensitive candor, "He does look kinda familiar, maybe like he's been on TV or something, but that 'Smurf' thing he's got going on makes it hard for me to put a finger on it. You recognize him, Jase?"

Jason Parker shook his head, though he had refused to take a genuine look.

"You didn't even try, dick brain."

"I don't have to—I don't know him."

"How do you know if you don't look?" Brad insisted.

"I don't know him, alright!" Jason shouted.

The response earned him a sincere and deeply furrowed scowl. "Okay, at least tell me how old you think he is. Or was, rather," Brad said, now fully studying the man's remains like he was buying a used car, displaying not even the slightest apparent regard for the life that had once burned within them.

Jason, knowing they would not leave this horrid place until he'd appeased Brad, reluctantly bent slightly at the waist, careful not to move his feet, and lowered his head a few inches closer to the body.

He shot erect again.

"I have absolutely no idea, Brad. He could be anywhere from forty-five to sixty-five. What's more, I don't give a shit, alright. Now can we please go?"

"Jesus, you're such a pussy! This is the coolest thing ever and you don't even appreciate the significance of it. I tell you, I can feel it, man. This is our lucky day." Brad scrutinized the exposed face for a long moment. "I'll bet you a buck he's somebody totally famous. Help me dig him out so we can see if he's got any I.D. on him."

Jason's eyes went instantly wide. "Screw you, man! I'm not touching the dead sumbitch!" He took a number of quick steps backward, placing himself now fifteen or more feet from the body. "Listen, I'm out'a here, Brad, no kidding. If I make it to the sheriff's office without you, you ain't getting one penny of the reward! If you think I'm kidding, just try me."

With that, Jason made a wide circle around his companion and the half-frozen corpse and scurried clumsily back up the hill, slipping several times as he retraced Brad's steps.

As he neared the crest, the cool air caressing the mountain range pierced his damp clothing like a thousand icy needles. He began to shiver and his teeth started chattering like dice in a cup.

It was going to be a long and uncomfortable hike back to the diner, he thought, not relishing the idea of making the journey alone. He surreptitiously glanced back at his buddy to see if he was coming, not wanting to give him the satisfaction of knowing that he was as frightened as he was cold.

Brad scooped snow back over the face to protect it from the warming sun that would touch this side of the slope within the hour and jammed his long walking stick firmly in the ground beside the body. He pulled a clean cotton handkerchief from his pocket and tied a square knot around the end of the stick.

As he was about to leave, he knelt again and admired the expensive watch. As if it had read his thoughts, the wind howled in angry protest of the interlopers who had remained too long in its realm. Somewhere nearby a pine branch finally yielded to the weight of the snow still clinging to its needles and cracked like a gunshot.

Now, it was Brad's turn to shudder. And to leave.

He stood at once, pulled the collar of his jacket tightly around his neck and quickly added a third set of footsteps to the slope. When he reached the top, he was only a few yards behind his less surefooted companion. He took a moment to note their exact position on his hike map before returning it to his coat pocket, cursing himself for having left his phone, with its native GPS app, in the car.

"Hey, wait up, Jase," he shouted after the younger boy. "You might fall off the trail again." The thought of easy money—lots of it—flooded Brad's mind. He couldn't help laughing out loud as he sprinted down the path toward the old diner at the trail's head, and a phone that would summon the sheriff and begin the 'reward' wheels turning.

TWO

T HE BRIGHT ORANGE RAFT disappeared from view as it plunged into the raging backwater of the "Snake," one of the most unpredictable rapids in Desolation Canyon.

Larry, an investment banker from New England and woefully out of his element, took the dare from one of his fellow rafters and attempted—unadvisedly—to stand through the cascading water, supported only by the thin nylon rope laced across the top of the flotation tubes. He might as well have been astride a raging bull.

At the first major dropoff, his less-than-enviably-fit two hundred pounds was pitched like a child's toy against the opposite side of the raft, narrowly missing another passenger, and then back again as quickly, coming to rest squarely on his back on the undulating rubber floor. A split second later, at the next drop, a hundred liters of chill, sandy river water that had collected in the raft joined him at its now lowest point. The icy deluge left him gasping for breath.

Despite being the middle of June in the American Southwest, where afternoon temperatures typically exceed the century mark, the water in the Green River had its birthplace in the mountains far to the north, the result of high elevation rains and recent winter thaws. As a result, the water along this stretch of river rarely exceeded forty-eight degrees in June. The Green River would be two states south of their present location before full immersion in it provided a soothing dip instead of a bone-numbing jar.

"I told you to stay down and hold on!" the boatman shouted over the roar of the furious brown water. She wanted to give death-defying Larry the cussing he deserved, and it took all her willpower to keep even one expletive from escaping past her pursed lips. In her 'I-mean-business' voice, she yelled, "I'm not joking, Larry. Now that you're down, stay down!" The job ahead redirected her thoughts; it would take all her strength and concentration to get them through the narrow channel without an incident far more serious than a soaking. She'd deal with the boneheaded banker later.

If they were both still alive at that time.

Larry, embarrassed, sodden to the bone, shivering, and now abruptly aware of his acute environmental displacement, nodded his silent concession. Other than his pride, he was unhurt. However, amid the turbulence and increasing instability of the raft, he had little choice but to remain seated in his icy bath.

Not even the seasoned guides in the group, Carolyn, Mike, Brian, or Alexia—Alex to all her friends—could have remained standing during this section: the most combative stretches of river the group would encounter in its seven days and six nights together.

The other three passengers accompanying Larry in Boat-1, an eight by twenty-foot inflated rubber 'donut' with a reinforced but flexible rubber floor, had wisely elected to do as Marie Matthews had previously instructed. At five feet, seven inches tall, beautiful in both face and figure, and as solid as an Olympic athlete, she commanded attention and respect, at least in this realm. They knew that it was wise to heed her words, and each knelt obediently at their chosen corners of the raft, clutching the lacing ropes firmly with both hands, their bodies pressed tightly against the fluorescent orange tubing. The geysers that continuously erupted from all sides of the raft looked like fountains of liquid chrome as the brilliant

June sun, illuminating the effervescent spray, imbued each in turn with a celestial glow.

Without warning, the right side of the Boat-1 struck a giant bolder just beneath the surface—at the far edge of the 'line' Marie had chosen through the rapids—and was promptly spun a hundred and eighty degrees, putting her back to the river's flow.

She instantly snapped her knees to her chest, released her gloved grip on the long aluminum oars, and spun half around in her center seat. Before the oar handles had moved more than a few inches, Marie once again had them securely in her hands, the rubber-impregnated Kevlar palms of her thick red and gray rowing gloves providing a glue-like grip even when soaked. After three summers spent tackling this liquid beast, the act had become second nature.

Marie once again had her back correctly to the flow, instinctively pulling on the left oar while pushing on the right with all her strength. An instant later the movements were skillfully reversed and the raft snapped magically back to her intended line. To competently steer the raft, which had no true bow or stern by design, one had to be facing down river. It wasn't so much that the boatmen were rowing their crafts as they were using the oars to steer them. The river was in charge of momentum; the boatmen in charge of riding the "line." Still, even with the muscles of a gymnast and the nerves of a SWAT team member, the river left each of the five boatmen on any given outing totally exhausted at the end of the day. Half from physical fatigue, half from ten vigilant hours keeping the paying clientele happy.

And alive.

A hundred yards ahead, the river appeared to literally explode into a huge fluid volcano, the caramel-colored water erupting ten feet into the air for a width of a driveway.

The noise grew deafening.

When encountered at eye level for the first time, "The Rattler" always forced an involuntary prayer for Divine deliverance past the lips of even the most resolute nonbeliever. Few, if any, remained genuinely agnostic when death—or the certain promise of death—stared them squarely in the eye. Even Marie, who had made this same trip more than a dozen times before, felt a knot forming in her chest as the familiar, yet always formidable, sight, announced its presence with the voice of a jet engine at takeoff. "Down!" she shouted at the three men and one woman in her immediate charge. "And hold on like your lives depend on it!"

It was neither an idle warning nor one meant to unduly alarm the passengers. On this river, the difference between life and death was always one foot. One second. One mistake.

The passengers didn't need to be reminded or warned again—each saw the obstacle that now lay directly in their path—and as it filled their eyes, each silently questioned the sanity of their choice of vacations. Why was this particular image not in the pretty brochure they had been sent? Probably for the same reason pictures of immense icebergs weren't in the Titanic's inaugural cruise pamphlet.

"What the hell are you doing?" one of the men yelled. "You're heading straight for it!"

Another mumbled a string of bewildered and half-formed obscenities as he tightened his grip on the rope lashing at his side.

Anne, the only other female in Boat-1, put as much of her petite form below the top of the tubing as possible. She had left the quiet, safe world of residential lending for the excitement and danger of the river. Now, it all seemed too exciting. Too dangerous. Too real. She wanted her safe desk and her endless stream of clients with sub-prime credit scores.

Yet, at the same time, she wouldn't have been anywhere else in the world but right here, in this very spot, at this very moment.

It was a feeling they all shared but would not admit even if they had been aware of it on a conscious level. It was why they hadn't gone to Epcot Center or Cancun.

Anne, though not overly religious, began to pray fervently, unable to remove her eyes from the frightening sight before her.

It was as if the massive object before them were some monstrous carnivore and she its next meal. It was "train wreck TV" at its most intense and there was no OFF button.

Larry, still stinging from his humiliating defeat and icy bath a few moments earlier, now appeared to be charged by the very idea of death. He knelt defiantly erect and shook his fists at the rock, screaming from his gut like a kid on a roller coaster. In the black echoing vaults of his mind, where his fear of death taunted him without respite, he commanded the familiar voice to be silent. His life, as long as he could remember, had been lived this way: challenging himself with death and then mocking it as it narrowly passed without collecting his outstretched token. Perhaps, though not brave as defined by Merriam-Webster, a battlescarred Marine might have understood Larry's actions and given them a fitting description that could exist without shame beneath the broad badge of "courage." Perhaps, as is so often the case, it was nothing more than raw fear disguised as courage that had no other way of being vented, of being exorcised. Whatever label it bore, it gave meaning to Larry's life while torturing his soul at the same time.

The spray lashed his face like a boatswain's whip as he begged silently for death to elude him just one more time.

Marie had learned the hard way that the most effective way of combatting fear is with action. Most people—most sane people, anyway—experience fear. It's what we do while we're scared out of our skin that defines our character. The best antidote to fear is action. It doesn't matter as much what you do as that you do something other than cower and shake. Perhaps that was why she focused so hard on the tasks at hand.

Oblivious to anything but the threat that lay ahead, Marie made a quick check of her 'line' and decided that, while not as perfect as on some previous passages she'd made, was still satisfactory, still safe. They were now running squarely at the boiling cauldron created by a shard of primordial granite the size of a station wagon jutting from the riverbed ten feet beneath them.

She knew—hoped and prayed at least—that the raft would again be catapulted past the rock just prior to the moment of impact, when it entered the hypercurrent which raced around it on both sides. That was the theory, at least. It had almost always proved sound and safe.

Almost.

Though all boatmen in all companies had heard vivid accounts of the McCarran incident in August of '05, no one in the rafting business would dare whisper a word of it in front of 'outsiders,' despite the fact that it had involved a competitive enterprise that no longer existed. Death on the river touched every boatman; they took a river death hard, as if somehow the water had won because it had been smarter, better, more clever, and they had lost because they had not been equal to the task.

Marie knew that if she tried to buy a little more room by moving them any closer to the canyon walls—only a short distance from either side of "The Rattler" at the river's narrowest point—that same hypercurrent would force the raft into the jagged, vertical granite ramparts, shredding it like tissue and hurdling a quintet of soon-to-be corpses into the brown torrent. This was one case when playing it safe was not the safe thing to do.

"You're heading straight for the damned thing!" Howard repeated. The man who shared the front with Larry shouted at the top of his lungs, certain he had not been heard the first time. He looked back over his shoulder at Marie for some reassurance that the situation was, despite all outward appearances, actually under control.

Marie simply winked at him.

It was not the response he had been seeking. In fact, it made him exponentially more nervous than he had been before a flash of Marie's perfect white teeth assured him she was quite aware of their collision course.

Had he chosen the raft of some lunatic with a death wish? Or, perhaps, like so many Americans today, this woman bore an inherent and intense disdain of lawyers, and planned to do her part for the 'cause' by plastering one of Chicago's most prosperous litigators against the granite monolith that lay immediately ahead. He suddenly wanted the security of his corner office and silently cursed the colorful sales literature that had depicted Desolation Canyon's Green River as a tranquil brook meandering its way placidly through Utah's vibrantly colored landscape.

Yep, straight for the damn thing, Marie agreed when Howard had turned back toward the front, her silent words more a prayer than a reply. Despite the broad "'company'" smile, Marie's muscles burned from the strain of the oars and her mind feverishly processed a thousand bits of data that came from three full, strenuous, and exhilarating seasons on this very river. She could taste the cold, sandy water on her lips as the spray pelted her face; feel the energy and power of the river pulsating beneath the tiny, vulnerable craft as if it were some monstrous mammal upon whose back they were astride.

One that seemed completely pissed off at the moment.

As it swept them along, the water moaned and cursed, its bass and thunderous voice reverberating the fears that lived within each of them.

Howard, rendered speechless by the inexplicable response he'd received from Marie, sank to the rubber floor in an effort to put as much of the soft pontoon as he could between his flesh and bones and the approaching granite.

Marie continued to make subtle corrections with her oars, simultaneously monitoring speed, angle, yaw, and list, as well as the feel of the river itself. At the last possible moment, she yanked the starboard oar completely into the raft with a powerful jerk. It slipped quickly across her bare thighs, its bright blue paddle just clearing the pontoon as the hypercurrent shot the pliable craft around the monstrous boulder now only a foot to their right.

She exhaled for the first time in a full minute.

A waterfall of frigid white spray completely showered Boat-1, soaking all five onboard and partially filling the raft before it popped into the relative quiet of the river that lay just beyond "The Rattler."

Marie maneuvered her boat quickly into the main stream of the current and as far from the canyon walls as possible.

There was a long moment of complete silence among the passengers after they had cleared the massive rock, then all hell broke loose.

"Oh, my God!" Howard bellowed in his loudest voice, rising to his knees again. "That was incredible! Absolutely incredible!" He reached back and squeezed Marie's knee, his heart pounding like a drum.

Larry took in a deep breath and nodded in silent echo of Howard's excited words. He had cheated death once again. "Awesome," he whispered reverently.

Anne had quit praying. She remained seated in the chill brown water on the rubbery bottom, simply grateful to still be counted among the living. For a brief moment, as she had passed the leading edge of the boulder, its surface smoothed and shaped from millennia of defiance to the river's ceaseless flow, she could have reached out and touched it. That quarter-second of absolute reality had now fractured itself into a timeless collage of oddly connected frames of light, color, and emotion. All sound had been stripped away. She realized that she had just stared death insolently in the eye and had lived to speak of it. The feeling was like nothing she had experienced in her life, and it electrified her body to the tips of her toes.

It was for each—after their banal, half-true, and far too predictable rationalizations had been shared at the commencement of the trip—the unspoken, perhaps not even fully understood, reason each had come to this river.

"You knew we weren't going to hit it," Anne said in awe.

Marie shrugged. "It's pretty much Job-One for all of us to see that none of you die a violent death while vacationing on the river," she said with her easy smile, her teeth practically backlit in contrast to her deep tan. Having prepared for one hundred-twenty-plus days of outside desert work by hitting the tanning bed during most of April and May, plus possessing the enviable ability to tan with remarkable ease, Marie's skin had acquired its familiar rich bronze tone of summer. "Recent studies indicate that dead passengers almost never recommend the vacation that killed them to their friends."

All five in Boat-1 let out a giddy, childlike laugh. The passengers because they had just done something uncivilized, unpredictable, unimaginable; Marie, because she had done it right one more time.

"Okay, you guys, grab your buckets and start bailing," she barked playfully, interrupting the spontaneous celebration. There was at present perhaps a hundred gallons of river water inside the raft, sloshing first one way then the other. Returning total control of the craft to the boatman was critical along the river, even in the most docile stretches. This present stretch was not truly docile, despite a mile or so of relative calm. It was time to bail; there would be ample opportunity at tonight's campfire to relive the past moment's danger and elation, the energy of collective recollection synergized by sixteen other passengers in the four boats that had yet to navigate The Rattler. "But remember what we discussed earlier," she added. "And don't forget, wait for my signal."

Each passenger grabbed one of the large plastic buckets that were lashed to the rigid aluminum support frame that spanned the center of the raft and began the task of bailing the boat. Over the next six days, the unfamiliar task would become automatic. The inflated, double layer rubber raft could not actually sink even if the water were at its gunwales—unless all of the separate air chambers had somehow been compromised—but it steered like a car with four flat tires when it had taken on too much water. It was also uncomfortable, if not impossible, to sit for any length of time in a near freezing waist deep bath, even with the desert sun glaring overhead. Marie knew that when the joy of not dying a moment ago had fully passed, her guests would quickly realize they were freezing their butts off.

Dry meant comfortable, and at several thousand dollars each for a week spent in two-person tents and undulating rubber boats, "comfortable,"whenever and wherever it could be found, was a very good thing.

When there was only an inch or so of water left in the raft, it would quickly be warmed by the broiling sun and would actually provide some measure of relief from the ceaseless heat. A foot of the icy river water, on the other hand, created an environment fit only for penguins.

Marie lifted her knees and spun quickly around again, now facing the remaining four boats in her group. And, after a dozen trips down this one river, it *was* her group. She had led the way, she had set the line, something that varied with each trip depending on water depth, ambient temperature, the ever-changing river bottom, and many other factors that only God was in charge of. Allowing only fifty yards between themselves, it was now each subsequent boatman's responsibility to follow that line exactly.

A familiar saying on the river was, "The best always lead so the rest don't bleed."The object was for the paying guests to go home with a lifetime of unequaled memories and with no one departing the river in a body bag.

Marie nodded in silent satisfaction that she'd upheld her end of the company's unspoken mantra. But, she reminded herself, she and her charge were only twenty percent of the outing. Anything could go wrong at any time.

In Boat-2, Alex Summers traced Marie's line flawlessly, as always. She also had a trio of seasons with the raft company under her belt. Unlike Marie, however, Alex had a new boatman just learning the river in the seat beside her; she controlling the starboard oar; the newbie the port, or left oar. As in Boat-1, Boat-3 and Boat-4 each contained a single seasoned boatman and four paying passengers. Boat-5 was piloted by "Old Man River," Mike Ohura, plus the second trainee on the trip. Ohura, at twenty-four, though several years younger than Marie, was already a veteran of six seasons on the wild rivers of Utah and Arizona, though only two seasons on this particular river. Still, despite not leading this expedition, Ohura wore the honorary title that had been bestowed on him by his fellow boatmen with pride.

Just as Alex had, the last three rafts in the group mirrored Marie's line perfectly, and each made it through the turbulent and challenging gauntlet of The Rattler without mishap.

As Alex's boat drifted within a few yards of the lead raft, in the slow, tranquil water where the river had widened, Marie called out to her. "Great job, Alex! You guys get as soaked as we did?"

Amid the adrenaline rush clamor of the passengers within her own boat, Alex brushed a forearm across her brow and wiped the sweat from her eyes. Even in mid-June, with the two hottest months of summer yet to come, the canyon floor often saw temperatures north of one-hundred-fifteen degrees. Today it was a relatively pleasant one-oh-five. "Not too wet," she shouted back. "But I was a foot or two closer to the left wall than you, I think. Less spray."

Marie nodded. "Not as wet, huh? That's good." She removed her red and gold 49er's cap and wiped her own brow. Upon that pre-arranged signal, her four 'soldiers' emptied the water buckets they had been concealing from view into the approaching enemy vessel.

Being the first day on the river, it was Boat-1's obligation and pleasure to initiate the other passengers in the longstanding and sacred rafting tradition of bucket fights. By the time the last boat had joined the fray, the group looked more like a mob of mischievous children than a collection of accountants, doctors, lawyers, and bankers.

It may have been the first water fight of the week's trip, but there would be many more.

THREE

B Y FIVE O'CLOCK, WITH all boats securely beached for the evening and nightfall still several hours away, Marie took a moment to stroll the sandy river's edge before helping her crew prepare dinner.

She had already given her guests eleven hours of undivided attention and loving care this day, as well as two elaborate meals, three snacks, four blisters, a pulled shoulder, historic insight, and volumes of photographic advice.

The next few blissfully quiet moments belonged to her alone.

As dictated by nature, rather than by time or distance traveled, each night on the river was spent in one of only eight or ten places along the ninety-five mile trek—depending upon the height of the river—large and flat enough to accommodate the dozen or more twoperson tents that had to be pitched.

Desolation Canyon, known for its nearly milehigh walls, narrow gorges, and the angry river that cut tirelessly and often unpredictably through it, offered one of the most breathtaking and exciting outings available for hire. For this reason, as well as the cruiseship-quality food and service provided by all of the licensed rafting companies, such trips rarely had a vacancy, even a single seat. The outfitter that Marie and Alex worked for couldn't recall the last time they'd launched an expedition with fewer than the twenty allowed guests. They could have sent twice as many boats down the river at each outing, but federal guidelines, plus an inherent desire by most outfitters to protect the environment while trying to share it at the same time, limited the number of guests that could be accommodated.

Marie had been away from the main group for nearly forty minutes when Alex caught up with her a half mile downstream from the campsite.

"All the tents are up," she offered softly, respectful of her friend's quiet time. "Mike and Carolyn have taken the group up to the old hermit's cave before we start dinner. Brian and the newbies are setting up the kitchen." The newbies' names would not be spoken until they had successfully completed their first month on the river, one of the many time-honored traditions within the rafting business.

For now, they were just the "newbies."

Marie nodded her approval as she sat on the bank a few feet from the water. She had always loved watching the endless movement of the river, constantly adjusting itself as it encountered obstacles, twisting and coursing relentlessly toward its unseen destination. Powerful. Unstoppable. Eternal.

When she had first sat on this spot, now three years earlier, the fascination had lain primarily in its sheer strength. While she now had even more respect for its awesome power, she had come to appreciate the more subtle aspects of the river. The more she lived and grew and learned, the more she saw her own life echoed in its rich brown waters.

"Quite a cast of characters, eh?" Alex added, flopping down beside her.

"Seems like a pretty good bunch." Marie's response was flat.

"How 'bout ol' Larry, eh? How come there's always one just like him in every group?"

Marie smiled at the question; she knew it was rhetorical. "I suppose we better get back and feed the beasts. They'll be starving after their hike." She turned her eyes from the river and looked at the other woman. "What is it tonight, Alex? Fish?"

"Yeah, salmon and scallops. Papa Joe even threw in two gallons of those tiger prawns you were admiring in Moab. Suggested grilling them in butter with a pinch of fresh garlic and some basil."

Marie brushed her sandy hands across the cutoff jeans she had pulled over her bikini bottom then twisted her long blonde hair into a quick knot, stuffing it back under her ball cap. "Thanks for giving me a little time to myself, Alex."

"Hey, no sweat. I know the first few days of June are always rough for you. I'm sorry the schedule couldn't be worked out so you could skip this rotation. Who knew Dena would need to have her appendix removed, eh?"

"It's all right," she said, then turning to Alex added, "And when have I ever skipped a rotation?"

The question required no response, though "never" was the only word that came to Alex's mind.

Marie looked deep into the young woman's clear blue eyes and then past her toward the water again. Since yesterday, her mind had stubbornly refused to put back the familiar, painful images it had dug out of the footlocker of her past. It would be like this for another day or two, and then slowly, without assistance or encouragement, would relent and allow her to return to the present. Each June, for the past three years, the scenario had been the same, and each year, the pain had lost a bit more of its original intensity.

But while the depth of pain had lessened, the images were still vivid, tangible, caustic. "There are moments when I can feel him right beside me, Alex, though not as much anymore. At first, you know, it was so real at times it scared the hell out of me. But now,"—she sighed deeply, lifting her head toward the sky for a moment as she thought—"I wonder if I'll even remember any of it one day. I don't know which would be worse: always having painful memories of what we might have had or having no clear memory of him at all." She shrugged. "Either way, it doesn't appear that I have much to say about it."

Alex produced a broad, warm smile. Maybe this time she'd get an answer to the unspoken question. "You realize, sis, that I don't actually have a clue what you're talking about, right? I mean, I realize you lost someone four years ago. He died unexpectedly, I gather. I know it was a man—no big secret there—but I don't think it was like a dad or brother. A lover, I'm guessing, maybe even a husband. And, all of this *is* just a guess on my part because you've never actually said anything specific about what's eating at you. Not a single word." It was time to lighten things up a bit. "And I've really pried hard at times, butted my nose right in, just like I'm doing now. We practically live together twenty-four-seven and I know nothing more about your past than I knew three years ago, when we first met." She decided to try the old reliable: guilt. "Marie, how can I think of myself as a real friend when you don't feel you can truly confide in me?"

Marie nodded her agreement that Alex had, indeed, tried her best to learn all she could about her friend's past for years—unsuccessfully. And she *was* a friend, a true friend, despite Marie's reluctance to share her past, or that fateful day so many months ago. In that respect, she had not singled out the woman standing at her side. No one knew. No one could ever know. It would simply be too dangerous for them.

And for her.

She brought her gaze back to the river; it had not finished speaking to her and she needed to listen to its healing song a bit longer. "Mind giving me just a minute more?" she asked apologetically.

Alex turned, brushed at the sand remaining on her shorts, and started back toward the campsite. "Not at all. Take your time, sis. They're not going anywhere, eh." She couldn't believe she still hadn't gotten the answer; she had used every trick in the book. *Oh, well*, she thought, *one day, maybe.*

31

By the time her friend had gone only a short distance down the beach, Marie called out to her. Though she hadn't intended to ever say anything specific about that time in her life—to anyone—she suddenly felt compelled to come clean to the closest 'sister' she'd ever had. Perhaps, as they say, confession would truly be cathartic; perhaps some of the painful memories would exit along with the words that described them. "Hey," she shouted over the roar of the water.

Alex turned back to face her. "What's up?" She knew what was up, however. She could see it in Marie's eyes, in the thoughtful knitting of her brow.

Marie walked quickly to her, taking both of Alex's hands in hers. "I need to tell you something, but you've got to promise not to freak out, okay?"

Alex hated it when people said things like that. It was like telling someone not to jump just before you fired a shotgun inches from their head. Impossible. She found herself offering a non-convincing, "Sure, no freaking out, I promise."

Marie looked to the water again for what seemed an eternity, then brought her deep brown eyes directly in line with Alex's. Tears had begun to stream down her cheeks and Alex could tell that whatever was on her friend's mind, she was having great difficulty putting it into words.

"Hey, girlfriend, you can tell me anything. Just say it. It won't seem nearly as bad after it's out."

"It's bad," Marie said, her voice shaky.

Beyond the nearly fanatical curiosity that had her nerves knotted like hemp rope, Alex was sincerely troubled by Marie's obvious pain, above that which she felt out of love for the closest friend she'd had since childhood. She had never seen Marie like this: unsure, emotionally drained, tenuous. In the years she'd known her, Marie had always seemed the quintessence of strength and certainty.

Except this week each year, she corrected. She was always a bit of a mess this week in June.

"How bad can it be?" Alex said, trying to give her friend the support she needed to continue. She desperately wanted to know the underlying reason for her friend's emotional distress, and the mere fact that she had never been able to get this close to the truth before drove her onward. "Look, sis, if you say it really fast, it'll be out there before you even know you've said it." Whether or not that had actually made any sense, it sounded perfectly reasonable to Alex. It didn't matter, dammit! She needed to know. She was so close.

Marie squeezed her friend's hands tightly and said, "It *was* a man, a lover just as you suspected, but he didn't die." The tears increased.

"Oh, my god, the bastard cheated on you?" Alex blurted, unashamedly lumping male infidelity into the same black pool as death.

"No, he did not cheat on me. He died."

"He didn't die, but he died?" Now Alex was totally confused.

Marie shook her head, squeezing her eyes tightly together as the next words came forward. "I mean he didn't actually die, like when you're sick or something." There was a long moment of silence during which Alex could barely keep herself from speaking. Somehow, she remained quiet, certain that if she spoke, the moment would vanish.

Finally, when Marie's eyes reopened, there was a cold, lifelessness to them that Alex had never seen before.

Not ever.

She realized that her hands were being squeezed hard enough to cause pain. As she was about to pull them away, Marie blurted out, "He didn't die, Alex. I killed him. And not just him, all of them. They're all dead. I killed them all. Six or seven... I don't know how many really." Her final words had been spoken in a whisper.

It was decidedly not the "Desperate Housewives" revelation Alex had sought for so long: the simplicity of carnal betrayal by a trusted lover or the sadness caused by the untimely passing of a significant other. As she freed her hands and stepped back from her friend, she saw that Marie's eyes had lost their icy chill and were again focused on the river to Alex's right. She looked spent, ready to drop right where she stood, but Alex felt no sisterly compassion at the moment, only bewilderment. And fear.

Fear was definitely there as well, in abundance.

"Okay, then," she said, taking a second step backward. It was followed by another. Then another. "Not gonna freak out, just like I promised." She let out a series of deep breaths, then realized she was, indeed, freaking out. "You take a little more time, Marie. All you want. Hey, we've got it covered. Don't worry about a thing. Just take it easy, okay. Take all the time you need. Sit, or you can remain standing. Standing's fine. Or sitting. Whatever you like," she rambled as she backed farther from Marie.

At a distance of fifteen feet, she turned and made her way quickly up the beach, wanting to run but doing her best to merely jog.

Marie said nothing more as Alex's form became at first a tiny shape then completely disappeared around the bend of the river.

It had definitely not been cathartic, she decided.

It had not healed her in any way. Not even minutely.

Not one single cell seemed to have benefited from the revelation, not one strand of DNA was better off than it had been a minute ago. And now her outburst, her disclosure, her long-kept secret, may well have driven away the only friend she had.

Had her words also just put Alex's life in danger? she wondered, pushing the thought away as soon as it formed.

"Well, so much for the truth setting you free," Marie said in ridicule to the river. "Never did care much for it anyway."

She would have sworn the river's roar had become a guttural laugh.

FOUR

OUT OF BREATH AND panting like a dog under an August sun, Brad Minick dug through his fanny pack in search of the change he knew was there. Despite the myriad of survival gear jammed into the small pouch, not one penny could be found. He cursed under his breath for having left both of their phones in the car with the girls, figuring since there would be no cell service on the mountain, why bother carrying the extra weight.

Either phone would sure come in handy now, as would a single quarter.

The handset of the only pay phone within ten miles dangled from the end of its coiled steel cord, its lack of a dial tone mocking them silently.

Brad heaved forward and rested his palms on his thighs, lactic acid burning its way through the muscles of his legs like a prairie fire. Driven by a strange amalgam of fear, excitement, and visions of instant riches, he and Jason had raced the last mile to the cafe that had been the starting point of their hike five hours earlier.

The boys had been dropped at the Tip-Top Diner by their girlfriends just before dawn. Neither Jessica nor Cindy had been

35

interested in hiking the steep, still half-frozen trail and had arranged to meet the boys on the opposite side of the mountain at dusk. They would try to find someplace to shop in the meantime.

Brad and Jason had been assured by a professor at school, who had made the hike a few years before, that they could meet their intended timetable if they kept a good pace and didn't stop too often along the way. Spending the night on the mountain would not be necessary unless they totally screwed around en route.

It was irrelevant now.

"Just, uh, dial 9–1–1," Jason wheezed impatiently, his breathing labored and painful.

"I would, butthead, but there's no dial tone. You can't call shit without a dial tone. Didn't you learn anything in kindergarten?" He coughed several times then spat on the decaying asphalt.

Jason scowled in response. He found himself shaking far more than the moderate outside temperature should have caused, and ran his hands over his damp jeans, surprised at how soaked they still were. It was over a hundred degrees in the valley, at Truman, twenty-five miles to the south, but near the summit of Dutch Mountain, the outside air was nearly forty degrees cooler. His soaked clothing only amplified his discomfort.

Brad extended the search for a quarter to his pockets, still to no avail. "Go see if there's a phone inside we can use."

Without a word, Jason darted the hundred feet to the front of the old diner and practically burst through the door.

The small green and white wooden structure, a cheap and decaying example of typical Fifties roadside architecture, had probably seen better days.

Perhaps not.

With almost sixty years of continuous service and its 'C' rating from the Department of Health hanging unabashedly over the greasy gas grill, it was probably a silent blessing that the lighting inside was so poor, the soiled windows now permitting only a portion of their original illumination.

It took Jason's eyes a long moment to adjust from the brilliant midday light burning outside.

When he could finally see clearly again, a dozen faceless eyes stared back at him from the dingy dining room to his right, like those of nocturnal creatures hiding from the day in some subterranean realm.

His own eyes took in each pair in succession as he slowly panned the tables.

"What'll ya have?"

Jason jumped at the voice that seemed to have materialized out of nowhere.

He turned toward the counter and saw a short woman, fifty or so, who was nearly as wide and thick as she was tall. She was dressed today as she was dressed every day of the week: dirty striped coveralls partially obscured by an even dirtier apron that would have read "Tip-Top Diner" if most of the letters had not been faded beyond legibility.

The few that now remained had a Braillelike texture to them, spattered with dried biscuit dough and mortared in place by a thick layer of grease.

Though her voice was scratchy and its tone as husky as any man's, the broad smile that generously spanned her round face put Jason at ease.

"Do you have a phone I can use, ma'am?" His words bore more excitement than he had intended.

The woman's head tilted slightly and her eyes narrowed a bit. "There's one right outside, hun, by the edge of the road. There's no way you could have missed it." The smile lessened.

"We tried that one, ma'am, but my friend and I can't seem to find any change. Could we just use the phone in here for one minute, please?"

"Sorry, hun, it's only for business. If I let *you* use it, I'd have to let everyone use it. I'm afraid you'll have to make do with the pay phone." She turned back to the grill.

"But, you don't understand, we have to call the sheriff. My friend and I just found some old guy in a suit buried in the snow and we..." His words stopped abruptly as he remembered the reward, then his head turned involuntarily to the right again. Each pair of eyes that returned his stare had widened a bit, though no one in the dining area chose to speak.

A large, weathered man in the far corner lit the cigarette he had just extracted from a crush-proof box, the yellow flame from the long wooden match drawing Jason's eyes instantly to it. The boy felt the tiny room becoming smaller, as if the walls were all moving toward him.

"You say what's buried where?" the woman asked incredulously, the smile now clearly gone. "Up the old Summit Trail?"

Jason knew Brad would be furious at his blunder. "Uh, I was only kidding," he responded lamely, forcing a smile. "I just needed to use the phone to call, uh, my girlfriend for a ride."

"Hell, that ain't much of a joke, son," the cook scolded, shaking an old wooden spoon she'd been holding in his direction.

Jason suddenly remembered the dollar bill he'd stuffed in his back jeans pocket before leaving the fraternity house. He withdrew the soggy single. "I forgot I had this," he said hurriedly. "Can you give me four quarters, please?"

The woman leaned forward and folded her arms on the counter. "I can't just open the register, hun, it's against policy. You'll have to buy something."

Jason couldn't imagine even one response befitting the absurdity of the situation. It felt like a scene from "Deliverance," a now cult classic from before he was born that the fraternity brothers downloaded one evening. It had scared the crap out of them all, as it had audiences decades prior.

He looked quickly for the gum and Certs display that was in every diner in the country. All except *this* one. "Like what?" he asked in frustration.

"I got some fried fruit pies here. Make 'em myself." She tapped the spoon proudly on a small display near the register.

The thought was vile. "How much?" He slid the limp bill toward her.

"Eightyone cents, including tax."

"But that'll leave me only nineteen cents!" he snapped before lowering his voice. "Sorry, but I need a *quarter* to use the phone." His frustration was matched only by his disbelief.

The woman studied the small plastic stand with its trio of shelves holding a dozen examples of her culinary wizardry. Each fried fruit pie had been lovingly tucked into a pocket of waxed-paper, the open end then folded twice and closed with a staple. A small piece of ragged masking tape had been applied to one side of each pouch and bore a single handwritten word in black magic-marker denoting its contents.

She selected one and laid it beside the bill. "You can have this coconut pie here for four bits. They don't sell as well as the peach and apple—they're my specialty, you know. This one's still pretty fresh."

"Great. Perfect. Fifty cents. I'll take it." He held out his hand for his change.

Without touching the register that "couldn't be opened," the woman stuck a plump hand into the top pocket of her coveralls—beneath her apron—and pulled out a fistful of quarters, dropping two of them into his palm.

"Thanks." Jason turned to leave, eager for the light of day.

"Hey, hun, you forgot your coconut pie."

With his body already partially through the door, Jason looked back and flashed a curt smile. "That's all right, just keep it."

When the door had slammed behind him, the woman put the pie back on the shelf and disappeared into her tiny office in the back of the diner, beside the cramped and cluttered pantry.

She moved some scraps of yellowing paper that had collected on the paneled wall above the light switch and dialed a number she had scribbled there nine months before. It was not the first time the number had been called by her, though not recently.

"Yes," came the attenuated response after two rings. The man made no attempt to hide his disinterest.

"This is Mattie at the TipTop Diner near Moon Lake Dam in Utah, just north of Truman. Are you the man who gave me this number?"

"No, ma'am,"—the man studied the hidefinition LCD screen in front of him. With the computing power at his disposal, more than enough to retrieve any stored data on any individual or group within the organization's voluminous database in seconds, her detailed file had appeared before she had spoken her first word, like caller ID on steroids—"but we're associated. What can I do for you today, Mrs. Blackburn?"

The quick mention of her last name no longer startled her as it had the first time she'd called. She knew the man on the other end was sitting at a computer. She'd seen such things in the movies.

"Some boy, probably a college kid from Salt Lake City, I'd bet—they start showing up about this time each year—just came in all excited and asked to use the inside phone."

"Really, the *inside* phone. My god, perhaps I'll alert the media," he said sarcastically. "I see you've called this number three times before today, Mrs. Blackburn."

"Yeah. The man who gave it to me told me to keep my eyes open and to call anytime I had something unusual to report. I'm only doing as he asked, just trying to be helpful."

"And in that spirit of cooperation, you believe some college kid wanting to use your telephone would be of help to us how?" He lit a cigarette and blew the smoke into the mouthpiece.

"This is different from the other times I've called, I'm sure of it." She delivered the words with confidence. "The boy said he and his buddy found some old guy in a suit somewhere near here, up on Dutch Mountain most likely, and he was buried in the snow. From his muddy boots, I'd say the boys had been out hiking, probably up the old Summit Trail. It starts right behind my restaurant, you know. The kids hike it all the time unless the heavy snows keep it closed." She took a deep breath. "Anyway, when I asked him to explain what he'd just said, he quickly changed his story and said he was only kidding."

The man was losing both interest and patience quickly. "He said he was kidding. And you don't think he was?" He didn't even know why he was still on the line.

"Look, mister, I've been feeding folks for thirty years or more and I've seen a lot of faces in my life. I've heard every line and lie that's ever been told—more than once, I can assure you—and I tell you this boy had the look of someone who'd just seen a ghost."

The man offered no response.

"Well?" She hated his rude silence.

He took another long draw on his cigarette, making sure she heard him exhale into the phone. "A man buried in the snow in the mountains is not exactly front page news, Mrs. Blackburn. In fact it happened—" He looked at the data on his computer screen that he'd pulled up while they had been talking; or rather, while she had been talking and talking and talking. "—twenty-three times in the last year alone. And that was just in the U.S.," he finished.

His patience had waned; he touched his finger to the END button.

"You're either not listening to me, mister, or you're not thinking very clear. The boy said the man was wearing a suit. A business suit. Now, I realize you may not know much about hiking mountain trails, but I'll bet you understand enough to know that you don't normally hike 'em in your Sunday best. Besides, the Summit Trail ain't been open since last September, the same month that other fella stopped by here and gave me this number. There hasn't been one person on that trail since that time. And the snow covering it hasn't melted in the last nine months, not 'till this week. If that's where the boys found the man, *in a business suit*—she repeated the words with emphasis to be certain she'd been heard clearly this time—that means he's been there since the last thaw, September of last year." She waited for what seemed an eternity before speaking again. "Now, is that the kind of information you fellas were looking for or not?"

The man looked to his left at the digital audio unit to verify that his earlier actions had, indeed, started it recording. "It may well be, Mrs. Blackburn." His voice had changed imperceptibly, though his pulse rate had elevated several counts. He pressed a button on the console, momentarily muting the phone. He switched on a mike beside his computer and spoke into it without waiting for a response. "Get me the Colonel—*now!*"

Mattie continued, unaware of the man's momentary distraction. "The fella that came to see me assured me there'd be good money in it if I ever came up with anything really important. Can I count on you to keep his promise?"

"You can," he said flatly.

She leaned her round body back in the old wooden desk chair. The thought of not having to put in fourteen hours a day at the diner to make ends meet filled her mind. Perhaps she would finally go on that Caribbean cruise. "How much are we talking about? I don't want no lousy five hundred bucks or nothing cheap like that for all my trouble. I really should have called the sheriff, you know, there being a dead guy and all. It's my civic duty. I don't even know who you fellas are or whether—"

"I assure you, Mrs. Blackburn," he said, cutting her off, "that you'll be well taken care of if your information proves of value."

"If it is the man you've been looking for, I want three, no, *five* thousand dollars, and I won't settle for a penny less." Her heart pounded. "I think that's more than fair. It's nearly a year I've been keeping my eyes open for you folks, you know. That's not even half minimum wage."

"Why only five, Mrs. Blackburn? Why not ten? Twenty?"

"Twenty? Twenty thousand dollars? You're telling me you'd give me that much for this information?" Someone in the dining room called Mattie's name; she covered the mouthpiece impatiently. "Keep your damn shirt on, you ain't gonna starve. I'll be there when I get there!"

"The actual dollar amount is of no consequence to us, Mrs. Blackburn, money is easy to come by. Good information, on the other hand, is priceless. Let's just say that you won't have a care left in the world if this is the piece of news my associates have been seeking."

Mattie's heart pounded like a kettle drum beneath the greasy apron and the striped coveralls. She was sure he could hear it.

She pressed the mouthpiece against her cheek.

"Before we could pay that much money, Mrs. Blackburn—"

"Please, call me Mattie," she interjected.

"Okay, Mattie. We would have to know the names of the two boys and everyone they speak with until a couple of my associates can get to your location. Can you take care of that for us Mat-tie?" He said, purposely exaggerating her name.

"The other man never said anything about me getting names or keeping an eye on no one. It ain't illegal, is it?"

Though she had voiced the question, his answer was entirely irrelevant. For twenty thousand dollars, she'd stalk the governor of Utah.

"Of course not, Mattie. Just find out their names and where they live. It would be ideal if they didn't talk with anyone but you and were still at your diner when my associates arrive in—" He looked at the map on his screen and did a rough calculation in his head, "—less than an hour. We'll want to reward the boys as well for their help, but that must remain strictly between the two of us for now, okay, Mattie?"

"That's not coming out of my part," she said firmly.

"Of course not, Mattie." He could promise her a 747; no money would ever change hands.

"All of this other stuff, you know, stuff the other fella didn't say nothin' about—it ought to be worth something extra." Her hand trembled on the phone; she could scarcely believe her own brazen words.

The man's lips formed a dry smile. "Do exactly as I have instructed and you'll be rewarded beyond your wildest dreams. Detain the boys, keep them from anyone else, and wait for my associates to arrive. You think you can do that?"

A feeling as close to orgasm as she'd felt in years coursed through her nerves. "Consider it done, fella. I gotta go now."

The other end was already a dial tone.

Mattie jumped to her feet and sprinted down the narrow hall and past the counter, placing her right cheek against the front window by the door. She swore angrily under her breath for having let the boy leave the diner. To her immense pleasure and surprise, she saw him, and his friend, she assumed, walking back toward the front door from the direction of the pay phone.

She quickly slipped back behind the counter.

The man who had called for her earlier, a regular at the diner, tapped his cup impatiently on the small, square wooden table in front of him.

She shot him a look that would insure no further interruption on his part, not if it took her another hour to get to him.

Jason pulled the door open and allowed Brad to enter first. The older boy immediately suffered the same light deprivation his friend had experienced a few minutes earlier.

After a moment, the boys dropped onto a pair of stools at the counter, their padded red vinyl tops now almost totally obscured by strips of wrinkled, silvery duct tape.

"What'll you boys have?" Mattie asked pleasantly, her chest heaving from the sudden physical exertion. The smile grew broader, the plump cheeks appeared as if they would burst at any moment.

The diner smelled of old coffee and burned bacon grease, but the boys were starving. Jason dug out his one remaining quarter and laid it on the counter. Brad looked at it in disgust; he had left his own wallet in Jessica's car along with his phone. "Just a couple of glasses of water," he said humbly.

"Water? Ain't you boys hungry?" she asked displaying what could have passed for genuine concern. "My boys were always eating, that's why I opened this place. I figured as long as I was feeding the five of them three meals a day, I might as well feed a few more mouths and get paid for it, right?"

The boys smiled, though her familial anecdote had not increased their fortunes by a single penny.

"We left our money in my girlfriend's car. I'm afraid water is all we can afford right now. We're waiting for someone. Is it all right if we sit in here until he comes?" Brad asked politely.

Jason, on the stool to Brad's left, looked past him toward the dining room. All eyes continued to stare silently back at them.

"Don't mind at all, boys. Sit here as long as you like. While you're sitting, though, how 'bout if I rustle you up a couple of cheeseburgers and some fries to go with your water? In fact, as chilled as you two look, I'll bet hot coffee sounds a lot better than a glass of tap water."

They both nodded silently but then Brad pushed the lone quarter toward her. "It sure does, but you're looking at our entire net worth at the moment, I'm afraid."

"Oh, hell, money ain't the end of the world, is it? It'll be on the house—my pleasure. You boys kinda remind me of my youngest two."

She grabbed a pair of her cleanest cups from beneath the counter and filled each with a generous portion of steaming coffee, then lovingly laid a couple of third-pound beef patties on the grill. She smiled generously at the boys before disappearing into the dining room with the coffee pot.

Outside, the wind moaned softly in the trees as the snow on the mountain steadily melted, creating tiny rivulets that rapidly disappeared into the black soil. By one P.M., the first warming light had reached the pallid fist, its shadow now stretching several feet toward the north, across the glistening, silvery shroud through which it thrust defiantly toward the heavens and the eternal justice which is believed to dwell there.

By dusk, R-W-G's impeccably dressed corpse, no longer protected by its veil of ice and snow for the first time in nine months, would become a most tempting feast for the creatures of the night.

When she returned to the front, the cook set the coffee pot once again on its burner, wiped her hands quickly on her apron, then leaned over the counter and extended her right hand pleasantly toward Jason. "Name's Mattie."

He thought about the overpriced and out-of-date confection he had been saddled with a few minutes earlier and wondered what had produced the unexpected bout of philanthropy in the woman who stood grinning only a foot and a half from his face.

Oh, what the hell. He was too hungry and too tired to give a damn about her motives. Free food was free food.

He took her outstretched hand; it felt cold to the touch. The serpent slithered under his shirt again and the small warning hairs on his neck stood at attention. "I'm, uh, Jason," he stuttered.

Though it had clearly announced its return, he could not positively identify the source of his disquiet. *Probably finding the dead body*, he thought. *That had to be it*. There was no pushing the image aside no matter how hard he tried.

"And I'm Brad," his self-assured, self-possessed friend chimed in, taking her hand and shaking it thankfully, followed by a short sip of his hot coffee. He, of course, shared none of Jason's foreboding. "Thanks for being so nice, Mattie."

She grabbed her spatula and gave the patties a quick turn. They sizzled and spat noisily against the hot, oily grill. "Glad to do it, Brad, Jason. You have no idea how much your being here at this moment means to me."

FIVE

TY SUMMERS STOPPED FIFTY yards from the south side of the diner, parallel to the crumbling asphalt of the parking lot where it met the surrounding hills. He placed the front bumper of his white Ford Expedition a few feet from the phone booth at the edge of the highway. The sheriff didn't have to bother searching for the boys who had phoned him with a breathless tale of bodies in the snow; they came scurrying across the parking lot before he had even switched off the ignition. He pressed the button and lowered the passenger's window just as the pair reached the vehicle.

"I'm Brad Minick, I'm the one who called you. Are you Sheriff Summers?" the boy asked hurriedly.

The sheriff nodded. He shook the outstretched hand.

"This is my friend, Jason Parker." Jason smiled slightly and gave a half-hearted half-wave. He was standing several feet behind Brad and seemed content to remain there. This wasn't as much fun for him as it obviously was for his buddy. There was something ominous and threatening in the air. He'd sensed it instantly upon finding the horrid purple hand and the feeling had not lessened with the sheriff's arrival.

If it would all be over soon, nothing could have suited him more.

Mattie Blackburn made a narrow part in the curtains covering the window on the southeast wall of her crowded office and peered out toward the SUV and horse trailer sitting at the far corner of her parking lot. She scribbled Sheriff Summers' name on the piece of paper that already bore the names of Brad Minick and Jason Parker. Her heart pounded and the feeling that she had somehow crossed the fine line separating right from wrong, or more appropriately, good from evil, filled her mind. She allowed the halves of the shabby rayon curtain to overlap again and dropped heavily onto her wooden chair, placing both hands to her heaving chest. A bead of sweat formed on her brow, coursed its way down the bridge of her nose, and dropped onto her apron.

Not going to worry about anything at the moment, she decided resolutely. She'd consider the morality of it all while she was cruising the Caribbean, eating someone else's cooking for a change.

Summers took a brief moment to evaluate the boys. They didn't seem like troublemakers to him, and they *had* remained at the diner as he'd instructed. Perhaps they had actually found a body in the receding snows. He sincerely hoped not, not only because it meant some unlucky bastard hadn't made it home to his family, and never would again, but also because the boys would see the man's face in their nightmares long after the adrenaline of the day had subsided. Possibly for the rest of their lives. After two combat tours in war zones around the world and twenty subsequent years in law enforcement, his own nightmares were a thick mélange of mangled bodies, nameless faces, and frozen stares.

Most likely, he thought, the boys had only seen a rocky formation that resembled a body. It happened all the time in the mountains. He had always considered that the altitude, where oxygen to the brain was less than at lower elevations, enhanced one's imagination. The sheriff stepped from the truck and met the pair at the front of the vehicle. In the trailer, Kate, his eight-year-old buckskin quarter horse, whinnied loudly, anxious to be free of her confines. Summers called out affectionately to his old mount and then turned his attention to the boy who had done the talking so far. "It's Brad, right?"

The boy nodded.

"Tell me exactly what you and your buddy saw, Brad. You were a bit sketchy on the phone." He rested a heavy boot on the reinforced winch mount and gave the youth a knowing look that warned against even the slightest exaggeration.

Brad was not put off by Summers' stern expression but it made Jason even more uncomfortable than he'd been, if that were possible.

"It was a man, sheriff, like I told you, buried in the snow. We were almost to Redmon's Ridge at the crest of Dutch Mountain when I—" he caught his friend's disapproving gaze, "—when Jason and I found him. You know the place I'm talking about?"

Summers indicated with a slight shake of the head that he was not familiar with that particular spot. He'd been on the mountain several times, on the Summit Trail specifically, but never had occasion to reach the crest.

"I'll show you," Brad said. He pulled his small hike map from his shirt pocket, unfolded it, and laid it on the hood, placing a finger on the spot he'd marked with his walking stick. "This is Redmon's Ridge, Sheriff, about two and a half hours up Summit Trail. The body is a hundred feet or so west of the trail, down a slight grade. I marked the spot with a long stick and a red plaid handkerchief. You shouldn't have any trouble spotting it, or reaching it from the trail," he added.

"It's a lot steeper than it looks, sheriff," Jason chimed in, recalling his inelegant fall before remembering he'd promised to let Brad do all the talking. He fell mute again.

Summers studied the map for a moment before extracting a small Kevlar pouch and a map tube from a pack in the back seat of the SUV. He laid the pouch on the hood and opened its Velcro flap, withdrawing an olive-drab military-issue GPS receiver and a folding straight-edge. He pulled a detailed map of the area compiled by the United States Geological Survey from the cardboard tube and spread it across the hood, keeping it in place with the GPS unit on one side and his heavy ring of keys on the other. After he'd plotted the cross point on the boy's smaller hike map, he transferred the latitude and longitude coordinates of the body's location to his larger, more detailed map, and then entered them into the GPS, providing him with exact direction and distance to the indicated spot.

If the boy's marked location was accurate, he should be able to ride directly to the body using the LCD display on the small GPS screen as a guide. In the remote mountains and forests of Utah, where even the most experienced tracker could become hopelessly disoriented and lost before he or she even realized it was happening, such technology had become commonplace.

And indispensable.

He looked again at Brad. "You're sure about this location. I've got no interest in riding halfway to Canada only to find out that you had your map upside down when you marked it."

"It's dead on, sheriff." He was resolute.

Jason disliked his choice of words.

Summers rolled the map and slipped it back in its protective tube. "What made you pick this particular trail, boys?"

"One of the professors at school told us it was a really cool day-hike. He'd done it some years back, but said it'd been closed for the last year or so because of unusually deep snows. When he told us he thought it might finally be clear enough to hike by the second week in June, we decided to give it a go."

"This isn't the second week of June," Summers noted.

"Yeah, we thought we'd get a head start, you know, be the first of the season to make the hike." Brad raised both eyebrows and formed a tight smile. "Being the first across would have been pretty cool, but finding a dead guy. Now, that's *way* cool."

Summers shook his head in silent amusement.

Jason, while no longer surprised by his buddy's complete absence of empathy, had still not grown comfortable with it. Though his clothes had nearly dried, he remained chilled to the bone.

"And you have no idea who the man you found is? You've never seen him before?" Summers said.

"Honest, sheriff, we were just hiking along and there he was, like he was sleeping. Only it was pretty obvious he wasn't sleeping, you know."

Jason shuddered.

Summers noted the boy's uneasiness and nodded at Brad's words. "How old do you think he is, Brad?"

"I couldn't say for certain." He looked to Jason for some input but got only a shrug of the shoulders for his trouble. "Kinda old, like somebody's grandfather, maybe fifty-five or so, I guess. He was definitely older than my dad." He again looked to Jason for confirmation and this time received a slight nod. "I think he's rich," Brad added.

The sheriff found the unexpected comment intriguing and cocked his head. "Why is that, Brad?"

"He's wearing a monogrammed silk shirt, an expensive suit, probably Italian, Armani or Gucci I imagine, and a diamond Rolex on his arm. Platinum," he added with a knowing smile.

Summers raised his eyebrows at the mention of the specific brand of suit and make and model of watch.

Brad noted the look of wonder. "My girlfriend is really into clothes, always reading *Italian Vogue* and shit—" He suddenly realized what he'd said and apologized. The sheriff only smiled. He continued. "And I'd kill for a watch like that." This time, he clinched his teeth at his choice of words. He knew cops didn't have sense of humor when it came to dead bodies. "Sorry, sheriff, just an expression. Really. We didn't touch it or anything," he said defensively. "I swear. It's still on his arm just like we found it."

"We didn't hardly touch a thing," Jason said sheepishly.

"Hardly?" the sheriff repeated, his stern look demanding a quick and accurate explanation.

"Okay, we did move a little bit of the snow covering the dude's face. That's how we got an idea about his age, but we didn't touch any of his stuff. You can search us if you don't believe us," Brad said defiantly.

"I don't think that'll be necessary, boys," Summers said. He was sure it had gone down just as they had described. He put the GPS receiver back in its pouch and attached its steel retaining clip to his gun belt. He withdrew a small digital audio recorder from his shirt pocket and checked that its battery was fully charged. It was the same reliable device he'd used as a detective in Salt Lake City years before and allowed him to collect a massive volume of data in a hurry without the bother of handwritten notes. He'd transcribe all relevant data to his computer when time allowed. He pressed RECORD. "I'm at the TipTop Diner near Moon Lake Dam on Lake Fork River Road, twenty miles north-northeast of Truman. I've been summoned here by two young white males, early twenties, claiming to have found a body on Summit Trail, two and a half hours north of Tip Top Diner, up on Dutch Mountain. Their data follows." Summers pointed the tiny recorder at Brad and told him to slowly spell his name and give his full address and phone number, then indicated for Jason to do the same.

The boys quickly complied.

When he'd made a few additional comments into the recorder, he pressed STOP and dropped the unit back into his shirt pocket, buttoning its flap after he did. It was obvious that Brad wasn't through. "Is there something you wanted to add, son?"

"I was wondering about the reward." The words almost shot from his mouth.

Summers grinned. "Reward?"

"Yeah, we figured any guy as rich as this dude appeared to be would have a lot of people out looking for him, no matter how long he's been missing. There's got to be a reward, don't you think?" Jason moved closer for the first time, but only by a single step.

"Could be a reward at that," Summers reasoned. "But I won't know until we find out who the man is."

"If there is—"

"If there is," Summers interrupted, "you'll be the first to know."

"And will it be ours? Ours alone?" he pressed.

"No reason to assume otherwise," Summers reasoned.

"Yes!" Brad made a celebratory gesture with his right fist. Even Jason smiled a bit for the first time. "Will you be needing us any more, sheriff? If not, we've got to call our girlfriends so they can pick us up here. They're expecting us to come out on the other side around sunset."

"Go ahead. I don't need anything else at the moment. I'll be in touch in a day or two. Thanks for being so thorough with the directions. It'll make my life a lot easier." Summers locked the SUV as Brad and Jason walked back toward the diner—Mattie had told them they could use the phone in her office if they needed to call someone to come get them. He yelled after them. "Hey." They turned to face the sheriff. "If you're still here when I get back, you're welcome to catch a ride with me into Truman."

They waved appreciatively and disappeared into the diner. Mattie had two generous slices of lemon meringue pie waiting for them. She needed to detain them a few minutes longer.

SIX

I N HIS OFFICE IN the center of the sprawling compound—simply referred to as "the ranch" by its two dozen inhabitants—his well-worn boots propped high on an old wooden desk, Colonel James Merkett listened to the digital audio recording for the fourth time. He was now more certain than ever that he'd been right to dispatch his closest teams to the diner. There had been something odd in Mattie Blackburn's voice, something that told him she might have just delivered him the item he'd been seeking for nearly a year, though with far less intensity recently than in the first few months following the crash.

He looked across the desk at his chief "squint," First Lieutenant Donald Shelton, head of covert technology for the Unit. Shelton and his team of Cyber Rangers had been so nicknamed by Merkett because of their propensity to stare for hours on end at meaningless lines of code or data on computer screens. Merkett understood none of it, didn't have to and didn't want to.

However, he fully understood and appreciated the awesome power it gave him.

He puffed on a cheap cigar in a well-chewed plastic holder as he switched off the player. "How 'bout it, Don? Think it's our boy?" Shelton was one of the only men on earth whose opinion he sought. The Colonel—for more than twenty years a member of the Army's elite Special Forces—was not given to uncertainty or lack of conviction. He did, however, value the insight and skills of the best hacker and computer wizard he'd ever met. To him, Shelton was a cyber-sociopath, with no regard whatsoever for the rights or privacy of anyone outside the Unit. He may not have used a knife or pistol as his weapon of choice to destroy the many lives he'd touched over the years that he'd been with the Unit, but in many cases, it would have been far better for the victim had they merely been eviscerated or had their brains blown out.

In one case, he had filled a congressman's personal computer with enough child pornography to get a dozen men sent away for life, and had then provided the 'anonymous' tip to the FBI that had led to the man's arrest and ultimately to his conviction. Alerting the media, also anonymously, had been unnecessary as they would have picked up on the despicable story soon enough, but having them at the man's home filming his humiliating arrest in the presence of his astounded wife and wide-eyed children had been a lagniappe too tempting to pass up.

Of course, the congressman had deserved having his personal, professional, and financial life torn asunder in one fell swoop. After all, he had cut Shelton off in traffic one rainy afternoon, and had then given the computer wizard the finger for merely blowing his horn out of reflex. Such societal unpleasantries simply could not be permitted in an orderly world, and order meant everything to a man of numbers and code.

When Merkett had learned of Shelton's completely disproportionate response to the congressman's actions and had questioned him about it, the cyber wiz had stated defensively that it had been a good opportunity to test some of his new software designed to plant digital information on any PC worldwide, by remote, and then automatically destroy all paths leading up to that event.

Oddly, the psychopathic explanation had satisfied the Colonel. What Shelton didn't fully realize or appreciate was that his absolute lack of morality and compassion for his fellow man were what Merkett liked most about him. Good computer technicians were a dime a dozen. True cyber-sociopaths were much harder to come by.

Shelton studied a satellite image of the Goodman crash site, taken in late September of the previous year, and expanded the view to include Dutch Mountain, more than thirty miles to the southeast. He leaned back in his chair, chewing on his bottom lip. "I suppose it's theoretically possible, Colonel, but it seems highly unlikely to me. The guy was twenty pounds overweight for Christ's sake, and hadn't walked farther than from his Lexus to the senate floor in the decade prior to the crash. The only regular exercise he got was humping his secretary."

"Angel Britt," Merkett said, recalling the woman's name.

"And don't forget the storm that whipped Utah's ass for two solid weeks beginning the very day he went down. I doubt there are five men in the Unit who could have survived long enough to make Dutch Mountain during that storm." He considered the brutal terrain that existed in every direction for miles from the site of the crash. "Hell, I don't think I'd like to try that hike on a sunny day."

Merkett blew a fat ring of smoke at the only window in the stark office. "You're forgetting one thing, Don."

"What's that, sir?"

Merkett stood and went to the window, directing his eyes to the southwest, to northern Utah three-hundred-seventy miles away. He could feel the same charge of electricity in his nerves he always experienced before a combat mission, when life and death rode on every decision. He spoke to the glass. "He had something driving him that few men ever experience in such undiluted form."

"Sir?"

"Revenge. The need to settle the score. I believe the bastard would have crawled through a river of broken glass and shit to carve out Wagner's heart in person."

"But he couldn't have known it was Wagner who betrayed him."

"Couldn't he? Ritchie Frye was supposed to kill them all, make it look like they died in the crash, and then jump to safety before the crash and disappear. With our help, of course. Goodman got the parachute away from him somehow, most likely by gunpoint. No chance Frye told him everything in exchange for his own life?"

Shelton thought about that. "Good chance, actually."

"Exactly. He was a big man, very detail oriented, but not overly brave. I admit I made a serious mistake there, one which I don't intend to repeat."

Merkett dropped what remained of his cigar into a waste can filled with sand and faced the other man, his words as hard as the gravel in his voice. "If it's Goodman, I want a lid clamped on it so fast and so tight that the maggots feeding off his rotting carcass will suffocate. Do I make myself clear, Lieutenant?"

"Crystal, sir."

* * *

Kate stumbled slightly when her right front hoof slipped in the stony soil, momentarily losing her footing. Summers locked in a breath and grabbed the saddle horn with his left hand, the same hand that held a half-inch nylon rope tied to Sam's halter. Such a minor misstep on Kate's part would have normally passed without notice, but Summers was acutely aware that on this particular trip, the ground fell away at an almost forty-five degree slope for several hundred feet on either side of their present location, leaving him, Kate, and Sam—a pack mule as sure-footed and strong as he'd ever owned—on a thin strip of trail no wider than a residential hallway. A fall from here might not be fatal, but it sure as hell would exact a heavy toll in broken bones before all of the rolling and tumbling had ended.

Soon, the narrow path would give way to a generous expanse of ground that sloped gradually to the valley floor, sprinkled with

Ponderosa pines and small clusters of Aspens—like most of the trail behind him. But for the next few moments, his life was in the hands of a creature who, if it could speak, would have undoubtedly said that it didn't particularly love the idea of a two-hundred-pound man on its back as it walked a craggy tightrope. Even the one under whose loving care it had spent its entire life.

"Easy, girl," Summers whispered soothingly. He used the reins to ease Kate a little closer to the center of the path, nudging her forward with the toes of his boots. Kate lunged once, then twice more, climbing the small stony rise like a veteran of the trail. The sheriff began to breathe easier as the scar of a path reluctantly widened.

Sam, Summers' fifteen-year-old red mule, though easily able to carry half his nine-hundred-fifty pounds in supplies—or bodies— was as step-certain as the native mountain sheep found throughout the area and strolled easily and obediently behind Kate, just as he had hundreds of times before.

Though Summers had only owned Sam for the last five years, he had spent his entire adult life in mountain service. To him, this relatively brief trip was a leisurely stroll in the park.

Once beyond the narrowest section of trail, Summers paused in a small clearing and removed the GPS receiver from its case, switching it on with the waterproof button on its side and ensuring that the internal antenna had a clear view of the sky. Within fifteen seconds, he had received timing signals from the four satellites necessary for minimal determination of latitude, longitude, and elevation. The LCD display changed from "acquiring" to a topo-graphical map showing the unit's precise current location. When the receiver had acquired a full complement of twelve satellites, usually within forty-five seconds of being activated, position and elevation would be displayed within a single meter anywhere on the globe.

Summers checked their current position relative to the spot Brad Minick had indicated, its coordinates having been entered as a 'waypoint' on the digital map. He studied the display for a moment, noting with pleasure that he had less than eight tenths of a mile to go.

Due north, fifteen minutes. Maybe less.

Having already spent an hour and a half in the saddle, he thought about stretching his legs and giving Kate a bit of a rest as well, but, after studying a sky that was forming an ugly, wide storm front fifty odd miles to the west, decided it would be more prudent to move on while they still had both the light and the weather on their side.

He checked the time: 3:15.

The storm that was threatening could easily make the Summit Trail by five, before they could reach the diner again. With GPS on hand, he had no fear of getting lost, even on a moonless night, but he didn't cherish the thought of being on the mountain after the sun had set. The snow-capped regions of Utah took on dramatically different personalities after dark. What little heat the upper elevations enjoyed during the day quickly yielded to the unforgiving forces of nature that had left them uninhabited and uninhabitable since the Rockies had defiantly thrust themselves toward the heavens a thousand millennia earlier.

Even with the best foul weather gear—which he owned but didn't have with him at the moment—Summers would not have willingly spent a stormy night on Redmon's Ridge.

They pressed on.

Twelve minutes later, Brad Minick's plaid scarf beckoned like a searchlight in a fog. Against the white hillside, it was easily spotted by Summers as he neared the location his receiver told him the body should be.

"Looks like the boys did all right, Kate." The buckskin responded to her name by chuffing noisily and bobbing her head up and down.

Summers stood in the stirrups and looked left and right for an access route to the dead man that would be easier than the path the boys had taken earlier. He could clearly make out three sets of footprints plus a wider track that indicated one of them had slid down the hill. No natural pathway existed. "Looks like we've got to do it the hard way, old Sam." The mule gave no indication he cared either way.

The sheriff dismounted and tied Kate's reins to a pine bough that just brushed the eastern edge of the path, then pulled his binoculars from the saddlebag and trained them at the base of Brad's walking stick. He could clearly make out a forearm and fist pointing rigidly toward the sky as well as the profile of a man's face and part of his upper torso; the lower half of the body was still partially entombed in snow.

"Seems the sun hasn't completely exposed him yet, Kate. Won't be long though." *Still a bit frozen was real good*, he considered in silent gratitude, not relishing the thought of a decomposing body filling his nostrils. As a precaution, however, Summers took a small plastic jar of Vicks VapoRub from his saddlebag and smeared a generous line of the greasy ointment across his top lip. The pungent fragrance raced through his sinuses, effectively preventing the passage of any other scent, good or bad, for as long as it remained there.

Kate turned her head away, not caring at all for the astringent aroma.

At the bottom of the grade, after Sam had been hitched securely to a large rock, and a weatherproof digital Nikon camera had been removed from the equipment case on his back, Summers stood several yards from the body snapping frame after frame of high-rez images. Despite the bright, clear conditions overhead, he used the small onboard flash to improve shadow detail and insure correct color balance in the intensely blue light of the mountains.

It was an all too familiar routine for the sheriff of Duchesne County, Utah, where three of the state's highest peaks were located. More often than he cared to remember, he'd been called upon to remove the body of some unlucky hiker who'd either underestimated the terrain or had overestimated his ability—or both. There were a thousand ways to die in Utah and Ty Summers had dealt firsthand with most of them.

Satisfied that he'd adequately documented the body and surrounding ground in its most undisturbed state, Summers moved in to shoot a close-up series. The image that formed in his viewfinder made him lower the camera from his eye and take a step backward. He dropped to one knee beside the corpse, its face now completely free of the snow Brad had thoughtfully put back in place.

"Son of a bitch," he said aloud but with genuine reverence. He recognized the man instantly as Robert Wayne Goodman, though he was always referred to, not only by friends but also the media, as 'Skipper' Goodman. The symbolic title given to him because of the yacht that he owned and piloted, often for weeks at a time.

Summers vividly recalled the senator's plane having crashed more than thirty miles to the north, across some of the most treacherous and difficult terrain in the Uinta Mountains. He also remembered the unparalleled manhunt that had continued without respite for more than a month after the crash, to no avail.

The body of the man who would have most likely been the next President of the United States appeared to have simply been swallowed up in the eternity of the mountains. Not a single trace of Goodman had been found at or anywhere near the impact site, though a hundred people had seen him board the plane that, according to Air Traffic Controllers in at least a half dozen different towers, made only one stop since that final takeoff, and that had been into the side of the mountain where all life had ended in a millisecond.

He also remembered that DNA testing had clearly shown there had only been four individuals onboard the senator's plane at the time of the crash, not the five everyone had expected: that of Lyle English, Goodman's pilot for more than a decade; Wade O'Connell, the copilot, new to Goodman's flight crew but a seasoned and respected flyer; Ritchie Frye, Goodman's bodyguard, also fairly new but with impeccable credentials; and Angel Britt, Goodman's secretary and executive assistant for many years.

But there had been no Goodman. It simply wasn't possible, both the NTSB and the FBI had testified repeatedly and resolutely, and yet that shared conviction hadn't altered the evidence.

Or more precisely, the *lack* of evidence.

One of the most powerful and influential men in the country had literally vanished into thin air without leaving a trace.

"What in God's name are you doing this far away?" Summers puzzled, referring to the site of the crash. "And in one piece?"

As he removed more snow covering the corpse and studied the scene, the sheriff quickly discerned a partial answer in the senator's tattered clothing and beleaguered appearance. While still just speculation, he surmised that Goodman had somehow made the journey on foot, in the middle of a violent winter storm that would have severely challenged even the most hardened Marine.

That did not, however, shed even a single candlepower of light on how he had exited his plane going two-hundred miles an hour— seconds before it became nothing but a debris field littered with aluminum bits and body parts—to attempt such a heroic feat of endurance and willpower in the first place.

Perhaps there had been a parachute after all, he reasoned, recalling the most logical—though entirely unsubstantiated—theory as to the senator's mysterious and miraculous absence from the plane. Such controversy had been the fodder upon which hundreds of Internet blogs had fed for months following the crash. However, after more than fifty-five-thousand man-hours of intense investigation, the FBI had not been able to uncover one sliver of evidence that a parachute existed, or had ever existed, that could be tied to Goodman, his plane, or anyone on the plane. Furthermore, in his nearly sixty years on earth, including his time in the military, the esteemed senator had never once skydived, not even in tandem.

Those reporters and conspiracy theorists who remembered Dan Cooper of the 1970s—AKA: D.B. Cooper, though neither were his real name—quickly likened Goodman's disappearance to that legendary skyjacker, though it was well known that Cooper had at least three parachutes from which to choose when making his miraculous escape.

That plus two hundred thousand in cash he'd just extorted from Northwest Airlines.

However, despite the fact that one had been a common thief, albeit a flamboyant one, with multiple parachutes from which to choose, and the other a revered member of the Senate and a Presidential candidate with no known means of exiting a plane in flight without death being an absolute certainty, the comparison had been made and the conspiracy blogs had flourished.

Summers thought about the diner, so near to Goodman's final resting place here, at his feet, and felt a surprisingly deep sadness for a man he'd known only via the media.

"You almost made it, sir," he said solemnly. "I don't suppose you had any idea how close you were to finding help." A frigid blast of air well in advance of the approaching storm front reminded the sheriff how precious time was; there was much to do and only two hours of good light left at best.

Summers finished the necessary photography and note taking, took an exact location reading with his GPS receiver, and then pulled one of the heavy rubber body bags from Sam's backpack.

SEVEN

T HE PLAIN BLACK CROWN Victoria eased cautiously off Lake Fork River Road and pulled alongside Summers' rig. The man in the passenger seat—dressed in a dark, well-cut suit, as was his partner—stepped from the vehicle as it slowed to a stop near the back of the horse trailer. He looked quickly inside and then moved to the truck, giving the driver a signal that meant it was also empty. They smiled at each other, celebrating their stroke of good fortune. The Colonel would be pleased to learn they'd arrived while the local 'Barney' was still out.

Now they needed to locate the boys who had found the body, learn everything they knew, and, most importantly, how much time they had left before the deputy's return.

The driver pulled the car into one of the parking places in front of the diner, next to an old green Jeep, and switched off the ignition. His buddy, having walked the short distance from where he'd gotten out, dropped into the passenger seat again. "How do you want to do this?" he asked.

"Nice and easy. The Colonel wants a real low profile until we know for certain whether or not it's Goodman. If it turns out not to be him, we thank everyone for their time and head back home.

No hits, no runs, no errors." He lit one of his last three remaining Marlboros from a badly wrinkled soft pack and offered the other man one. It was declined, as usual.

"And if it is Goodman?"

The driver took a deep and pensive drag, keeping the smoke in his lungs for a short while before letting it ease from his nostrils. "That'll change things, won't it?"

Mattie Blackburn watched with intense interest as the Crown Victoria circled the parking lot and the passenger stepped out beside the sheriff's rig. Between catering to Jason and Brad for the last two hours and waiting on a steady flow of regular patrons, she'd kept an eye on the highway like a kid might watch the fireplace on Christmas Eve. Twenty thousand dollars. The number played in her mind like a favorite tune. She hastily positioned herself at the front of their car when they didn't get right out, not certain if she should move past the front bumper.

Amused, the two men just stared at her with casual indifference.

When they didn't jump right out and greet her, she moved to the driver's side. "Are you the men that other fella sent, the fella I spoke with on the phone? Did you bring my money?" Her words were breathy as she framed her face in the open window. If they had been a couple of insurance salesmen from Salt Lake City—instead of who they were—they would probably have rolled up the glass and hurriedly sought another dining establishment.

But they weren't insurance salesmen from Salt Lake or any other city. They could be, of course, if required. On a recent occasion, they had been FEMA field agents; on another, NTSB accident investigators. Today, they were with the Federal Bureau of Investigation.

The driver reached inside his jacket with his right hand. "Are you Mrs. Blackburn?" he asked flatly. She nodded, but didn't like not being able to see his eyes behind his dark sunglasses. He withdrew his I.D. and held it in her face for a brief moment before closing it arrogantly again. "FBI ma'am. I'm Special Agent McGhee and this is Agent Witherspoon. Are the two boys still inside?"

"You mean Brad and Jason. Really sweet boys. Kinda remind me of a couple of my own, my youngest two. They're on their second dessert, waiting for their girlfriends, Jessica and Cindy, to arrive. Since they weren't able to—"

"Yes, ma'am, that's fine," McGhee interrupted, not wishing to spend any more time chewing the fat with Aunt Bea than necessary. "Now is there a place inside where my partner and I can speak with them alone?"

Mattie appeared to give it some thought. "Not really, not if you want any real privacy. Everything's pretty tight in there except in the dining room, but there's a handful of folks eatin' right now. They'll probably all be leaving before long, though. If you'd care to wait, you're welcome to use that area. I just put on some fresh coffee."

"No ma'am. We need to speak with the boys as soon as possible. Would you mind sending them out without alerting the rest of your patrons to our presence?"

"No, I don't mind." Mattie hesitated a second but couldn't help herself: "Did that other fella say anything to either of you about my money?" Her pulse quickened.

McGhee had no idea what she was talking about, but figured he knew the right answer to keep things moving along. "Yes, ma'am, he did, and we were instructed to inform you that everything is being taken care of even as we speak. I'm sure he'll be back in touch with you very shortly, probably within the hour."

Mattie's scalp tingled. "Oh, you're just the sweetest man. I'll send Brad and Jason right out." She disappeared into the diner. McGhee thought he saw her skip-step, evoking a pig-like snort from him.

When the door had closed behind her, his partner rapped him on the shoulder with his knuckles. "What's that for?" McGhee asked.

"Wither-spoon?" the other man declared in disgust, stretching out the name.

"Yeah, you like it? When I was having the creds made up, it just sort of came to me." He gave 'Witherspoon' a twisted smile. "I think it suits you."

"Kiss my ass. It sounds like it belongs to a tent preacher. I knew I should have looked at them before we left. Next time, I'm in charge of names."

"Yeah, whatever." McGhee reached for a cigarette and was about to light it when the boys exited the front door of the diner and looked in their direction. He pushed the smoke back in its pack and the pack back in his jacket pocket. "It's show time. Play nice, at least at first," he admonished his partner.

Witherspoon straightened a bit. "Me? I always play nice."

McGhee shot him a look of complete incredulity, earning a muffled, "Screw you," from his associate.

Brad and Jason stood on the stoop, the front door slamming behind them. The sun, while not as bright as it had been hours earlier, made them squint and wrinkle their foreheads. Jason shielded his eyes with his hand. The two men exited their vehicle and stood like a pair of Brooks Brothers mannequins by their respective doors.

"Right here, boys," Witherspoon called, motioning them toward the black sedan. The boys moved quickly down the steps to the car. He opened his back door for Brad while Jason reluctantly entered the back seat on the driver's side.

Once inside, McGhee started the engine and drove to the far side of the lot again, paralleling the sheriff's vehicle, and as far from the diner as possible without getting back onto the road. An eighteen-wheeler chugged noisily up Highway 35, thick black diesel smoke belching from its twin exhausts. Following it, a young couple in a new BMW seemed welded to the truck's rear bumper, the driver—with growing impatience—itching for an opportunity to pass. In a minute, both had disappeared over the hill to the south leaving the parking lot quiet except for the soft purr of the Ford's powerful V-8. McGhee switched it off.

He and Witherspoon turned partially in their seats, facing the boys. Neither removed his sunglasses, adding immeasurably to Jason's misery—he was now positive he had an ulcer in the making.

The man in the passenger's seat spoke first. "Good afternoon, boys. I'm Special Agent Witherspoon and this is Special Agent McGhee. We're with the FBI."

"Mind if we see some I.D.?" Brad asked.

"Of course not, boys," McGhee obliged, and he and his partner thrust a pair of perfect FBI credentials into the back seat, coming to rest only inches from each of the boys' faces.

Jason shrunk an inch in his seat, though his buddy was charged by the appearance of the federal law enforcement agency. *This guy must have been someone really important. The reward is gonna be huge,* he thought to himself. Jason knew exactly what Brad was thinking by the wide-eyed expression on his face.

Brad quickly gave the men both of their names and addresses, and as before, found himself speaking into the microphone of the small digital recorder that had been placed on the seatback between them. He knew in his gut that they had stumbled onto something bigger than just some well-dressed dead guy with a fancy watch. The Feds, for god's sake! The thought, fueled by four cups of Mattie's high-octane coffee and two pieces of sugar-filled lemon meringue pie, made him feel like he was going to explode right there in the back seat.

Unable to miss the boy's heightened, almost agitated state, McGhee said, "Calm down, son. There's nothing to be nervous about."

"I'm cool," Brad quickly assured him, though every cell in his slender frame was experiencing a sugar and caffeine-charged buzz of epic proportions.

"That's good. Now, first, how long has the deputy been gone?"

"You mean the sheriff, Sheriff Summers," Brad corrected. He looked at his watch. "A couple of hours, I guess."

The men had not expected the county's top cop to be handling the removal personally, but gave no indication that the news was even mildly troubling. "Can you tell us how far the body is from here, Brad?"

Brad took a deep breath and collected his thoughts. "It took Jase and me a little more than five hours to get there and back, I guess, but we were on foot and we took our time going up. We ran like the wind coming back down, though."

"I imagine you did," Witherspoon said.

"I figure the body is about four or five miles up the trail, maybe a bit more." Brad sought confirmation from Jason, but the other boy remained mute.

The men looked at each other. Figuring the sheriff had no more than an hour's work at the site, and allowing for the difference in speed between the boys on foot and the sheriff on horseback, their timetable was approaching critical. "Tell us about the body," Witherspoon said.

"What do you want to know?" Brad asked.

"All of it. Don't leave anything out, no matter how inconsequential it might seem to you. It's our job to make sense of such trivia. Understand?"

Brad didn't care for the man in the passenger seat. "Yes, sir," he agreed.

Jason nodded agreeably but didn't speak.

Brad recalled for the two men every detail he could remember, as well as giving them the hike map he'd marked. When the expensive watch and R-W-G monogram were mentioned during his nearly breathless ten-minute delivery, the men looked at each other briefly, their nods of approval and sly, knowing smiles barely perceptible.

Jason added nothing to the excited monologue other than an occasional nod. When Brad had finally finished and slumped back in his seat—the caffeine and sugar rush having ebbed momentarily—both men knew beyond a doubt that Goodman's body had finally been found. The driver looked sternly at the pair. "What about his cell phone, boys?" McGhee's voice was completely flat and as serious as that of an executioner.

Now it was the boys' turn to study each other in silence. "What cell phone?" Brad asked.

"We didn't see any cell phone," the boys said in unison.

Witherspoon pressed, his tone elevated. "You're telling us you found no cell phone on or near the body?"

"No memory card, no thumb drive, no DVD, not even so much as a CD?" McGhee pressed.

"No, sir, but we didn't really look all that hard. There wasn't anything in plain sight, that's for sure."

"Not a damned thing that would hold a video?" McGhee pressed.

"No, sir. Not unless he had something in one of his pockets, but we didn't look in any of them," Brad assured them.

"It's just like we told the sheriff," Jason added, the fear of rotting in federal prison now looming over him—at least in his fragile state of mind—"we didn't touch the guy. Not at all. I mean, we scraped some of the snow off his face to see if we knew him—"

"And *did* you know him?" Witherspoon snapped sharply, startling them.

Both boys shook their heads.

"No, sir," Jason added weakly. "We thought, you know, that we might have seen him on TV or something, but—"

"But what?" Witherspoon said, his face as hard as stone. "Did you know him or not?"

"No, sir," Jason assured him.

"No, sir," Brad added a second later.

Witherspoon's stare intensified, alternating between the boys as he tried to determine whether or not they were telling all they knew.

They were, he decided.

McGhee, the man ultimately in charge of the investigation—at least at this moment—decided not to press the issue. The boys could know nothing of the cell phone's significance, he reasoned. If it had not been in Goodman's possession when he left the plane, all the better. It had logically been destroyed in the massive conflagration that consumed the plane's fuselage and everything within it.

On the other hand, if the video was somewhere on the corpse—in whatever form it might exist—and the sheriff now held it as part of the general evidence collected at the scene, that presented a problem. Not a huge one, he reasoned, but it would certainly not be the simplistic act that taking it from a pair of intimidated college kids had represented. Their creds would stand up to the closest visual scrutiny, they always had, but what if the sheriff decided to call the local FBI Field Office or even D.C. for some boneheaded reason? They knew a local 'Barney' was seldom a true professional, and, as such, could often be both unpredictable and unreasonable.

Either way, it was time to report what they had learned to the Colonel.

Brad summoned his courage as the men sat silently staring into the back seat, their eyes moving in tandem between the two boys. He knew this was meant as pure intimidation and he wasn't having any more of it. They were the heroes here, not the villains, dammit. They'd found the guy everyone had apparently been looking for, now they were entitled to get whatever was coming to them.

"Was this guy famous or something?" he asked.

"You just told us you didn't recognize him," Witherspoon said, repeating the boy's earlier words. His eyes narrowed and the stony expression returned.

Brad said, "We didn't, I swear. I mean we still don't."

Jason silently agreed, his head moving side to side.

"Should we have?" Brad asked meekly.

"Probably not. He wasn't famous, not the way you kids think of it." Both men were silently pleased that the boys had no sense of the magnitude of their discovery, though it mattered little, if any, at the end of the day.

The thought of money continued to flood Brad's mind. "Is there a reward for finding this dude? Sheriff Summers seemed to think there might be." He crossed his fingers. Jason was in a self-imposed trance, the words that floated between the front and back seat now barely discernible.

McGhee thought for a second, missing barely a beat. "Yeah, a big fat reward, Brad, thousands of dollars, but it's federal. It can only come through us, not the sheriff. You know what that means, boys?"

Brad was already spending the money in his mind; Jason's eyes had lost their glaze. "Federal? I don't understand," Brad said.

"It means you've told the last person you're ever gonna tell about the body. If you breathe a word about what you saw up on the mountain today to another living soul, and that includes your family, girlfriends—*anyone*—you not only won't get shit, you'll end up in a federal prison."

"What *can* we say about it?" Brad asked, wanting to know if any latitude at all existed.

"You can't say a damn word!" Witherspoon snapped, then checked his tone. "If anyone asks either of you anything, simply tell them you changed your mind about hiking the trail today. Tell them the snow was still too deep."

"I don't understand why we have to lie," Jason murmured timidly.

"Without going into detail, son, let's just say that it's a matter of national security. Now do you understand?"

Both shook their heads indicating they did not.

"That's okay, you don't have to understand. You only have to do exactly as you're told. You have any problem with that?" Witherspoon removed his dark glasses revealing dull green eyes within narrow slits, like those of a reptile.

Brad was taken aback by his severe expression while Jason quit breathing altogether. "No problem whatsoever, sir," Brad assured him.

Jason signaled his consensus with a single nod.

Brad then added in his sincerest voice, "Hell, mister, we ain't saying shit to anyone about even being here today. As far I'm concerned, we went to the mall with the girls."

"Now you've got the idea, son," McGhee smiled. "With an attitude like that, the reward's as good as cash in the bank."

As McGhee mumbled something cryptic to his partner, an Acura coupe pulled in front of the diner, its attractive driver chatting animatedly with another young woman in the passenger seat sitting with her back to the side glass. The driver was Brad's girlfriend, Jessica; the passenger Jason's girlfriend, Cindy. The young women had planned to go shopping while Jason and Brad played Lewis and Clark, but had been summoned by Brad an hour and a half ago—from the pay phone—and were now back at the diner to retrieve their boyfriends at the same spot where they'd left them at sunrise.

Jason had wanted out of the car since he'd first entered it, and with his girlfriend and passport to freedom having just arrived, wasn't interested in waiting another second. He already had one foot on the asphalt before his first word was spoken. "We've got to go now. We won't say a word, we swear." Without awaiting a response, he finished exiting the car, closed the door soundly behind him, and sprinted toward the bright red Acura.

Brad shrugged his shoulders and produced a dumb expression, looking alternately between the men's faces for permission to leave. "Not one word to anyone, I swear," he repeated. "I really like the idea of cash and I don't think I'd care for prison even a little bit." He hoped his lucid grasp of the situation would reassure the two agents. When the only response he received was Witherspoon recovering the hard, narrow eyes with his Ray-Bans, he joined Jason.

Within a minute, the Acura was speeding south, down the mountain and ultimately back to Salt Lake City. The moment the diner's chimney had vanished from the rear glass, Jessica and Cindy had been sworn to secrecy.

"You get the tag?" Witherspoon asked, handing his partner the small recorder.

McGhee smiled as he repeated the license plate number into its microphone.

Goodman had been found.

It was time to call the Colonel.

More importantly, they knew, it was time to move the plan forward after months of sitting on their hands.

* * *

Ty Summers stopped along the trail, less than a mile from the diner, and checked the heavy bag he'd tied to Sam's back an hour earlier. It was the second time he'd repeated the ritual since reaching the ridge trail again, tightening the lashings as the senator's body—strapped ignominiously across the mule like a sack of feed corn—became less rigid within the warmth of its thick, black rubber cocoon.

"Sorry, sir," he said as he pulled tightly on the nylon ropes. "I know it's not exactly a limo, but it's the best I can do under the circumstances." Summers realized it was not a very fitting conveyance for "the man who would be king"—as the pundits had often referred to Goodman when rumors of his bid for the Presidency began to fly in the spring of the previous year—and the sight of the once great man strapped like a slain deer across the hood of a Jeep bothered him more than he'd expected. This was not his first body retrieval, not even his hundred-and-first, but there was little doubt it would be his most memorable.

He remounted his horse and looked back at Sam, who bore his famous cargo without the slightest complaint and with even less indication that he understood the importance of the moment. "If it's any consolation, sir—though I doubt you'll give a shit at this point, eh—I think you'd have made a hell of a good president."

Great, I'm talking to a dead guy, he grinned in silent amusement as he gently touched the toes of his boots to Kate's flanks. The big quarter horse chuffed once and then moved forward without further encouragement.

Summers studied the rapidly approaching storm and knew it wasn't going to pass them by. "Let's go, big girl. If we hurry, we'll both be snug in our beds before the worst of it hits, eh."

Kate added a bit of energy to her stride as if he had understood every word.

EIGHT

I T WAS DUSK IN the canyon when Marie Matthews rose from her sandy seat at the water's edge and started for the campsite. With its mile-high walls and narrow gorges, darkness fell on the river more than ninety minutes before it robbed the last light from the plateaus and mesas five thousand feet above.

Personal problems aside, she had a group to feed, entertain, inform, and protect from the elements. She could do none of those things a half mile down the beach.

Alex, certain in her gut that her best friend was not actually a serial killer, despite her bizarre and troubling admission, had explained away Marie's uncharacteristic absence by telling all who asked that the 'boss' had a migraine. "She gets them bad sometimes, always has. It's just the desert sun," she'd added to lend authenticity to the lie. She assured them that Marie would be her old self after she'd had a little time away from the bustle and noise of camp.

The latter more prayer than lie.

Alex truly loved Marie, not only as the sister she had never known but also as the mother she had barely known. Their age difference was less than ten years, Alex having just turned twenty-two, but Marie had always seemed far wiser and more together than anyone Alex had ever known—regardless of age.

Except this week each June, she continued to remind herself.

She would have bet her life that her friend's murderous admission had been nothing more than stress-induced rambling. Surely she hadn't actually killed anyone, certainly not several people, despite having stated it as fact.

Marie's words had blindsided her, however, and had, indeed, freaked her out totally for awhile, despite her promise to remain calm and level-headed no matter what.

When she saw Marie again, soon she hoped, she would apologize to her for her reaction and beg her forgiveness. That's what friends did after all: they listened; they stood by your side; they took the bad with the good. *But a murderer*, she thought, pushing away the ludicrous notion as soon as it had formed.

It was enough to drive one mad.

Marie materialized quietly out of the inky blackness of a starless night and strolled toward the campfire, around which two dozen physically exhausted, yet spiritually super-charged, carolers tried their best to put words and harmony to the long version of *American Pie*, Don Mclean's pop classic of the early seventies. It wasn't working any better with this group than it had with any of the others she'd led down this river, their attempt at musical concord rarely more than the vocal equivalent of a sack full of bagpipes being crushed.

Still, the words were mostly on track—she'd heard them enough times to know them by heart—and they weren't the absolute worst group she'd ever heard.

Perhaps only the second or third worst.

Alex spotted Marie when she was still a hundred feet south of the campsite, just as the faint glow from the roaring fire gilded her from head to toe in flickering amber hues. She jumped up and ran to meet her.

As the two women embraced, Marie began to apologize profusely for her outburst, almost drowning out Alex's own heartfelt petition for forgiveness. The two stopped speaking in mid-sentence and just smiled affectionately at each other. No further words of contrition needed to be exchanged. They both understood.

"You know that I didn't really take everyone's life, right?" Marie said. "It's just that I feel so—"

"Of course I do," Alex interrupted warmly, pulling her friend to her again. "I know you're not a killer."

"Well, that's not entirely true," Marie corrected. "But the worthless son of a bitch I shot had just..." A lump formed in her throat and the words failed her.

"It's okay," Alex assured her. "Obviously, we have a lot to talk about around this, but hey, this is a really good start, right."

Marie nodded.

"So, what say we get you fed—I saved you some salmon and a double handful of the best shrimp—and you can tell the 'kiddies' one of your famous ghost stories before bedtime. Sound like a plan?"

"Yeah, sounds like a perfect plan."

They walked, arm in arm, toward the fire and the joyous group now absolutely massacring Jimmy Buffet's *Margaritaville*.

"Tell you what," Alex said as Brian and Carolyn rose to greet them, when she still had a few private seconds left with her friend before she had to again share her with everyone else, "the minute we get back to Truman, let's grab some real girl clothes—not these river rags—and spend a couple of days in Salt Lake City shopping, eating all the wrong foods, hanging out with boys, and spending our hard-earned money like we didn't have a care in the world."

Marie could only nod.

"You lead and I'll follow, just like always," Alex added. It was an expression the women had shared for three years; not signifying submission but rather a well-deserved and warmly offered respect.

The tears again rimmed Marie's cocoa brown eyes.

The other boatmen reached their companions, followed by a quartet of passengers who had just spotted their newest hero, the woman who'd pushed them all to the very edge of oblivion before deftly yanking them back to safety. Amid the cacophonous mélange of well-wishing and back patting that ensued, Marie managed to say, "I'd love nothing better. You're a truly great friend, you know that, right?"

Alex smiled broadly then disappeared toward the camp stove.

* * *

McGhee held the cell phone to his right ear, waiting for Colonel James Merkett to pick up. He withdrew the nearly smashed pack of cigarettes from his inside suit pocket and shook it to force into the ragged opening one of the remaining Marlboros. If fact, there was only one cigarette left; he reminded himself to get another pack from the trunk.

Witherspoon, bored beyond description, searched the car's glove compartment for something to eat. Anything. He was starving, and he always ate when he was bored.

And right now, he was bored shitless.

"I'm going in for a burger," he said. "Want one?"

McGhee looked amused. "Should I see if the Colonel wants pickle and mustard on his?"

The hungry man reconsidered the soundness of his decision to leave at this particular moment and continued to rifle through the glove box.

Unable to find so much as a flattened packet of ketchup or a half-eaten roll of Tums, he returned his attention to the data he had been entering into his cell phone; the Colonel would immediately want everything they'd learned since arriving at the diner. He was certain Merkett would be pleased with the information they had managed to collect in the short time they'd had to work.

His stomach let out a long, deep rumble that earned him a disapproving stare from McGhee. He turned his palms upward and wrinkled his brow as if to say, "What?"

"Give it to me short and sweet," Merkett said when the call had been put through to his office by the ranch's switchboard operator, choosing to use neither of the names of the men he had dispatched to the diner. Not that it would have mattered, their current names being as fake as the breasts of most Hollywood starlets, but it was standard operating procedure. Stateside or not, this was still a military operation and would be treated as such at all times. Anyone violating protocol would answer to Merkett personally.

The operator, like all in the Unit who dealt with audio, video, or data, were Shelton's men, experts in the field of encryption, decryption, surveillance, counter-surveillance, and the many disciplines directly related to computer technology and the Internet.

All calls coming into or originating from the ranch were monitored electronically by Shelton's team and simultaneously copied to thumb drives after having been heavily compressed and encrypted. There were no exceptions, not even for the Colonel. There had been but one breach of security since they had departed Afghanistan the previous year, but it had been so potentially devastating—remained so potentially devastating to this day—that the ranch had become more secure than Fort Knox since the discovery. Without the benefit of secure phone lines, it was SOP for those calling 'home' to use cryptic language and bidirectional anonymity during all phone conversations. It was highly unlikely that anyone—more precisely, any agency—was actually monitoring the phone lines coming into the ranch, or any of the dozens of cell phones in use by operatives within the Unit, but one lame assumption of absolute loyalty by all within the elite group had almost tanked the whole plan before it had begun.

It would not happen again, and when the traitor responsible was finally apprehended—as he surely would be one day—Merkett had sworn to peel his skin from his body and tack it to the wall in front of him before slitting his throat and feeding his remains to the hogs.

The men in the Unit knew it had not been an idle threat.

"It's him, sir," McGhee said succinctly.

"Degree of certainty?"

"One hundred percent, sir."

"Data." It wasn't a question.

"Transmitting now," McGhee said, indicating for Witherspoon to forward the information that he'd sent to his cell phone from their taped conversation with the boys. This included the license number and detailed description of the vehicle in which they'd departed only minutes earlier.

His partner complied, touching the SEND button of the small LCD screen and delivering an encrypted version of the data—in this case to the Colonel's office computer—via a highly obfuscated version of the standard text messaging application normally found on the phone. This program, more clever than any currently in use by even the most well-funded covert agencies in the world, converted the normal text data into a mishmash of mind numbing gibberish that would take a team of military cryptologists a year to decipher without the key.

By then, the program's self-scrambling algorithms would have changed the encryption sequence no less than a hundred times, relegating whatever had been learned from one or two intercepted transmissions to little more than detached pieces of intel awash in a sea of disconnected mumbo-jumbo.

Fortunately for the Unit, the man charged with deciphering such data was also the man who'd written the ultra-sophisticated program. At the receiving end, Merkett would see all encrypted text messages in real time and fully decrypted, having already passed through Shelton's extraction and conversion routines.

"I'll hold," Merkett said. Shelton stood over his shoulder, peering with great interest at the window on the HD display where the information would appear.

McGhee swapped the phone to his left hand and withdrew the last Marlboro with his right, stuffing it between his lips. The soft pack was then crumpled into a tight ball and tossed to the floorboard on Witherspoon's side. He punched the cigarette lighter in the middle of the dash and held it depressed for ten seconds while the other end of the phone remained silent. When he withdrew it from its socket, it glowed cherry red. He touched it to the end of a Marlboro that looked more like a piece of twisted driftwood than a cigarette and drew in a deep breath.

When the Colonel still hadn't spoken by this time, he said, "Sir?"

"Stay on the line," came the terse response.

Within fifteen more seconds, Shelton's program had worked its magic and all of the information that had been collected by the diner team appeared on the Colonel's computer.

"Can I surmise from the description of the vehicle and its female occupants that you no longer enjoy the company of the two boys?"

McGhee knew at once from the Colonel's tone that they should have detained Jason Parker and Brad Minick. He cursed silently under his breath.

Witherspoon made a questioning gesture, unable to hear both sides of the conversation, but McGhee waved him off impatiently.

"That's correct, sir. In our opinions, it seemed more important at the moment to—"

"You don't have opinions," he barked. "You follow orders. You follow procedure." By this time, Merkett was on his feet facing the window in his office.

McGhee could feel his dark eyes staring at them from across the expanse of mountains that lay between the ranch and the diner. This moment held none of the pleasure and "job well done" they had anticipated.

"Yes, sir," came his anemic response. "Should we—"

Again he was cut off in mid-sentence. "You have help heading your way," he said brusquely, referring to the backup team he had been wise enough to dispatch. "They have already been forwarded the relevant information and will clean up. In the meantime, do you think you can take care of the remaining items on your list?"

"Absolutely, sir," McGhee assured him.

"Well then, do it. The items that you dropped are of little consequence compared with those that remain to be collected. I want nothing left undone. Clear? A mistake at this juncture will cost more than you're prepared to pay, I'm afraid."

Merkett looked at Shelton to assure himself that Bravo Team had already been forwarded the vehicle's information, as well as full descriptions of its four occupants.

It had.

Witherspoon knew at once from his partner's pained expression that the Colonel was not pleased with their actions thus far. All thought of food vanished as his stomach instantly soured, silencing the rumble that had heretofore continued to make its presence known.

McGhee understood that Merkett had not been referring to the fiscal cost of another mistake on their part. He didn't relish the thought of his own hide being nailed to a wall at the ranch, if only metaphorically.

The Colonel may have tolerated mistakes about as well as his bowels would have tolerated broken glass, but in McGhee's years with the Unit, disloyalty had been the only sin that carried with it a death sentence as certain as sunrise.

"The package should arrive within the hour, sir. We have much to do between now and then."

"So why the hell are you still on the phone with me?" Merkett hissed.

The other end went dead before McGhee could press the END button.

NINE

THE PHONE IN MATTIE Blackburn's office rang just as she pressed a flattening iron to a half slab of bacon that was frying on the grill. It would keep the thick slices of salty pork from curling and shrinking as they normally would without benefit of the two-pound weight. She wiped her hands on her apron and practically flew from the kitchen.

"Hello," she said breathlessly. It had been an exciting day thus far and the best was yet to come. Hopefully, this was the call she'd been waiting for.

"We need you to clear the diner as soon as possible. Preferably, within the next ten or fifteen minutes. Can you do that, Mattie?" McGhee questioned.

"Sure, I guess. But why? Normally I don't close before—"

"Because we need you to," he said impatiently, then reconsidered his tone. "We can't risk handing you such a large sum of cash with that many people around. Of course, if you would prefer a check."

"No. What I mean to say is yes, sure, ten minutes. I'll take care of it."

McGhee smiled. It was always greed that got 'em. Got 'em every time. "Excellent. My associates will be there with your reward money by then," he lied, "and I know how anxious you are to receive it. Now, be sure," he cautioned, "not to arouse any suspicion. And one more thing, Mattie..."

"Y-yes," she stuttered. Her heart was making enough noise to be heard in the dining room. She could smell the bacon turning to charcoal on the old grill but couldn't have cared less.

"No calls, Mattie. Your phone is now being monitored and if a single call leaves the diner between now and the time my associates arrive, I'll simply tell them to drive on by. Do I make myself clear?"

"Ten minutes. No calls. Get everyone out. Don't arouse suspicion. No problem. Got it." Her heart felt as if it would burst and sweat soaked her scalp.

"Wonderful," he said as he terminated the call.

Witherspoon took the cue and exited the vehicle, taking the keys to the trunk with him.

Fifty feet away, the Tip-Top Dinner was about to close early for the first time since Christmas Eve.

With no real explanation or courtesy, even to her most loyal patrons, Mattie Blackburn successfully cleared the small eating establishment with two minutes to spare, saying simply—a long wooden spatula punctuating her words—that she was tired, was going home early, and had had enough of cooking and clients for one day.

While not normally given to outbursts of psychotic behavior, Mattie was nonetheless seen by most of her clientele as a bit eccentric at times, and her abrupt decision to terminate the business day a few hours early had not been taken by anyone as a precursor of impending doom. At most, those expecting to dine there, having wiled away the afternoon over coffee and gossip, would have to migrate to one of their other haunts for their evening meal.

Outside, McGhee and Witherspoon had witnessed in amusement what could only be described as the departure of rats from a sinking ship, so quickly had the patrons vacated the diner. *Gets 'em every time*, he chuckled to himself, slitting open the new pack of Marlboros with his thumbnail that Witherspoon had retrieved from the trunk along with the field bag that now lay on the seat between them.

Witherspoon checked his watch. "If the boys are right about the location and the time Barney left to collect the body, I'd say we have just over half an hour to finish inside. Plenty of time." He unzipped the heavy Kevlar bag and withdrew a small aerosol can, no larger than one typically used to fill a butane lighter. "Gotta love this bitch," he said, referring to Shiva, the nickname for the short-lived semi-paralytic gas contained within the canister. "Sure makes life simple."

"Makes *death* simple," McGhee corrected with a sinister smirk. He rifled through the field bag, ensuring that, among other items they might need, were two pairs of wide-mouth pliers and a time delay igniter.

This particular ignition timer, made almost entirely of non-metallic composites that would completely disintegrate in even a small fire—leaving behind none of the usual evidence associated with less sophisticated and less costly devices—was a favorite of the Unit not only because of its simplicity and reliability, but also its ability to disappear after it had done its work. When they'd finished here, the cook would be gone, the disgusting "choke and puke" of a diner would be gone, and most importantly, all evidence of their involvement would be gone.

As would they.

Later, despite some insurance adjuster or fire investigator arguing that arson had almost certainly been the cause of the inferno that had claimed poor Mattie Blackburn and her beloved roadside café, it would be put down in the books as a tragic accident originating from a gas leak in the antiquated plumbing and ill-kept fixtures that literally defined the Tip-Top Diner.

A settlement check would be cut, a family would grieve the loss of its matriarch, and life would return to normal for most of Truman before the ashes had cooled.

Such was life.

Such was death.

"Let's go," McGhee said, taking the bag and reaching for his door handle.

"Forgetting something?" Witherspoon said, handing him a small mask similar to those used by auto body shops to keep volatile organic chemical fumes present in paint and primer from prematurely shortening the lives of their employees. These particular masks had an additional filter treated with a proprietary compound that would neutralize Shiva's effects when encountered.

McGhee took the mask and, after a final glance around the parking lot to ensure theirs was the only vehicle remaining within sight—other than the Expedition belonging to the sheriff and Mattie's old Impala—he and his partner strolled quietly up the steps toward the front door.

Working furiously at the stove, Mattie Blackburn used a heavy food scraper to remove the remnants of the scorched bacon from the wide stainless steel grill top that had seen its best days three decades earlier. Her back to the counter and front door, she labored at a chore she had done scores of times in mindless toil.

Her thoughts were on money. Mounds of glorious green cash. Sacks of the stuff of which dreams are made. She didn't even hear the men enter, though this as much the result of intentional stealth on their part as oblivion on hers.

When a cooling waft of air on the back of her neck finally told her that she was no longer alone in the diner, she turned quickly, certain a patron had slipped back in, despite the CLOSED sign prominently displayed in the front window, and was about to despoil her once in a lifetime shot at winning the lottery.

"Out!" she barked, spinning toward the door, scraper at the ready. "Can't you read?" In the second before her legs failed her as surely as if her spine had been severed, and she collapsed face-up in an uncomfortable-looking heap on the grimy floor, all she remembered seeing was an outstretched hand holding an odd-looking

86

spray can, small and silver in color, not completely unlike those found at the perfume counter in the mall. It had made a "pssst" sound just inches from her face and then the floor had jumped up to meet her.

If there was anything to be grateful for, the fall to the hard floor had caused Mattie no pain, despite a fractured right radius and four shattered fingers of her right hand which, unfortunately, had ended up beneath the plump cook as she dropped. Shiva worked her magic on the central nervous system as expertly as the best anesthesiologist, though infinitely more quickly, while leaving a recipient of her kiss completely conscious and fully aware of his or her surroundings.

The absence of pain, however, did nothing to lessen the horror Mattie Blackburn experienced as she quickly realized she was being methodically murdered.

"Want to stage the body before we burn it?" Witherspoon asked as he locked the front door and closed the only blind that had remained open. His mask made his words sound as if they'd been spoken by someone with a clothespin over his nose and a mouth stuffed with cotton.

McGhee studied the woman's position on the floor and shook his head. "Totally believable that she collapsed right here in the kitchen while cleaning up for the day, overcome by the gas fumes before she could find the source or make an exit."

Though not necessary, Witherspoon bent and shot an additional blast of the compressed gas directly into Mattie's face. She saw it coming, of course, but could not even blink in self-defense. She would not be able to move a finger or make an utterance for help for the better part of an hour.

Twenty minutes too late, he thought.

"You love that shit, don't you?" McGhee said, shaking his head.

His partner stood erect again and only smiled.

"If you're through screwing around, we've got work to do."

They waited the requisite half minute for the gas to rise and dissipate before returning their masks to the field bag. As Witherspoon grabbed the pliers and quickly loosened the main gas line feeding the ovens and grill, just to the point that a gentle hiss began to emanate from the fitting, his partner extinguished all pilot lights and ensured that no other sources of ignition existed that would alter the timing of the explosion that would occur when the timer reached zero.

In forty minutes, the wooden structure would be filled with enough gas to float it into outer space like the Goodyear blimp. That is, if Propane were more like helium and less like nitroglycerine in nature. Because it didn't behave at all like helium, it would not be the Goodyear blimp that carried the cook away in just under three-quarters of an hour, but rather a reincarnation of the Hindenburg.

An essential element of Shiva's appeal was that Mattie Blackburn would be breathing normally at the time of her death, proving conclusively—through scorched lungs and a charred airway—that she had been alive and well when the inferno claimed the diner. Furthermore, her cooked remains would be free of any evidence of a struggle, which both men knew could be uncovered by a competent coroner these days, if such telltale signs of an "assisted death" existed.

Everything would point incontrovertibly to a tragic accident.

Satisfied that all was in place within the diner, the men stowed the last of the items that had been taken from the field bag and moved to the door. As McGhee took the shoulder strap of the field bag with his left hand, and the door knob with his right, Witherspoon parted two of the horizontal blinds to the left of the door.

"Shit," he said, stopping his partner's movements cold.

"What?"

"Cops."

"The sheriff?"

Witherspoon shook his head. "Patrol car. Deputy."

McGhee leaned to his left, squinting through the narrow opening in the blinds. "Shit," he echoed.

"Now what?" Witherspoon asked.

McGhee thought quickly as he watched the patrol car ease into the parking slot to the right of their Crown Victoria. "If the son of a bitch comes to the door, I suppose we'll just have to let him in," he said, lowering the field bag quietly while simultaneously removing his pistol from its shoulder holster. He reached into his right front pants pocket and withdrew a matte-black sound suppressor, an inch and a quarter in diameter and six inches long. It perfectly matched the finish of the 45-caliber automatic and screwed quickly into the threads that had been milled into its barrel. While not a nearly total silencer as so often depicted by Hollywood, it would nonetheless effectively eliminate most offending sound for approximately a half dozen shots, at least beyond a few dozen yards. By then, the internal baffles and suppression material would be all but destroyed by the immense pressure of the blast they were designed to contain. All subsequent shots would become increasingly loud until, after only about a dozen to fifteen, no appreciable reduction in noise would be gained by its continued presence on the end of the barrel.

He looked back at the grill and could smell the gas beginning to fill the room. He realized that a shot, even through a silencer, would emit enough of a spark to blow them all to the moon. "Shit," he repeated, motioning with his head toward the kitchen.

"Well, this shit just keeps getting better and better," Witherspoon groused in angry frustration, at once appreciating their precarious predicament. It never ceased to amaze him how quickly a perfectly good plan could turn into a pile of dog crap.

With no words and only a few quick gestures of his handgun, McGhee—knowing it would be unwise to take his eye off the deputy for more than a second—indicated for his partner to kill the flow of gas and switch off the ignition timer. The place would still contain a dangerous level of Propane within its tinderbox walls for half an hour or more, but at least no more of the highly explosive gas would be added until they could stabilize the situation.

"Open a back window," McGhee whispered, but Witherspoon had already disappeared from the kitchen to the office in the rear, the same thought having crossed his mind. With luck, and a little breeze outside, the gas would dissipate more quickly.

Much more quickly, he prayed.

In his hand, the patterned grip of the pistol began to feel moist.

Outside, the deputy sat eerily still in his cruiser, though occasionally answering or placing calls on the radio with the corded handset. When not on the radio, he alternated his stare between the empty Crown Victoria to his left, the diner with its premature CLOSED sign in the window, and the far end of the parking lot where the sheriff's vehicle and trailer sat parked.

While the license plate on the Crown Victoria would never lead the authorities to the ranch or any person within its borders, it would also not lead them to any law enforcement agency or government entity.

McGhee realized that their suddenly-crappy situation was most likely going to end in a gun battle, and the thought excited him while souring his stomach at the same time. The final scene in *Butch Cassidy and the Sundance Kid*, where Paul Newman and Robert Redford found themselves in a small adobe hut surrounded by the entire Brazilian Army, filled his mind.

Or was it the Bolivian Army?

Despite having seen the movie eight times or more, he couldn't remember at this moment.

"It already smells better in here," Witherspoon said quietly, stepping over Mattie's motionless form and interrupting McGhee's stroll down memory lane.

Mattie Blackburn, horrified at her world turned inside out, could only stare at the ceiling like a fish on a carving table. It must be a nightmare, she kept telling herself. Soon, she would awaken and see her beautiful money all around her. She prayed and wept, the tears clouding her vision as they pooled around unblinking eyes before running down her cheeks.

"We still have company?" Witherspoon asked, returning to the window but not touching the blinds.

The other man only nodded, careful not to move a muscle of his left hand. Like his partner, he realized that the slit in the blinds could not change shape or size even a fraction of an inch without turning a potentially volatile situation into a sure-fire shootout. It was precisely the kind of thing that cops look for when assessing threats, even in a tiny community like Truman, Utah, and such a change would not go unnoticed or its ominous meaning unappreciated.

Even if he waited until the deputy looked away before he let the blinds fall together again, the mere absence of an opening previously there would become a red flag, a harbinger of evil tidings. When people were not up to no good, things like that simply didn't happen. He held the thin aluminum slats steady, cursing under his breath while trying to make up his mind whether or not it would be more prudent to simply rush into the parking lot and end the cop's life with a single shot to the head.

TEN

A S TY SUMMERS CRESTED a small rise, he could just make out the chimney of the diner and its familiar triple clay pot stack, and said a silent thank you to the heavens for not yet opening the swollen gray sky and unleashing its frigid torrent on him and his small caravan. He hated working in the rain, hated being cold and wet to the bone and unable to do anything about it, and despite having done it more times than he could count, had never gotten used to the unpleasant feeling.

Three minutes later, Kate's hooves had touched the asphalt of the diner's parking lot.

Still hoping to get Goodman into the back of the Expedition and his mounts stowed in the trailer before the sky opened up, the sheriff made quick work of the tasks at hand. Within two minutes, working quickly and expertly, he was again behind the wheel of the SUV for the first time since lunch.

To his amazement and extreme pleasure, he was also still dry.

As he checked the small catch-all bag on the seat beside him to ensure that he had not accidentally lost a photo memory card out on the trail, or had dropped some piece of evidence in the parking lot as he hurried his mounts into the trailer, he found himself wanting a cup of hot coffee as bad as he could ever remember having wanted one, even Mattie Blackburn's continuously-reheated swill.

The siren that whooped ten feet away, just as he was about to shove his keys into the ignition, told him that the coffee would have to wait. He rolled down the passenger's window as one of his deputies, Andy Kilburn, did the same with his driver's glass.

"Sorry, sheriff," Kilburn began apologetically, "saw you loading your gear and was about to lend you a hand when a call came in. We've got a real bad one at Cougar's Rift."

"Not again," Summers said flatly. He knew the spot only too well. Hardly ninety days went by without at least one vehicle exiting Highway 35 at that treacherous spot, only to end up a thousand feet below in a craggy scar in the earth, named Cougar's Rift, that seemed to have been put there by God for no reason other than to snare and devour automobiles. Despite a half dozen caution and reduced speed limit signs, as well as numerous attempts by the highway department to erect all manner of barriers, nothing had been truly effective in stemming the flood of victims. No one who breached the railings had ever survived, but he still found himself asking about fatalities. He said a silent prayer that *this* time someone had miraculously escaped death.

Andy nodded, his face tight and his brow creased. "Hard to say how many, but when I talked to Doug a few minutes ago, he suspected at least three, maybe four. The vehicle appears to be a red late model Acura or Honda. Hard to tell at this point. He got as far down the slope as his rope would allow, about a hundred feet, and was able to put some glass on the carnage," he said, referring to binoculars. "Could make out three shapes amid all the twisted metal. No movement. Couldn't get a read on the tag, either. We'll have to go down."

Sergeant Doug Rozier was Summers' chief deputy, as good a cop as he'd ever worked with, even during his years in Salt Lake City. However, despite his skill as a law enforcement officer, and his extensive training in mountain search and retrieval, this was a task that would require all of their efforts. The small, sparsely populated county of Duchesne, Utah, didn't enjoy a huge force of deputies, only eight in all, and with one out with the flu and another vacationing in the wine country of California with his wife, it was going to be a long night.

Just at that moment, a bolt of lightning blazed with the intensity of a camera flash and the resultant clap of thunder shook the SUV. Drops of water the size of butter beans began to drum their cars. The storm that had promised its arrival all day was about to fulfill that commitment with a vengeance.

"Lead the way, Andy," Summers said, the realization that he was going to get soaked to the bone after all of little consequence now. *What was wet compared with dead?* he thought with a sadness that seemed deeper than he would have imagined. He was now glad that he hadn't eaten. Prying mangled remains from crumpled automobiles, often one severed limb at a time, could bring up the latest meal in even the most hardened first responder. He fastened his shoulder harness, then turned again to his deputy, "I'm right behind you, but I won't be able to make your speed with this rig in tow."

Kilburn nodded, then raised his window and sped off, siren blaring and emergency lights reflecting off a million raindrops as the heavens opened up in earnest, releasing their long-held burden with complete indifference to the misery of the creatures onto which they fell.

Summers switched on his own lights and siren and made a tight U-turn that would put him on the highway in the wake of his deputy. "Sorry for the unscheduled stop, Skipper," he said aloud, addressing the senator's remains that he knew were rapidly thawing in the rear of his vehicle. "I'll be as quick as I can."

Because of the extremely high profile and perishable cargo in the back of his Expedition, the sheriff knew he couldn't stay for the full extraction of the Acura or Honda—or whatever the unfortunate vehicle had been before it pirouetted, spiraled, and tumbled down nearly a quarter mile of jagged granite walls that defined Cougar's Rift. Still, he needed to be there long enough to ensure that his men had everything they would need to get in and out as quickly as possible. He would also coordinate their efforts with the capitol to see if they could spare a few State Troopers to lend a hand.

He reached for his cell phone and dialed Will Cameron, long-time friend and the local coroner.

"Will, it's Ty," he said when the doctor answered on the second ring.

"I know, I know, don't plan on an early dinner," Cameron said with alacrity and a touch of good humor. He had already been informed by Linda Taylor, the dispatcher at the Sheriff's Office, that his services would be needed shortly. Linda hadn't provided much detail about the most recent accident at Cougar's Rift. In truth she hadn't known much when she'd called, but the details were irrelevant to the coroner. Will Cameron had lived in Truman all his life, except for medical college in Salt Lake City and the six years he'd spent as a Navy flight surgeon during the Vietnam War, and had seen more victims of that treacherous hairpin curve than he could remember. Not once had there been a survivor.

He didn't expect today would be any different.

"So, I gather Linda called you about the accident," the sheriff said as he navigated the tightly winding road that snaked its way west from the diner, losing more than three thousand feet of altitude in less than ten miles. It was not a road built for the faint of heart or the foolhardy. He quickly placed a small Plantronics headset over his right ear, linked by Bluetooth to his cell phone.

"A few minutes ago," Cameron replied.

"Sorry to keep you late."

"Not the first time; won't be the last."

"That wasn't the reason for my call, however," Summers said. He was forced to brake hard just before a sharp left turn when he found himself a bit too fast in the approach; he'd momentarily forgotten about the four thousand pounds of extra weight coupled to the Expedition. *Sorry Kate, sorry Sam*, he thought as he heard them shuffling for stable footing in the trailer. "I recovered a body on the old Summit Trail, near Redmon's Ridge. Still mostly covered by snow, it's in great shape from what I can see, though he's been up there a while. About nine months exactly would be my guess."

The reference to a specific length of time puzzled the physician. It was out of character for the veteran investigator who normally waited to be told things like that. "Someone you know?" he asked.

"Oh, yeah, and so do you."

Cameron dropped heavily into his huge office chair and propped tired feet up on his old oak desk, crossing his ankles while trying not to shove too much of the backed up paperwork onto the floor in the process. It wasn't like Ty Summers to play games, so this must be a special occasion. He decided to play along. For the life of him, however, he couldn't remember anyone he knew who was missing or unaccounted for, certainly not for three-quarters of a year. "You got me, Ty. Can't think of a single soul other than Henry Gibbons."

"Pastor Gibbons?" Summers laughed out loud. "Hell, no, Will. I swear, you must be the only person in the state who doesn't believe he's on a beach in Mexico with his secretary and a barrelful of parish cash."

For several months the previous year, the story of the missing pastor of a prosperous local Presbyterian church, his missing secretary—twenty years his junior—and tens of thousands in missing collections, had created quite a scandal. It had not been a story, however, that Cameron had paid much attention to, being a Mormon and not being predisposed to gossip by nature. He rolled his shoulders and rocked his head side to side to work out the day's kinks. "You sure I know the deceased?" he said wearily, still puzzled by the sheriff's comment.

Summers made the next series of curves without killing himself or his livestock, though his cell phone now lay on the passenger's floorboard. "Let's just say you'll recognize him at once," he grinned, knowing his old friend had been a huge fan of the senator from California. "It's Skipper Goodman, Will. In the flesh."

At the other end of the line, Will Cameron was on his feet.

* * *

Inside the Tip-Top Diner, McGhee and Witherspoon had watched silently as the deputy put his cruiser into REVERSE and backed away from the diner, though the whole while the deputy's eyes never left the narrow slit in the blinds in the small window beside the front door.

They knew they could not be seen, that it was human nature to direct one's attention toward any opening, no matter how large or small, much as one always looks toward any source of light in darkness. However, they had taken little comfort in this knowledge and the fixed gaze, even from behind nearly black Ray-Bans, had given them the sense that the deputy had not only been able to make out their faces as clearly as if they'd been standing in a lineup six feet away, but that he could also see the evil intent in their hearts.

"Where's he going?" Witherspoon asked incredulously, as if his partner possessed some profound gift of insight that evolution had failed to bestow upon him.

McGhee's response was a hard and unpleasant stare.

"You think the sheriff's back?" his partner pressed, unfazed by McGhee's sour attitude. It was normal.

"Most likely," McGhee grunted.

"Shit," came the abrupt response that summed up their present situation in a word.

McGhee merely nodded in agreement, finally allowing the blinds to fall together fully. He quickly snatched a paper napkin from the small chrome holder on the counter and folded it several times until it closely approximated the thickness of two fingers. This wad of paper was swiftly wedged in-between the same two horizontal slats he'd held apart for the last twenty minutes. Not exactly the same gap, he puzzled, but close enough if the deputy returned. He shook his left arm to get the blood flowing again.

As the long-still limb began to tingle with fresh blood flow, he heard fat drops of rain begin to peck at the tin roof of the diner. In a hard downpour, he imagined the sound would become deafening. He produced a faint smile: rain was good. As he was about to tell Witherspoon to make his way out the rear window and alongside the outer wall opposite the direction the deputy had driven, he heard not one, but a pair of sirens split the early dusk. They were in for it now. When he raised his pistol and stuck his face in the narrow opening once again, Witherspoon withdrew his own automatic and affixed its silencer.

"How do you want to do this?" he asked.

"In their faces," McGhee said resolutely. He wasn't about to become the object of a standoff, not armed with two short-barreled pistols and extremely limited ammunition. Since it was now obvious they wouldn't live to see the morning, unless they had a streak of luck that would make them instant millionaires in Las Vegas, or unless they wished to spend the next dozen years in a state prison—which was not an option either was willing to consider—a quick and decisive assault on the cops the minute they pulled in front presented itself as the only logical move.

McGhee could hear his partner's breathing grow more rapid and told him to calm down, that this was no different than a half dozen similar situations they'd encountered in the Mid-East.

Witherspoon sucked in a deep breath and expelled it rapidly through flared nostrils. "I'm good," he reported confidently.

McGhee knew the other man wouldn't fail to perform in a firefight. He never had even when the odds had been far worse than now. Still, as he massaged the grip of his 45-automatic, ideal for taking down a human at short distances but not worth a damn against vehicles or at range, he longed for an AK-47 or M-16 and a couple hundred rounds of armor piercing ammunition.

They'd make do just fine with what they had, he decided. However, surprise meant everything now. He realized that the cops, whatever their suspicions, were not prepared to assault the diner, guns blazing, until they'd attempted to ascertain the exact nature of the threat before them. Assuming, of course, that any threat actually existed. In fact, this was most likely nothing more than a couple of Feds acting strangely, something Feds typically did. As the local law enforcement officers—in that wonderful moment of indecision as to the best course of action to take—sat pensively in their vehicles outside the front door, he and Witherspoon would erupt from the diner and kill them both as dead as yesterday's news. Then, they'd accelerate Mattie's death and the destruction of the diner and get the hell out of Dodge.

It was an imperfect plan at best, but it sure as hell beat prison.

At the exact moment he'd accepted his fate, the deputy's cruiser shot across the parking lot and onto Highway 35, disappearing over the hill to the west. It was closely followed by the sheriff's Expedition, trailer in tow, albeit at a less frantic pace.

It appeared they were not going to die this day after all.

But, as he swore under his breath, considering the full implication of the sheriff's departure, neither were they going to collect Goodman's body as planned. Or more importantly, as ordered.

McGhee didn't know which he feared more: having a shootout with the cops or placing another call to the Colonel with bad news.

"Gas her again," he said, gesturing with his head toward the cook. He unscrewed his pistol's noise suppressor, holstered his weapon, and tossed Witherspoon a mask.

He fastened his own mask over his mouth and nose as he set about closing the office window and restoring the previous gas leak. It was time to get the hell out of there before their luck ran out permanently. As he passed the small ignition timer, he set it for twenty minutes.

Witherspoon knelt before the prostrate proprietor and, using his thumb, wiped the tears from her swollen, red eyes. One lid tried to blink at his touch and he knew McGhee was right: she was slowly coming around.

"Why the tears, Mattie, my love?" he asked. "You should be thanking us. Just look at the life you've got here." He looked around the grimy kitchen, shaking his head in disgust. "Honestly, you can scarcely call it living by any measurable standard. Am I right?"

Mattie Blackburn couldn't have answered the maniacal figure looming over her even if she still possessed the motor function to speak. Her heart, unaffected by the paralytic gas, was on the verge of bursting from fear she hadn't realized was possible to experience. It didn't matter that the woman hadn't responded to his question; it had been rhetorical.

When he wasn't wreaking havoc or dispensing destruction, Witherspoon fancied himself an intellectual, equal to any university professor he'd ever encountered—to his way of thinking, anyway. And, by his own admission, light years above the average serial killer, a normally loathsome category—societally speaking at least—into which he didn't mind being lumped at all. To his way of thinking, those responsible for the most deaths during any historical period were always the best remembered figures of their day. Human beings have always exhibited an uncomfortable relationship with mass murder, vocally expressing their abhorrence of such brutality while silently maintaining an unblinking fascination with it. He wasn't about to depart this life, if at all possible, without leaving his own indelible mark.

One day, soon perhaps, he would let the world know everything that he'd accomplished in his pursuit of that goal in such a relatively short period. The thought made him grin.

He patted Mattie's cheek patronizingly, maintaining *his* wide smile as he did. "I realize that we may have startled you earlier, when we came in unannounced, and I apologize for any discomfort that may have caused. Of course, not knowing who we are or what our intentions may be, you are rightly puzzled, dare I say frightened." The grin widened into a full smile. "Fear not, Mattie for we mean you no suffering. None whatsoever. In fact, both being in beneficent moods, my partner and I have decided to spare you from all of *this*." He let the last word linger, to emphasize his disdain for the horrid little diner.

He donned his mask as Shiva blew a final, soft kiss into Mattie's face. "And, since being consumed by fire is such a painful way to go, or so I have been told, how fortunate for you that you're not going to feel a thing."

The irony of it all suddenly struck him: cooking the cook. He began to laugh out loud, and the sound that emanated from the painter's mask had an otherworldly quality to it. Mattie prayed that the intense pounding in her chest would take her long before the flames.

ELEVEN

TY SUMMERS PULLED HIS Expedition into Will Cameron's driveway and switched off the ignition. After leaving Doug Rozier and Andy Kilburn at Cougar's Rift, once the State boys had arrived to lend them a hand, he had swung by the barn beside Headquarters to drop off Kate and Sam, both having had their fill of winding mountain roads and abrupt stops.

Despite the intense downpour that had begun twenty minutes after he'd arrived at the accident site, and which had, for the next hour, emptied rain from a woolen gray sky like the very bowels of heaven had been slit, he had made quick work of stabling the mounts, stowing the trailer in its shed beside the barn, and then dropping by the house. There, he slipped into dry clothes: comfortable jeans and an old *Utah Jazz* sweatshirt in place of the saturated uniform.

From there, he drove quickly across town, above the posted speed, but without lights or siren—not wishing to draw undo attention to himself and his precious cargo. Eight minutes after leaving his home, he had arrived at Cameron's medical offices on Seventh Avenue.

He knew that the world-class three-ring circus would come to town soon enough, the very moment the media got wind of Goodman's discovery. And while Truman had been spared virtually all of the previous media storm, when news of the senator's plane going down had been initially reported—being too far from the impact site to garner interest from even the most hard-pressed reporter—it would be fully in the eye of the hurricane now and would remain there for God only knew how long. But however long it was, it would be too damn long.

He'd seen something like it once while a detective in Salt Lake City, when a religious compound southwest of town, belonging to a polygamist splinter group of the Mormon Church, had been raided by state and local authorities after charges of child molestation and pedophilia had been alleged by an anonymous caller, a minor currently living in the compound.

The media had swarmed over the property and surrounding area like locusts to a wheat field, and had not left until the public finally lost interest in the story. It had taken weeks for the initial fascination to wane and further coverage only threatened to erode ratings.

Ratings, he scoffed. *What the networks wouldn't do for ratings.* Being the focus of unwanted media attention at the dawn of modern news gathering had simply been annoying—disagreeable at worst—when there were a mere three or four reasonably restrained networks to contend with. Today, with a hundred times that number of ravenous channels needing to be satiated every day—their drug-like cravings fueled by audiences that suffered from shared attention deficit disorder after decades of gore- and excess-filled sound bites—it had become positively insane.

Every story that promised to elevate a channel's audience stock by even a fraction of a point created a feeding frenzy among competing networks that took on epic proportions.

This is gonna be worse, he thought. Much worse. A media tsunami. A perfect storm.

The sheriff stepped from his vehicle and stretched his tight muscles, thankful the rain had subsided for the moment. Will Cameron was already crossing the clinic's wide front porch, pushing a gurney as if he were competing in a marathon.

The scene made Summers chuckle. "Wasting no time, I see," he said as the well-used stretcher wheeled down the handicap ramp toward the SUV.

"You certain it's Goodman?" came the out-of-breath response.

Summers nodded that it was the famous man, indeed, which only served to speed the gurney's progress toward the Expedition.

The sprawling three-story clinic, a meticulously-restored and lovingly-kept Queen Anne Victorian, was comfortably situated on a high bluff overlooking the Duchesne River a hundred feet below. Its more than ten acres of land, with dense woods and the river to the north, provided peaceful isolation while still being convenient to patients and only minutes from everything they could want in town. When Will and Joan Cameron returned to Truman after the Navy and purchased the home, it had served both as his medical offices and their private residence; the clinic and office occupying the first floor and the residence the second. The third floor had initially remained attic space, filled to overflowing with a mix of patient records and out-of-season clothing.

In time, as the practice grew and Will took on the added duties of County Medical Examiner, the Cameron's relinquished more and more of the residential area until they had squeezed into the third floor like a pair of aspiring artists sharing a cold water flat in Soho. Joan finally put her foot down—something she rarely did—and told her husband that she didn't intend to spend one more Christmas living like Anne Frank.

It was time to move.

While the clinic still occupied the ground floor, patient scheduling, insurance, accounting, and patient records had been moved to the second story and now consumed that entire level. The once-cluttered third floor had been converted into very efficient storage of files deemed of no further use at present, generally the result of a patient's death. A long but narrow darkroom, where x-rays taken during the course of the day were developed and analyzed, had also been squeezed into the upper floor.

The doctor and his patient, but not overly acquiescent, wife had built a lovely home in the country club community of Westwinds, right on the golf course, and had lived there for more than two decades. Now sixty-one, Will Cameron hadn't slowed down a bit, spending no less than a dozen hours a day in his clinic or at the hospital, and despite having lived for twenty-four years within spitting distance of the seventh green at Westwinds, had not once to this day held a golf club in his hands. "Perhaps when I retire," he would say whenever asked.

Will Cameron loved medicine, loved helping people. But most of all, he loved the diversity and excitement that each day spent in the medical field brought, this one being no exception.

In fact, by day's end—though neither he nor the sheriff knew it at the moment—it would prove to be the most eventful day of their lives.

"How did this all come about?" he asked when the gurney abruptly came to a stop at the rear of the SUV. "How in God's good name did you end up with Skipper Goodman's body?" As the sheriff was about to answer, Cameron blurted out, "Oh, hell, never mind, we'll get to all that soon enough. Open the hatch and let me have a look at him."

Summers pressed the appropriate button on the remote control he'd just fished from his right trouser pocket and the Expedition's hatch opened with a mechanical "clunk-clack." It began to rise slowly and deliberately. Will Cameron helped it along with an enthusiastic pull, its automatic lift system apparently providing insufficient speed to satisfy his burning curiosity.

The moment he could fit himself into the back of the SUV, he took the slider of the oversized nylon zipper on the body bag and pulled rapidly toward the enclosure's middle, enough to reveal the head and upper torso of the body contained within. Lying on his left side in an exaggerated arc, looking more like a boomerang than most 'stiffs' he encountered on a regular basis, lay the mortal remains of Robert Wayne 'Skipper' Goodman, one of the most powerful and charismatic men to enter politics in a generation. Even now, nearly a year after his disappearance and assumed death, his influence could be felt in both houses of Congress.

"Son of a bitch," he said reverently, then looked to Ty Summers as if to ask, "Are you seeing what I'm seeing?"

Summers wrinkled his brow and nodded his head, fully appreciating his friend's wonder and puzzlement.

"There *was* a parachute," Cameron said thoughtfully, noting the superb condition of the body and recalling the most logical theory put forth to explain the complete absence of the senator's remains at the site of the crash. By contrast, many had argued that the senator hadn't even been on the plane, and was now hiding abroad, despite the dozens of witnesses that had testified under oath that they'd seen him board that fateful morning. Still others postulated that the senator had somehow caused the crash before he parachuted to safety, presumably to cover up the fact of his long-time alleged affair with his secretary, Angel Britt. Of course, all of this had been nothing more than pure speculation. Even the parachute theory had been just that, a wild guess.

Until now.

"No other explanation to my way of thinking," the sheriff said. "He got down soft and easy somehow, at least compared with hitting the ground at two-hundred miles an hour. A parachute does it for me since I'm not a big fan of miracles, as you know."

The doctor nodded, but didn't move his eyes from Goodman. As he did a rapid triage examination of the remains, his experienced mind was noting, studying, and cataloging a hundred disparate bits of information, all of which would become part of the final autopsy report in some form or another. "He's in extraordinary condition, almost as if he simply went to sleep and didn't awaken. Clearly, he didn't impact the ground with any force."

"Nope. And he may have done just that; I found him nearly thirty miles south of the impact site and I would guess that he walked the entire distance. Probably dog tired, freezing, and starving."

Cameron continued to nod his agreement. "I see Sam brought him out," he said, tracing the arc of Goodman's body with his left index finger. He'd been friends with Ty Summers for many years and had assisted in numerous remote body retrievals during that period. Kate and Sam were as well known to him as his own horse, Tennessee and his Persian cat, Solomon.

"I would have used the department's ATV with its onboard stretcher, but knew it wouldn't make it all the way to Redmon's Ridge. Too many places that only a horse or mule can go. Sorry for, well, bending him a bit." Summers shrugged his shoulders and appeared genuinely apologetic.

"I think it's safe to say the ride down didn't do him any harm."

"No, he's pretty much as dead as he was when I found him. How long before you know what actually killed him?"

"You in a hurry on this one, Ty? I mean, other than for the most obvious reasons?"

Summers brow knitted heavily. "You might say that, Will. Saw some feds up at the diner up on LaMotte Peak and I suspect they were there to assert jurisdiction and claim Goodman's remains. I left before we had time to exchange pleasantries."

The mention of Feds converted the doctor's studious expression into a frown. "How long before they arrive?" he asked.

"I'm actually surprised they weren't here waiting on me," Summers said. "I stopped for half an hour at Cougar's Rift and then ten more minutes at home before coming here. It wouldn't take too much on their part to learn that I was ultimately heading here with the body."

"Probably stopped to eat," Cameron said hopefully. "Surely they can't expect to show up unannounced and just leave with the body," he said, then added, "Can they?"

Summers shrugged. "Never know with the Feds. Remember, this guy had just announced that he was going to make a run for the Presidency, and we both believe, along with about a hundred million other folks, that he would have stomped into the ground anyone the Republicans threw at him. The win would have redefined the term 'landslide election.' In addition, his family has more money and 'yank' than the Kennedy's had even in JFK's day. Given that, I'd say the Feds can pretty much do whatever they want to do, or have been told to do, and we're gonna have to shut up and take it." The sheriff dropped his keys back in his pocket and stared up at the night sky. Not a star in sight, though the rain had not yet returned.

It would, he knew. Soon.

"Besides, I'll be pleased to get him off my hands and back to Oz," he said, referring to Goodman's home state of California. "We're going to get enough of the carnival as it is, just being the ones who found him. The longer his remains stay in Truman, the nuttier it will get. Hell, in a week, they'll have you graduating from Harvard Medical one day and training under a voodoo witchdoctor the next. They'll have me born in three different states with six illegitimate children and a transgender mistress. I've seen it. It's the craziest thing you'll ever go through. I say, the sooner they take him off our hands, the happier we're all gonna be."

Cameron looked at his watch: 7:20 pm. He didn't have much time and he wasn't going to let the most famous guest to ever grace his autopsy table be taken from him without a thorough examination and lots of "pictures."

As if reading his mind, Ty said, "I wouldn't go chopping on this guy just yet, Will. Our jurisdiction isn't gonna last five minutes once they know for sure we have his body, and his family will be highly pissed, maybe even litigious, if some hick sawbones carves a huge 'Y' in their golden boy's chest."

Cameron didn't even wince at the slight to his medical standing. He knew it was only meant, by a good friend, in the context of the moment and as it would be seen in the eyes of the Goodman family. Billionaires tended to be 'elitists' and didn't generally look with favor upon interference by anyone they felt either lived or operated below their lofty standards of excellence. The post mortem would be done in Sacramento and the results would be exactly what the Goodman family lawyers wished them to be.

Nothing less. Nothing more.

"I suppose I better at least ensure that he doesn't start decomposing before they come, eh." With that, he closed the body bag and grabbed the two handles at the head end, pulling smartly and expertly toward the gurney like someone who'd done it a thousand times. Before Summers could take the straps at the opposite end and lend a hand, Goodman was onboard the gurney and already being strapped in place.

"You're getting too old for all this," Summers said as he took the leg strap and pulled it tight. "You'll give yourself a hernia one day, or worse."

"Not likely; got a ticker now that's better than a Swiss watch and a back that would make Sam jealous. However, if you'd like to offer your help pushing this rig up the ramp, I'd be of a mind to accept it."

Without complaint, Summers took the left corner of the gurney while Cameron pushed on the right. In less than five minutes, though both men now panted like four-pack-a-day smokers, Skipper Goodman's body had been delivered to Autopsy and had been removed from the rubber bag that had protected his remains since being extricated from the snow. The body bag had been scoured for any remaining physical evidence and the 420 milliliters of water that had accumulated within the cocoon—the result of thawing— had been emptied into a wide-mouth, clear-glass jar and labeled appropriately.

The table in Examination Room Six, reserved exclusively for those patients who would not be getting better—ever—was made of heavy stainless steel measuring four feet wide and seven feet in length. A quarter-inch-wide lip, nearly two inches in height and smoothed at the top, bordered it completely. It served to keep all particulates, solid or liquid, within its confines.

Goodman had been placed on his back and the arc-like curvature that had resulted from the mule ride down the mountain had diminished considerably. What remained, however, still kept his head and shoulders elevated more than six inches from the table, his far heavier hips, legs and feet winning the gravity battle.

"Hold that end," Cameron said, motioning for the sheriff to grab the senator's ankles as he put a hand firmly on each of Goodman's shoulders. "I'm going to try to remove the last of this bow."

Summers did as he was told as the doctor applied steady pressure to the upper torso. Goodman's body slowly yielded to their efforts, and in ninety seconds, lay fully prone. The coroner and the sheriff stepped back for the first time and stared silently at the once-great man in what could only be described as a moment of shared veneration. To both of them as to millions of other Americans, Skipper Goodman had been the most electrifying leader to grace the political arena in decades. He had represented a rebirth of sincerity and idealism, an exorcism of the old and a promise of what could actually be when a government put the genuine needs of the many above the greedy desires of the few.

No wonder he didn't live to see any of it come to pass, Cameron had often said after the crash. Those in power always preferred the status quo.

Summers was the first to break the silence. "It's just like I thought when I first saw him on the mountain. He doesn't look as much dead as asleep. As if he finally gave up, laid down, and simply closed his eyes for the last time. I've seen it too many times, the cold does that to you after a while. You lose the will to go one step farther, even when you know the end is only a few steps away. In his case, I'm sure he had no idea where he was in relation to help. Poor bastard had to be colder than I can even imagine."

"Hypothermia," Cameron said. "It'll kill you quicker than a bullet and quieter than poison."

Just then the sheriff, who stood on the opposite side of the table from Cameron, noticed something that struck him as particularly odd, and he moved in close for a better look. "Take a look at this, Will. I'd swear he's got something clenched in his fist."

The coroner had seen hundreds of cases of rigor in his career and expected that was what had garnered the sheriff's attention. He moved around the table to gain access to Goodman's left side, and at first glance, the posture seemed completely in keeping with the effects of rigor. However, when he lifted the senator's left forearm and moved it a small distance from the body, exposing the palm, the hand did, indeed, appear to be tightly clenched—unnaturally so. He grabbed his reading glasses and studied the hand further, turning it first one way then the other, at least to the extent the half-frozen muscles would permit. "Nothing appears to be protruding from either end of his fist," he said. "Whatever it is, if it is anything at all, it would have to be quite small. My guess is that it's merely a rigor-induced tightening of the fingers."

"Look at his right hand," Summers said.

The doctor did so at once and noticed that it bore no resemblance to the left whatsoever, the fingers and thumb being fully relaxed in posture.

"Why such a difference," Summers asked, "if rigor is the cause?"

As he had done with the left, the doctor lifted the opposite forearm for closer examination but immediately noticed that it had sustained a severe break, bisecting both the radius and ulna. He lowered it gently, wishing to inflict no further injury to the corpse before a thorough examination could be made.

"Right arm is completely fractured," the doctor said. "Probably couldn't have made a fist if he'd wanted to, at least while he was alive." Still, he knew rigor didn't care about pain, and if the left hand had involuntarily balled into a tight fist, the right should have mirrored that behavior, certainly far more so than the posture

111

it currently exhibited. "It is a bit odd, I'll give you that. At this point, I'd lean more toward the left hand being the anomaly, as you suggest, than the right." He turned his attention back to the fisted left hand. "Bet I'll have an answer to that question and many more in no time."

"I'll take that bet," Summers said. "If the Feds aren't here in the next half hour, at the outside, I'd be more surprised than if Skipper sat up and started talking. Time is something definitely not on your side, old friend."

Being reminded again of the inevitable and unwelcomed presence of the Feds, Will Cameron was about to ask the sheriff to leave him in peace when the sheriff's cell phone broke the silence.

Summers fished it from his front jeans pocket and answered it by the third ring. The display indicated Headquarters.

"Sheriff Summers," he answered in his official voice. It was Linda Taylor. For the next twenty seconds, he listened without speaking as she recounted the latest tragedy in what was rapidly becoming the most bizarre twenty-four hours of his life. When he hung up, Will Cameron could see that his old friend had not been told that he'd just won the lottery.

"What now?" he said, though the larger part of him did not want to know. Not now. He had his plate filled with the most exciting case of his career, the clock was ticking like a time bomb, and for the moment, didn't want to be bothered by the day to day aggravations of life and death.

Still, he found himself awaiting an answer.

"You know the Tip-Top Diner, right?"

"Sure, Mattie Blackburn's place. Why?"

"It's gone."

"Gone? What do you mean 'gone'?" He couldn't get his mind around the word.

"I mean totally gone, no longer standing. From what the fire marshal told Doug Rozier, it appears to have been some kind of gas leak. Whole place blew up like Mattie'd been hording dynamite.

What wasn't blown to splinters for a hundred yards in all directions burned up in the fire. Only the Colorado Low we had this evening," he said, referring to the intense rainstorm, "kept the whole damn forest from going up with it."

"Thank God for small miracles," Cameron said, but he could tell that the other shoe had yet to drop. "Please don't tell me the place was packed for dinner."

"That's what's so odd about this; the diner was apparently closed."

That news surprised the doctor—who'd eaten at the Tip-Top Diner a hundred times—more than the explosion itself. In fact, most who'd eaten at Mattie's place were amazed it hadn't burned down long before. What wasn't caked in grease was coated in oil. It was the kind of eatery that cholesterol-conscious people had nightmares about, much as a vegan breaks out in hives when passing a butcher shop. "Why on earth was Mattie closed on a Saturday evening?" he puzzled. "That normally her best day of the week. Was anyone in the diner? How about Mattie? I hope she wasn't still in there. Has anyone talked with her yet?"

Summers held his hands up to stop the onslaught of questions. "Easy, boy. You know exactly as much as I do at this point. Guess I'll head back up there to see what I can find out. And don't forget, you've still got that accident headed your way as soon as my guys retrieve the bodies."

"Cougar's Rift," Cameron muttered.

Summers nodded. "Looks like we're both in for a very long night, Will." He looked at Goodman, who was now thawing and dripping onto the stainless table like ice cream on a summer day, then back to his old friend. "Don't get creative, Will. Just poke around, make a few quick notes, and then get him back on ice before we have a jurisdictional and legal nightmare on our hands. Remember what I said about his family. Big money can bring big problems."

"Just a cursory examination to see what I can learn before the Feds drop in and spoil all the fun."

"Good. Now promise me." The sheriff knew his friend too well.

Cameron crossed his heart with the index finger of his right hand. "Scout's honor," he said in jest, but when he didn't get the chuckle he'd expected, realized the sheriff's mind was on another planet. He could not let the troubled scowl on Summers' face pass without comment. "What? There's something else, isn't there? Something you haven't told me yet."

Summers took a long, deep breath and tried to put order to a jumble of thoughts that all jockeyed for attention. He made deliberate eye contact with Cameron, as if to punctuate his next words. "I have a really bad feeling about this whole deal all of a sudden, Will. You know how much I hate coincidences, or rather, how little I trust them. Mattie's place blowing up the same day Skipper is found, practically within sight of each other. That's just way too much coincidence for me."

He suddenly remembered Brad and Jason, the fraternity brothers who had found Goodman, and an unsettling feeling swept over him. *God, no, not the kids*, his mind shouted as the gruesome accident at Cougar's Rift came back to him like a scene from a horror movie. "Gotta go, there's something I have to check on right away," he said, pulling his cell phone from his pocket and bolting from the room. "Lock up behind me, Will. I mean it," he shouted as he ran toward the front door.

"Call me. I don't care what time it is," Cameron yelled back.

He heard the front door slam and a few seconds later the Expedition bolted down Seventh Avenue, its siren splitting the night.

With his attention immediately back on Goodman, Cameron wheeled a portable Siemens x-ray unit around the autopsy table so it would be in position to shoot the senator's left side. He put one of his largest exposure plates between the body and left forearm and hand, then elevated the wrist from the table with a gelatin wedge that would not appear in the x-ray.

As he carefully aligned the laser positioning crosshairs with the center of the tightly balled left fist, a smile formed on the medical examiner's face like that of a kid opening a much-anticipated present on Christmas Day. Aloud, as if Summers were still in the room he said, "Okay, Skipper, it's about time we got a peek at whatever it is you're holding there."

TWELVE

BY DINNERTIME, THE PIONEER Grill in Truman was enjoying an above average crowd, even for a Saturday evening. While the heavy rain had prompted a few timid souls to stay at home, opting for a homemade meal or pizza delivery, the added clientele that would have normally eaten at Mattie Blackburn's diner more than made up for the weather's attrition.

Charlie Everett, publisher of, and head reporter for, the *Duchesne Register*, the county's only thrice-weekly newspaper, sat in a booth along one wall, sipping coffee and writing a story from the notes he'd taken that afternoon. No matter how hard he tried, the story of the bake sale at the First Baptist Church benefiting the victims of recent tornados in Oklahoma—paltry news by even the small town standards of the *Duchesne Register*—was going to be boring, boring, boring.

Nothing ever happened in Truman, in the entire county for that matter, and all the clever metaphors and euphemisms wouldn't create a serial killer out of thin air or land an alien spacecraft in the town square.

To his credit, Charlie Everett didn't pray, even secretly, for a genuine tragedy to befall his hometown, merely for the purpose of providing some brief respite from cookie-cutter, boring as white bread, editions that seemed to issue from his presses each Monday, Wednesday, and Friday as similar in look and feel as if from a Xerox machine. On the other hand, if the Fates decreed that a mass murderer was in Truman's cards, while he would hate it as a concerned citizen, as a reporter, he would be in journalistic heaven.

About the most exciting thing to capture the attention of the town in recent memory was the return of a native son, a Marine, safe and sound from the war in Iraq, a Medal of Honor around his neck. It had been a proud day for Truman, to be sure, but the excitement had lasted only three issues. Then, as always, gas prices, the upcoming presidential election, and whether or not we were actually in a recession or merely an economic slowdown filled the pages not otherwise packed with grocery ads, auto sales, and real estate listings.

"More coffee, Charlie?" the waitress asked as she stopped at Everett's booth, coffee pot in one hand, a stack of menus in the other.

He smiled up at the pretty blonde, "Thanks, Nikki."

"Hot on a story?" she asked as she topped off his cup, noting his scribbling.

"I wish." He reached for the Splenda and tore the top from the small yellow packet of sweetener. "Church bake sale. Whoopee do. Maybe I'll hold the presses." He emptied the powdery contents into his cup and began to stir, his mind back on the story. As boring as it was, a deadline was still a deadline, even in Truman, and he had at least a dozen more stories to research and write by press time tomorrow afternoon.

As Nikki moved on to the next table, she smiled pleasantly back at him, though not sympathetically. She didn't feel sorry for anyone with a job that paid more than minimum wage plus lousy tips. She'd kill to be doing news stories, even on church bake sales. At least that way, she could move out of her parents' home and perhaps even get a new car. The thought made her giddy.

117

Though he was deep in concentration, groping for the perfect adjective to describe the assortment of baked goods he had sampled earlier in the day, he heard voices coming from the booth to his left. A single phrase stopped him dead in his tracks: *a man's body*. Words not often heard in sleepy Truman, Utah. He slid closer to the dividing wall and listened intently.

Separating each pair of booths were paneled dividers about a foot thick, eight feet deep, and five feet high. Copper-lined planters ran the entire length, beginning at the wall, and were filled with a wide array of synthetic plants that provided a pleasant, albeit fictitious, environment year round. The dividers also afforded occupants of the individual booths far more privacy than could be enjoyed at adjoining tables on the dining floor.

Normally this was what Charlie liked most about his favorite booth.

At the moment, it was what he liked *least*.

Unable to hear sufficient to his needs, or at least his curiosity, Charlie Everett finally folded his spiral notebook and scooted to the end of the padded seat.

"Pardon me, gentlemen," he said as he stood before the booth where the intriguing snippet had originated, "but I couldn't help overhearing a portion of your recent conversation."

In less than five minutes, he had gotten as much of the story as he needed at present, had poured down the last of his lukewarm coffee, had left sufficient money on the table to cover the food and a tip, and was speeding toward Will Cameron's clinic.

When he arrived, the ludicrous bake sale not even a memory, he bolted up the front steps and rang the buzzer impatiently.

"Come on, come on," he moaned as he continued to press the black plastic button.

Charlie Everett had known the physician and Medical Examiner for most of his life, but they weren't close friends. Their relationship was cordial enough, even pleasant, but had never grown beyond the occasional business encounter, necessitated by intersecting careers. To Everett's mind, there was no particular reason for this; Cameron was a pleasant enough fellow and his wife was a jewel. It was just one of those things that happens sometimes. No real explanation, but also no real regret. The demands of day-to-day life simply didn't allow for every potential relationship to blossom into a genuine and lasting friendship.

When his repeated attempts to summon the doctor went unanswered, he pulled his cell phone from his jacket pocket. After a few seconds of scrolling through his expansive contact list, he located the clinic's number and pressed SEND.

No answer, despite being able to hear the phone on the receptionist's desk tolling loudly with each matching appeal from his own phone.

He pressed END and returned to his contact list. Finding Cameron's unpublished cell phone number, he pressed the SEND button again.

This time, it only rang once before being answered.

"Hello," came the timid response.

"Will?" Everett asked.

"Who's this?"

"Charlie Everett."

"Jesus, Charlie, you scared the crap out of me."

"How so?"

"It's nothing. Forget it. Is that you at the front door?"

"Yes. Sorry to drop by so late, but I'm working on a story." Complete silence was the only response. "A dead guy buried in the snow up near Redmon's Ridge, or so I was told. Anything to it?" Again, a silence so long and deep that Everett looked to see if he'd lost service. "You there, Will?" he finally asked.

After twenty seconds of deafening quite, the front door shot open and Will Cameron stood in the opening, looking exactly like a man of senior years who had just run down several flights of stairs. The doctor had been in the darkroom on the third floor when his cell phone rang. "You alone?" he asked panting heavily.

The reporter assured him he was.

119

"Come in quickly."

"What's up, Will?" Everett asked.

When the door had been closed and locked behind them, the Medical Examiner motioned with a beckoning hand for the reporter to follow. Not a word was spoken as the two men hurried across the first floor and down the north hall toward Examination Room Six.

"Ready for the story of your life?" Cameron finally asked as he stopped and turned to face Everett, his back to a wall of cooling drawers in which the deceased were safely stored while awaiting final disposition.

Everett could only nod; his pulse rate had most definitely elevated since arriving at the clinic.

With that, Cameron took the handle of Vessel-1 and pulled it out enough to reveal the head and upper torso of its most recent occupant.

"Mother of God," Everett said, as the pencil fell from his hand.

* * *

When the sheriff set foot on the front porch of his home on Old River Road, it was no longer Saturday. In fact, Sunday had arrived, unnoticed, more than three hours earlier. It had brought with it no day of rest for the bone weary sheriff and his deputies, Doug Rozier and Andy Kilburn. As far as each was concerned, the two days had coalesced into each other with such chaotic fluidity that they might as well have been one forty-eight-hour day.

As he stood beneath the wide porch overhang and out of the downpour that had returned in earnest halfway back to Mattie Blackburn's place—or what had been left of it—he shook rain from his arms and hands and stamped his feet to shed as much water from them as possible before stepping onto the hardwood floors. He ran his fingers through his thick gray hair, matted from the downpour, squeegeeing it as much as possible. Content that he was presently as dry as he was going to be until he could put his hands on a bath towel, he dug in his jeans pocket for his keys. When he'd closed and locked the heavy oak door behind him, and was finally in the sanctuary of his home, total exhaustion, both physical and mental, began to creep out of its box and clutch at him like quicksand, trying its best to drag him into unconsciousness. If he hadn't been as wet as someone who'd actually gone swimming in his clothes, he would have collapsed on the living room couch, probably not awakening again until sometime the following afternoon.

He somehow managed to reach the master bathroom without passing out, and, after a shower hot enough to boil eggs followed by some wonderfully dry clothes, actually felt that he could stay awake long enough to complete the paperwork that had to be filed before he could call it a day.

Or two days, he groused, but quickly realized that no one cared. "Remember the Eleventh Commandment: Thou shall not whine," he muttered sarcastically to the weary man staring back from the mirror.

While not much of a drinker by any measurable standard, though neither was he given to long periods of abstinence—at least not by intent—there were times when Ty Summers enjoyed a snifter of brandy or an ice-cold beer as much as anyone.

This was one of those times and he poured himself a double of his favorite cognac: Hennessy XO. It was a small luxury he afforded himself without consideration of cost.

Despite still being tired to the point that focusing for any extended period would soon prove impossible—this he knew from years of experience—he had important work to do before he could sleep, while the details of the day were as fresh in his mind as they would ever be. He had been right about the bodies found at the bottom of Cougar's Rift. Though the extensive physical damage to all four occupants would require dental record matching before positive identification could be made, he was absolutely certain in his gut that the two male occupants had been the boys in search of reward money, Brad and Jason. Logically, therefore, the female victims were the girlfriends who had come for them.

No dental records could be obtained until noon at the earliest. He looked at his watch—eight and a half hours if everything moved along like clockwork, which it seldom did with government agencies. However, the license plate of the vehicle, as well as its VIN, perfectly matched a red late model Acura registered to Jessica Beckman. According to the notes he'd made in the parking lot when he'd met the boys, that was the name of Brad's girlfriend, the one coming to pick them back up at the diner.

He drained half his brandy in a long swallow and sank into a thickly padded leather chair at the desk in his study, at the rear of the house. On the wide maple desk, just to the right of the computer monitor, his favorite picture in all the world rested comfortably in a plain silver frame. The sight of it at the end of the hellish day locked the breath in his throat, but then, it always did, even on the best of days.

Smiling warmly back at him was his beloved wife Elizabeth, her proud Native American blood evident in the rich ochre color of her skin and her raven black hair that she always wore long and straight. He was glad Alex had gotten her mother's looks; in photos at the same age, the two could have passed for twins. It was still hard to imagine that she'd been gone almost eight years now. In the photo, her arms were wrapped tightly around their beautiful daughter. Alex was still in braces then, grinning ear to ear, but careful not to let her 'hardware' show. She was always so self-conscious about her braces, repeatedly telling her parents that she would never ever do such a horrid thing to *her* children, if she ever had any children, which was highly unlikely since no boy would ever look twice at a girl with a 'grill' like hers. She was destined to spend her entire life in a convent, celibate and miserable while all of her friends married musicians and movie stars. They had completely ruined her entire high school experience and she would never forgive them.

Ever.

Ever, ever.

And so it went until the hated braces finally came off during the Christmas holidays of her Junior year. Then, miraculously, her natural good looks and slender, athletic build, which had developed curves in all the right places during the 'grill' period of self-imposed social isolation—topped off by the most gorgeous set of perfectly-straight pearly-whites Alex had ever seen, totally better than any of her friends—suddenly made her one of the most popular girls in her high school.

What wonderful, generous, and brilliant parents she had.

The only regret, shared by both of them, was that Elizabeth had not lived to see the perfect smile their little girl now possessed, but Ty believed that Elizabeth somehow knew, just as he believed he would see her again and forever when his own time came.

He caressed the frame between his thumb and fingers and longed to see his daughter; a quick glance at the calendar on the wall told him that she would be home in six days, when her current two-week river tour ended. It would be wonderful to see Marie as well, as she had become both big sister and surrogate mother to Alex in the three years she'd lived in the apartment above their garage. As soon as the girls arrived, he would take them to dinner, or better still, stay at home and fix them the finest meal they'd eaten in a month. Then he'd open a nice bottle of cabernet, sit back on the couch in the living room, and let them regale him in turn with side-splitting tales about "babysitting adults" on the Green River. God, how he missed their company, which was absolutely true, but he also knew that most of the melancholy he was presently feeling was the hole left in him by his wife's passing.

Another long pull on his brandy and he placed the empty glass beside the picture. *Snap out of it, Summers,* he admonished himself. *One short hour of work and then you can sleep.*

He punched the power button on the LCD display and fired up Microsoft Word. No need to switch on the computer; it was never turned off except for an occasional reboot. He detested that long wait while the system came up to operational readiness and therefore refused to subject himself to it every time he sat at the keyboard.

He interlocked his fingers, turned his palms outward, and cracked all twenty-four finger knuckles at the same time. Being careful to omit nothing, even when it was only supposition, conjecture, or suspicion on his part, he began to lay out the bizarre events of the day in intricate detail, beginning with the call Linda Taylor had received from Brad Minick from the pay phone at The Tip-Top Diner yesterday afternoon.

Less than fifteen hours ago, he thought. Jesus, how fast life can change.

As he typed, using only practiced index fingers to peck out a steady forty words a minute, the string of coincidences that had seemed only loosely connected earlier in the day now seemed to weave a story of conspiracy and intrigue that boggled his mind. Maybe he was wrong this time, he considered, trying to maintain a fair sense of professional objectivity. Not about whether the kids killed in the car crash were Brad and Jason, or whether Mattie Blackburn's place going up in a violent conflagration had been the result of carelessness or shabby maintenance but about the events being interconnected. Perhaps they were just what they appeared to be, a couple of unfortunate accidents that had nothing to do with each other, and nothing whatsoever to do with Skipper Goodman finally being found.

"You're tired, Summers, not blind and stupid," he said in ridicule of his previous thought. "You know damn good and well this was no coincidence." He looked at Elizabeth's face in the picture, "And another thing, sweetheart, where the hell did the Feds go? Pardon my French."

As he chewed on his lip and contemplated a second brandy, he suddenly remembered he'd promised to call Will Cameron the minute he left Mattie's place. Instinctively, he reached for the phone, but set it back down when he noted the time on its display.

Will may have said that he didn't care what time it was when he called, but Joan sure as hell would care. "It'll keep till morning, old friend," he said to the empty room. "Nothing earth shattering is going to happen between now and then."

As he continued to peck at his notes, he heard a vehicle pull into his driveway, its headlights painting rapidly changing patterns across the front curtains.

"What the hell?" he said more curious than alarmed. Still, as he rose and made his way to the front door, he tucked his service automatic into his jeans and pulled his baggy sweatshirt over the exposed hand grip.

When he put a wary eye to the peephole in the center of the door, he chuckled under his breath. "Well, speak of the devil," he said, pulling the heavy door open fully. "I was just wondering what in the wide world had happened to the two of you."

THIRTEEN

T HE TRENDY INDIGO BAR and restaurant on G Street, one of the best places to see and be seen in D.C., was only a brief stroll from the Capitol and, consequently, enjoyed more than its share of power brokers and "beggar lice"—the two always found together, like hound dogs and ticks. With the dinner crowd having come and gone hours ago, the eclectic eatery had grown comparatively quite, at least for a Saturday night. From the standing-room-only crowd three hours earlier, there remained but a handful of patrons, drinking quietly, though earnestly, as they took turns restructuring the Republic and rewriting the Constitution.

Those who weren't delivering the central sermon at a particular table listened in feigned deference, hanging on every word like the good little sycophants they were. Obsequious servility, more saccharine than a double helping of chocolate mousse, was the most commonly served dessert in the establishment.

Along the four walls that framed the main bar area, where many of the guests preferred to dine in a more relaxed setting, large-scale flat-panel displays could be tuned to any of three hundred or more digital channels. While dinner was being served, they were, as a rule, switched off, allowing the evening meal to be enjoyed in relative serenity, without the distractions that preoccupied most patrons on most days. They were all turned on, of course, whenever management decreed that keeping their wealthy and powerful clientele informed of a breaking news event took precedence over helping them digest a meal that cost more than many Americans paid for groceries in a month.

On this particular evening, all sets had been off during dinner, this being just another boring Saturday night in the land of excess. Oh, sure, the paparazzi had photographed some celebrity shock diva 'borrowing' a designer fur coat from a fellow prima donna at a Los Angeles late night hot spot—taken completely by mistake, of course. In the financial sector, unemployment had gone down in the precious month, nearly offsetting the rise from the month before. On Wall Street, yet another over-funded and under-producing tech firm had failed, evaporating tens of thousands of retirement dreams even as the CEO fell to earth on a breeze thanks to an eight-figure "golden parachute." And finally, in the Middle East, a hundred students and teachers had been killed by seven armed gunmen while simultaneously, on the opposite side of the province, six more U.S. Marines had fallen victim to IEDs.

All of these events had been deemed by restaurant management to be of such little news value that even collectively they hadn't warranted disturbing the evening feast. Hence, all screens had remained black until well after 10 pm, and even now, at nearly midnight, only two of the dozen sets showed any picture. One, closest to the bar, had been tuned to ESPN, covering a Yankees-Padres game on the West Coast, the outcome of which no one seemed to care a damn about except, apparently, the bartender. Sporting a well-worn Yankees cap, his pleased expression reflected the Yankees' four-run lead in the fifth. The other flat panel displayed CNN Headline News, in case anyone might wish to catch an informational snippet as it flashed in silence beneath a mime anchor, the sound having been muted.

At a table in a remote corner of the bar, as far from the front door as possible, and therefore as far as possible from the ceaseless noise and bustle of the masses who came and went all evening, three men in expensive suits and loose ties sat sipping thirty-year-old scotch, having already consumed between them one fifth and the greater portion of a second. Costing more than a thousand dollars a bottle, the Macallan single-malt was ordered by Indigo a full case at a time. It had long been a favorite of the "big dog" regulars, those with real money to spend, not just high credit limits on maxed-out credit cards. Like most in the bar, these three men were deeply immersed in the culture of American politics—and politicians—as well as the myriad and colorful subcultures that had evolved within that most coveted of all professions since the Revolution.

Over the course of the last hour, the scotch drinkers—Democrats each to the marrow of their bones—had begun enumerating, for the millionth time since his hat had been thrown in the ring, the egregious and meticulously-catalogued failings of the Republican frontrunner. The fear that each silently felt at the thought of not controlling the White House for the next four years, and beyond, was as real as the fear of cancer. While no one had yet been announced—Goodman's death having put an unexpected wrinkle in their election plans—there was still time; the convention was weeks away yet. With an overall approval rating that teetered precariously near single digits, making the current Republican president the most unpopular chief executive in a century, they saw it as highly unlikely the GOP would be able to make even a respectable showing in November, to say nothing of actually holding on to the White House, regardless of the Democratic opponent.

Only a miracle could save the Republicans, even with Goodman's passing, and none of them believed in miracles.

In their hearts, they each felt certain that a great and long-awaited change was about to occur—at last. The first order of business, once a Democrat was at the helm and the Congress was again controlled by their party, would be a swift end to the protracted and costly fighting the Middle East.

Still, as the trio of 'Hill' veterans knew only too well, the American public had failed to do the expected, logical, or intelligent thing on more occasions than they cared to remember.

Despite the pallets of money that got consumed putting forth profound and meaningful messages, elections were just crap shoots whose outcomes were always less certain than a jury verdict.

The one television that was tuned to CNN hung on a wall at the back of Clark Corello—personal secretary to J.D. Wagner, Massachusetts senator and Chairman of the Senate Intelligence Committee—and Louisiana senator Martin Walburn, a long-time friend and associate of Wagner. The muted TV image was, however, directly in Wagner's line of site, and occasionally, as his interest in the verbal assassination of the Republican president waxed and waned, exacerbated by the four tall glasses of Macallan he'd consumed since dinner, he would steal a glance at the screen.

As Clark Corello droned on about the war and the cost to the American people in both economic and human terms, Wagner's attention was drawn to a vaguely familiar image hovering over the shoulder of the reporter. He squinted to identify the picture and make out the words beneath it but the scotch, the late hour, and his seventy-one years of hard living conspired to keep the TV screen as fuzzy as a highway billboard through a rain soaked windshield.

Wagner lowered his head and squeezed his eyes shut, then brought his hands to his face and massaged his closed lids with his fingertips.

"You okay, J.D.?" Martin Walburn asked, though he wasn't the least bit concerned. He'd seen his old friend tired before. Drunk, too, and on more than one occasion. "Ready to call it a night?"

Wagner continued to rub his eyes as if he hadn't heard the question.

"Want me to call for the car?" Corello asked. Under a pleasant June evening, the three men had walked from the Capitol to the restaurant, but had never planned on leaving by foot. Both of the senators had a limousine at their beck and call twenty-four-seven. Corello reached for his cell phone.

When Wagner raised his head and squinted at the TV screen again, his vision had cleared enough to instantly grasp the gist of the story that CNN was currently reporting. Though Goodman's eventual discovery had always been a remote possibility, he'd thought it as likely as finding the Loch Ness Monster swimming the Potomac.

"My god," he stammered in a voice barely audible. All the worst imaginable scenarios that could play out in the coming days flashed before his mind's eye like a horror movie in ultra-fast motion. He couldn't imagine a single outcome that heralded a storybook ending for either Corello or him. Suddenly he forced his chair back from the table, stood on wobbly legs, and disappeared from the bar before either of his companions could react.

Initially, both Corello and Walburn sat aghast in their thickly-padded leather chairs, unable to speak, unable to even comprehend what they had just witnessed. Despite having left in a hurry, but otherwise without incident—no tables overturned, no fellow patron knocked to the floor—the entire bar seemed to be in a buzz over Wagner's departure. At every table, the quiet murmurings were now audible, even excited, conversations. Throughout the bar, people stood and slowly made their way toward the table where the three men had just sat sipping vintage scotch, as if drawn by some invisible force.

Corello shot from his seat and began to make his way through the bar in the tracks of his obviously distraught employer when he suddenly realized that all eyes were not focused on Wagner's exit, but rather on the TV in the corner of the room, the one on the wall behind their table. He turned his attention to the screen and the images and headlines which filled his eyes froze him in place as surely as if he had just been cast in bronze.

"SKIPPER GOODMAN FOUND!" the words announced in block type that seemed to blot out the entire screen, virtually obliterating everything not part of those nineteen simple letters. He didn't need to hear the announcer's commentary to understand that a world of shit was about to hit the fan.

Wagner's fan.

His, too.

He wove his way through the bodies that seemed to have multiplied in the last minute and returned to the table where Martin Walburn stood speechless, his eyes now glued to CNN. Throughout the bar, all twelve large-screen displays were being switched to one news channel or another, from Fox to CBS to MSNBC. Someone began shouting for the bartender to un-mute the volumes, for god's sake, and almost at once, the room which had been as quiet as a study hall a minute before seemed to explode in a cacophony of authoritative voices, all different in tone and inflection but each saying the same thing: the body of the most powerful man in America had finally been found. Now, at last, answers about his untimely and mysterious death could be found.

Perhaps the discovery would only generate more questions than answers, others speculated.

With such little notice, despite nine months for potential preparation, it seems none of the news organizations had had enough forethought to put together anything more in-depth than banal quips and predictable sound bites: snippets from previous speeches, often-seen moments from Goodman's career, both in business and in the senate, replayed and rehashed. While much was known about Goodman's life, virtually nothing was known about his death.

Tomorrow, the emerging story would begin to dominate all news channels as well as the printed word. In the succeeding days, as competition for audience share reached fever pitch, the pressure for real answers to the questions that finding the former Presidential candidate's body, perfectly intact—if you don't count being dead, of course—would plague every government agency from Homeland Security to the FBI to the NTSB.

Corello took the bottle and poured himself a final scotch, then dropped back into his seat like someone who had just had his legs cut out from under him.

"This is not good, Clark," Martin Walburn said in hushed tones. "Not good at all. We both know Skipper's death was no accident, despite what the official FBI report said."

Corello nodded in silence.

Walburn returned to his own seat, pulling his scotch toward him. He cradled it in both hands against his chest like a wino on a winter's night with a screw-cap bottle of Mad Dog 20/20. "Whoever killed him isn't going to take this news well."

"Oh really, you think, Marty," Corello said sarcastically before draining his glass.

"He was on his way to meet with J.D. when his plane went down," Walburn said, recalling that morning. "It had to be something really urgent to put together a meeting like that, face to face I mean, with no advanced notice whatsoever. Why not just call? Why the last-minute flight in the midst of a snow storm? Had to be crazy important, right? You know what it was about, Clark?"

Corello stared at his empty glass. "Maybe it wasn't the kind of message you can deliver over the phone."

"You mean something of national security?"

"That's a broad term, Marty. Means different things to different people." His tone was brooding, fatalistic.

"But you know what they were meeting about," Walburn said. It had not been a question this time.

Corello nodded somberly.

"Well?" Walburn insisted after an intolerable silence. It felt like minutes had passed when it had only been a few seconds.

"Well, what?" Corello barked. His angry response had been noticeably above the din of the room, despite the volume of the dozen televisions and a score of excited patrons whose collective level was now equal to that of a Super Bowl party. He leaned toward the other man and said in a more reserved tone, "You want to know what got Skipper killed and will probably get J.D. and me killed before the sun rises? Is that what you want, Marty, because if it is, I'm just about in a mood to grant you your wish. Nobody likes the idea of dying alone, including me."

It had not been the response Walburn expected or wanted. He stammered, "Uh, no, not really. Just forget the whole thing. Forget I even asked."

"Just what I thought."

"What are you going to do?" Walburn pressed. "Where'd J.D. go?"

Corello stood, his legs feeling like rubber. He was certain they would not support his stocky six-foot frame. In slurred tones, he said, "Probably the same place I'm going, as far from any spot on earth someone might expect to find me."

"That's crazy; why not just go to the FBI? They'll give you protection; that's what they're here for." Walburn now stood, putting his hand on Corello's arm. He had known Clark for many years and had a deep respect for the man, as well as an abiding friendship. His mind raced; he didn't even know from whom Clark and J.D. needed protection, if they needed protection at all. Perhaps, more logically, both men were merely giving in to unreasonable paranoia.

What he did know with certainty, though, was that both men displayed a fear in their faces that he had never seen before. Not once in all his years.

Corello gave a twisted smile, pressed his tie flat against his shirt with a few quick swipes of his right hand, then buttoned his jacket. "Protection? There is no protection from these men. Hell, they took down the most powerful man among us with less effort or thought than it takes to swat a mosquito, and left not a single shred of incriminating evidence. You think for a moment they could do something like that without significant help from very powerful people. People more powerful than the FBI?" He moved shakily around the table, bumping into one chair after another, then turned back to Walburn. "No thanks, I like having my fate in my own hands. If I were you, my old friend, I would take one of your annual junkets to some foreign country, stay gone for a couple of months, though I doubt that will buy you much if they decide to come after you, too."

"Come after me? I don't know crap about any of this, Clark. I'm not even sure I agree with you about the crash. For all I know, you and J.D. are just a couple of crazy drunks with vivid imaginations. The FBI said the plane went down as a result of pilot error. Period! End of story! You're the ones who've had the elaborate conspiracy theory all these months; who think the crash was no accident. I never said any of that, I just went along with you two because you're friends. They can't possibly want anything from me because I don't know anything," Walburn argued vehemently, as if Corello were judge and jury and this his only chance at escaping a certain death sentence. Despite his vociferous denial that he could be connected in any way, even minutely, to Goodman's death, his whole body shook visibly.

Though the two men appeared to be in the throes of a full-blown argument, or at the very least a heated dispute in the midst of an ever-growing crowd, not a single patron paid them the least bit of attention. Each was either fixated on the images and words now pouring forth from the various reporters, or engaged in his or her own discussions or theories surrounding Goodman's death, the once red-hot story now sizzling again.

Corello held the back of an empty chair for stability. "I hope you're correct, Marty, and you may well be, but by staying here you're betting your very life that you're right. Mark my words, at this point, it doesn't matter what you know or don't know. All that matters is what these men *think* you know." He stumbled halfway across the room then turned a final time to his old friend. "If these men, whoever the hell they are, decide to come after you, you might as well kiss your ass goodbye because you're gone." He made a magician's gesture with his hands, bringing them together with a clap and then rapidly apart, palms forward, exposing an emptiness as if a white dove had just been freed. "Gone," he repeated in a whisper.

Then, like a magician, he disappeared from the bar.

* * *

The old woman moved with careful toddler steps, more a shuffle than the deliberate walk of someone who didn't fear a shattered hip from every rise and fall in the pavement. Her trustworthy walking stick tapped the sidewalk ahead of her twice with each pair of steps she managed, not unlike someone her age who was also suffering an acute loss of vision, though not yet fully blind. Bent severely at the waist, head almost in line with where her bust had been in her youth, the enormous dowager's hump that rose from the old woman's back made her look more like the Hollywood stereotype of a decrepit octogenarian than a real person.

As the tap, tap, shuffle, shuffle moved her down G Street as slowly as a glacier, she grew quite tired and decided to rest for a few moments in front of a well-lighted establishment into which people seemed to be steadily streaming. There didn't appear to be a single parking space along either curb as far as the eye could see, but she would have been the first to admit that she didn't see as well as she once had.

The old woman took her small purse, always kept in the hand opposite her cane—since there was no way its strap would remain on shoulders as bowed as a McDonald's arch—and laid it on one of the two stone planters which sat below the huge windows flanking the bar's front door. They were too high for her to rest her diminutive frame, but the simple act of relieving herself of the weight of the purse, though small in design and empty of contents when compared with the steamer trunks carried by the average working woman today, seemed heavenly.

It was the little things in life that she had come to appreciate in her later years.

The young, well-dressed man—who exited the bar like there was a fire inside—paid no more attention to her than had any of the of patrons who'd entered in the last few moments. Invisible, that's how she felt. Old folks like her were always invisible to anyone younger than they, which, at her age, was pretty much anyone not looking up at dirt.

As he practically fell down the four granite steps, coming to a shaky stop on the sidewalk only three feet from her, the old woman said in a motherly tone, "Young man, I really don't think you should be driving in your present condition."

Clark Corello turned in foggy disbelief toward the scratchy whisper of a voice that seemed to originate from somewhere behind him. It was like a voice from a dream. He brought his blurry vision to bear on a diminutive form leaning against one for the stone planters and said, "Excuse me, ma'am." With most of the illumination coming from the windows at the figure's back, all he could make out was a tiny silhouette and a sliver of a face, as wrinkled and pallid as a mummy. He moved closer, bending down to get a better look at the old woman, though why he didn't know. He had to get the hell out of town, now, and taking time for a busybody grandmother, no matter how well intentioned her counsel, wasn't part of the plan.

When his own bewildered gaze met her milky-eyed stare, she repeated her admonition then punctuated her words by poking him in the knee with her cane.

"Ouch, dammit!" Corello said, rubbing his leg. "I heard you the first time. Who the hell are you?"

Apparently not at all pleased by his tone and lack of regard for her words of wisdom, the old woman pulled her purse from the planter, tapped her cane twice on the sidewalk, and shuffled off in the direction she'd been heading before her rest, without another word to the rude young man she'd merely tried to help.

When she'd shuffled a few yards east on G Street, slowly moving toward Seventh, Corello pulled his cell phone from his pocket and tapped in the number for Capital Cab, a number he knew by heart. As he entered the third digit and groped for the fourth, he began to feel lightheaded and nauseated. Perspiration poured from his brow, stinging his eyes as he tried to focus on the keypad. No use, he had to sit down for a moment. He knew he'd had too much scotch, way too much, but he'd been drunk before and had never been incapable of dialing a goddamn phone number.

"Shit!" he barked at the phone as the remaining digits escaped him. The dizziness grew, as did the feeling that he was going to vomit at any moment. His mouth watered uncontrollably.

As his legs gave way, he reached out his left hand to grab the same planter the troll-like good Samaritan had just relinquished but depth perception failed him completely and he missed the stone cap by a full foot. Instead of his fingers securing the cap for support, they grabbed only a handful of air and he fell forward, his face striking the granite top with the full force of his body's weight behind it. His nose splintered at once and blood flooded his mouth and sinuses, but the intense pain that would have resulted from the devastating blow never registered in his brain.

Clark Corello was already dead.

As the old woman rounded the corner at Tenth, a black Crown Victoria with windows as dark as obsidian eased to the curb a few feet ahead of her. The back door opened and a man the size of a Frigidaire stepped out, leaving the door ajar. He motioned for her to accept the ride.

Without a word of either protest or gratitude, the woman carefully moved her diminutive form into the back seat, followed at once by the big man. Even before the door had slammed shut, the vehicle was again underway.

"Have you been naughty again, Meagan?" the man in the front passenger seat asked as they sped away.

The old woman straightened a bit and rested both palms on the smooth, rounded top of her cane. Her back ached terribly. To no one in particular she said, "I suppose that would depend on your definition of naughty." Her right thumb massaged the small activation button, cleverly disguised as a knot in the hickory staff.

When depressed, it would cause a stainless steel needle, smaller than a human hair, to instantly protrude from the rubber tip at the pavement end of the cane, just enough to penetrate several layers of clothing and the skin beneath. Simultaneously, a minute dose of synthesized curare, genetically engineered to deliver a hundred times its original lethality, would be forced by compressed air through the needle's core and into the blood stream of the victim; it all occurred in less than the blink of an eye. Certain death would ensue within sixty seconds.

While potentially detectable during an autopsy, if exactly the right combination of tox screens were first ordered and then performed to perfection—which occurred during every CSI episode on TV, but rarely, if ever, in the real world of forensics where too little money and too many cases governed laboratory protocol—death was generally attributed to a massive stroke.

Her mind wandered in nostalgic recollection of all the stories she'd read about "kill canes" like hers, made famous by the KGB during the Cold War. Unlike the predecessors of her preferred tool of assassination, which now only existed in books and museums, hers had not been designed around mechanical systems, with springs, pneumatic pistons, and miniature hydraulics or elaborate linkage tying all of the killing parts together. Her generation of "bang stick," as they were affectionately called by their owners, was a marvel of microprocessors and lithium power.

Still, despite its NASA level of sophistication—it had, after all, cost more than a good used Mercedes—she wished she could, just once, take a mark down with one of the grand old tools of the past. She doubted that those who followed in her footsteps would have the same sense of history and respect that she possessed. The times they were a changing, as Bob Dylan had once said, and not for the better to her way of thinking.

"So, now you're a philosopher," the man mused, snapping her out of her daydream.

"Not so much a philosopher as one simply immune to such conventional labels, I suppose," she answered with a sardonic smile. Her voice was no longer the crackly whisper of someone on the back side of eighty, but had gained a robustness which might even be called sensual.

He turned and made eye contact with the woman. "No problems with Corello, I gather?"

"Of course not," she said without emotion. She looked at the small gold watch on her left wrist. It had been just under three minutes since she'd injected the inebriated man. "He should be getting stiff by now."

"And Wagner?"

"Sheila phoned me a minute before Corello exited the bar. Seems the esteemed senator from Massachusetts missed his subway. Too bad the subway didn't miss him. I understand it was quite a mess. Sheila reported no issues with witnesses. Besides her, Wagner had been the only person at the stop when he, shall we say, fell onto the tracks. Clean and easy. He really shouldn't have drunk so much. It's bad for one's health."

The two men in the front seat looked at each other, their pained expressions a mix of revulsion and admiration as they imagined the gruesome scene and understood that both deaths had been carried out with surgical precision and impunity by two petite women who, combined and fully dressed, weighed less than either of them.

"Remind me to never piss you off, Meagan," the driver said.

"Hey, that's not nice, I'm a sweet old lady. I wouldn't hurt a flee. For *free*, anyway," she added in a chuckle. "It's the folks who hire me that you'd better never piss off. For my part, my only loyalties lie with dead presidents."

She pulled the gray wig from her head followed by the wireless ear bud that connected to her cell phone. When she'd stowed both carefully in the large bag the refrigerator had handed her, she began to pick at the silicone and latex that had been used to artificially age her. She stuffed the rubbery fragments into a gallon-sized Ziploc bag; they would be discarded later. Within ninety seconds, the driver had put twelve blocks between them and Indigo Bar and the old woman was younger by nearly two-thirds of a century. "And, speaking of dead presidents," she said, her upturned palm extending between the front seats.

The man in the front passenger seat reached into his coat pocket and withdrew a bulging envelope, handing it to the young woman. "With the General's sincerest thanks. Sorry about the short notice."

Without counting the contents, she stuffed the envelope into her handbag, then added that to the carry bag between her feet. "As long as he's willing to pay for rush, you'll get no complaint from us. I assume—"

"You assume correctly," the man interrupted, anticipating her question. "Twice your normal fee."

That bit of happy news garnered a broad smile as the woman separated the walking stick into three pieces and pushed each section with great care into its custom-made leather case, also handed to her by the huge man to her right. Then she removed her long-sleeve blouse and withdrew the inflatable hump that had deformed her back, stuffing the thick rubber bladder into the bag along with the other prosthetics, cane, and support gear. Her dark gray wool-blend slacks were slipped off and added to the bag.

She was now wearing only a bra and small, white cotton panties, but she didn't seem to give it a second thought. The three men knew better than to gawk, despite her generous breasts and shapely figure: it could well be the last sight their eyes beheld in this life.

She withdrew a stylish silk shell from the garment bag the huge man had put on the seat between them and pulled it over her head, then added a pair of complementary linen slacks, also from the garment bag.

When she could once again pass for a successful, young businesswoman with a slightly oversized carry bag, the man riding shotgun said, "Where do you want us to drop you? Back at your place?"

"Better take me to Sheila's, I'll crash there. You know it?"

"In Burtonsville, right?"

"Yeah, Prince John Place."

He looked at the driver who said he knew the address; they would be there in twenty-five minutes. When a sinister thought forced a broad grin, he said to the woman, "How many of Sheila's neighbors would be shocked to discover they have a world-class assassin living among them in their perfect little suburban neighborhood?"

Meagan leaned back comfortably in the seat, arching her back repeatedly as she rocked her hips side to side. It was the first time she'd been able to straighten her spine in an hour and the bones cracked and popped as they realigned themselves. Of all the characters she assumed in her profession, the old lady was the hardest to do for an extended period. Oh, well, for more money than most of her neighbors earned in a year at their boring nine-to-five jobs, the discomfort was insignificant. She'd get a hot bath tonight and a massage in the morning. In another twelve months, eighteen at most, she and Sheila would be able to retire to the islands in the style they now only enjoyed while on vacation, six or eight weeks a year. After that, they'd take only one job a year, only for long-standing clients, and then only if the money was just right.

As she exchanged her low-heeled orthotic walkers for a stylish pair of Emilio Pucci pumps, costing easily as much as the suits these men were wearing, she said, "You know as well as I do that people see exactly what you give them to see, that they believe exactly what you tell them to believe, especially if it's already what they want to see and believe. If their minds weren't all filled with Disney movies and sappy sitcoms, and they were actually aware of the world that truly existed around them, what you and I do for a living would be a hell of a lot harder to pull off. Am I right?"

"Absolutely," he agreed. "Let's hope John and Jane Doe never wise up."

"Never gonna happen," she said, then added philosophically, "They're totally content to live in the world they want, the world they actually think they have a hand in shaping: no questions, no problems. It's perfect."

"I hope you're right," he said to the passenger glass as the picturesque city raced by postcard images.

The woman grinned knowingly as she began to peel away the latex that had aged her hands to match her face.

PART 2:
CONTAINMENT

"A good plan, violently executed now,
is better than a perfect plan next week."

George S. Patton, U.S. General
(1885–1945)

FOURTEEN

HEN MARIE AND ALEX crested the final hill on Highway 191 that led into Truman from the southwest, with home only a mile away, Alex let out a giddy laugh: "Oh, my gosh, I can't wait to climb into my own bed tonight and sleep until noon tomorrow. I don't know why, you'd think I'd be used to it by now, but I'm so tired of sleeping on that stupid air mattress I could scream."

"I know exactly how you feel," Marie agreed with a wide smile. The grin had not been produced by what her best friend had just said, but how she'd phrased it. While Marie considered herself an accomplished cusser, a self-proclaimed potty-mouth—equal to any sailor if push came to shove, or the mood simply struck her—Alex attended BYU, a deeply religious Mormon university, and had taken their teachings and beliefs to heart. While she had never chastised Marie for her language anytime a colorful execration would issue forth with little or no real provocation, sometimes just because it seemed to be the most appropriate adjective or verb at the moment—to Marie's way of thinking, at least—she didn't

145

practice the art herself. In fact, their three-year association had actually yielded a surprising side effect: Marie's day-to-day language had almost been completely purged of excess expletives, most notably the "f---" word, while Alex's had not suffered adversely in the process. "It'll be almost as good as soaking in my own hot bath instead of sponge bathing in a liquid freezer, especially since I won't have two dozen pairs of eyes watching my every move twenty-four-seven. Hell, I may even take my clothes off."

The women shared a good laugh over Marie's last comment. While on the river, bathing was always a group activity, primarily because the pre-arranged overnight camping spots, which had to accommodate thirty or so weary travelers, were seldom larger than the average front yard. With such tight quarters, bathing consisted of scrubbing as much of your body as you could modestly reach while still wearing a bathing suit, or could stand to scrub to any adequate degree while immersed in water the color of cappuccino, moving like a runaway freight train, and only slightly warmer than melting snow.

Effective in a pinch for keeping you "socially acceptable"—*barely*—but hardly the method preferred for personal hygiene before an important date or if one were to be the maid of honor in a wedding.

"I'll bet a week's pay that my dad is planning on taking us out for dinner tonight," Alex said as they approached the last turn before home. "What do you feel like?"

The drive up from Moab, where the raft company had their headquarters and from which all tours originated and ended—at least from a provisioning and equipment maintenance standpoint—normally took just under four hours, but the women had stopped on the way to eat lunch at a favorite spot just outside of Helper, Utah, consuming another thirty minutes along with the best tacos in the state. While neither was especially hungry at the moment, the prospect of a real "sit down" dinner after two weeks in the wild, despite the severely limited culinary choices offered in

Truman, was always looked forward to with as much anticipation as any Thanksgiving feast or Christmas dinner.

Since Ty Summers had never failed to take the two of them out to eat the first night back after a two-week stint—in the three years that they had worked the river circuit together—it was a pretty safe bet.

"I think I'd like Italian tonight," Marie announced, patting a flat, toned stomach that had just made a growling noise loud enough to be heard in the back seat.

"Suits me; I'm up for anything. I don't think my dad will care where we go either. He's always so glad to see us." Alex turned to Marie and made deliberate eye contact with her, and Marie sensed a melancholy in them that was uncharacteristic in her bubbly friend. "He really cares about you, you know? I do, too, but no news there, eh." She put her hand on Marie's shoulder and gave it an affectionate squeeze. "Thanks for being the person you are, sis. And thanks for always looking out for me."

*　*　*

"Grab your gear, we're going to Truman," Merkett said over the ranch's intercom system. "I want Charlie, Delta, and Echo Teams ready to leave in fifteen minutes." He turned to Donald Shelton and said, "Bring all your shit, Don. I have a feeling we're going to need it."

"But, sir, it's over. Done. Neither Alpha or Bravo came up with a thing. It's my opinion, there isn't anything left to find. Whatever Goodman had with him, it's no longer of any concern to us. Besides, Alpha Team is still in place and appears to have the situation under control."

"Those two clowns? Simple-minded killers, both of them. Good for nothing but wet work. Not a whole brain between them. We're counting on them covering our butts from three hundred miles away and you and I both know they couldn't cover their own butts with a tarp. They haven't come up with squat in a week. I'm getting a very bad feeling."

"Sir, maybe they haven't come up with anything because there simply isn't anything to come up with." Despite his confident words, 'squint' Shelton began to fill his portable computer cases; everything he'd need to do electronic eavesdropping, Internet probes, signal interception, and data manipulation.

"Bet all our lives on it? Yours?" Merkett asked, filling a 'war' bag with two Beretta 9MM pistols, a 7.62MM M40A3 sniper rifle that had already been broken down for easy transport, a 5.56MM SOPMOD M4 fully-automatic assault rifle, and spare magazines enough for all. "You know that there's no way through this deal if we don't achieve absolute victory. Anything less means our heads. You wanna gamble on that?"

"No, I don't think I would," Shelton said, understanding that they weren't going south on a sightseeing tour—this was a military operation on American soil, an operation during which blood would be spilled. It was time to wrap things up so the master plan could get back on track. Apparently, the Colonel had every intention of "locking the door" himself.

In fourteen minutes, fifty-two seconds ahead of schedule, Colonel James Merkett and twelve of this best men were onboard a pair of Bell UH-1N "Twin Huey" helicopters, their dual Pratt & Whitney engines thumping like bass drums gone mad in the afternoon sky. Before dusk, they would place their feet on the ground in Truman, Utah.

"We have ground transport ready?" Merkett asked of Donald Shelton, his voice crackling over the headset.

"Took care of it before we left, sir. We're good. Should have three SUVs on the tarmac when we touch down."

"I want to be in and out by twenty-two hundred hours. It's time for this shit to end. I'm tired of waiting for the other shoe to drop."

"Low key, sir" Shelton asked.

"Covert, overt, same difference as long as it's over once and for all. The best defense—"

"Is an aggressive offense," the Lieutenant finished.

"Right," Merkett smiled.

"Consider it done, Colonel. They won't know what hit 'em."

* * *

Sensing there had been more to Alex's words than a simple "thank you," possibly much more, Marie said, "Hey, not still weirded out about that little outburst of mine back at camp, are you? I mean, you don't have to be worried about me or anything. I'm fine."

"Yeah, I know," she said reassuringly. "But, since you brought it up," she continued, drawing out the words, "we still have a lot to talk about on that subject." She intensified her stare almost to the point of interrogation. "Right?"

Marie nodded but wished she had never opened her mouth at the river.

"Anyway, that didn't have anything to do with my thanking you for looking out for me."

"Hey, girl, we look out for each other. Always have," Marie added, grateful that the conversation had not continued in the direction it appeared to be heading.

"I know, it's just that..." she said with a shrug of her shoulders, not finishing her thought. She turned back in her seat to watch the road.

Marie now understood. There had been no need for Alex to explain. What Marie knew was that she had become best friend, half-sister, and surrogate mother to the younger woman. It was a role she had not been seeking when they had met three years ago, but it was one she hadn't run from either. Alex—her father, too— were easy to like, easy to know, as easy as any two people on the planet, she imagined. They were a pair of open books from which you got exactly what you saw, no matter how deeply you read.

No secrets, no troubled past, no skeletons in the closet; of this Marie was as certain as she had been of anything in her life.

She wished she could have said the same about herself. About her own life, or at least the life she'd lived prior to Truman. In her mind, it seemed like forever ago, and at the same time, like yesterday.

Perhaps, one day, she'd take them both aside and tell them all about the real woman who lived above their garage, who shared meals with them, and who had been so warmly and genuinely befriended. Maybe then their friendship could be based, at least from that moment forward, on truth and trust, the foundation blocks upon which all solid and lasting friendships had to be forged.

Perhaps, one day, she'd just pack her bags and disappear while they slept and not have to deal with any of this crap. She was good at running, but then, practice makes perfect.

The past from which she'd tried to escape for so long always seemed to rear its ugly head at the most unexpected and unwelcome times.

Like now.

Dammit! Why couldn't Alex have just said "thanks" and leave it at that? Why did she have to be such a sweet kid, the kind of person Marie believed she might have become if life hadn't slapped the shit out of her every time she turned around at that age?

As Marie was about to say something she was sure she would regret the moment the words left her mouth, Alex announced, "Italian sounds perfect. Good idea." She patted the dash with her hands like a nervous drummer, in perfect sync to the music Marie hadn't realized was still playing in the background: Kenny Chesney was singing about living in fast forward.

The sudden urge to come clean, to turn the little white coupe into a rolling confessional, passed as quickly as it had come, like a morning fog evaporated by the first rays of sunlight. Marie didn't know whether she felt relieved or disappointed, but whichever it was, she let the feeling pass without giving it a voice.

In another minute, she had turned off Old River Road and into the long asphalt drive that led to the Summers' home, pulling her three-year-old Honda Accord coupe up behind the patrol car already in the driveway.

"Good, daddy's home," Alex said with excitement, tossing her seatbelt aside and reaching for the door handle before the car had even come to a stop. "We'll unpack later." With that, she exited the car and began to stretch travel-stiff muscles, shaking her long, tan legs alternately like a runner before a marathon.

"No argument here; I'm certainly in no hurry to do two week's laundry," Marie said, switching off the engine and joining Alex on the walkway.

Together they moved quickly up the wide stone steps and across the front porch, anxious to be home. As they approached the huge oak front door, Marie was filled with a sense of 'family' she hadn't felt in more years than she could remember.

Or perhaps, chose to remember.

Though for the past three years, since arriving in Truman, she had actually lived in the small apartment over the garage, which was detached from the house, she had eaten almost every morning and evening meal with the Summers, Ty and Alex. They had treated her like family from day one, even telling her after she'd paid the first month's rent that she could stay for free; in fact, they had insisted on it. While she already paid only a pittance for rent when compared with the other places she'd investigated before hearing of the cozy apartment above the garage, she had equally insisted that she be allowed to continue to do so, for her own self-esteem if nothing else, or she would have no alternative but to find accommodations elsewhere.

Since neither Alex nor Ty had wanted Marie to leave, they relented. It hadn't taken long for her to figure out that from that point on, Ty had given back far more money each month feeding her than her paltry rent contribution. Every time she brought up the subject, however, he would say that it cost no more to feed three than it does two. A ludicrous argument, of course, but the same one she would have used in their place.

Hard to successfully argue with good folks who had their minds made up to do good things. What do you say in rebuttal? "I'd rather you consider me nothing more than a renter and ignore me at every turn instead of treating me like family for no apparent reason other than the fact that you're truly good people."

Even when Marie came home with groceries on her own, stocking the pantry to overflowing, a hundred dollar bill would wind up mysteriously in her purse where none had previously resided.

Of course, she'd put the money on the desk in the den, or in one of Ty's uniform shirt pockets, but it would always reappear in her purse by day's end.

And so it went: they would give, she would give back. In every sense but technically, they *were* a family.

She had never told them that she was more than capable of paying not only her own way, but theirs as well, for that would have raised more questions than she had been prepared to answer—was *still* prepared to answer.

Better for them that they remain happily oblivious to such things. Safer for them, at least.

Marie knew as surely as the sun rises in the east that her past would catch up with her one day, and she didn't intend to allow the devil to exact any "collateral damage" when he finally came to collect her soul. If fate decreed that she must die for past sins, so be it.

She had no death wish, to be sure, but neither was she willing to sacrifice a single innocent life simply to buy her a little more time.

FIFTEEN

O N OLD RIVER ROAD, an inky-black sedan cruised with the deliberate ease of a killer whale, its occupants cocksure that they, like the orca, represented the pinnacle of the food chain, and as such, were threatened by nothing or no one. Their speed, neither too fast nor too slow for the quiet rural setting, would have elevated the adrenaline level in no one working in their front yard or walking the family dog.

When they glided by the pastoral residence with the wide covered porch and galvanized tin roof that was home to Sheriff Ty Summers, former Chief of Detectives with the Salt Lake City Police Department, and his daughter, Alex, a senior at BYU, their speed didn't change one mile per hour. They had seen what they'd come to see: the daughter and her friend were home, right on schedule.

Witherspoon checked the screen on his laptop to satisfy himself that audio was being received from the four miniature microphones they'd placed throughout the house a week earlier, and smiled at the outstanding signal they were getting. "These new transmitters are so damn sweet," he said with obvious satisfaction.

McGhee glanced at the LCD screen for as long as he dared, while still keeping the Crown Victoria on the road, and nodded approvingly. Now all they had to do was listen and wait.

* * *

"We're home," Alex announced as soon as her foot touched the entrance hall floor. She heard footsteps coming from the back of the house and crossed the living room to meet her father half way. She needed one of his great bear hugs.

"Hey, Alex. Marie," Doug Rozier said warmly appearing in the doorway that led to the den, though it was obvious to Marie that he wasn't pleased to see them. It was not unusual for Ty's chief deputy to visit; in fact, he was a regular guest at the Summers' home, but Sunday afternoon was not his normal time to come calling. A sense of dread begin to clutch at Marie's soul.

"Where's my dad?" Alex asked, looking around the deputy in anticipation of seeing her father round the corner from the den at any second.

The look on Doug's face was one that Marie had seen too many times, and it made her legs turn to Jell-O.

Without answering, Doug reached out and squeezed Alex's shoulders with both hands.

"Doug, where's my dad?" she repeated, but this time with a touch of dread in her voice. When his eyes rimmed with tears, Alex fell to her knees, shoulders slumped, head bowed, more a heap of a person than a vibrant young lady. "Oh, God, no," she said in a voice that was soft and flat but lacking emotion, as though there was no heart left in her with which to color her words. "Is my daddy...?"

She could not finish the thought.

Marie knelt and wrapped her arms around her stricken friend. She wanted to weep like a baby, to curse at God, to smash something, but knew these were selfish feelings that would not serve the needs of her closest friend in her most dire moment. She had to be strong, for Alex. Maybe it was only an accident and everything was going to be fine.

"I'm so sorry, Alex," Doug said, and with those four words, the floodgates opened and there would be no closing them until the last tear her body could produce had been exorcised. Alex doubled over like she'd been kicked in the stomach and began to sob uncontrollably. She was joined by Marie, also a pitiful font of tears despite every attempt to remain a Gibraltar of support.

Perhaps, after all, the best support she could provide at this very moment was to yield to her feelings, honestly and deeply, without regard for propriety or circumstance; to fully experience the pain they both felt in all its ugly and dreaded dimensions. Perhaps control of any kind at a time like this was a total illusion and not even possible unless one didn't possess a heart. Whichever it was, or if it was something altogether different, the tears came more easily and more intensely than she had imagined was still possible with all that had happened in her life.

Or maybe, precisely *because* of all that had happened in her life: wounds and losses that she had not yet mourned sufficiently for her own healing to begin.

Doug sank into the old leather chair that had always been Ty's favorite and wiped his eyes with the sleeves of his uniform shirt. He had shed his tears for his boss and dear friend days ago. Soon, their tears, too, would end and they would want answers, though he understood that no knowledge, no matter how detailed or insightful, had ever been able to bring back a single loved one in all of history. Today would be no exception, but answers would still be sought. The need to understand the reason for a death was deep in the human psyche, even when that understanding changed nothing, not even the slightest little thing. For now, there was nothing he could do or say that would help either woman with the pain they were experiencing. As much as he wanted to ease them through this process, he also knew that it *was* a process, and as such, could be hurried no more than wine could be made to ferment in a day.

155

He thought about the irony of Ty's death, and it seemed the harshest cruelty of all. After the loss of his beloved Elizabeth, Ty Summers had packed up his teenage daughter and all their earthly possessions and had moved to the sleepy little town of Truman, Utah, confident that he could serve out the remaining years of his law enforcement career in Mayberry, USA, where not only would his daughter be safe, but so would he. It wasn't the danger of the job that he feared but the toll the job so often collected. He'd buried more than one fellow officer in his lifetime and never wanted to put Alex through that, not without the support of a mother. If that meant leaving a job he loved, the tariff was small.

When Doug had asked him about the abrupt career change, once their friendship had grown to the point where such personal confidences began to be shared, Ty had expressed his concerns honestly and openly with his chief deputy. "You'll understand when you have children, especially a daughter," he had said, but added, "If death wants you, it'll find you wherever you live. You can't run from it; you can only make choices."

When wracking anguish at last dissolved into a quiet despondency that seemed to resonate through the home as surely as a scream, Alex rose from her fetal position on the floor and sat on her heels, arms hanging lifeless in her lap. A moment before, Marie had gained some sense of composure, albeit tenuous and as thin as a fly's wing, and continued to envelop Alex in a loving embrace. She could not tell if the younger woman was even aware of her presence, but conscious perception wasn't important at the moment. She knew that Alex's soul was aware of her presence, of her concern and caring, and nothing else mattered.

Finally Alex spoke. "What happened, Doug?" The voice, barely above a whisper, had regained none of its life.

Doug Rozier took a long and labored breath before speaking, letting it exhale slowly through his nostrils. "Last Sunday morning, around nine a.m., Andy spotted a damaged guardrail on Duchesne Road, about a mile southeast of town. It looked to him like a vehicle had struck the retainer at speed, but there was no vehicle in sight. When he stopped to investigate, he spotted Ty's Expedition a few hundred yards off the road at the bottom of a small gully. By the time he reached the car, it was already too late. There was nothing he could do."

As he spoke, Alex's hands had gone to her face, covering it fully, as if blocking the world from view would somehow prevent all of this from being real.

"What happened?" Marie asked.

"Not really sure. No sign of another vehicle being involved," Doug said.

"What, he just drove off the road?" she said incredulously.

His brow knitted into deep furrows. "There were other, uh, considerations," he finally managed to say, though he was clearly uncomfortable with this admission.

"Like what?" Marie pressed.

Doug looked to Alex when her hands returned to her lap and her eyes repeated Marie's question.

"There appeared to have been alcohol involved."

"What! That's bullshit!" Alex said defiantly. "My father would never drink and drive. Who came up with that lame-ass theory? You, Doug?"

"Alex, I know you're upset, we're all—"

"Don't patronize me, Doug. Don't you dare patronize me. You're damned right I'm upset, my mother's dead and now my father. You and I both know he would never drink and drive. Period. End of story. There's got to be some other explanation." She looked at him as if to say, *okay, tell me what really happened*.

Doug looked to Marie for some level of understanding and shrugged his shoulders, turning his palms upward in bewilderment as if to indicate that he had nothing else to offer. "Alex, I'm sorry but there was a very strong odor of alcohol on Ty when we got to him, and we found an empty bottle of brandy in the kitchen when we came to the house later that morning. Only one glass."

"So," Alex snapped. "Having a drink doesn't mean *drunk*. For all you know, the bottle was nearly empty to begin with. He often had a brandy on Saturday night, you've shared one with him more than a few times, but he's never been drunk a single day in my life. Have you ever, I mean even one time, seen my father drunk? Have you, Doug?"

Doug shook his head; indeed, he had not.

When Alex had resorted to profanity not once, but three times in the last sixty seconds—a decade's worth of foul language for her under normal circumstances—Marie realized that the stress on her had to be incredible, unimaginable.

Though Marie hadn't consciously summoned the memory, the image of her sitting in a crowded room, not unlike this one, and hearing that she, too, had just been orphaned, flooded over her like hot magma, singeing her nerve endings and torturing her spirit. She closed her eyes and forced her mind back to the moment. "What was his blood alcohol level?" she asked.

The look on Doug's face said that he had no idea.

"You didn't check it?"

Again, the upturned palms.

"Why in God's name not?"

The news that Doug now had to deliver was not going to help either the mood of the moment or provide the answers the women wanted. To his mind, however, it was probably better to get it over with, while they were both still down, than to wait until they had gotten to their feet, literally as well as figuratively, only to be knocked flat again. He took another deep breath, this time exhaling quickly as if to steel his nerve. "We didn't get a blood alcohol level because Will Cameron died the same day. Apparently he suffered a heart attack while at his clinic early Sunday morning."

If a sparrow's feather had dropped on the hardwood floor at that moment, it would have made the sound of a ceramic vase crashing through a glass table. The room had become as silent as a vacuum. As devoid of sound as space itself.

Between the beginning of her sophomore year in high school and the beginning of her sophomore year at BYU, Alex had worked at Will Cameron's clinic in nearly every capacity. In high school, she had come every day after school, first as his receptionist and then later as lab assistant and darkroom tech. When she went away to college, she had spent the first summer performing the same tasks, but knew she would not be returning to the clinic the following June. She loved the job and the Camerons, thinking of Will more as an uncle than her employer, and of Joan as a kindly aunt, but she'd been offered a chance to spend her summers outside, working for the rafting company, and the idea had thrilled her at once. Alex had always been an outdoors person.

When Marie arrived in town and took up residence above the garage, she'd inquired about any jobs that might be available in the area. The timing couldn't have been better: Alex recommended Marie to the Camerons. As she imagined they would, both took to her at once, and for the last three years, she had worked from September to May at the clinic, doing the same jobs Alex had previously performed.

When Alex had told Marie about her summer job offer, she'd signed up as well without a word of encouragement being needed. Though Alex had not worked for Dr. Cameron for three years now, she had stopped by his clinic every chance she had, and their relationship had remained close.

The news of his death knocked the last wind out of her, and she ran to the bathroom to vomit.

Marie let her go without trying to stop her. She knew she was spent, done, though she also knew her friend would not harm herself, even in this moment when optimism and belief in the future—two of Alex's defining qualities—were as fractured as the human spirit could imagine. There was always a limit to what a body could give in any tragedy and Alex had just been slammed face-first into that emotional boundary.

To her surprise, Marie realized that the greatest sensation she felt wasn't increased pain or loss of hope, but a bristling of the small telegraphic hairs on the back of her neck. They had always proven as reliable a warning system as the best radar in the U.S. arsenal. "What time Sunday morning?" she asked.

"What?" Doug said, his attention fixed on Alex as she vanished down the hall toward her bedroom and adjoining bath. When the bedroom door slammed shut behind her, he turned slowly back toward Marie.

"I asked you what time Will died Sunday morning?"

"Not sure exactly. Joan found him lying on the floor in his office about sunrise. She awoke earlier and realized he'd never come to bed Saturday night. When he didn't answer the phone at the clinic, or his cell phone, she drove over to see if he was there."

"My God, how is she doing?"

"About as well as anyone who'd just lost her mate and best friend of five decades."

"Lousy, huh."

"Yeah. Pretty much."

"Who's checking on her?"

Doug ignored the question but stood and looked down the hall. "We need to do something," he said, referring to Alex.

"I'll go to her in a minute," Marie said. "Right now, she needs space to wrap her mind around all of this. Half an hour ago, she was looking forward to Italian with her dad. Now, she has his funeral as well as the funeral of a close friend to look forward to. Shitty deal no matter how you slice it."

"Actually, we buried Will on Tuesday," Doug said, with an apologetic look that said he hadn't meant to correct her. "The Sheriff, Alex's dad I mean, is still at the clinic, in the morgue. I knew we couldn't do anything more until she had a chance to see him, you know, one last time."

"Thanks for that, Doug. How bad is he? I mean..." Marie stammered. There was no way she was going to let Alex see her father in some catastrophic state. The image would never leave her mind, not in a hundred lifetimes. All Doug had said was he'd been in an automobile accident at speed. Marie knew that could well mean physical damage that would make Hollywood's most graphic battle scenes pale by comparison.

At first Doug was not sure what Marie meant, but then the meaning of her words struck him. "No, it's okay, really. He just looks like he's asleep. Some pretty severe bruising but that's to be expected. Doctor Caruthers from Mercy Hospital helped out; he signed the death certificate. Said the impact with either the guardrail or the culvert where the Expedition came to rest broke Ty's neck. No seatbelt. It was instantaneous, thank God. Small blessing. He looks good, really," he repeated for reassurance.

"No airbag?" Marie wondered. She wasn't sure she'd actually uttered the words, but when she looked to the deputy, she could see that he was mulling over the question in his mind.

Doug massaged his chin mindlessly between thumb and forefinger, forming the skin into a dimpled crease below his lip and then forcing it smooth again. Finally he said, "No, there *was* no deployment; first I've thought of it, really." Then with a shrug, "Guess the angle was wrong or something."

The hairs on the back of Marie's neck were now fully erect. "You don't find that odd? I mean, the impact was severe enough to snap the neck of a man built like a pro linebacker and yet not severe enough to set off the airbag sensor?"

The deputy shook his head, not in disagreement but in shared wonder. "You're right, it makes no sense." He gave Marie a hard look. "Hey, you suggesting it wasn't an accident?"

"Your words, not mine."

"Yeah, but it doesn't take a rocket scientist to know what you're driving at."

This time, Marie only shrugged.

"Who'd want to kill Ty Summers? Everyone in town loved him. He could have been mayor if he'd wanted to be. Besides, there wasn't any sign of foul play."

"Look, Doug, I'm not implying that you and Andy didn't do your jobs investigating Ty's death, but there are just too damn many coincidences here to suit me. I don't like it, not one bit."

This time, Doug shook his head in disagreement. "Nope, I can't agree with you, Marie. First, whether Alex, you, or I care to admit it, for whatever reason, Ty took a late night drive on a curvy mountain road with a bellyful of booze and missed a turn. There's not one shred of evidence to suggest that anyone else was in the SUV at that time or that another vehicle had been involved. The airbag is another issue, I admit, but one that doesn't alter the events. Second, it was raining like the end of the world at the time of the accident; had been most of the day before. That particular curve isn't easy to navigate at noon on a sunny day, especially if you happen to be going a bit too fast and are a bit impaired."

"You don't know that for sure."

"Yes, we do, Marie. Listen, the last thing on earth I'd ever do is slander Ty's good name, and this is never going to appear in the official report, you have my word on that, but he smelled like a brewery. If he wasn't over the legal limit, then he poured the entire bottle of brandy all over himself before getting behind the wheel."

"Or someone else did," she said in a half whisper, her comment not really meant to be heard.

"Like who?" he barked impatiently. There was nothing wrong with Doug Rozier's hearing, and right now, what he heard was not improving his mood.

Marie looked defiantly at him. "That's for *you* to find out, isn't it? I'm not the cop here."

"Really? Sounds like you're trying to be one to me."

"Why, just because this all seems wrong? Inexplicable?"

"It's not inexplicable, Marie. You just don't like the explanation."

"Then give me one I can live with, Doug," she practically shouted.

Doug shook his head in obvious displeasure. "Finally," he said through clenched teeth, finishing his original train of thought, "when his oldest friend in Truman gets the news, he keels over from a heart attack. Everyone knows Will had a bad ticker, including you, right?" He paused to gauge her reaction but couldn't read her expression with any degree of certainty. "I suppose you don't like that theory, either."

Marie knew she'd pressed too hard. Doug was a friend and a good cop. Still, it didn't add up in her mind: two plus two wasn't coming anywhere close to four. "Okay, I admit he'd had some issues with his heart lately, but for a seasoned medical examiner to drop dead merely upon hearing the news of a friend's death is preposterous."

"Some issues?" Doug said incredulously. "Jesus, Marie, he had a quadruple bypass last year. Almost died on the table. Have you forgotten that already?"

Marie had not forgotten, how could she. But the dedicated small town doctor had come back to the work he loved in record time and with no apparent ill effects from the surgery, despite Joan's admonition that he retire, or at the very least, work only half a day. He'd done neither, but he'd also had nothing but good reports from his attending cardiologist in the months that followed.

To her mind, Will Cameron had returned to work as sound as any man his age she knew, and with an attitude that seemed to resonate an amour de la vie. People who loved life as much as he simply didn't drop dead when they got bad news. She wasn't buying any of it, but she also realized that her own past was probably responsible for much of her paranoia. She reminded herself that just because you were paranoid, however, it didn't mean they weren't out to get you.

Now, the question was, who were *they*? "Fine," she conceded, "he had serious issues with his heart, but—"

"But nothing," the deputy interjected, cutting her off. "Don't go all crazy on me here. You're exhausted and emotionally devastated.

You've just lost an important and valued person in your life with no warning at all. It's natural to feel a bit paranoid"—there was that damned word again she cursed silently—"unexpected death does that to us. Don't forget, I lost a great friend, too, and if there was one molecule of evidence indicating foul play, I'd be all over the investigation like stink on shit. You couldn't tear me off it, but there's not. Now, go to Alex and see what you can do for her. She's going to need you."

Marie smiled at his attempt to interject a bit of levity into the tension of the moment. "Sorry," she said. "I guess you're right."

"No need to apologize. I understand, believe me."

"Can we see her dad later today, I mean, if she wants to?"

Doug put his arm around Marie's shoulders and together they moved toward the front door. "Just give me a call; I'll drop everything and take the two of you myself."

"Thanks, Doug. I mean it."

"Sure. I'll see myself out."

As she heard the door close behind him, she looked toward Alex's room and wondered what she could possibly say that would make any difference at all at a time like this. She tried to remember all the things that had been said when she'd lost her folks at that age. Not the trite little clichés spoken by people who didn't really know you or care about you, but who felt they were expected by everyone else in the room to say something sensitive and insightful, but the things that had actually helped.

She took a deep breath and put her ear to the bedroom door.

SIXTEEN

WITHERSPOON PULLED NERVOUSLY AT his lip. "She's gonna make trouble," he said as he and Mc-Ghee watched Rozier's patrol car make its way down the long, winding drive and then turn east onto Old River Road. From their vantage point, the deputy couldn't have seen their vehicle even if he'd been looking for it. The shadows created by the dense stand of pines under which they'd parked had effectively swallowed the black sedan as surely as if it were a shadow itself.

"She's gonna do nothing but cry and whine like a little girl, just like the daughter," McGhee said. He was chewing on a wooden toothpick, moving it from one side of his mouth to the other for the hundredth time. "She's a nobody, a complete nothing who lives over a garage. On her best day, she couldn't cause us as much trouble as a homeless person. We could snuff out her meaningless life and not one person on this huge planet would give a rat's ass."

Witherspoon looked unconvinced.

McGhee spit the mangled toothpick out the driver's window and grabbed a fresh one from the small box in front of the instrument cluster, inserting it between his teeth. "I'll tell you what, though. If she gets too bothersome, you can do with her whatever you want. She's yours."

His partner raised the volume of the microphone monitoring the girl's bedroom when he realized the rest of the house had grown quiet. It had been muted earlier when the disgusting sounds of Alex Summers puking repeatedly had filled the Ford. "You know, after a boring-ass week in this shit hole of a town, I believe I'll take you up on that, even if she doesn't cause any trouble. I may even kill her first so I don't have to listen to her whining anymore."

McGhee shook his head in amusement. "You're a sick bastard, you know it."

"Absolutely, but don't tell me you haven't thought about doing the daughter. The first time you laid eyes on her picture in that back room, I saw the look on your face. She's one sweet piece, eh."

The thought had intrigued McGhee for a week; it intrigued him still. He liked innocent young girls, unlike his partner who preferred "seasoned women" as he put it, but for now, his mind was focused on the next forty-eight hours. When they had found Goodman's body at the clinic on Saturday night, more than a week prior, it had been searched thoroughly, turning up no trace at all of the item they were looking for. In their terminology, the body had been "clean."

An hour earlier, their initial interrogation of the coroner had resulted in his sudden and unexpected death from an apparent heart attack, before they could learn anything. That was actually a good thing, McGhee had reported to the Colonel—who agreed with him for once—because mysterious marks on Cameron's body from hours of torture would have raised unanswerable questions, possibly even bringing in the real Feds. The sheriff had not been as cooperative—suffering no premature cardiac infarction—and even after three hours of the most intense 'bloodless' torture and interrogation they knew how to inflict, refused to offer them anything of value; anything they didn't already know. Upon orders from Merkett, they had snapped his neck and had then staged the accident on Duchesne Road to make the wounds he'd suffered during interrogation plausible.

Just like with the coroner, Summers had proven a dead end. Either he had been the cleverest and most dedicated liar they'd ever met, equal to any defiantly patriotic prisoner of war, or he'd had nothing to tell.

They believed the latter.

That Sunday just past noon, the senator's body had been retrieved by relatives and a host of attorneys and state officials from California, despite Doug Rozier's feeble protest—in his 'wet paint' capacity as acting sheriff—that none of the requisite 'official' paperwork had been filled out. It had been done with great political fanfare amid one of the most bizarre media circuses any city in North America has ever witnessed, to say nothing of sleepy little Truman, Utah, where such things not only didn't happen, they had not even been imagined possible by its residents prior to that moment.

An extremely tense week followed during which not one word of the General's master plan had been reported by the media, and not one member of the numerous agencies under the umbrella of Homeland Security had paid anyone at the ranch a visit. That meant, in the Colonel's estimation, that whatever information Goodman had with him when he boarded his plane the day of his death—the information that was meant for senator J.D. Wagner in Washington, chairman of the Senate Intelligence Committee—was either consumed in the crash or exited the plane with him. If the former, problem solved, on with the "show." If the latter, however—and prudence dictated that they assume the worst case scenario—then the damning information was still out there, somewhere, which meant it was most likely between the spot near Redmon's Ridge where Goodman's body had been found and the clinic. A thorough search of the senator's body by McGhee and Witherspoon had revealed nothing, nor had the simultaneous and equally thorough search of the clinic.

Of course, before the college students who'd found Goodman had been sent to a fiery grave—along with their unfortunate girl-friends—Bravo Team had satisfied themselves, and Merkett, that they knew nothing other than what they had told McGhee and Witherspoon at the diner. Which was to say, they had known nothing of any real value.

If the sheriff or coroner had found what the Colonel was look-ing for, though it was highly unlikely given the thoroughness of the searches that he and Witherspoon had conducted after questioning and then killing both men, there was a possibility, however slight, that the daughter or her friend would lead them to it. They both lived at the Summers residence and they both worked for, or had worked for, Will Cameron. That made them the only two people in Truman who could possibly put an end to their quest.

Exactly how they would do that remained a mystery to them both, but theirs was not to reason why. Theirs was simply and faithfully to do or die. Both knew the potential cost of their chosen profession and neither balked at the prospect of dying in the "line of duty." The Colonel had ordered them to remain in Truman a few days longer and learn all there was to learn from the two women but not to torch the town in the process: Unit-speak for maintain-ing a low key.

They had dealt with the last two people who were known to have come in direct contact with Goodman's body. Now, all they had to do was wait and watch.

But, just as with killing, that was a task at which they excelled.

SEVENTEEN

THE BEDROOM DOOR OPENED as soft as a breath, like a mother checking on a flu-stricken child who had finally drifted off to sleep. On the queen-sized bed, Alex lay on top of the covers as still as a corpse, her eyes open wide and unblinking, fixed on a spot on the ceiling. Or, more likely, on a remote star deep in the cosmos that only she could see. "How you doing, buddy?" Marie asked in a whisper.

Her concerned words elicited no response, not even a blink.

Marie moved to the bed and sat beside her friend, gently brushing the tear-matted raven hair from her face. "I guess this makes us real sisters now."

At first, her words had less apparent effect than if they'd been spoken to a mannequin, but then the younger woman turned her head slowly toward Marie, eyes as dry as the sun parched desert sand. It didn't appear to Marie that Alex could ever cry again, as though her eyes no longer possessed the ability to make tears. She cocked her head as if trying to comprehend what had just been said to her. "I don't understand," she said, her voice a whisper.

Marie took both of Alex's hands in hers and squeezed gently, searching for just the right words. "I realize before now I haven't told you very much about my past, and that isn't really fair, especially at a time like this."

To Marie's amazement, Alex said, "That could make the Guinness Book of World Records in the category 'Understatements of the Year,' don't you think?" Alex's full lips wore a trace of a smile that quickly widened into a grin as she saw Marie echo her expression. In another second, they were both laughing out loud as though her comment had been the funniest thing they'd ever heard.

Even in the midst of the worst tragedies the human spirit is forced to endure, no matter how stoical or sturdy the individual, it eventually cries out for relief from the torment. This is often manifested in odd, even bizarre, behavior by those in pain: some plummet into a black hole of denial and live for weeks, months, or even years in a make-believe world where the tragedy hasn't yet occurred, unconsciously going about their days as if life were perfectly normal. Others act out with destructive consequences, abusing alcohol or drugs or both in hopes of assuaging their wounded souls. All Alex wanted to do was not hurt anymore. Her attempt at humor had not been deliberate or even realized at first, but it proved to be the perfect medicine to bring her back from the brink of hopeless despair, that metaphorical cliff's edge on which she had just seconds ago been perched, ready to leap at any moment to her emotional death.

"God, I'm so sorry, Alex," Marie said when their laughter had finally subsided. She squeezed her hands more firmly than ever.

"I know, and I love you for that."

"It'll be okay, you understand that, right? I know it doesn't seem possible at the moment, but it will be okay. It just takes time."

Alex's mind did understand that she was not going to actually die just because her father had, though her heart would have disagreed vehemently at the moment—and would for weeks. Healing would come, just as it had after her mother's death. She nodded at Marie's words, sitting up with her back to the headboard, arms wrapped tightly around her knees. "What did you mean earlier?" she asked.

Marie shifted her position on the bed to allow Alex to sit up, then folded her legs, yoga style, and sat opposite her. The pictures that had found their way into her mind's scrapbook and had then been stored safely away; the images that hadn't been viewed in years now had to be brought into the light once again. She had not wished for this, having at last gained a peaceful sense of equilibrium between hated recollections and remembering loved ones—most of the time, anyway—but she couldn't tell Alex of their bond if she didn't, in fact, bring the images that linked them into the light. What had seemed so easy to say a minute before now stuck in her throat like stale dry bread. "I lost my parents when I was in college, almost exactly your age. Both of them on the same day." She didn't cry with this revelation, those tears had been shed many years ago, but the images that flashed before her mind's eye seemed to tear at her soul like buzzards ravaging a dead animal. The past became the present more quickly than a thought. "So, I guess that makes us sisters. Orphan sisters," she said in a small voice. "Not exactly a sorority either of us would have willingly pledged, but here we are."

Alex had never heard her closest friend talk about her family. On the contrary, Marie had steadfastly refused to even discuss the subject whenever it had arisen. She had always figured that there had merely been "bad blood" there, as in so often the case in families these days. We had become a country where dysfunction more typically characterized families than did any other trait. She had never imagined that Marie was completely alone in the world, just as she was now, and felt more sorry for her for some indescribable reason than she did for herself, though only a moment before, she had considered herself the most unfortunate waif ever to have been born.

"How did it happen?" she asked, this time reaching out to Marie.

"That's not important, really. Just know that I have been where you are, and you will survive it if you don't give in to self-pity." She saw Alex's brow knit into a tight furrow. "Hey, don't think for a minute that I'm saying this doesn't suck. It sucks bad, and it's gonna hurt like hell for a long, long time. There will be days when you'll reach for a phone, just to call your dad to share a tiny bit of the day with him, and will realize halfway through dialing his number that he isn't going to pick up. Never again is he going to pick up. At that moment, you'll feel like someone punched you squarely in the solar plexus. It'll take your breath away."

"I know. I did that a couple of times after my mom died," Alex said, her voice cracking. She knew that her friend wasn't just using sympathetic words but spoke from personal experience. People who tried to express solidarity with another's loss, when they had no real connection to such loss, always spoke in grandiose terms, never acknowledging the infinite gossamer threads from which life is woven, and by which life so tenuously clings. Sure, you always missed your wife at Christmas, or your husband on your anniversary, but it was remembering how they liked a half packet of sweetener in their iced tea instead of cane sugar that tore your heart out when the waitress set a single glass of the amber brew in front of you at dinner. "I really don't think I can go through that again," she said soulfully.

"Sure you can. It's just like being on the river."

Alex didn't connect the dots and her furrowed brow said so.

"Think about it this way: what if the hundred miles we cover each trip were somehow compressed into a single mile, with all of the rapids and boulders in your face back to back without a break?" Marie said.

Alex's pained expression said that such a thing would be incomprehensible, frightening beyond description.

"Exactly," Marie said, realizing she'd made the connection. "And as much as it seems, right at this moment, that you're going to have to experience all the loss and pain you'll feel in a lifetime, back to back with no respite, you won't. These first days, just like the first rapid you ever navigated, are going to scare the hell out of you, but then there will be calmer water, maybe even a long stretch where you can catch your breath. The next rapids won't seem as intimidating, no matter how soon they come or how steep they are, because you know there will always be calm water before and after, just like on the river."

Alex closed her eyes and lowered her forehead to her knees, hiding her face from view. She didn't speak for a long moment during which Marie feared she'd lost her again. As her mind groped for something else to say, though she had already played her best hand, Alex sat erect again, her expression calm, her eyes brighter than they'd been in an hour. Marie knew that the breath she exhaled was loud enough to have been mistaken for theatrics but it had been genuine relief.

"I want to see my dad," Alex said in an even voice. There was no hint of the apprehension in her tone Marie had expected when this moment came.

She said a silent prayer of thanks and kissed her friend on the forehead. "I'll call Doug; he offered to take us, and I really don't think either of us feels much like driving right now."

"No, that's perfect. It'll give me time to make myself a little more presentable. Don't want him seeing me looking like this. I must be a sight," she said, trying to put her long black tresses back in place using her fingers as combs.

Marie knew Alex had not been referring to Doug, but her dad. Alex didn't want her father to see her looking anything less than perfect, just as he remembered her, as he always thought of her. She understood that sentiment perfectly. "I'll tell him to be here in an hour. Enough time?"

Alex indicated that it would be and moved to the bathroom. In the doorway, she turned back to Marie. "You'll help me get through this, won't you, sis?"

Marie was deeply affected by her words, but the idea of not being at her best friend's side, every step of the way, no matter how long it took, had never entered her mind. "Absolutely. Hey, girl, we're family. All that either of us has left. That's what families do, right? Stick together whenever the world turns ugly."

If she'd been able to cry at that moment, Marie's words would have brought tears to Alex's eyes.

EIGHTEEN

D OUG ROZIER EASED HIS personal car, a Dodge Magnum, in behind Marie's white Honda coupe and put the gear selector in PARK, leaving the engine running. He'd gotten a second call from her less than a minute earlier and she had assured him that they wouldn't keep him waiting once he arrived; Alex was almost ready. True to her word, the front door opened almost at once.

When the women stepped onto the front porch, he was amazed at the transformation. When he'd left the house two hours earlier, both women had been dressed in shorts and t-shirts, their sneakers stained from months both on and in the river, their eyes swollen and red from crying. Now, Marie was dressed in black slacks and a thin white scoop-neck pullover, her two-inch heals bringing her height just short of six feet. With her long blonde hair falling casually across her shoulders, neatly styled but not fussed over, she looked great, professional, and he immediately wondered why he'd never asked her out.

Perhaps he would when all of this was behind them, though he understood that 'someday' was some indefinable mark on a calendar that had yet to be printed. You never truly put something like this behind you; it merely becomes a tolerable pain that quietly nags—like a pebble in your shoe—in the background of your mind. Perhaps in a few weeks, he amended. *God, she looked incredible*, he thought, almost forgetting the reason for this most recent visit.

Alex, in a simple white sleeveless dress that fell just below her knees, appeared ready for Sunday services. He couldn't remember the last time he'd seen Ty's little girl in anything other than grungy shorts and a pullover or t-shirt. She, too, was stunning; a truly good looking kid. No, he corrected, remembering that she was no longer a teenager—a beautiful *woman*. Too bad the perfectly applied makeup and cheerful summer dress couldn't hide the pain that seemed to have aged her lovely face several years in as many hours.

"You ladies look really great," he said, holding open the door for Alex who thanked him and sat quietly in the front passenger's seat.

"Thanks, Doug," Marie said, taking her place behind Alex. He closed her door as well and moved quickly around to the driver's seat.

"I have to say something to you two before we go, by way of an apology, really."

"You don't owe us any apology," Marie said, believing the deputy was referring to the suggestion that Ty had been inebriated at the time of his death.

Alex didn't speak, either because she hadn't fully processed his comment or because Marie had put words to her own thoughts.

"No, I do," he insisted, turning in the seat so he could see both of them. He addressed Alex: "When we discovered Ty, your dad, I mean, you know,"—she didn't respond and her blank expression made him shift uneasily in his seat—"the first thing I thought of was finding you and telling you in person. I immediately called the raft company to see if they could tell me where you were on the river, and find out if there was any way of getting a message to you. Of course, there wasn't. They said you did have a radio with you, but it was used only for emergencies on the river, not monitoring the airways for something wrong at home."

"We never really turn it on except the first day to test it. Then it's switched off and stored in one of the waterproof food lockers," Marie said. "Even if someone died while on the river, there'd be no place for a helicopter to land to get them out. It's not possible until the last afternoon when we reach Swasey's Beach, and the canyon walls drop away. Before then, it's way too steep and the wind that follows the river would make trying to maneuver a helicopter in there a death wish. I'm not even sure why we carry it."

This, too, Doug had learned from the company. "Then, when they said you'd be back in late Saturday, but were planning on spending the night in Moab before heading back this morning, I figured it was best to let you get here before telling you. Partly because I didn't want you to hear news such as that over the phone, but also because I didn't want you making that long drive after learning, you know, that your dad..."

He hadn't needed to finish.

Alex squeezed Doug's knee and gave him the biggest smile she could muster, which was barely a smile at all. "I know you did all you could, Doug. I'm really glad you told me—us—the way you did, you know, in person. I'll always appreciate everything you've done this week." When she moved her hand and sat gazing out the windshield, he knew that he'd said all she could hear at the moment.

* * *

Maintaining a safe distance between their vehicle and the Dodge Magnum, McGhee and Witherspoon strolled toward Seventh Avenue at a leisurely pace. There was no need to hurry or attract unwanted attention; they knew exactly where the trio was heading. With all of the rooms the women would logically enter having been bugged with highly sensitive microphones—no larger than a dime and easily concealable—they could sit outside the clinic and eavesdrop with impunity on all that was said within its walls.

They had not been able to plant any listening devices in either Rozier's patrol car or his personal vehicle. This fact annoyed them as the three mourners made their way in silence—at least as far as surveillance was concerned—toward the clinic and Summers' remains. It did not, however, cause them undo alarm. Since there was no way any of the three in the Dodge could have known about the bugs planted throughout the house, the garage apartment, and the clinic, there would be no reason to suspect that they would say anything in Rozier's vehicle that hadn't been said, or wouldn't be repeated, in a location where surveillance did exist.

Arriving at their destination within five minutes of leaving the Summers' home on Old River Road, McGhee was surprised to discover that they had arrived before their quarry. As soon as they had backed into their predetermined listening post, however—chosen not only for its proximity to the wireless microphones, which had a limited transmission range, but also for the excellent concealment it afforded them—the Dodge and its trio of sorrowful souls pulled into the clinic's driveway.

"We're not going to learn anything here," Witherspoon said, bored as usual.

"Maybe, maybe not," McGhee said, extracting a toothpick from the box. He was temporarily out of cigarettes and wouldn't be able to get any more until the women had gone to bed for the evening, hours from now.

"I say they don't know shit."

"Not now, perhaps. But they might uncover something we didn't."

Witherspoon gave an incredulous scowl. "Like what? They're not gonna accidentally find a cell phone stuffed up the sheriff's ass that we overlooked."

"Really? I don't remember looking there. Did you stick your head up the sheriff's ass while I was in another room?"

"Hell no! I'm just saying we covered it. You couldn't have hidden a flea in that building, more or less something as large as a phone."

"Maybe. Still, we don't even know what we're looking for. Perhaps we stared right at it and didn't even know it," McGhee said, the toothpick making its way from the left side of his mouth to the right with annoying regularity. If Witherspoon hadn't grown immune to his partner's bothersome tick after several years together, he'd have jerked it out and stuck it in his eye.

"Unless I was on crack at the time, and I don't think I was," Witherspoon said sarcastically, "I distinctly remember being told that we were to locate Vanover's cell phone and destroy it at all cost."

"Really? I don't remember that conversation."

"Bullshit! You were standing right there. The Colonel said—"

"What Merkett said," McGhee interrupted, "was that Marec Vanover appeared to have recorded the meeting where General Longmont went over the all the details of the operation, and that he apparently used his cell phone to do so."

"Yeah, so just like I said, we're looking for a damned cell phone. You know, you're not usually this slow on the uptake."

McGhee ignored the jab. "Not necessarily," he continued. "The recording may have started out on a cell phone, but most have very limited internal memory—like Vanover's—not suitable for long video recording, just a few seconds usually. That means if Vanover made a half-hour video of that damned meeting, and according to Shelton we have to assume he did, then it was recorded on the phone's internal memory card. To make matters worse, Vanover's particular phone uses a very tiny memory card, not much bigger than a thumbnail. Easily hidden. Also easily transferred to another medium."

"Like a DVD. That's why you were asking the boys about DVDs and CDs and all that shit."

McGhee nodded. Of the two, he was far more technologically savvy, though not as quick to pull a trigger as Witherspoon; not that the thought of killing made him squeamish. Simply put, he preferred gadgets to guns.

"Why not just post it on 'My-Space' or whatever and get it out there for everyone to see?"

"And give away for free what you can sell for a bundle?" McGhee said.

"Right. That's why he chose Goodman. The bastard's loaded."

"That video is exactly the kind of information Goodman would have paid a fortune for. Assholes like him always love playing the big hero."

"Bringing that video to light would have made him a *super-hero*," Witherspoon said.

"And would have spelled the end of us all. Will *still* be the death of us all if we don't get our hands on it."

"But we've looked everywhere," Witherspoon said wearily. He understood the gravity of the situation, but they'd done everything possible, looked in every conceivable location.

"Not in the *last* place," McGhee said as he spit the toothpick out the window. It looked like a piece of frayed twine. God, he wanted a cigarette.

"What last place?" his partner asked, not understanding.

"Whatever you're looking for is always found in the last place you look. My bet is that we simply haven't found that last place yet."

"And you think the girls will? After all we've done?"

"Maybe, maybe not. In either case, if we don't have it in our hands by tomorrow night, we're going to kill 'em both and burn the clinic and their home to the ground. Kill deputy 'do-good' for insurance. Then we'll disappear without a trace. At least that way, we'll be pretty sure we've covered every possible base."

Witherspoon watched as the trio from the Dodge crossed the massive front porch and closed the front door behind them. The first microphone picked up their footsteps on the hardwood floor like hammer blows on a wooden table. He dropped the volume. "But not before we have a little fun with the girls, right?"

"Of course," McGhee assured him. "Just like I promised."

NINETEEN

LEX REMAINED AS STILL as a statue beside the open morgue drawer, as she had been for the last ten minutes, staring down in silent disbelief that her father was actually gone. He was covered from his broad shoulders to his bare feet with a thin white sheet, and except for a bruise on his right cheek, no more serious than he'd gotten a hundred times riding the back country on his beloved Kate, he might have merely been asleep on the stainless steel tray. He simply couldn't be gone, her mind shouted angrily, he'd always been such a strong man, a Marine, a cop. Weak people died, old people, sick people, people who didn't have anyone to care about them. Not daddies with little girls left behind, who now had to muddle through the rest of their lives alone.

Marie continued to stand beside her dearest friend, left arm around her shoulders, pulling her gently to her for support. Neither had spoken since arriving, but then, what was there to say? To Doug Rozier's amazement, neither of the women shed a single tear. He had no way of knowing that there were no tears left. They were weeping like wounded children in their hearts, but the tear ducts were as dry as attic dust.

Finally, Alex put her right hand to her father's forehead and stroked it gently, lovingly. Apparently she had prepared herself for the chill that met her fingertips, or perhaps her nerves were so frayed that they no longer responded to any temperature, and could have just as easily been thrust into a fire without notice. Whichever the case, she didn't instantly withdraw her hand when her warm flesh met his icy skin.

Marie looked to Doug, standing on the opposite side of the extended drawer, and mouthed the words, "Let's go," indicating with a point of her chin that they were to leave Alex alone with her father for awhile.

He nodded and moved slowly toward the door.

Marie lowered her arm from Alex's shoulders and said, "We'll be just down the hall. Take all the time you need, sweetie. Okay?"

Alex continued to rub her father's forehead in silence but nodded once that she had heard and understood.

Within the spacious clinic, on the first floor at the northwest end of the long hall that contained the five examination rooms, what would have logically been Examination Room Six had been converted into the autopsy room and official county morgue. Besides the usual equipment associated with the performance of autopsies, one wall contained six coffin-sized pull-out drawers. Each was cooled by a separate commercial refrigeration unit and glided effortlessly on heavy-duty stainless steel roller bearings. An occupant of the facility could be expected to remain in a safe state of non-decomposition for weeks if need be, though this had never been the case. At present, despite the ability to accommodate a half dozen decedents, Ty Summers was the morgue's only guest.

Joining Doug outside Autopsy, Marie further indicated with a gesture of her left index finger that they were to move a bit farther from the doorway lest their voices be heard. He followed her like an obedient puppy.

When they'd moved two doors down, into the empty but spacious Examination Room Four, Marie looked back down the hall to see if Alex had followed. She had not.

Doug sank into the only chair, but at once stood and left it for Marie, opting instead for the patient table covered from head to foot in sterile white paper. It crinkled noisily beneath him as he hoisted himself onto the table, and he was certain the racket had been sufficient for Ty, himself, to have heard. "Sorry," he mouthed.

Marie, who's attention had been elsewhere, turned back toward Doug when he spoke. "Huh?" she said, only half hearing his apology.

"Nothing." He shifted his position and the stiff paper complained loudly.

"What now?" she asked.

He cocked his head, not sure what she meant.

"Officially, what comes next?" she clarified.

"Oh, sorry." He looked at the doorway to be sure Alex hadn't suddenly materialized. "The State boys are sending down an assistant Medical Examiner from Salt Lake City to do the autopsy on Ty either tomorrow morning or first thing Tuesday. They had some important case going on up there, both sides wanting evidence reexamined; expert testimony on the witness stand for hours on end. Couldn't get anyone down until now." He shifted his weight again and again the paper made more noise than he had imagined possible from mere paper. He lowered himself to the floor and stood opposite Marie, door to his left. "Shouldn't take more than a day to wrap everything up and then we can have the service."

"I suppose an autopsy is mandatory."

"Yeah. Everything points to it being an accident, but we have to know for sure. Who knows, you may be right."

"I didn't say it wasn't an accident, Doug. I only said there was no way Ty was drunk. I guess, if it turns out I'm wrong, it'll have to appear in the official report."

He put his hand on her shoulder. "Yes, I'm afraid so, but I give you my solemn word the report will remain sealed." He looked to the door: they remained alone. "Alex will never hear a word of it, trust me. All she'll ever know is what she knows right now, that her father died in an automobile accident."

"And if it turns out not to be an accident?" Her eyes narrowed.

To that question, Doug Rozier had nothing to say.

* * *

It was nearly dusk when the trio finally left the clinic. Alex had remained at her father's side, despite being in a thin summer dress in the icy chill in the autopsy room, for more than two hours. During that time, neither Marie nor Doug had spoken to her, though together or separately, both had checked on her several times.

To keep from going stir crazy, Marie had wandered around the clinic, its familiar walls almost a second home to her after three years. She knew every fixture, every light switch, every box of cotton swabs.

It wasn't so much any one large thing that eventually gave her pause, but a combination of dozens of small things, infinitesimal nuances of change, that had accumulated in her subconscious as she strolled the halls and visited the various rooms in the former mansion. Everything was in its place, and yet almost nothing was precisely where it should be. She couldn't put her finger on it, but the entire clinic was, well, just wrong.

Finally, she spotted Doug, who by then was sound asleep in Will Cameron's office, his head resting on folded arms atop the small mahogany desk. All of the waiting, with nothing to do but watch a friend grieve for hours on end in statue-like silence, had lulled him into that kind of sleepy state that classroom lectures always seem to induce in high school.

She gave him a gentle tap on the shoulder.

"Ready to go?" he said hurriedly as he sprang to his feet, knocking over a large coffee mug and spilling its contents across the desk and onto the floor. Mildly disoriented, he'd slept like the dead, if only for ten minutes. He began to collect the various items that had gone helter-skelter when Marie told him to stop, she'd get it.

"No, not yet, relax; didn't mean to startle you," she said. He sat back down as she knelt and swept the various items that had struck the floor into a neat pile. "I just checked on her and she's still standing there, like a zombie. Hasn't moved a muscle." When the small pile of pencils, keys, paper clips, and push pins had been gathered, she filled her hands and deposited them back into the oversized coffee mug. To this she added the balance of the items that had remained on the desk.

"Sorry," he said, holding the cup for her.

Marie just shook her head, her obvious concern for larger matters knitting her brow. "I don't think she's going to handle this as well as I'd hoped."

"Yeah," Doug said. "An orphan at twenty-one. That's rough."

Though the words cut through Marie like a saber, she sucked in a deep breath and let the pain pass with an exaggerated exhalation—just as she'd done a thousand times in her life. She, too, had been orphaned at that age, but of course, this was not known to the deputy, and there was nothing to be gained by sharing this personal insight with him. On the contrary, there was much, perhaps everything, to lose. The more anyone knew about her past, the easier it would be to narrow down the search for her true identity.

That was out of the question.

Carefully, she formed her thought into words, not wanting to be seen as having totally lost her mind to conspiracy theories. She remembered his earlier warning covering that subject. "Doug, when you found Will last Sunday morning..."

"Right where you're standing," he said, pointing to the spot between her feet.

Without conscious thought, she moved a step backward. "Were there a lot of people in here, you know, milling around?"

"No, just me, Andy, Joan Cameron, and another deputy. She was a mess. Oh, yeah, the EMS guys came, too, of course, but they were in and out in no time. Only thing they touched was the body. Will was clearly deceased and there was nothing to be done but take him to the funeral home." He pondered her question in silence for a moment, then said, "Why?"

"Oh, no reason really. Just curious," she lied. *If not Doug's people, then who*, she wondered.

It had been another half hour before Alex had been ready to go, and then only after Marie had coaxed her gently. Closing the morgue drawer, knowing it would be the last time she'd ever see her father, had been the hardest thing she'd ever done.

The Dodge moved toward the Summers' residence in perfect silence, much as it had made the journey to the clinic hours before. As they passed the Day's Inn on Grand Avenue, Marie noticed the large portable satellite dish in the parking lot, a television broadcast van connected to it and also hitched to the trailer that towed the dish. Both were spotless, having been painted gleaming white with the huge letters, CNN, in contrasting black across the face of the dish and the sides of the van. Standing beside the van, she saw a camera crew with tripod and portable lights, the news anchor, an attractive Hispanic woman in an expensive suit, delivering some standup monologue.

"What's with the media van?" Marie asked.

Doug Rozier glanced to his right as he slowed for the upcoming traffic light. "CNN. Last to leave, I guess. Most of the others pulled out on Wednesday."

Marie studied the scene as the Dodge rolled to an easy stop at the red light. "I don't understand," she said, unable to make the scene explain itself and finding no plausible reason for the news giant to be doing a remote broadcast from Truman, Utah.

"Oh, sorry, my bad," Doug said. "Forgot you guys were on the river when all this started."

Her expression told him in no uncertain terms that he hadn't helped her confusion one bit.

"Goodman," he said.

"Goodman?" she repeated, though hers had been a question.

"Yeah, some kids found Skipper Goodman's body up near Redmon's Ridge last Saturday. The national media went crazy, as you might imagine." The light changed and the Dodge moved away, slowly reaching traffic speed. "Must have been a hundred of those dishes in town most of last week. Probably looked like a mushroom farm from the air." He smiled at his little joke but Marie failed to join him. Her mind was racing, as was her pulse.

"Robert Wayne Goodman? The politician?" she said.

"None other. The man that was probably going to be the next President of the United States. His plane went down—"

"Yeah, I remember," she said, severing his thought. "Kinda hard to forget."

"Sorry."

"You said some kids found him."

"Yep. Two fraternity brothers from BYU. Came up here for the day to do some hiking. Probably wanted to be the first of the season to cross the ridge. Anyway, they practically stumbled over him."

"But I thought he died in the crash, forty or fifty miles from there."

"More like thirty, but yeah, everyone thought he had died in the crash, even though they never found a trace of his remains. The conventional wisdom was that he'd been thrown clear of the main debris upon impact and the storm that followed hid his remains. They looked for weeks, dozens of special teams and hundreds of volunteers, but nothing, nada. Like he'd vanished from the face of the earth." Marie's condescending nod and smile told him that he was, once again, repeating well-known facts. "Sorry," he repeated.

"Who brought him down?" she asked.

"Ty. He took Kate and Sam up right after lunch, after meeting with the boys, and had him down by late afternoon." He looked into the back seat to see how Alex was doing, but she was still staring out the window, no indication she had heard a word either of them had said since leaving the clinic. As he made the last corner before Old River Road, he added, "Things got kinda crazy after that."

"I guess it did. With the accident and Will's sudden collapse..." Her voice tapered off to a whisper as she formed the words. Coincidences—she hated them.

"Yeah, but before any of that, we had the accident at Cougar's Rift. Bad one. Four kids went over. Never had a chance."

"Local kids?" she asked, hoping she hadn't known any of them, then feeling terrible because someone had: they had been someone's children.

"No. In fact, it was the same kids who'd found Goodman earlier in the day. Their girlfriends, too, though we didn't find out who the two girls were until late Monday. Probably got so excited about finding Skipper Goodman that they didn't pay attention to the road, and Cougar's Rift doesn't give second chances."

"Four of them," Marie said in a whisper. It hadn't been a question. She felt like a huge snake was making its way slowly through her bowels.

"Yep. We found beer in the car. Mountain roads and alcohol are a bad combination." As soon as he'd said it, he expected Alex to smack him from the back seat. He braced for the impact, but none came. When he pulled into the driveway and behind Marie's Honda, Alex bolted from the car without a word. "What an asshole," he said, speaking of himself.

Marie's mind was traveling at light speed, a kaleidoscope of images and words trying to knit themselves into a conspiracy theory of biblical proportions. She fought to keep them from overwhelming her, but was having little success. Her heart slammed against her chest wall like a jackhammer. She said, "Did Ty take the senator's body to the clinic?"

"Sure, just like always," Doug said.

Marie could no longer speak. No one on earth could successfully explain away the bizarre string of 'coincidences' that had transpired in her tiny, little town over the last eight days. *Oh, God, not again,* she prayed. *This can't be happening again.* She felt as if she would throw up at any moment.

"Excuse me, Doug, please. I have to go. Thanks for—" Her words were cleaved by the passenger door slamming behind her.

TWENTY

THE BLACK CROWN VICTORIA assumed its position of concealment amid the pine shadows, a clear view of the Summers' home visible through the windshield. Once again, they had taken the alternate route to Old River Road, only this time, they'd arrived almost simultaneously with the deputy's vehicle. For a moment, they were afraid they'd been spotted surreptitiously backing into their make-do lair, but a quick glance through the powerful Canon Image-Stabilizing binoculars, that had a semi-permanent home on the dash, affirmed that the attention of the driver and his passengers had remained fixed on their own problems.

"That was close," McGhee said, laying the binoculars back on the dash. He fished for a toothpick. With another evening ahead of them that promised to be as boring as watching cement harden, he had half a mind to go for a carton of Marlboros and resume surveillance when they got back.

"Wonder what they talked about in the car?" Witherspoon said. He was still miffed that he hadn't gotten a chance to bug everything in town. Not only couldn't they have foreseen all the possible locations the women might visit, there had not been enough of the

190

tiny, but extremely expensive, long-range microphone-transmitters available.

"Who gives a shit," McGhee said, growing irritable. He needed a cigarette; the toothpicks were no longer cutting it. Besides, he was beginning to feel like a termite.

"I'd just like to know. They didn't say anything worth a damn in the clinic and I was just wondering, that's all. No need to bite my head off."

"They didn't say shit because they don't know shit. They are a couple of dumb little girls." He put the vehicle in DRIVE. "I need a smoke."

* * *

Marie slammed the front door and raced across the living room to the half bath beside the kitchen. She barely made it to the bowl before she lost what little she still had on her stomach. As she wiped her mouth with the back of her hand, she leaned against the wall, keeping the toilet in plain view. The serpent that had been in her bowels was definitely not gone; in fact, retching appeared to be exactly the stimulus it had needed to begin writhing like it was in the throes of death.

"Oh, God, please let this all be just dumbass paranoia, just like Doug said. I really can't go through this again," she prayed as her mouth filled with water. She leaned over the bowl but only spat a few times, despite the upheaval in her guts. When she dropped back to the floor and against the wall again, her forehead had broken out in beads of sweat. She yanked a long length of toilet paper from the roll and crumpled it into a loose ball, blotting the salty droplets before they could sting her eyes. Her skin felt cold to the touch despite her certainty she would spontaneously combust at any moment. She remembered her mother telling her that menopause was like that.

"Mom," she said in a broken whisper.

She pushed the image away at once.

"You okay," the soft voice asked from somewhere above her.

She turned to see Alex standing in the doorway. Instead of rising to meet her, Marie extended her hand and gently pulled her friend to the floor beside her.

"What's up, girl?" Alex asked. "What can I do?"

Marie only shook her head, but knew her haggard appearance must present quite a sight—a total departure from only ten minutes ago. However cheerful she might attempt to be, her face would make a lie of it. She had to say something, but how could she involve this sweet little girl in her wild, insane fantasies? How could she begin to tell this sheltered child that the world was not really a nice place, that boogie men did exist and not just in the movies?

Her eyes darted around the ceiling of the small room, from corner to corner, as if a wasp had just flown in and she needed to keep an eye on it. Nothing, she quickly concluded, but then, they would never be that overt. She felt sure they couldn't be seen, though she didn't know why on earth she'd reached this completely unsubstantiated conclusion.

She was dead certain, however, that every syllable they spoke could be heard.

Had been heard. From the very moment they'd set foot in the house.

The whole house had probably been bugged from the moment Goodman's body had been found. The clinic, too. God only knew where else. *But why?* she puzzled. *What was there to gain? And why kill everyone? Who were these bastards?*

She knew she might never know their names, but she knew she would meet them soon enough—she and Alex both—just as her father and Will Cameron had. Just as the four kids who died at Cougar's Rift had. Just as... *how many more?* she wondered as the snake writhed and knotted in her guts.

She put her arms around Alex's neck and pulled her tightly to her. What came next surprised the young woman more than anything she'd heard in her short, sheltered life.

Marie put her mouth to Alex's ear and whispered as quietly as possible while still making herself heard, "I need you to trust me and not say a word. Not one word, Alex. It's not safe to talk here. We need to get in my car and leave now. Can you do that? Can you trust me and just go with me without speaking? I'll explain everything in the car."

For the longest moment, Alex just sat in shocked disbelief, not moving so much as a muscle, remaining held in Marie's arms like an infant. Finally, her own mind sensing—knowing somehow—that all was not right, she said in a voice as faint as Marie's, "You lead, I'll follow. Just like always."

Without a word, the women stood and Marie led Alex to her bedroom, then went to her tall chest of drawers. She pulled some comfortable jeans from a drawer and a clean t-shirt from another, then a pair of sneaker socks from yet another, laying all on the bed and indicating for Alex to change into them as quickly as possible. Alex began to undress at once.

Next, Marie again put her mouth to Alex's ear and asked if there was any money in the house. Alex nodded there was and removed a thick wad of bills from her lingerie drawer. With no housekeeper, cook, or siblings, just a trusted friend and a loving father, the money had always been as safe there as in Fort Knox. Marie didn't bother to count it, but stuffed it into the front pocket of Alex's jeans. Then she put her finger to her lips to indicate that Alex was not to speak, though the younger woman had already figured that out. In a clear and distinct voice Marie said aloud, "Hey, sis, I'm going up to my room to put on something more comfortable. What say we fix a couple of sandwiches in a few minutes and then watch a movie? I'm starved. Sound good to you?"

Marie then indicated for Alex to respond out loud, which confused her to no end. Still, she didn't miss a beat and said in a matching voice, "Sure, yeah, that sounds great. I'm starved, too."

Then Marie put her finger to her lips again and wagged it as if to say, "Not another word." Alex nodded in total mystification and continued to remove her dress.

In seven or eight minutes, Marie had returned from her garage apartment wearing jeans and a white oxford shirt, the thick rubber soles of her hiking boots squeaking noisily on the tile and hardwood floors as she crossed the kitchen and living room on her return trip to Alex's bedroom.

Alex was just tying a pair of gray and blue Saucony running shoes when Marie returned. She showed the thick stash of cash that she'd taken from her apartment and then stuffed it back in her jeans pocket.

Alex started to say something but Marie's wagging finger was up at once warning against it. She took Alex's hand and led her to the kitchen. There, they made a noisy showing of rummaging through the refrigerator in the business of sandwich preparation. Not a word was spoken during this entire time and Alex was beginning to think that her friend had lost her mind completely. Trust was one thing; this was bordering on following Alice down the rabbit hole.

Suddenly, Marie blurted out, "Oh dammit. I left my purse at the clinic." Startling Alex as much as if someone had just popped a balloon behind her back. Marie added, "Doug said that ME from Salt Lake City would be there in the morning and I need to get it before they get there. Wanna ride with me? Won't take long." She shook her head indicating for Alex to answer in the affirmative.

"Uh, sure. We can be back in ten minutes. No need to even put this stuff up, right," she adlibbed, shrugging her shoulders as if to ask if she'd done right. Marie gave her a thumbs up and headed for the front door, her friend totally confused but following close behind, as usual.

*   *   *

"What in the world is going on," Alex mouthed in silence when the Honda pulled from the driveway.

"It's okay to talk now," Marie said. "They couldn't have gotten to my car. It was in the company garage in Moab the whole time."

Marie mashed the accelerator and the small white coupe made good time down Old River Road. She didn't speed away, however, in case they were being watched.

"They?" Alex repeated. "They who? What are you talking about? What did you mean it wasn't safe to talk in my own home? Who's listening? Why would they—"

"Be quite, Alex!" Marie snapped, cutting her off in mid-sentence. Her abruptness startled the younger woman. Marie had never spoken to her in such a harsh tone. By the hurt expression on Alex's face, Marie could tell at once that she'd been too abrupt. She understood that all of this had to be unbelievably confusing to her naïve friend. Earth shattering, in fact. Hell, it was mind boggling to her and she'd been through this before. *Maybe not this, exactly,* she corrected in her mind, but she knew instinctively what was happening, even if only in the most oblique terms. She rounded the corner at the end of the street and studied her rearview mirror. They were not being followed. Not at the moment, anyway. She also knew that would change.

She made the right onto Grand Avenue and fell in with the sparse late afternoon traffic heading for dinner or services at one of the dozen local churches. "I'm sorry, Alex, but you're going to have to trust me on this. There's something very wrong going on and I believe we're right in the middle of it."

The muddled expression on her passenger's face demanded a deeper and more plausible explanation. Clearly, Alex didn't have a clue what was happening, and if she were to be trusted—and absolute trust between them was essential for their survival—she had to be brought up to speed, at least as far as Marie could bring her given what little she knew. Or rather, what she suspected. She tapped the brake, moved into the right lane of the two that headed east, and swung the white coupe into the parking lot of a small strip center. On Sunday evening, every business was closed. She left the engine running and continuously scanned the windshield and rearview mirror for any sign that another vehicle was more interested in their activity than in food or church.

When they'd come to a complete stop, Marie said, "Were you listening to our conversation in the car coming back from the clinic? What Doug and I were talking about, I mean?"

Alex shook her head. "I heard you two talking but I don't think—"

"That's fine," she cut in again. "Listen, here's the deal, short and sweet. And when I tell you, I don't need you going all crazy on me, okay?" This clearly didn't elicit a look of unquestioning support Marie would have wanted. Alex didn't answer, didn't nod, only narrowed her eyes as if to say, "You're scaring me here."

Marie looked both directions out of nervous concern more than because she truly expected to see a camouflaged Humvee pull alongside and a dozen armed men jump out and riddle her vehicle in a fusillade of armor-piercing bullets. "Remember Skipper Goodman?" she began. Alex nodded and started to speak. The finger went up. "His plane crashed somewhere north of here last fall. The authorities always suspected foul play, though they could never prove it. Worse, they never found his body, even though a dozen witnesses said they'd seen the senator board the plane, fueling all kinds of conspiracy theories about what had happened to him."

Alex continued to nod that she remembered all of this. It had been the talk of the entire university for most of the fall and winter before becoming only a footnote by the spring semester.

"Your dad found him not far from here." Marie said the words then waited for the importance of what she'd said to sink in.

"My dad?" Alex was connecting no dots.

"Yep. Well actually some college kids from your school found him, but Ty brought his body off the mountain. Took it to the clinic hours before Will died."

Not typically slow on the uptake, but also not a veteran paranoid like her older friend, Alex failed to grasp the significance of any of it.

Frustrated, both because of her own soul-scraping fears and also because she needed Alex to comprehend, Marie practically shouted, "They're all dead, Alex. Dammit, everyone who touched Goodman's body since it was found is now dead."

This time, the dots not only connected, they collided in a barrage of emotions. Where tears would normally have been, only red, swollen eyes could be seen: dry as sawdust but full of hate. "Are you saying that someone *killed* my father?"

"That's exactly what I'm saying. I'm so sorry, Alex, but we don't have time to lose it here. I suspect they're coming for us next."

Amid her confusion and anger, Alex managed to hear and partially comprehend Marie's words. "What? Us? Why would they want to kill us?"

"I have no idea, but it makes perfect sense."

"No it doesn't! It makes no sense at all!" she shouted. Her hands were at her mouth, her slender arms trembling both from anger and from fright.

"It does if you're them."

"Stop that! You keep saying *them*. Who the hell is *them*?"

"I don't know, we may never know. Right now, we have maybe an hour before they begin to suspect we're on to them. Once that happens, the shit will really hit the fan. By then, we need to be on the road and out of sight like we never existed."

"What are you talking about?" Alex said again, her mind unable to wrap itself around such words. "My father's funeral is in two days—"

"And ours will be in three, dammit!" Marie yelled. "Listen to me, Alex, this is not a game. I've dealt with men like this before and they don't play games. They shoot to kill and won't hesitate to do anything necessary to protect their interests."

"You're scaring the hell out of me, Marie. How do you know such things?"

"Let's just say that I do and leave it at that. Listen, I love you. I'll never let anything happen to you if it's humanly possible to prevent,

I swear, but we need to do several things in the short time we have and I can't do it without your help. I need you to be here, now, with me. Not in some world where good guys wear white hats and always vanquish the bad guys. That's Hollywood bullshit and it will get us both killed. We cannot possibly hope to beat them with our muscles, so we're going to have to do it with our minds. Understand?"

Hell no, she didn't understand, Marie thought. *How could she?*

Alex said, "We should go to the police. Doug can help us. If what you're saying is true, we need to go to the police right now."

Marie shook her head as she again looked fore and aft for any threat looming on the horizon. Oddly, they seemed to be of no interest to anyone at the moment, as if they were invisible. She turned her attention back to Alex. "The last time I went through something like this, the bad guys *were* the police. It's not safe, at least not until we have some idea what this is all about."

"The *last* time?" Alex said incredulously.

"Yes. I was involved in a huge conspiracy a few years back where a lot of people got killed. Got me shot and almost killed." She rubbed the old wound on her upper arm and Alex turned her attention to it.

Though her shirt sleeve covered the resulting scar at the moment, Alex could have described it perfectly from memory. "You told me that was from a motorcycle accident."

"Yeah, well I lied. I've lied to you about a lot of things, but not about this. This is real, dammit, and it's serious shit. Listen, we've got to get to the clinic and find out what Will was working on when he died. I'll bet my ass it's got something to do with this business and if we find it before they do, we have a better than even chance of using it to save our lives."

"You're crazy, you know that? You've lost your mind," Alex said, continuing to process the most bizarre conversation she'd ever had in her life; ever imagined possible. Oddly, what incensed her most was Marie's admission that she'd lied to her, and that admission seemed to make a lie out of every word that now exited her mouth.

"Fine, let's say I'm crazy, but you've known me for years and you know that I mean it when I say something is serious shit, right?"

Her words earned her a barely perceptible nod.

"Then believe this: you have nothing to lose by playing along with me for a few minutes, and everything to lose if you don't. Is that clear enough?" The hard expression on Marie's face told her she was not open for any discussion on the subject.

Unable to think of anything to say that was going to change the mood or direction of the moment, certain that Marie had snapped from the emotional toll the death of her father and Will Cameron had exacted, Alex conceded. "What do you want from me?"

"When I was waiting for you at the clinic, you know, while you were with your dad, I walked all around the place to kill time. Everywhere I looked, stuff had been moved. Not like in the day to day operation of the clinic, but like someone had gone through the place looking for something. It's like they moved everything in the place and then put it all back, but not quite where it had been before."

"Looking for what?"

"No idea, that's the problem. If they found whatever it is, they're long gone, but if they didn't, my bet is they're still around."

"And you think they're spying on us, hoping we'll lead them to whatever it is?"

"Exactly. I would in their position." Marie put the Honda into gear and pulled back onto Grand Avenue.

"How do you know all of this?" Alex asked once more, this time expecting a real answer.

Instead of getting a satisfactory explanation, Marie said, "When I was in Autopsy, I noticed that there were several empty x-ray plates lying on the counter."

"Will would never have left them out like that," Alex said, knowing firsthand what a stickler for neatness and preparation her former boss was.

199

"Right. Not in a million years," Marie agreed. "He was practically anal about having all the equipment and supplies ready to go at a moment's notice. His Navy training, I suspect. Several empty film holders out on the counter could only mean one thing: that he used them on the night he died, before—"

"He could refill them," Alex finished.

"Right again."

"But why? Were they for my dad?"

The Honda made the last turn before Seventh Avenue. "I don't think so. According to Doug, Will had already suffered a heart attack, if it *was* a heart attack, before he could have even seen your dad. It had to be for Skipper Goodman."

Alex was having so much trouble taking it all in, the reasoning behind it all. She had no experience with conspiracies and things. "Why?" she asked feebly.

"The 'why' behind it all is always the sixty-four-thousand-dollar question. For now, let's assume it's all about money."

"Money?"

"Sure. The motive behind 99.9 percent of all human tragedy is greed, lust for money. Always has been. I'll bet my life on it." As soon as Marie spoke the words, she realized the ironic truth of her statement. She *was* betting her life on it. Alex's, too. However, if she was correct, they'd done absolutely nothing to get into this fix—other than being in the wrong place at the wrong time—and there was nothing other than what they were doing, right now, that was going to get them out of it. Assuming, of course, that there was any getting out to be found. Just because you had a burning desire to live, didn't mean you were going to. She thought of Ty and Will, and then about the four young kids who'd never had a real shot at life. Yet they were all gone now, killed after touching the body of Robert Wayne Goodman as surely as if he'd been infected with Ebola or hemorrhagic fever. Quicker, actually.

She pulled into the clinic's drive and switched off the engine. "Listen, Alex, if I'm right about everything, and it's too risky to assume anything else for now, they will surely have the entire clinic wired. Probably enough of their little microphone bugs to hear everything we say anywhere in the building."

"How do you know this stuff?" Alex continued to question.

"I don't really know very much about the electronic surveillance part, only what I've read in books and on the Internet, but it's all real. There are microphones smaller than a pea that can pick up sounds in a room the size of a gymnasium and then transmit that signal for a quarter of a mile or more. Truly scary shit."

All of it had the younger woman frozen in her seat. The last thing she wanted to do was go back in a building filled with pea-sized listening devices planted by men out to kill them for money. It was all so insane, so much like a bad dream and not at all like the life she'd lived up until a few hours ago. Why couldn't it all just go away? Why couldn't her father make it all vanish, like he'd always done with the monsters under her bed?

Marie recognized the "deer in the headlights" look on her friend's face and shook her shoulders with both hands. "Alex!" she shouted, bringing the other woman back into the moment. "Stay with me. This isn't going away just because you want it to. We have to look quickly, both of us, you hear me, and locate whatever it is that these bastards are so dead set on finding."

Alex nodded her understanding.

"When we get inside, I'll tell you to look for my purse and you say, 'okay.' Then we'll head up to the darkroom to see if we can find that missing x-ray film. Understand?"

More silent nodding, but the scared stiff expression still blanketed Alex's face.

Marie was sure Alex would follow, like always. "Let's go," she said, quickly exiting the car.

TWENTY-ONE

HEN MCGHEE AND WITHERSPOON backed into their hidey-hole again at the top of Old River Road, the fresh carton of Marlboros on the console between them along with a cold six-pack of Coke—beer wasn't sold in Utah on Sundays, if it was sold at all—they didn't miss Marie's white Honda at first. McGhee lit a cigarette and exhaled noisily, enjoying the first smoke he'd had in half a day. *Should have bought two cartons*, he thought.

As Witherspoon toyed with the laptop, moving the digital sliders up to their highest point in an effort to pick up conversation in the Summers' home, he said, "Must be sleeping or something. I'm not getting shit except the ticking of that damned grandfather clock. That's one loud bastard, you know it."

"Nah, they wouldn't be sleeping at this—HOLY SHIT!" McGhee spat out as the realization that their quarry had eluded them struck him like a Freightliner. Merkett was going to kill them both, and he wasn't thinking of the girls. He flicked the cigarette out the open driver's window and slammed the huge Ford sedan into DRIVE.

"Where do you think they went?" Witherspoon said, closing the lid on the laptop and fastening his seatbelt. He knew that wherever McGhee was headed, the drive wasn't going to be a stroll in the park. "Maybe they just went out for something to eat. You think?"

As he was about to say that he didn't have a friggin' clue where the women had gone, McGhee's cell phone rang.

"What," he practically shouted into the mouthpiece.

"Something wrong, McGhee?" James Merkett asked, a touch of annoyance in his voice.

"Uh, no, not really, sir. We were just—"

"What are the girls up to?" Merkett asked. "This very minute, I mean."

McGhee saw his life flash before his eyes as he pondered his answer. He realized that the next words to exit his mouth had better be honest, succinct, and without a hint of excuse attached to them if he and Witherspoon hoped to see tomorrow. "They went straight home after visiting the girl's father in the morgue. We left to get something to eat, only gone about five minutes, and when we returned, they were gone." He bit his lip and awaited the worst.

"Okay," Merkett said calmly. "You two head for the clinic to see if you can intercept them there. Anyplace else they went won't be a big deal, but if they went back to the clinic, that could only mean one thing."

"On the way now, sir," McGhee assured him. "Should be there in five minutes. What do you want us to do if we find them?"

"If you find them?"

"Excuse me, sir, *when* we find them." By this time, he'd practically bitten through his lip.

"Detain them by force, but don't kill them yet. This ends tonight, but not before I have the chance to chat with them."

"We'll call you the second we have our hands on them," he assured the Colonel.

"That won't be necessary, Sergeant. We should all be at the clinic within fifteen minutes."

*   *   *

Once inside the clinic, Marie and Alex went straight to Examination Room Six, just to satisfy themselves that Marie hadn't imagined the empty x-ray plates. She hadn't. A half dozen of them were sitting right where she remembered. She pointed up with her index finger, indicating that they should head for the darkroom on the third floor.

The mansion on Seventh Avenue, now a clinic and morgue for the small town of Truman, and former residence of Joan and Will Cameron, had once belonged to a wealthy family who'd struck it rich in the silver business before going bust a few years later. Built in the late 1880s, it was a huge wooden structure with high ceilings on all three levels, rising to more than eleven feet on the first floor and only a foot shorter for each of the consecutive floors.

Although in superb condition, completely free of termites and wood rot, it was nonetheless a massive collection of kiln-dried lumber covered in two dozen coats of oil-based paint. In short, it was a five-thousand square foot tinderbox just waiting for a match to send it to the moon. For that reason, Marie had repeatedly petitioned the doctor to install a state-of-the-art sprinkler system. At the very least, on the third floor where the electrical systems and HVAC had been retrofitted to the home in succeeding decades, the place where a fire was most likely to originate. Despite her insistence that she had no desire to be the first—and probably only—victim of the massive funeral pyre on Seventh Avenue as she worked in the darkroom on the top level, the best Marie had been able to earn was a modest concession from the aging physician. It had never had a sprinkler system in its one-hundred-twenty-plus years, so none was needed now.

Marie and Alex paused on the landing at the top of the stairs while Marie's fingers searched for the hall light. They found it quickly. The stairs, which they'd just ascended, emptied out into a narrow carpeted hallway which bisected the entire third floor, with

HVAC and storage on the right, or south side, and the darkroom on the left. This floor had once been the make-do residence of the Camerons before Joan had insisted that she felt more like a wicked stepchild living in the attic than the lady of the house. They had moved shortly thereafter.

Marie pushed the door open and together she and Alex entered the spacious room. Except for a little clutter, it was exactly as she'd left it two weeks prior. *No, not exactly*, she corrected herself as she saw, once again, telltale signs that this room, too, had been given the once over. Whenever she wasn't actively on the river, Marie continued to work at the clinic five days a week. Her last day had been the Friday before their most recent river tour, sixteen days ago.

"Look," she said, pointing to the sink. "He did develop some film." The brown glass bottles of chemicals that were used for the development, fixing, and preserving of x-ray film were still in the sink, though the heavy stainless steel trays in which the film was submerged for processing were now empty and had been left upside down to drain. "Never in a million years would Will have left this stuff out."

"I wonder what he did with the negatives," Alex said, joining Marie at the sink.

The darkroom, which measured just under eight feet wide by nearly twenty feet long, occupied less than a fourth of the top floor, leaving the majority of the space for the storage of written patient records as well as the heating and air conditioning equipment rooms. Within the darkroom's narrow confines, dozens of old file cabinets lined the south wall, with each drawer filled to overflowing with a lifetime of medical images: broken collar bones, sprained ankles, wrenched knees, and a myriad of other middle school and high school sports-related injuries. Despite the sheer quantity of negatives—Marie had once estimated the number at more than ten thousand—the filing system was incredibly orderly, another testament to the years Will Cameron had spent in the Navy: a place for everything and everything in its place.

When none of the negatives were to be found in the drying oven, she went immediately to the filing cabinet that would have logically contained the images she was seeking. She understood Will Cameron's personality pretty well, and if the insatiably curious doctor had taken film of senator Goodman, and she couldn't imagine a more plausible explanation for the relative 'clutter' in Autopsy, then that film would be filed by date and patient I.D. in cabinet-86, the one currently in use based on chronological order. The unique patient code, another quirk of the late doctor, had been developed using his own simple, but effective, algorithm. "To preserve patient integrity," he had said while teaching the system to Marie, "In case the images ever fall into unauthorized hands." She couldn't imagine that trafficking in old patient x-rays was, or ever would be, high on the local "top ten crimes" list, but she'd learned Cameron's system and had employed it with military rigidity and surgical precision.

"What was last Saturday's date?" she asked of Alex.

"I don't know, the seventh I think. Yeah, that's right because today is the fifteenth." Alex moved beside her, half out of curiosity and half out of the fear of being alone, even if only by a few feet.

Marie pulled open the last drawer she'd been working with before leaving for Moab and flipped through the manila envelopes. There were about a dozen of them, but she quickly found what she'd been looking for, right where it ought to be: the last file on the last day of Will Cameron's life. The patient code, 1w6r1n0a2m7d0o6o0g, confirmed that she had been correct, Goodman had been the reason for the empty plates in Autopsy. "Got it," she said excitedly.

Alex glanced at the self-adhesive label that had been affixed to the top right-hand corner on the large manila envelope and quickly read the neatly typed patient code, which she also understood instinctively. "That's the film for Goodman, RW, taken on the seventh of this month."

"Yep, just as I thought," Marie said, hurriedly pulling the black and white images from the envelope. Inside were six sheets of 14x17 Agfa x-ray film which she quickly spread out across the huge viewing box that occupied nearly seven feet of wall opposite the filing cabinets. She was only able to fit four sheets end to end, and she chose the first four in sequence based on their order in the stack. When she flicked on the fluorescent lamps inside the viewing box, Robert Wayne Goodman seemed to come to life before their eyes, albeit in somewhat ghoulish terms and absent all color normally associated with the living. From left to right, the esteemed senator from California appeared in perfect anatomical chronology, with his feet at one end and his head at the other. Between those endpoints were most of the two-hundred-plus bones that make up the human skeleton, with only the arms absent from view. It was almost as though a single six-foot x-ray had been taken of the famous man.

Marie held the last two remaining sheets up to the overhead light to ensure that they were, indeed, the missing limbs. Satisfied, she turned her attention to the view box. "This guy looks like he fell off a building," she said as she noted the dozens of small fractures in his feet, legs, and ribs.

"More like out of an airplane," Alex said, studying the film as well. Both were used to seeing hundreds of patient x-rays, and while not Radiologists by any stretch of the imagination, knew a fracture when they saw one.

"Yeah, that's right," Marie said. "He did fall from the sky, didn't he?" Despite her most concentrated efforts, she saw absolutely nothing worth killing for, nothing even worth mentioning. She could clearly make out his belt buckle and a few coins in his pocket, probably less than a buck all told, and there were a pair of dog tags around his neck on a beaded chain, but that was the sum of it. "Wasn't Goodman in the Marines like your dad?" she asked.

"No, I think he was a Green Beret or something like that."

"That explains how he was able to go so far with all these injuries," Marie said. When she still couldn't find anything of value, she pulled the first two sheets down and replaced them with the two showing the forearms and hands. "Ouch, damn," she said, seeing the shattered right forearm. "That one hurt like hell."

Alex leaned toward the film. "What's that in his hand?" she asked.

At first, Marie didn't see a thing, then realized her friend was looking at the left arm, not the right. Within the palm of the left hand was the perfect silhouette of a key, the fingers clinched tightly around it. Solid objects appear white on an x-ray; this shape was completely opaque, indicating metallic content. "It's a key," she said, stating the obvious.

"I can see that now, but why a key? Why on earth would he be clutching a key when he had to know he was about to die," Alex wondered.

Marie's mind spun like a top and her thoughts fought to recall something she'd seen earlier in the day. But where? "Dammit," she moaned aloud. "I've seen this key."

"Really? Where? When?"

"Today, I'm certain of it, I just can't remember where. Dammit!" she repeated in frustration. Then it came to her. "Oh, yeah, now I remember. Stay here," she ordered, indicating for Alex to remain right where she was. "I'll be back in a minute. With that, she disappeared from the darkroom.

The black Crown Victoria pulled in close behind the small white Honda and the two men inside let out a collective sigh of relief. McGhee looked at his watch: 6:13, Merkett would be here in eight minutes or less. "Let's go," he said, exiting the vehicle, pistol in hand.

Witherspoon pulled his 45-caliber automatic from his shoulder holster and affixed the silencer. "Right behind you, buddy." As he passed the Honda, he shot out both of the passenger-side tires, their instant exhalation of air significantly louder than the bullet report that had rendered them useless. However, both men doubted that the noise had been heard more than a few hundred feet away, and even then, might easily have been mistaken for distant thunder.

It didn't matter either way, this would all be over in a few minutes and they would be gone from this boring backwater town before nightfall.

Marie reached Will Cameron's office in under thirty seconds, racing down the stairs two and three at a time, her heart pounding much harder than the exertion would have caused by itself. In the empty old home, it must have sounded like a herd of buffalo stampeding across a wooden bridge.

Once there, she immediately grabbed the coffee mug Doug Rozier had knocked over earlier in the day and spilled its contents once more across the desk, this time being careful to keep everything off the floor. After a few seconds of rummaging through the mess, she plucked the item she'd been seeking from beneath a clutter of paper clips. "Got you, you sucker," she said excitedly as she made a fist around the small brass key, much as Goodman had done in his last moments. The irony of it was not lost on her. "What the hell does this unlock?" she said aloud. "And what in God's name is behind the door."

As she was about to head for the stairs to retrieve Alex, wondering now why she'd left her there in the first place, she heard two distinct "pops" back to back, each followed by a loud wheezing sound. Carefully, she peered from the window in Cameron's office and saw two men making their way up the front steps, guns drawn, her Honda lame in both right feet.

Oh, shit, this is really bad, she thought as she raced for the stairs, her heart now pounding so hard she was sure it would break through her chest. *Really, really bad.*

TWENTY-TWO

AS MARIE CLOSED THE darkroom door, which featured no lock of any kind and unfortunately wasn't made of three-inch bullet-proof titanium as she would have liked, Alex said, "Did I hear firecrackers outside?"

With only a curt smile for an answer, not wishing to frighten her friend any more than necessary—lest she be left with an immovable zombie on her hands again—Marie placed the small brass key against the backlit x-ray, rotating it until it aligned precisely with its pure white counterpart: a perfect match, just as she'd suspected.

Okay, so now she knew what they were after. Now, all she had to figure out in order to stay alive long enough to have another double latte at Starbucks, to say nothing of seeing her unborn grandchildren graduate from college, was who 'they' were and what in God's good name the key was all about. While she was at it, she had decided to unravel the mysteries of the Bermuda Triangle and the origin of the Sphinx—both of which seemed no more daunting than the tasks currently at hand.

She quickly stuffed the key deep into her front jeans pocket and went to Alex. "Sweetie, you know the bad guys I was telling you about? They're here. It's time for us to go."

Just as she feared, Alex immediately became as rigid as stone, hands at her mouth, eyes wide and glued to the darkroom entrance like a little girl fixated on a closet door, certain that at any moment a huge scaly beast with fangs the size of steak knives would appear and devour her quicker than a piece of Halloween candy. "Oh, God," was all Alex could utter.

"Look at me, girl. Stay with me." Marie stood directly in Alex's line of sight, but at first it seemed as if she'd magically become invisible during the last ten seconds. "Alex," she said more forcefully, gently squeezing the frightened woman's chin between her thumb and forefinger, forcing her to make eye contact. "Stay with me, girl, don't go off to that weird place you sometimes go. I need you to help us save our lives, just like on the river. This is just like on the river, Alex, do you understand me?"

After what seemed an eternity, during which time Marie didn't hear the front door open and shut so much as she felt it in the souls of her feet, Alex finally said, "Okay," in a voice that was barely audible. She started for the darkroom door.

"No, sweetie, that's the wrong way," Marie said, taking her shoulders and turning her toward the far wall.

At first, Alex just walked toward it mindlessly as if the intent were to break through the plaster and lathe and fall to the ground below. Halfway down the bowling alley of a room, she said, "Where are we going? We can't get out this way."

"It's okay, buddy, trust me." Marie continued to push her nearly catatonic friend.

When they reached the far end, completely opposite the only door in the room, Alex turned around, a look of terror turning her face ghostly pale. "There's no way out," she repeated.

With that, Marie knelt at the wall and moved an empty cardboard box that had contained manila envelopes. "Remember when I told Will that I wouldn't work up here without a fire escape, and he told me that it would kill the esthetics of the place—like I gave a shit about that with my ass on the line?"

Still so pale that she seemed almost transparent, her skin looking as thin as breath on a winter day, Alex managed to say, "You said he allowed you a minor concession, whatever that means."

Marie pulled at a small pewter knob on the wall, about knee height, and an almost invisible panel swung open. It measured three feet by three feet and pivoted on cabinet-style hinges which were hidden from view when the panel was closed. It was nothing more than a pint-sized door cut in the exterior wall, with a matching door on the outside of the home. The exterior panel had been clad in the gingerbread shingles that were true to the home's era, and was practically invisible from the yard below, even upon careful examination. With a quick turn of an interior knob and a gentle push, a perfect hole now existed in the darkroom wall, large enough for any nonplus-size person to use for escape in the event of a fire. "Say hello to my little concession," she said, mocking the Al Pacino line in *Scarface*.

Alex stared disbelievingly into the hole and could clearly see the ground in the early evening light thirty feet below. "I'm not jumping," she said adamantly. Alex wasn't crazy about heights.

"No one's jumping, for God's sake, there's a ladder." With that, Marie lifted a plank in the floor, just beneath the half door, and withdrew a heavy-duty rope ladder, its thick nylon stringers and rungs neatly coiled into a tight bundle and tightly secured to the floor rafters. In half a minute, it had been lowered through the three-foot opening, its bottom rung just inches from the ground. Though Marie had not tested it personally when it was finally installed last January, the company which did the work guaranteed it would support the weight of three average men. Not that she believed either Alex or she would tax that claim, even together, it was comforting to know it provided ample room for forgiveness, just in case she had packed on a few extra pounds over the winter. "Out you go," she said.

"You first, like always," Alex insisted.

"Not this time, kid. I have some things left to do up here and you need to get the hell out before our company discovers where we are. Now go."

"I'm scared, Marie. Scared shitless."

Marie couldn't help smiling at the little profanity, so appropriate for the occasion but so out of character for her young friend. "I'm going to make a potty-mouth out of you yet it seems. Now just grab the top rung and swing out, but don't make a sound going down. Thank God there aren't any windows on this particular part of the home. If you're quiet, they won't have any idea we've even left the building. When you hit the ground, wait for me but stay tight against the wall. Don't go moving around and attracting attention, understood?"

Alex nodded her understanding, but didn't appear the least bit happy about any of it.

"Just like on the river," Marie assured her. "One step at a time."

When Alex had disappeared from view, Marie peered out the portal to see if everything was going as planned. Alex was making steady progress down the snake of a ladder, albeit at a slower than desirable pace, and would be on the ground in another minute or two.

Confident that Alex would be fine, Marie raced back to the x-ray view box, knocking an empty chemical bottle off a shelf midway across the room. It crashed to the wooden floor with a thunderous boom and crack, sounding a hundred times louder in the tension-filled atmosphere than it had been in actuality. Still, it had been loud enough and there would be no further concealment of their whereabouts. The two men would be making a beeline for the third floor, guns in hand.

"Dammit to hell," she swore under her breath as she reached the view box. She yanked the film from the screen and stuffed all six sheets into their manila envelope, but instead of putting them back in the appropriate drawer, she went to one in the middle, completely out of sequence, and stuffed them in the midst of a thick stack of x-rays from a decade ago. Hopefully, she reasoned, even if they figured out why the women had been in the darkroom, they wouldn't as easily uncover the same information they had. Maybe it would buy them a few hours, maybe even a day or two. She could only hope and pray.

When the worst case scenario played like a horror movie in her mind's eye: getting caught by 'them' with the key in her possession, Marie fished it from her pocket, the first place they would look in a search. She thought for a moment then quickly unbuttoned her white cotton blouse, revealing an ivory bra. Carefully, she slipped her hand into her left cup and pressed the small brass key deep into the recesses of the bra, completely under her breast, at the bottom where the underwire met her ribs. Once in place, she rubbed her hand across her breast, on top of the nylon and spandex that comprised the fabric of the bra, and satisfied herself that not only was the key safe from accidentally falling out, but also that it would not be found merely by "patting her down." It would take a full strip search to uncover the hidden treasure, and she didn't intend to allow that, even if it meant her death.

As she hurried to button her blouse, she moved quietly to the door to peer out the small peephole that had been put in the door's center rail years before. The sight that met her eye froze the breath in her lungs, and was the only reason she didn't scream out loud like a frightened little girl whose older brother had just jumped out of the shadows. Less than three feet away, a well-dressed man, the size of a living room couch, had his left hand outstretched, ready to turn the doorknob, a gun as large as a piece of field artillery—even if optically exaggerated by the convex lens in the peephole—elevated and ready to kill anything in its path.

Without moving, she immediately sought a weapon, hoping for a large-caliber machine gun or howitzer of her own, but had to settle for one of the heavy stainless steel trays lying in the developing sink when nothing better could be found.

She pulled it tightly to her chest and pressed her back firmly against the wall, in the narrow pocket that would be created when the door swung open. Hopefully, this bozo wouldn't do as killers and cops always did in the movies and look immediately behind him for someone hiding in that space. If, however, that was the man's intent, she was more than prepared to instantly crack his skull with the thick steel pan.

Slowly, the door eased open, the long, silenced barrel of the 45-automatic leading the way into the unfamiliar space, like some alien probe in a science fiction film. For a split second, Marie had the brilliant idea of throwing her entire weight—all one-hundred-twenty-four pounds of it—against the door, forcing the man to cry out in pain and drop his weapon as the slamming door broke his arm. The very moment it formed in her mind, however, the ridiculous plan evaporated. Men like this didn't cry out in pain. Besides, she couldn't hope to get enough leverage and speed in the short distance she had to work with, to say nothing of being half the man's weight, to move the bastard two inches, more or less hard enough to fracture bones or cause him to relinquish his piece.

As the door continued to swing open, Marie found herself being pressed against the wall, the space rapidly becoming significantly smaller than she'd anticipated. If he opened it one inch more, he would realize that there was an object resisting his efforts, something soft and killable. She held her breath as sweat trickled down her back and between her breasts.

Finally, the man with the gun moved into the room, the door stopping just a few millimeters short of colliding with the steel tray held against her chest. If it wouldn't have meant immediate death, Marie would have let out a sigh of relief. Instead she held her breath and listened: the man had taken several steps into the room, but had then stopped, apparently surprised at not finding the room occupied.

Then, to her horror, the door began to move slowly away from her, the pressure of her thigh muscles, compressed when the door had been opened against them, now acting as springs to close it. *Oh, shit!* she said silently, *I'm dead*, but there was no way to grab it and remain concealed without making enough noise to reveal her presence at once.

Almost fully exposed now, the door more than half closed again, Marie knew one of two things was about to happen, and neither was good: either the man would look to the far end of the narrow room and realize there was an inexplicable hole the size of a car trunk in the wall, at which time he would race to the opening and put a bullet in Alex's brain, or he would surmise that the women had made their escape through that far portal and would race to intercept them on the ground level, at which time he would immediately see her and put a bullet in her brain. In either case, death awaited one of them in less than a second. *I really hate this shit!* she cursed to herself as she kicked the door the rest of the way closed while simultaneously bursting forth from her hiding place with developing pan held high.

Witherspoon turned at once and raised his pistol to fire, but the three-pound tray found his forehead and the bridge of his nose a millisecond before he could squeeze the trigger. He went down instantly, striking the wooden floor with a tremendous thud that sounded like a safe had just been overturned.

Pan still held high, ready to administer another crushing whack to the skull, Marie stood over the prone figure with a look of a woman more pissed off than afraid, yet more afraid than anyone should have to feel in two lifetimes.

Though the man was apparently going nowhere for the moment, she felt certain she hadn't killed him. A thin stream of blood issued from both nostrils, though not as much as she would have expected given the intensity with which she'd leveled the heavy pan against his cranium, and both eyes were rolled up in their sockets, leaving only the milky-white, vein-laced sclera visible.

"Screw you, asshole," she said aloud, but had barely gotten the words out of her mouth when she heard another man shouting the man's name and demanding to know what the hell was going on, followed by heavy footsteps making double-time up the stairs from the ground floor.

She immediately switched off the overhead bulbs, throwing the west end of the narrow room into total darkness, and stepped carefully past the unconscious man.

Guided by the waning evening sunlight, still streaming in through the fire escape opening, she made her way quickly toward the opening. When she spotted his Glock automatic lying a few feet from his limp body, she scooped it up, stuffing the surprisingly heavy weapon into the waistband of her jeans as she continued to move. In another ten seconds, she was out the opening and onto the ladder. A quick glance down verified that Alex had done as instructed, and was waiting patiently, if nervously, for her.

Hoping once again to purchase a few precious seconds of head start, Marie pulled the inner door shut as much as possible, though the ladder's half-inch thick ropes, which now crossed the lower threshold of the opening, prevented it from closing completely.

It would have to do.

She descended as rapidly as her quivering arms and legs would permit, grateful to feel Alex at the bottom of the rope, pulling downward and providing some welcomed stability. Descending a thirty-foot rope ladder in a hurry was like trying to descend a spiral staircase covered in Mazola. Possible, but ugly.

McGhee hit the darkroom door like a storm trooper, blasting it almost off its hinges before diving to the floor inside the narrow space, his outstretched pistol ready to dispense death to anything that moved.

Nothing, near total darkness other than a sliver of pale golden light some twenty feet distant.

He rose carefully to one knee, then to his feet, his 45-automatic moving to meet every groan and crackle the old structure made. With his left hand, he found the light switch and lit the room, immediately wary an attack might follow.

None came.

Instead, he saw his partner lying in a heap on the floor, ten feet distant, just beginning to stir. Blood oozed from his nose and the top of his forehead. Quickly determining that they were alone, he barked, "What the hell happened to you?"

Witherspoon sat up and rubbed his nose, then his forehead. "One of the bitches decked me. The blonde, I think," he mumbled, his head still spinning like a top.

"Where's your piece?" he asked, realizing it was nowhere to be seen. The thought of it being in the hands of the two bitches pissed him off to no end. Regardless of what Merkett had said, he was going to kill them both the moment he laid eyes on them.

Witherspoon didn't respond, but looked at his right hand as if surprised to find it empty. McGhee went to him and helped the bigger man to his feet. "Where the hell'd they go?"

Again Witherspoon seemed to be shaking cobwebs from his brain and didn't answer at once. Then he pointed to the far wall and said, "There."

At first, McGhee was baffled, then he realized that the sliver of sunlight had to be coming from some type of window. "Shit!" he yelled, racing past the other man. When he neared the small door, he pulled another pistol from the outer pocket of his suit coat. It was a smaller caliber gun than the heavier-gauge weapon in his hand, and held fewer bullets in its clip, but as his backup piece, it had always served him faithfully.

He threw it to Witherspoon.

"Go! Get down there and cut them off. They'll probably try for the nearest neighbor. You've got to stop them. I'm going after them from here."

Weapon in hand, head almost clear, the burly man with the broken nose moved with surprising speed across the narrow room and down the third-floor stairs.

The red in his eyes wasn't blood, it was the purest hatred he'd ever felt in his life. The bitch who'd blindsided him was about to die, and her death wasn't going to be quick or pleasant.

TWENTY-THREE

ESS THAN EIGHT FEET from the ground and scrambling for all her worth, Marie suddenly had the purest sensation of being watched she'd ever felt. Immediately, she looked upward, her dark cocoa eyes staring into the barrel of a Forty-Five. God, the hole in the end of the gun appeared as large as a soup can, the expression on the face of the man aiming the weapon at a spot directly between those lovely brown eyes was as hard as granite, as mad as a rabid wolf.

Without a second's thought or hesitation, she released both hands and plummeted backward, the nylon ladder at once springing upward a full ten inches from the sudden loss of her weight. It had not been enough to knock the weapon from his hand, as the developing tray had done to his partner, but it was enough to spoil his aim.

As she struck the ground with an organic thud, knocking the breath completely from her, she managed to roll toward the east wall, beside Alex. Two rounds fired in rapid succession struck the ground precisely where she had fallen, but to no avail. Grabbing her own weapon, the pistol taken from his associate, Marie pointed it upward and fired three shots in equally rapid succession, striking the jam of the outer opening and forcing the man to fall back into the room or be hit. She still wasn't the world's greatest shot, but over the last three years, in complete secrecy, she'd fired numerous weapons at the shooting range just south of town, expending thousands of rounds at distances ranging from arm's length to several hundred yards. The fusillade, even from the silenced weapon, had been enough to gain them a few precious seconds. The man upstairs wouldn't be sticking his head out again until he was certain they had fled.

"Go!" Marie shouted, rising to her feet and shoving Alex nearly hard enough to send her toppling.

Without a word, and thankfully not frozen in terror, Alex continued in the direction she'd been pushed, picking up the pace with each step. Once, just before they rounded the northeast corner of the building, Marie looked back over her shoulder and fired a single round, just for good measure.

As bullets flew his direction, McGhee fell back into the darkroom, striking the plank floor hard on his butt and free hand. "You whore!" he screamed. "They're headed north, toward the woods!" he then shouted toward the open door, loud enough to be heard throughout the building. "Cut them off!"

Rising to his knees again, he poked his head a few inches through the opening in the wall, only to be greeted by a single slug splintering the jamb less than a foot away. "You worthless whore!" he swore angrily, landing on his ass again.

Witherspoon had made it to the second floor landing when he heard his partner yelling that the women were heading north, not toward a neighbor on the south as they'd assumed. He turned right and raced into an office with a large north-facing window, quickly spotting the fleeing women less than forty yards away, but dangerously close to disappearing into the dense woods. The late evening light painted the left side of their bodies in hues of honey and orange, outlining them perfectly. *An easy shot from here*, he thought as he shattered the window with the borrowed pistol. As the glass fell away, he fired half a dozen rounds as quickly as he could pull the trigger while still maintaining an accurate sight picture. It didn't help that the girls, one of them half his age and the other younger by a decade, were running like Olympic cross-country contenders.

As they raced across the wide expanse of lovingly-tended lawn that formed the north border of the property, the security of thick trees, and bushes with leaves as dense as the fur on a squirrel, was just a few yards away. Marie heard angry bees whizzing by their heads and then the recognized but hated "crack-thud" as the slugs smashed into branches and earth ahead of them. A split second later, the report of the gun found her ears.

Suddenly she noticed an odd crimson mist fill the air, precisely where Alex's head had just been. As her mind tried to process the bizarre image, the younger woman fell forward, striking the earth as if she'd been tripped. Rag doll arms made no effort to check her fall, her chest and face taking the full brunt of her body's collision with the ground.

The horrific sight instantly sickened Marie.

She dropped to her knees and spun to face Alex's killer, emptying the remainder of the weapon's clip into the large window along the north wall of the house with blind fury and reckless abandon. She continued to pull the trigger even after the muffled popping had ceased.

Though none of her shots had drawn blood, several rounds struck the window and thin exterior walls only inches from the shooter's head, shattering glass and splintering wood and plaster. The hailstorm of lead forced Witherspoon to seek the relative shelter of the floor, his hulking mass hugging it as tightly as a rug.

"You bitch!" he seethed as glass rained down around him.

With the slide locked back, indicating that the empty weapon was now no more useful than a rock, Marie pitched it aside, turning her attention to her stricken friend.

A quick glance confirmed her worst fears: Alex had suffered a head wound, her gorgeous raven hair now tangled and awry, her skull oozing blood. She turned the slender figure over, cradling Alex's limp body in her arms, and wiped the sticky red essence and matted strands of hair from her angelic face.

"Oh, God, Alex, I'm so very, very sorry."

The tears flowed freely, making it difficult to see, but she didn't bother wiping them away. Her heart was as shattered as this poor young woman in her arms, and she wished at that moment there was a single round left in the pistol. Then, this could all be over in an instant and she would never again have to witness a loved one die. A nauseating feeling of déjà vu swept over her, and all she could do was continue a tearful apology for not having kept her promise to protect this precious life, even if it meant her own.

Several angry bees again swarmed around her torso and head, only this time, one of them stung her, knocking her flat on her back. The left sleeve of her white cotton shirt immediately turning damp and red, the pain in her shoulder like the flame of a welding torch was being held against the skin. She started to cry out, practically biting through her lip instead.

"They're down!" Witherspoon shouted through the shattered window. "They're both down near the edge of the woods. Run!"

Content that he'd done all he could from his current position, and being unable to reload a weapon for which he had no spare ammunition, Witherspoon darted for the stairs and the ground floor. In the rear of the clinic, McGhee was just stepping from the fire escape ladder, weapon again at the ready.

In fifteen seconds, both men realized they would have the women in their hands, and all this crap would be over and done.

Unable to do anything more for Alex, and determined anew to keep the bastards from winning this deadly game at any cost, Marie rose to her feet and disappeared into the protection of the forest. As she clutched her damaged shoulder with her right hand and tried to fight off the disorientation that intense pain brings with it, she could just begin to hear the Duchesne River less than a half mile away.

Four minutes. Maybe three.

The problem was, it was also a hundred feet down.

* * *

Arriving at the body of the Summers' girl, Witherspoon looked to his partner, who'd arrived only seconds earlier, and said in disbelief, "Where the hell'd the other one go? I hit her, I saw her go down."

"Apparently not," McGhee corrected, kneeling beside the younger woman's body. Roughly, and with no regard for her whatsoever, he thrust his hands into each of her front pockets in search of their prize. All he got for his efforts was a Samsung smartphone and a few hundred dollars in twenties and tens. Both he stuffed into his jacket pockets. He grabbed the neck of her blood-stained t-shirt with both hands and with one violent pull, tore it from collar to waistband, exposing her thin white bra, its spandex material also dappled with red. As crude and clumsy as a drunken freshman on his first date, he squeezed and mashed her breasts like a baker kneading dough.

"This is no time to cop a feel," his partner complained, realizing that they were losing precious seconds. "But it is time to go."

"Kiss my ass. My 'ex' used to hide money in her bra, like no 'perp' was gonna ever look there. Yeah, right."

"And..."

"Nothing, not even a mole." Flipping Alex's body over as roughly as a butcher handling a side of beef, McGhee dug into both back pockets: again he came up empty, without so much as a single penny or scrap of paper. "Goddammit!" he swore, his anger palpable. "The other bitch must have it." For pure spite, he planted his shoe squarely on the dead girl's hand as he headed after her friend. The bones cracked like dry twigs.

Retrieving his empty Glock-30 and inserting a full ten-round magazine, Witherspoon raced after his friend who by then had disappeared into the woods, less than a minute behind the last remaining contact with Robert Wayne Goodman.

And his damned video.

Better still, she was probably wounded and they were as mad as hell. They'd catch her alright. And when he finally got his hands on the skull-cracking blonde, he would be the one to put a bullet through her heart.

As they vanished into the forest, neither McGhee nor Witherspoon noticed the trio of black Suburbans that pulled into the clinic's driveway.

"That way, sir," Nate Fisher said as he pointed toward the woods fifty yards to their left. He'd seen the man they were presently calling Witherspoon running into the trees from that position just as they arrived.

Merkett exited the passenger's seat and studied the two flat tires on the white Honda, then glanced through the side glass of the Crown Victoria as he passed it. The bag in the front seat brought a look of intense displeasure.

He stepped into the center of the small group that had collected beside the middle SUV. "In and out in five, boys," Merkett said with casual authority. He chambered a round in his Beretta 9MM automatic and flipped off the safety before reinserting it in its holster. "This shit ends now."

TWENTY-FOUR

THE DENSE POCKET OF forest ended sharply at the river's edge, even more abruptly than it had begun at the north border of the clinic's manicured lawn. If not for the small clearing, no larger than a two-car garage, Marie would have run right into thin air, plunging a hundred feet to the Duchesne River.

She steadied herself as she stared down in horrified wonder at the churning water so far below, its rich emerald color in stark contrast to the muddy brown hue of the Green River. Suddenly, the irony of the name struck her as incredibly funny, though she also realized the comedic moment—so out of pace with the reality of the situation she was in—was triggered by the massive endorphin release her body had generated from the intense sprint through the woods and the bullet in her shoulder. It also made her suddenly dizzy and she dropped to one knee to keep from toppling over the edge.

Her left shoulder burned like hell itself and the long sleeve of her cotton shirt, rolled up at the elbow, was now entirely sodden with blood. She looked at her upturned palms and realized they were also smeared with crimson, though not from her own vital essence but from the blood of her dearest friend. Several strands of matted black hair clung to her fingers and the sight sickened her. She quickly wiped her hands on the grass.

When she heard shouting between the two men who were approaching like a runaway freight train from behind her, she knew there was only one option: if she could make her way over the edge and onto the craggy rock face, perhaps she could disappear from view before they realized where she'd gone. Maybe, just maybe, they would assume she'd either run off the edge in her frantic flight and had plunged to her death or they had somehow lost her in the dense woods; that she'd made a turn to avoid the river that she, having worked at the clinic for three years, had to know lay dead ahead.

Most likely, she reasoned, they wouldn't immediately assume she'd attempted a "no-ropes free climb" down a ten-story granite wall. If she were lucky, more lucky than she'd ever been in her life, they would backtrack on their route and try to reacquire her.

Or, she considered, they would see her climbing to safety and fill her brain with lead before she had a chance to escape or fall to her death, a far more likely outcome of the foolish endeavor.

The plan was thin, as transparent as the shadow of a ghost, but better than kneeling in place and waiting to be murdered. She prayed that her shoulder, on fire but apparently not broken, would hold out as she lowered herself over the edge.

Thankfully, the surface of the cliff was mostly granite marbled with other igneous rock, not the crumbly sandstone and gravel composite that comprised so many river banks in this region. This was due to a violent tectonic shift eons before, when an entire mountain split right down the middle, the west face—the one on which she now descended—retaining its mostly solid, primal rock structure while the opposite shore had been weathered away into granite chips and small fragments of sedimentary stone and sand. Half Dome in Yosemite was perhaps the most famous example of the same anomaly, though on a far grander scale, its vertical crest rising more than four-thousand feet above the valley floor.

Step by careful step, fingers and toes groping for every reliable purchase amid the fissures and crags, she slowly descended the face.

Just as she heard the men, their shouts now only a few yards from the clearing, she realized she was sufficiently below the ledge to at least be out of their initial view, though not far enough toward safety to risk dropping the remainder of the way and trusting that she wouldn't shatter every vertebra in her spine when she and river finally met.

The two killers were now just above her, pacing back and forth and cursing out loud at having lost the bitch. She detested these men, complete strangers to her, and wished she could somehow meet them on an equal playing field—then she'd show them what a bitch she could be. Not wishing to make the slightest sound that might reveal her position, she froze in place, hugging the wall as tightly as possible, despite fingers and toes screaming for relief and muscles and tendons burning beyond human endurance.

Just when she was sure she could not tolerate another second, her head exploded in a fury of pain that defied her ability to comprehend it. Had the glowing embers of a fire been poured down on her as during the siege of some medieval castle? Had a bullet just entered her brain? Was this what Alex had experienced only two minutes before? Whatever it was, it was truly beyond understanding or endurance; she released her fragile fingertip grip and her hands shot toward the origin of the pain, knowing full well that by trying to assuage the torment in her head, she was condemning herself to death by falling.

She didn't fall, however. She didn't even drop an inch. In fact, to her horrified amazement, she was actually rising, being pulled upward by her hair. Her hands finally encountered the source of the virulent agony and her fingers clutched and tore at the huge hand that held her golden tresses in a death grip.

With a final resounding jerk that wrenched enough hair from her scalp to make a doll's wig, the man who's nose and skull Marie had bashed with the developing tray yanked her slender form back to the grassy clearing, depositing her in a heap on the ground between his feet. Before she could curse him for his brutality, he took a double handful of her locks and snatched her to her feet.

"Screw you, you son—"

She didn't even get the words out before his massive fist plunged so deeply into her stomach that his knuckles probably met her spine. Again, she found herself between his feet, only this time on her right side, vomiting violently while also trying to find a wisp of breath with which to fill her lungs. Beneath her blouse, the blood from her shoulder wound created a small stream that coursed toward her breasts.

"Screw me?" he bellowed. "No, screw you bitch!" With that he pulled his Glock 45 and pointed the barrel at the center of her face, his finger caressing the trigger. He couldn't wait to end this whore's life.

"Put that away," came a deep, hard voice from behind them.

Marie managed to look up from her fetal position, as a man, dressed entirely in black, stepped into the clearing. He was flanked on both sides by at least half a dozen men, all scary looking as hell, and all dressed like death itself.

Recognizing the voice of his commanding officer, Witherspoon immediately holstered his weapon. "Sir!" he responded smartly, turning to face the man.

"Stand her up," Merkett said, and again the big man complied, jerking Marie to her feet and standing behind her, her arms pulled back and locked in his powerful grip.

"Take it easy, you son of a bitch!" she snapped when her left shoulder screamed for relief. It only earned her increased misery as he pulled her elbows nearly to the point of touching behind her back. At that moment, she swore she'd kill him.

Marie stood facing a man she'd never seen before, but also a man in an expensive suit that she was sure was the same person she'd fired at in the darkroom opening.

She glared at him but he only smiled in return.

Turning her attention to the man obviously in charge, despite no insignia or indication of rank among any of the killer squad, she said, "Who the hell are you, the leader of this pack of dogs?"

Merkett was amused by her pitiful, but totally predictable, defiance. "Let's just say I'm here to collect the item you took from the clinic, the item either Cameron or Summers found on the good senator and we'll leave it at that."

"You're going to kill me, aren't you," she said, chin held high. It had not been a question. He cocked his head and seemed amused. "So why not tell me what the hell I'm being killed for? What can it hurt?"

He thought for a moment, his face in a studious scowl. Then he said with a voice that displayed no emotion at all, "Listen, sweetie, this isn't some Hollywood B-movie script where you delay the bad guys long enough to somehow escape. We're going to take the item we came for, kill you quickly, and then leave—one, two, three." He took a deep breath and exhaled slowly. "You're not knowing the reason why couldn't matter less to me."

Marie had thought that the previous men frightened her, but this cool bastard almost made her wet her pants. He had eyes like a reptile and skin as dark as shoe leather, having obviously spent considerable time in the sun. *Probably the Middle East*, she imagined. And if this son of a bitch wasn't bad enough by himself, there were six men with him—one from each team having remained with the vehicles—who looked like they belonged on *America's Most Wanted*.

Her mind fought to formulate a plan. "Humor me. It's not like I have a lot of escape options. Right?" She kept eye contact with the leader and waited for some sign that he might yield to her request. While it was very unlikely to change her current status in any useful way, if she could somehow learn anything of worth, it might prove to be of immeasurable value if she did manage to escape.

Who was she kidding? She wasn't going to escape. She was going to die, just like this man had said. She looked at the nine men around her, between them enough collective firepower to start a war, and laughed inside: *Oh, well, now you know when, where, and how. Only question remaining is why.*

Merkett again smiled. "Perhaps. But first, give me the item I'm after. Then maybe we'll talk."

"Listen, I swear the only thing I took from there was my ass, and look at all the good that did me." She thought of Alex and fought back tears.

He shook his head. "Not true. You have the item I want, and if you won't give it to me voluntarily, I'll simply take it from you." He pulled a long knife from a belt holster and allowed the scalpel-sharp edge to catch the last light of the afternoon sun. It looked as long as her arm. "Shall I begin by cutting off your pants or your shirt?"

From behind him, she heard a smattering of lascivious snickers. *There are worse things than being dead*, she reminded herself, not wishing to consider what this unsavory group would do to her if given the time. Where were the damned cops? Surely the gunfire from earlier had made enough noise to wake the dead. "Okay, wait, that's not necessary," she said. "I'll *show* you that I don't have anything on me at all. Nothing. Alright?"

He made an enigmatic gesture with his long blade and immediately her arms were released. The shoulder which had started to become numb again signaled extreme disapproval with its rough treatment. She grabbed it with her right hand and massaged it repeatedly. She could feel the wound beneath her fingers as well as the penny-sized hole in the fabric.

"If you don't mind," Merkett said, pointing at her jeans with his blade.

Marie quickly reached into her front pockets and turned them outward, spilling her car keys and the wad of cash she'd taken from her garage apartment onto the grass. The man to her left in the expensive suit scooped it all up at once.

Nathan Fisher took everything from McGhee and examined the keys carefully. He quickly ascertained that there was nothing on the ring that could hold video information, just a collection of keys, a tiny survival-style can opener no larger than a postage stamp, and a small LED flashlight less than an inch long. "Not here, Colonel," he said smartly.

So this bastard, this "Colonel," was some type of military officer, she thought, watching the man who had just spoken cram the money in his shirt pocket. Her damn money!

"Going somewhere?" Merkett asked flatly, having noted the unusually large wad of bills. It had been her "quick cash"; nearly two thousand dollars intended for "weekend shopping emergencies." The sight of it being stolen without so much as a "thanks" pissed her off like she'd been slapped in the face.

"Sure, the Bahamas," she said sarcastically, hoping to infuriate these assholes even more than she already had. Hey, if she were going to die anyway, she reasoned, why not have a little fun on the way out? "Alex and I"—the name caught in her throat—"we just love Paradise Island. You ever been to Atlantis, Colonel Mustard? Or is it Sanders?" She watched for his reaction.

She didn't have to wait long.

"The back pockets!" Merkett growled angrily, his even temper suddenly inflamed. The man behind her immediately dug his meat hooks into her jeans, probing for the item they were looking for but also massaging her butt in the process. She was definitely going to kill this bastard the very first chance she got.

He withdrew his hands. "Nothing, sir."

Merkett nodded and touched his shirt.

Before Marie knew what had happened, the big man behind her had ripped her blouse violently from her, throwing it at the feet of the Colonel. White plastic buttons struck the ground like tiny hailstones. Merkett picked it up and felt the two front pockets. Again, his quest ended in frustration. His curdled expression said that he was no longer having any fun playing this game.

Standing before the group of killers in a thin, sexy spandex bra and low-cut jeans, her firm, ample breasts rising and falling from adrenaline-laced fear with seductive regularity, Marie felt completely naked. She looked down and discovered that what she thought was sweat trickling between her breasts was actually a steady stream of blood from the bullet wound. It had stained both cups of her bra where they and her generous cleavage met before continuing downward, first pooling in her navel then darkening the waistband of her jeans.

She glanced at her left shoulder and could plainly see that a bullet was not likely buried in her deltoid muscle. It appeared that the brass-jacketed round had drilled a half-inch hole in that muscle and had then passed cleanly through. Though it still bled freely from both the entrance and exit holes, and she had probably already lost a full pint of blood, at least she wouldn't have to go digging around for a buried slug with her pocket knife.

If she had a pocket knife.

If she lived long enough to need one.

Great! she thought, annoyed as hell. *Now I have a matched set of the damned things. Just what I always wanted.* She was referring to an almost identical wound in that same arm, three inches below, where another bullet had passed through both the biceps and triceps muscles three years earlier. Neither had shattered the bone, however, and she was grateful for that blessing.

The clearly furious Colonel, whoever the hell he was, focused his attention on her breasts, thrusting his knife in their direction. "Hold her," he barked, and once again, her arms were yanked behind her back like a steer being wrangled for branding. As he stepped toward her with the clear intention of removing her bra with his ridiculously long bayonet, to see what treasures might lie beneath—besides the obvious pair that had every man's attention fixated on them—Marie decided she'd had enough. *There are definitely worse things than death*, she reminded herself.

Timing her move with split-second precision, she waited until the knife-wielding bastard was only two feet away, her arms held perfectly rigid and behind her by Alex's killer, then drew her knees to her chest while contracting her legs as tightly as possible. With a thrust whose primal power originated from three years' hard work on the river, pulling oars with both arms while pressing in the opposite direction with rock-hard legs eight hours a day, she buried her hiking boots squarely in the Colonel's chest, then shot her legs straight out like a pair of hydraulic pistons.

In the blink of an eye, both she and the man holding her disappeared over the edge. She never uttered a sound as they fell, but the big man screamed like a little girl until the river silenced his cries.

Merkett, initially caught off guard by the unpredicted and suicidal move, recovered his composure quickly and stepped to the edge of the cliff. He was just in time to see both bodies strike the river below. Every man in his group stood at his side in disbelief, staring silently into the abyss.

"I'll be damned," McGhee said, as the bodies disappeared beneath the water. "What a crazy bitch."

When he was certain the woman was not going to miraculously swim to the opposite shore and stare up at him with a mocking look on her face, the middle fingers of both hands fully extended and wagging defiantly, Merkett sucked in and quickly exhaled a deep breath through his nostrils. He looked at McGhee and asked casually, "Who's cigarettes are those on the front seat of your car?"

Caught completely by surprise by the off-the-wall question, McGhee didn't have time to think about his answer, or the consequences of his words. "They're, uh, mine, sir," he stammered.

Without another word, Merkett thrust his killing blade up to the hilt in the man's solar plexus, its tip projecting upward nearly to his esophagus, his heart cleaved in two. He was dead where he stood, not a drop of blood exiting the wound as his heart was silenced in mid-beat. As the corpse dropped to the ground, he said simply, "Nasty habit, smoking. It'll kill you. Remember that, boys."

Not a syllable was uttered in response, though a half dozen pairs of eyes watched without blinking as he knelt and wiped the blood from his blade on the sleeve of the dead man's six-hundred-dollar suit.

He stood and turned to his men. "Alright, get this piece of shit into the trunk of his car and let's get the hell out of here. Delta Team, get down to the river and collect those two bodies, before sunrise if possible. We can't have some early morning kayaker find the woman or this asshole's partner, and we still need to get our hands on that damn video. Charlie Team, burn this place to the ground, the Honda, too, then take two men and burn the bitch's home and garage to the ground. I don't want so much as the mailbox left standing, understood."

He turned his attention to First Lieutenant Tom Pickard, head of Echo Team. "Tom, cover every possible place in town where someone would take a body they found floating in the river, alive or dead. If you see the woman or our man, I want to know at once."

Pickard took his team and melted into the woods.

"Sir?" Captain Nate Fisher said. "What if Matthews doesn't have the video on her. From what I could see, there wasn't any place left to hide it, I don't care how small it may have been."

"You may be right, Captain. I truly hope so. When Delta Team locates her body, they will either find the video or they won't. Either way, it's all good at this point. Containment is complete."

"What about the Summers girl?" Fisher asked. They would pass her body again as they made for the Suburbans. "Want us to put her body in the clinic before we torch it?"

Merkett shook his head. "Leave the little bitch where she fell."

When he was the last man standing in the small clearing, Colonel James Merkett pulled his cell phone from his pocket and pressed the first number in his speed dial list. The line was not encrypted, so logic and security concerns dictated that their conversation sound enigmatic and ordinary.

When his call was answered on the second ring, General Clayton Longmont said without preamble, "How's the party going, Jim? Everyone having a good time?"

"Not too bad, sir," Merkett said. "We did have two last minute guests who weren't invited, but they were politely asked to leave and did so without complaint."

"Did either of them bring a present at least?" Longmont, even more than his immediate subordinate, was ready for this fiasco to be over.

"The last woman to leave had a present, we believe, but she departed before we could get it from her. However, she promised to deliver it by morning and I believe she'll make good on her word."

"Great. That's most generous of her. Be sure to pay my respects to everyone there. Sorry I couldn't make it. Can I assume with the party being over, that you will be returning to work on Monday? I'm anxious to get on with our little project."

"No obstacles appear to remain, sir. The project," he repeated, "should be on track again. I'll call you the moment the boys and I get back to the office. We have a bit of clean-up to do here first. Small stuff; won't take long. You know how cranky the locals can be when you leave a mess."

That he did, whether the locals were in Iraq or Iowa. "It's all good news, Jim. We've been on hold far too long." Without another word, Longmont terminated the call.

With the requisite update out of the way, and feeling for the first time in three quarters of a year that things were finally back on track for the originally-planned October execution date, James Merkett looked down at the distant river, its waters now blue-black in the early light of evening.

"I'll give you this, Marie Matthews," he said with an admiring smirk, "you sure as hell went out on your own terms. That was the gutsiest move I've ever seen. Not sure any of my men would have had the balls."

He gave a mock salute, then turned to join the others.

TWENTY-FIVE

PAUL BURKS HAD COME to Utah countless times to relax and enjoy the splendid fly fishing its numerous cold-water streams and rivers afforded. While he had not allowed the sport to get into his blood the way it had so many of his colleagues, he nonetheless looked forward to the two weeks each year when he could just kick back and do nothing all day but try his best to coax a rainbow, brown, or cutthroat trout into his net by bobbing a tiny man-made insect on the water's surface. More pragmatist than purist, he bought his flies online instead of tying each by hand: a tedious, labor-intensive, and highly-skilled obsession that was as much artful black magic as science. By eight o'clock, with the sun almost gone, it was time to call it a day.

Originally from San Francisco, Burks was a clinical psychologist with a small but highly profitable family practice on Santa Rosa Avenue in Sausalito, at the northern end of the Golden Gate Bridge. Life was good for the divorced forty-four-year-old. He was remarkably fit for his age, had all his hair, good friends, an enviable string of lovers, and with an ex-wife who was the CEO of a successful software company in Menlo Park, an hour south of Sausalito, had not been saddled with the debilitating alimony payments or property settlement that had nearly bankrupted many associates and even more clients. As an added bonus, the couple, who'd met in graduate school and had fallen in love at once—only to fall out of love even more quickly—had brought no children into the insanity and turmoil of the Twenty-First Century.

Remaining childless had been a matter of strategic planning rather than dumb luck—the birth control choice of most newlyweds. Paul Burks preferred a life that was neat and well ordered; surprises were the result of sloppy planning or poor communication. Or both. A life without surprises is a life without tragedy, he reasoned. While the unexpected divorce the year before had blindsided him, to be sure, he had quickly put all the associated emotional clutter into neat little boxes in his mind and heart, and life had returned to a blissful state of "pre-marital" normalcy in no time.

Life was indeed good for the good doctor, even if he had only caught two trout worth keeping this day. Oh, well, they'd make a fine meal tonight. He'd try some other place along the river tomorrow and maybe have better luck.

As he reeled in his line and made for the west bank and his temporary camp at the water's edge, his mind was on which wine to enjoy with his brown trout dinner. He never liked to repeat wines on a fishing trip, even with similar or identical entrees most nights, and since he had only himself to satisfy on vacation, he could be completely selfish in his choice. He'd brought a mixed case from his extensive wine cellar, ranging from an inky-black Monastrell to a nearly colorless Sauvignon Blanche.

"I think a nice Adrian Fog tonight," he said aloud, remembering that he'd brought two bottles of the 'cult' Pinot Noir from the tiny, but exclusive, Sonoma County vintner. It was one of his favorites.

Despite considerable effort, his progress through the rapidly moving, waist-deep water was impeded by his thick and cumbersome chest-high waders, allowing him to move no more quickly than a man weighing twice his one-hundred-ninety pounds.

With pan-seared trout and a superb bottle of wine filling his thoughts, he almost didn't see the large, oddly-shaped object that approached from his right, carried on the current but just below the surface like humectant driftwood. When his peripheral vision detected an object in the pristine stream, as incongruent as an iceberg on a city street, he spun to get a clearer view of it.

"Oh, SHIT!" he shouted excitedly, tossing aside his twelve-hundred-dollar handmade rod as if it were of no greater value than a hillbilly's cane pole. He tried to sprint back to the spot he'd just left, but his ponderous waders made it impossible for him to intercept the man's body before it passed just inches from his outstretched hands. It was like moving in depressingly slow-motion.

His heart pounded not only from the heroic but fruitless half-minute of all-out exertion, but also from the horrid image of the man disappearing from view. Though obviously dead, and probably beyond all human help, the inability to do anything at all on his behalf froze the dedicated, if somewhat self-indulgent, psychologist in mid-stream. Immediately, he pulled his cell phone from the waterproof pocket in the bib of his waders and punched in 9-1-1.

Just as the line connected, he was struck hard from behind. The phone was instantly knocked free and disappeared from view in the swiftly-moving current. "What the hell!" he shouted, turning to face his attacker.

Instead of a trout thief brandishing a Louisville Slugger, the half-nude body of a young woman, as blue as the sky had been an hour before, bobbed and banged against his torso, like a skiff tethered to its dock during a hurricane. As he was about to spew forth a string of profanities, his mind instantly incapable of anything more clever than base expletives, he lost his footing, fell backward, and submerged.

At once, the lifeless torso passed over him on its mindless journey downriver. In the bottle-green miasma of the river, he could clearly see her slipping beyond his reach.

With all the strength he possessed, he thrust both hands upward and behind him, like a trapeze artist reaching for a bar, just managing to hook an index finger in one of her belt loops. His tenuous grip lasted but a second before the current tore her from him again.

Still beneath the water but continuing to grope and grapple for another piece of the woman, any piece at all, he felt her sodden jeans slip though wet fingers without any purchase at all being made. Just as her feet passed his hands, he somehow managed to seize a boot; only one boot, but it was enough.

Holding on as if his own life depended on it, Paul Burks allowed the movement of the woman's torso to pull him to the surface. Choking and coughing, he rolled onto his stomach while still keeping his hands deadlocked on the one hiking boot. Thank God, he thought, that her footwear was the type that laced tightly around the ankle, and not the stupid slip-on or Velcro closure type. It they had been, she, too, would have literally slipped through his fingers.

His back to the current, he planted his own feet firmly in the stony riverbed and pulled her steadily to him. With Herculean effort, he finally held her to him. As he suspected, there was no sign of life at all.

Using a fireman's carry, heaving her limp form over his shoulder so that her torso hung across his back and her head and arms were at the lowest point of carry—praying this would begin to expel the untold liters of water she'd ingested into her lungs—Paul trudged ahead like a man trying to push a stalled car uphill. But, just like the mother who manages to lift a burning station wagon from the child pinned beneath it, the shock of adrenaline coursing through his system gave him the added strength to reach the west bank.

When his thick rubber soles met the sandy shore, he fell first to his knees then onto his face, the twenty gallons of icy river water now inside his waterproof waders, coupled with this woman's dead weight and his exhausted muscles, proving too much even for a momentary Superman. Unable to stand with her again, scrambling on his knees and one supporting arm, he moved her steadily up the bank, toward his camp spot fifteen feet away.

Finally, he was able to lower her onto her back on a patch of relatively flat ground, a mix of short grass, small pebbles, and sand. Her bluish color had not improved with her extrication from the chilly water, but then, it had only been a minute. Maybe less.

He ripped his waders off and threw them aside, knowing that he could not possibly do what needed to be done with them impeding his movement, sapping his strength. He would need every ounce of it for what lay ahead.

He then knelt beside the woman and pushed her forehead down gently with his left hand while elevating her chin with his right. When he was satisfied with this initial step, he pulled her mouth open and assured himself that she had not swallowed her tongue. "Good, she hasn't," he said aloud, then pinched her nose and blew two deep breaths into her lungs while placing his mouth fully over hers. Her chest rose and fell just as he'd hoped. Still no response, but he hadn't expected any.

He interlocked his fingers, left hand atop his right, elbows locked, and placed the heel of his right palm in the center of her sternum. Again satisfied with the correctness of his procedure, he began the steady rhythm of chest compressions at a one-hundred-per-minute rate, careful to depress the sternum at least two inches with each downward thrust. Thirty compressions, two quick breaths, and the cycle began anew. There was no letting up now until help arrived or the patient came around. That was the CPR mantra of the American Red Cross.

Since his cell phone was at the bottom of the river, and help was at least half an hour away by back roads, he had no choice but to continue the monotonous and grueling cycle until he succeeded in restoring life, or until he passed out.

It was exhausting work, often described by those who'd been through it as the most physical effort they'd ever expended, or ever hoped to expend, in their lives.

As he continued the seemingly endless routine, he began to consider the consequences of his actions. Assume for the sake of argument that he succeeded in reviving this young woman—despite statistics that said the likelihood of a positive outcome after an extended period of oxygen deprivation was less than one-percent—what then? Would he succeed in restoring life to a body that no longer had sufficient brain function to even realize it *was* alive? And what if his muscles were simply no longer able to continue, only seconds before she responded and began to breathe on her own?

The dilemma, which seemed to have no reasonable answer and which promised no positive outcome, fought its bloodless battle in his brain, yet still he pressed thirty times and breathed twice, pressed thirty times and breathed twice. For a quarter of an hour he continued, until he could go on no more. With arms that could not lift themselves, he stared down at the beautiful young woman before him and started to curse the heavens. Instead, he slapped her face hard enough to rock her head to the side. "Wake up, dammit!" he shouted. "Wake up! Wake up! Wake up!"

His chin sank to his chest and his eyes rimmed with tears. When the woman coughed violently and spat half a liter of river water in his lap, he almost jumped out of his clothes. "That's right!" he continued to shout at the top of his lungs. "Come on back! You can do it!" He slapped her face again, on the opposite cheek, and again she coughed and expelled a huge volume of water. Quickly, he rolled her onto her right side and pounded repeatedly with the heel of his hand at a spot directly between her shoulder blades.

More water. More coughing.

In the near total darkness that had fallen during his extended effort to revive the woman, Paul could just hear her breathing on her own, but he could no longer tell if her body bore the unearthly azure hue it had when he'd begun.

He bent and put his ear to her lips. "Yes!" he said excitedly. She was breathing.

Shallow, but on her own.

Freezing and shivering in his own soaked clothing, he knew she had to be in far worse shape. God only knew how long she'd been in the water. Again, the thought of having saved her life only to condemn her to a lifetime as meaningless as a statue, screamed for him to consider the consequences of his actions; to let her die if that was God's will.

"Screw it," he said to the inner voice of warning. "She's alive, that's all I know. There's no going back now."

With her breathing somewhat stabilized, it was now time to keep her from succumbing to hypothermia, the next great obstacle she had to face. If he could get her body temperature up to near normal, and quickly, she stood a chance of making it to the next step.

A slim chance, perhaps, but at least it was a chance. He thought about the man he had not been able to reach and understood now that if he had succeeded in getting to him, this beautiful young woman would have paid for that success with her own life.

He looked up the hill to where his Range Rover sat parked, its outline just visible in the twilight. "I'll be right back," he said to the woman who lay quietly on her side, her breath as shallow as someone in a coma.

TWENTY-SIX

WHEN PAUL BURKS REACHED his Range Rover, he threw open the back hatch and dug through a veritable store's worth of survival gear in search of the large drawstring duffle that contained his trusty North Face sleeping bag. He'd owned it forever, but having been the very best money could buy, he'd never seen the need to replace it. Designed to accommodate one in sumptuous comfort, it was spacious and extra-long, providing ample room in the foot for clean clothes to be kept warm and dry. Few things could be more disheartening than crawling out of a toasty down bag on a cold winter's morning only to be faced with clothes that had grown as stiff as an oak plank in the frigid night air.

Because he was staying at the cabin of a colleague on this most recent trip to Truman, he had not anticipated needing his extreme weather gear in the June warmth of the Utah flatlands. However, a quick change in his vacation plans, which often occurred for no reason at all other than the whimsy of the moment, might have taken him to a high mountain lake where evenings, even during the summer, often approached zero. The unmatched thermal properties offered by the goose down filler and synthetic composite shell that composed the sleeping bag would warm her nicely. He grabbed a broad-beam camp light and slammed the hatch, then rushed back to the nearly frozen young woman.

Thankfully, she was still holding her own, but when he knelt and listened more carefully, blocking out the din of the river, decided that her breathing had actually grown shallower and less frequent. To make matters worse, in the amber glow of the camp light, he could see that she was now shivering violently, a clear sign that hypothermia was setting in. Every moment lost now would mean increased risk of her falling into a deep unconsciousness from which only death would provide release.

Working quickly and with determined resolve, he stripped every thread of clothing from his body and dropped the soggy garments on the ground at his feet. He was not going to let this woman die now that he'd gotten her this far.

Dropping again to his knees, he tore at the laces of her hiking boots, but lengthy submersion in the Duchesne had made the knots nearly impossible to loosen. Worse, his fingers had grown numb and clumsy. Finally he worked through one set of laces, then the other, removing both boots and tossing them on the pile. Her khaki Thor-lo socks came next.

When he rolled her gently on her back to allow access to her jeans, she coughed several times but otherwise remained silent and unresponsive. He undid the one button at the waistband and lowered the zipper to its stop, then grabbing a handful of denim at the seams of both legs, about midway down her thighs, carefully eased the loose-fitting jeans down across her hips and buttocks and finally off her legs entirely.

With her now clad in nothing but an ivory bra and matching high-leg briefs, he considered leaving the underwear in place. He felt the fabric: it was as cold as ice, clinging skin-tight around the most blood-rich portions of her anatomy. Leaving them in place would be like trying to stay warm in a car going down a winter highway with your head stuck out the window. The bra and panties were added to the growing pile of sopping clothes and footgear.

With the sleeping bag unzipped almost to its foot, Paul made quick work of placing the frigid figure inside the soft cocoon, then slipped in beside her and zipped them both in tight. Cuddling like spoons in a kitchen drawer, he pulled her close to him, allowing his considerably greater body heat to flow into her. Almost at once, her teeth quit chattering and she no longer shook from head to toe like a rabbit in a panther's gaze. Inside of five minutes, she lay perfectly still, her breathing again deep and even, though she still remained unconscious.

As each minute passed more slowly than the previous one, Paul could feel her skin and underlying muscles begin to reach normal temperature. It was taking far longer than he'd imagined, with more than forty minutes having already passed. It seemed like hours. He repeatedly checked his wristwatch, its luminous dial clearly discernable in the soft light, though the reason for this ritual made little sense to him even as he observed a second hand that now appeared to be moving backward. He knew this process was going to take exactly as long as it was going to take; not one minute more, but certainly not even one second less.

Rubbing his hand up and down her arm to help speed the warming process, Paul's fingers encountered an injury he hadn't noticed earlier. He pulled back the thick covers and allowed the camp light to illuminate her left shoulder, front and back. Squarely in the center of her deltoid muscle was a hole about the size of a Magic Marker, a matching hole of equal size in back. Both were clean, even sterile looking, and neither appeared to be actively bleeding. The skin around each hole was puckered and wrinkled from prolonged exposure to water, much as a child's fingertips look after hours in a swimming pool. He had no idea what to make of it, and attributed it to a puncture of some sort, probably a submerged stick or piece of metal she'd encountered in the river. The wounds would need medical attention, to be sure, but they were not a serious concern at the moment.

When he pressed his hand against her chest to gauge her breathing, as he'd done six or eight times so far, he realized for the first time that he was aware of her right breast against his palm. Her nipple was still hard and erect from the cold, the skin soft and inviting. "Stop it, you idiot," he chided himself, returning his hand at once to her midsection, just below the ribs. He couldn't get in any trouble there, he reasoned, but the image of her exquisite form pressed against him persisted, and fought for control of his thoughts. He played back the day's fishing in monotonous detail to keep his mind occupied and his anatomy in check, a sort of mental "cold shower."

A few minutes before nine p.m., he finally heard the sound he'd been praying for since pulling her lifeless shape from the Duchesne River: coherent words passing her lips.

She moaned softly, though more like someone in a hypnotic state than truly awake, repeating the words, "I'm so sorry, Alex, so very, very sorry."

He'd inquire about Alex and about the man he'd failed to save in due time. "And about how on earth you came to be in the river in the first place," he said aloud, studying her face for some indication that he'd been heard. At least for now, she was apparently aware of nothing but the voice in her head pleading for forgiveness.

Though he'd done absolutely nothing wrong, having in fact saved this woman's life not once but twice, Paul knew enough about human behavioral response to understand that he needed to be anywhere other than in this cocoon with this perfect stranger, the two of them as naked as the day they were born, when she finally awakened. He felt certain this would be any moment now.

Slipping quietly from the down bag, he was careful not to disturb her any more than necessary. Standing in the open again, the relative chill of the evening breeze, though still in the mid-eighties, felt like a blast of arctic air on his bare flesh. He sprinted up the hill and found clean, dry clothes in the back of the Range Rover, then dressed hurriedly, discovering that his only footwear option that wasn't drenched was a pair of Crocs. These he donned sockless and returned to the woman's side.

No sooner had he sat down, with the soft honey-colored glow of the camp light painting her face and hair, the woman opened her eyes and stared blankly at the lamp. For several seconds, it seemed as if she were trying to adjust to its intensity, as she blinked repeatedly and squinted as if it were the afternoon sun.

"It's okay," Paul said in his best therapist's voice. "You're okay. You're safe. Take all the time you need. My name is Paul and I'm here to help you. You're perfectly safe."

* * *

When the small, plastic camp light finally came into clear focus and was no longer the proverbial light at the end of death's tunnel, Marie began to get her mind around the bizarre and incredible fact that she wasn't fish food. Still laying on her side, wrapped in the down sleeping bag, she said, "Impossible. It can't be."

"What's impossible," a voice asked softly from beyond the lamplight. For the first time, Marie realized she was not alone or in a dream. The voice clearly startled her and her expression showed it. "It's okay, you're safe," the voice repeated. "My name is Paul Burks, I'm a doctor and you're perfectly safe with me here. Can you tell me your name?"

Now that it was also in focus, she studied the face of the strange man across from her, trying to determine if it belonged to any she had seen in the clearing on the ridge, however long ago that was. Certain that he had not been among the group of killers, she said, "Where am I?"

It was always the first question disoriented people needed an answer to and he'd prepared his answer in advance to provide as much information, in a non-threatening manner, as possible. Neat and orderly; the sooner he could get his life back in that mode, the better. In a voice oozing concern, he said, "You're on the west bank of the Duchesne River near Truman, Utah, about a mile south of a point known as Eagle Ridge. Can you tell me how you happened to be in the water?"

Eagle Ridge was the highest point on the Duchesne River for fifteen miles either side of Truman, and had been the cliff from which she'd fallen—*no, correct that*, she noted—from which she'd pushed that murdering bastard.

At once, Marie sat up, the sleeping bag falling from her shoulders and arms. She grabbed her chest with both hands, her sternum feeling as if an elephant had stepped on it; her ribs aching as well. Then she realized that she was completely naked, and while the reality of that fact surprised her somewhat, it did not shock her. She spent the bulk of each summer in a skimpy bikini, sixteen hours a day in the midst of strangers from every state and a dozen foreign countries. While not a prude by any standard, the discomfort of the moment prickled her flesh. Casually, she pulled the cover across her again. "Where's the man?" she asked. She noticed that the man's expression had not changed either when the sleeping bag had fallen or when she'd covered herself again, unlike the thugs on the ridge, whose eyes almost came out of their heads the moment her bra was exposed.

She didn't know him, certainly didn't trust him, but neither was she frightened by him. In fact, he'd just scored a big point with her in her book. Most of the raft trips were spent with middle-aged men ogling her breasts whenever they thought she wasn't looking, which of course she was as are all women whenever this happens. She loved men, but they could be such jerks at times.

"Who, the man with you?" Paul asked.

Marie nodded. "A man in a gray suit."

Paul took in a deep breath; he didn't want to have to deliver such bad news, not with this lovely woman so recently in a life-threatening situation, but realized he had little choice. The anxiety of not knowing what had happened to her husband or lover, or whatever role he played in her life, would actually be worse than getting a hard dose of reality and then being allowed to grieve. He exhaled slowly and evenly. "I'm sorry, but I wasn't able to reach him in time."

"You're saying he's dead," she stated rather than asked.

Paul nodded. "I'm sorry."

"Where's his body? Where it is right now?" she pressed.

The questions caught him off guard, seeming a bit macabre, but he attributed them to the stress of the moment. "I suspect the river has carried it some miles distant." He pointed to the south, the direction of the current. "However, I feel absolutely certain that—"

"Got you, you worthless bastard!" she shouted, fists clenched in defiance. Again the covers fell. "I told you I would," she said, pulling them back across her bare breasts. The look on her face was one of sheer elation and victory.

In all his nearly twenty years of clinical practice, including weeks of volunteer work at state hospitals for the criminally insane, Paul Burks, PhD, had never gotten such an unexpected reaction to the news of a death. Clearly this woman was in the throes of a psychotic episode, perhaps even a dangerous one, threatening to more lives than merely her own. It was time to get her better medical care than he could administer along the Duchesne River.

As he was about to speak, Marie said with urgency in her voice, "What time is it, Paul?"

Though troubled by the sudden direction shift in her mood and thought process, he looked at his watch. "A few minutes past nine," he said, then, "And it's time that we got you to the hospital, young lady. You've had quite an evening."

Marie did the math quickly and realized it had been more than an hour since her meeting with the "Colonel." By now, they would have had ample time to get to the west side of the river—*her* side of the river—the east being too steep to provide access for most of the river's journey south. She knew they would do everything necessary to locate her body and the 'item' they know she had on her when she entered the river; probably the body of the man in the suit as well, not wanting to leave behind that kind of evidence. "Oh, shit!" she exclaimed, groping her breasts with both hands: no bra. "Where's the key? Where's the damned key?"

As a frightening montage of horrid images formed in her mind, the last day playing back in fractured bits and pieces of fear and carnage, she knew that without the key, Alex's death will have been in vain, and her own life no longer stood any chance of surviving at all.

"This one," Paul said, holding a small brass key in his outstretched hand.

With no regard for her present state of undress, Marie leaped from the sleeping bag and snatched the key from his outstretched hand, clutching it tightly in her fisted grip, holding it to her heart, "Thank you, God," she said. "Thank you, thank you, thank you."

More than ever, the psychologist was certain this very strange woman was on the brink of a complete nervous breakdown. Or worse.

Realizing she was now standing completely nude less than two feet from a total stranger, Marie reached down and pulled the sleeping bag to her body, but continued to stand. "Who are you?" she asked, wrapping it across her shoulders and folding her arms tightly to her.

"My name is Doctor Paul Burks. I'm a clinical psychologist from Sausalito, California. I—"

"I thought you said you were from San Francisco," she said, the small hairs on her neck at once catching the inconsistency in his story.

"I am, I was born there, but my office is just a bit north of there in the community of Sausalito. It's just on the other side—"

"I know where it is," Marie said, again cutting him off. The explanation satisfied her and the warning hairs stood at ease again. "Why are you here?"

Grateful that the conversation had moved in a 'normal' direction, he said, "I am on vacation, trying to get in a little fishing. I'm staying at the cabin of a colleague not far from here." He studied her expression as she seemed to take in every syllable he spoke, like they were in a foreign language and not understood. To lighten the mood, he said, "Never thought I'd catch a beautiful mermaid," then smiled at his own little joke.

Processing every word, grasping at every straw of survival that she could clutch, Marie said, "Upstream or downstream?"

"What?" Paul asked.

"The cabin," she explained.

"Oh," he said and pointed toward from the lights of the town that painted a milky haze across the night sky northeast of them.

It was upstream, the opposite direction the Colonel and his men would have to head if they were to have any hope of finding her body in the swiftly-moving river.

And the 'item' she had taken from them, whatever the hell that was. She'd come to the conclusion that they had no idea the 'item' was a key, or Colonel Sanders would have simply used the word. He would have said, "Give me the key, bitch, not give me the 'item' we're after." He was on the hunt for something, a deadly quest to be sure, but apparently had no clue as to its identity. *How can that be?* she wondered. "Another damned mystery," she mumbled under her breath. "This is beginning to piss me off."

As her mind returned to the moment, she nodded approvingly. "I want to go there now," she said, then looking at the pile of soggy rags at her feet added, "Do you have anything I can wear until my clothes dry?"

"The only thing that might fit is a pair of sweatpants and an old sweatshirt. I keep them—"

"Perfect. Grab 'em." When he didn't rise at once from his comfortable spot on the sandy soil, she said, "Would you please get them for me, Paul? I can't exactly go around wearing a sleeping bag."

It had not been the lack of courtesy that had him glued in place, but the sense of urgency in the woman's voice. For the fourth time, she'd switched conversational directions so fast that he could barely keep up. "If you tell me your name first."

Though she had no time for games with Colonel Mustard and the rest of the bozos from *Clue* on their way at this very moment to finish what they'd started an hour ago, she also realized that they might lose even more time at this game if she didn't yield. She considered holding her ground and insisting that he get the damned clothes—now!—and they'd do all the "getting to know each other shit" at the cabin. "My name is Marie Matthews," she said calmly. "I live in Truman." Then to hurry him along, she added, "Thank you for all you've done for me. I can never hope to repay you. You're my newest and best hero."

As she'd expected, he rose at once and darted for the car, returning shortly with dry clothes. When he'd handed them to her, he scored a second major point by turning his back to her as she dressed. *Maybe he's a nice guy*, she thought as she dropped the sleeping bag.

Standing nude in the amber light again, she made a quick assessment of her shoulder wound. While the burning pain had never fully gone away, it had become tolerable, probably the cold water. *Good*, she thought, *the bleeding has stopped*. Realizing that there was no time to take care of her shoulder at the moment, even if she had the means with which to do it, she dressed quickly. Maybe there would be a first aid kit at this friend's cabin; she could deal with it then.

With the thick sweatshirt and pants knocking the wind-enhanced nervous chill from her body, Marie said, "All done."

Paul turned around and began to loosely roll the sleeping bag into a usable state for transport. "Better?" he asked.

"Heavenly. Thanks. I like sweatshirts that are way too big." She put the key between her teeth and bit down, then pulled the waistband drawstring as tight as it would go, bunching the large man's sweatpants into furrows around her twenty-four-inch waist. She removed the key. "Pants fit fine, too."

He noted the extra foot of fabric gathered at the waist and said, "Yeah, like a glove."

Key again locked between her teeth, not wanting to allow it out of her sight even for a second, Marie dug through the pile of soggy clothes and removed her bra, panties, socks, and boots, wrapping them all in her jeans. "Let's go," she said moving at once toward his car, bundle in hand.

Paul grabbed the camp light and sprinted to join her. "Please listen to me, Marie. You had an horrific experience tonight. You nearly died. It took me more than a quarter of an hour to revive you, then you tried to go into hypothermic shock."

"Oh, that explains a few things," she said.

Puzzled but growing more used to the wild ride with each passing moment, he said, "Explains what?"

"My sore ribs and sternum." She touched the area that hurt the most with the fingertips of her right hand. "And my being naked in a sleeping bag. I was taught that when someone exhibits signs of hypothermia, it's imperative that you elevate their body temperature at once, by any means available. Paul, did you share body heat with me as the manual suggests?" She knew he had, or probably had, and was grateful for all he'd done. A little fun with him for a moment or two because of it wouldn't hurt anything. She gave him the look of a mother who'd just caught her son in the cookie jar.

More embarrassed than he had imagined possible at this stage in his career, or life, Paul's blush, even in the yellow camp light, answered Marie's question and made her grin. As he was about to explain, she said, "Thank you, Paul, from the bottom of my heart," then gave him a kiss on his reddened cheek. "Now, let's gather up everything, and I mean every single grain of sand that could point back to you, then get the hell out of here."

"Marie, please listen to me, you need medical attention, if for no other reason than for that injury to your arm. It's pretty bad and it's going to need a good dose of antibiotics and stitches, maybe even surgery." His expression was one of genuine concern.

She stepped even closer to him and gave him a look that said what she was about to say was dead serious. In less than half an hour, he'd already come to recognize it. "That injury to my arm is a bullet wound, Paul. The man who shot me, who tried to kill me and who did kill my best friend, was the same son of a bitch who floated down the river just before you grabbed me. I killed him and damn near killed myself in the process, but thanks to you, I'm still kicking. However, if I go to the hospital now, or at any time in the foreseeable future, I'll be dead for sure. In fact," she put her palm against his cheek, "if we both don't leave here at once, Paul—you *and* me—no doctor on earth will be able to save us."

Paul Burks had seen crazy people before, many times in fact, but he couldn't tell with any degree of certainty if this was one of those times. "Okay, Marie," he said evenly as he began to police the area for every item he'd brought from the vehicle since first making camp at sunrise. "We'll do it your way for now."

TWENTY-SEVEN

A S THE RANGE ROVER moved along the narrow and winding back roads that had led to the river's edge, Marie continued to play back the day's events in her mind. Perhaps she'd heard or seen some important clue that was the cornerstone of this riddle, and only needed to bring it to the surface of conscious thought so that she could study it, learn from it—use it to save her life. More likely, she didn't know squat, would never know squat, and would be dead at the Colonel's hands inside of twenty-four hours, the damned key a mystery to her even if she managed to see Heaven.

Which, with the way she had started cursing again, was highly doubtful, she assured herself.

They had carefully picked up every scrap of potential evidence that might link Paul's vehicle to the campsite, at least as far as they could play "CSI-buster" by the beam of a single three-cell flashlight. Still, it had been a good job and had taken only a few minutes. Most of his gear had been in the Range Rover anyway, except for the sleeping bag, some fishing gear, clothes, waders, and live-well with two medium-sized trout in it. The fish had been set free and the rest collected. The last thing Marie had done was to take a leafy branch and sweep most of their footprints away, though this had been a halfhearted effort with her chest, arm, back, knees, elbows, shoulders, hips, feet, neck, and head aching like she'd just fallen a hundred feet into a river.

Her heightened sense of worry and dread had not diminished with the cooperative effort, however, and she thought hard to imagine what they'd left behind that would come back to haunt them sooner rather than later. There was always something; you could never remove all evidence you'd been somewhere, even if for only a brief time.

"Care to talk about what happened?" Paul said, interrupting her forensic analysis of the day's events.

"About what?" she asked, knowing there were probably a hundred things about which he could be speaking. She'd let him be specific rather than her spewing forth answers to questions not yet asked.

"We could start with who's after you."

Marie shrugged.

"Okay," he said, "how about *why* these people are after you?"

Again, she answered his question with a shrug.

Not deterred, having encountered this same reluctance to respond in many patients, Paul said, "Fine, then tell me about Alex." That struck a nerve and he knew it at once by her pained expression. When she didn't volunteer anything right off, he decided to goad her. "What did Alex do to get herself killed?"

If Marie could have dropped him with a single look, the one that contorted her face at that precise moment would have been the weapon with which to do it. "She didn't do a goddamned thing to get herself killed, you son of a bitch! Unless you want to find out what car keys in the eyes feels like, you'll take that back." Her breathing was intense, a match for her tone. She sat staring at him, her back against the passenger's door.

Good, he'd gotten her talking at least, now he needed to steer the conversation in a more positive and informative direction.

"Sorry, but lack of information causes a person to jump to all kinds of conclusions. Unless you tell me something to the contrary, I'm stuck here with nothing but my initial impressions." He glanced at her expression in the console lights as he tried to keep his eyes on the twisting dirt road. When he saw her eyes and mouth soften a bit, he said, "Help me out here, Marie. I really want to understand. I didn't save your life just to piss you off." It had been a cheap shot, meant to create guilt, and he knew it would be an effective one.

Finally Marie's posture eased and the fists she'd made with her hands relaxed and returned to her lap, though the key in her left palm was again being massaged like Grecian worry beads. "She was a really sweet kid. The best. Like a little sister to me. Everyone loved her."

"Tell me what happened." He drove cautiously, avoiding as many of the divots and washouts as possible.

Suddenly acutely aware of their painfully slow speed, she snapped, "Can't this piece of shit go any faster? Hell, I could run alongside and make better time. You want me to drive?"

Hell no, he didn't want her to drive, was she crazy? Then he checked his train of thought: whether or not she was insane had yet to be determined.

Not put off by her outburst, actually expecting it, Paul pressed for answers. "Marie. Tell me who is trying to hurt you? How did you come to fall into the river? Who was the man who drowned? Who is Alex and how does she figure into all of this? What's with that key in your hand?"

"Enough, already!" Marie said sharply, hoping to silence the onslaught of questions. "Give me a minute and I'll tell you as much as I know, or rather as little as I know, but the key is of no importance other than sentimental value. Forget the key; I thought I'd lost it, that's all."

Realizing her response sounded totally lame, and had, if anything, only served to focus his attention more closely on the damned key, she tried to get his mind onto other things. "You have to believe me, Paul, I don't really know who these men are, but there are at least ten of them, probably more. They killed my best friend, Alex, shot her in the head for simply being in the way. They also killed her father, Ty Summers, who was the sheriff of Truman. Staged a fake car accident and tried to make it look like he'd been drinking. They also killed Will Cameron, the coroner; made that look like a heart attack." She caught her breath. "Oh, yeah, and four college kids from BYU. Another car accident. God knows how many others. And now," she added with a dramatic pause, "they will be coming for us. That's why we must get away from the river. We must get to the cabin where we can think and plan."

While there was no way for Marie to be certain the Colonel and his men would even have the means of tracking down her rescuer, the consequences of not assuming they could, and would, were too disastrous to consider. Better for now to have Paul believe he was up to his neck in her problems. *Better for me*, anyway, she thought.

Though not a hero, but certainly no coward, Paul immediately didn't like the sound of the word "us" in her conspiracy scenario. "You mean 'you' right? They will be coming for you."

Marie shook her head slowly. "Not anymore, I'm afraid. It's now *us*."

As Paul was about to express his great displeasure with the way things were going, Marie said, "Do you have a gun in the car or back at the cabin?"

With the situation spiraling from bad to worse in a hurry, Paul could only utter, "A gun? Uh, no. I don't believe in guns."

"You don't believe in guns?" she said incredulously. "They're not Bigfoot or the Easter Bunny, Paul. They exist, they're real, and when the bad guys have lots of them and you don't have even one, you're totally screwed."

Even if he'd had a gun, this wide-eyed "seer of boogiemen" would be the last person on earth he'd have given it to. In an effort to keep her focused, Paul said, "Do you at least have any idea *why* these men, whoever they are, would want to hurt you and all the others?"

Turning to face the road again, she lied, "No, I have no idea and I'm through answering questions." Marie knew she could not reveal the importance of the key, even though she didn't understand its importance herself.

No way. Never. The key was all she had; the only means of defeating these bastards. Lose that tiny edge, no matter how small it might be, and all would be lost.

She glared again at the speedometer and locked her teeth together. She was tired of questions and she was tired of crawling along this dirt road. "I swear to God, Paul, if you don't press down on that gas pedal, I'm going to throw you from this car and leave you for the bad guys."

When he looked to see if she were kidding or not, the blood in her eyes immediately doubled their speed.

*　*　*

When they finally reached the borrowed cabin, a truly rustic, massive-log design from the outside, with wide porch overhangs and a tin roof, Marie was pleasantly surprised to find its interior fully stocked with all the modern amenities. There were smooth stone floors and granite countertops, stainless steel appliances and even a washer and dryer in a nook between the pantry and the back deck.

"That's what I'm talking about," she said, yanking open the door to the Maytag washer. Inside of a minute, she'd sorted their various river-soaked clothing and had the first load going. Surprisingly, she found an unused bottle of Woolite in the cabinet over the washer and pulled it down, taking it into the bathroom with her to clean her lingerie in the sink. She preferred not to wash her rather expensive bra and panties with her jeans and socks and his cotton Dockers and pullover.

When she caught her reflection in the large mirror that hung in the dining area, the image that returned was even worse than she'd imagined possible, and that mental image had been bad enough to consider changing her address to The Black Lagoon. Golden hair that had never looked so bad even during a two-week river tour lay matted and flat against her head, like spring wheat killed by a summer storm. Her face was swollen, its skin hyper-hydrated from having marinated in the Duchesne River for half an hour, looking horridly like a drowning victim. And last but not least, her eyes were as bloodshot as those of someone who'd recently died by strangulation. The petechial hemorrhaging in both scleras was far more pronounced than on the morning after the worst drunk she'd ever been on in her life, and that was saying something.

"Wow, girl, you look like shit warmed over," she said aloud with a chuckle, and headed off to the bathroom with her Victoria's Secret in hand. After closing the drain and pouring a capful of Woolite into the basin, she added cold water and then scrubbed her lingerie until it was as clean as it would get.

Then, breaking a solemn vow she'd made the first time she'd paid sixty bucks for a bra or twenty bucks for a single pair of panties—to never dry such expensive underwear anywhere but on a line—Marie crossed the hearth room again and tossed them into the Maytag dryer, setting the controls to air fluff, no heat.

"You hungry?" Paul asked as she darted across the room again. The laundry was on the opposite side of the cabin from the bedrooms. *Whose dumb idea was that*, she wondered. He was rummaging around in the kitchen of the eight-hundred-square-foot cabin looking for something to fix. It was located just to the left of the front door as you entered, and along with the large hearth room, dining area, and laundry nook, comprised the north end of the cabin. To the right as you entered, the south end of the cabin, were two pleasantly large bedrooms, each with an attached bath, and each with a door that led onto the huge side porch. One bedroom was known as the "tub room" because of the claw-foot tub in its bathroom, while the other had been dubbed the "shower room" for similar reasons.

Marie hated taking baths, the thought of sitting in the same dirty water and pretending you were somehow getting clean never made any sense to her. Of course, she loved soaking in a hot tub until she wrinkled like a prune, generally with a bottle of wine and an interesting man close by, but the last time she'd done that was—she tried to remember—*at least three years*, she thought in a moment of melancholy. "Going to scrub this nasty hair of mine before I can even think about eating," she said, and disappeared back into the "shower room."

By the time Marie had finished in the bathroom, including adding a half bottle of the Visine she'd found in the medicine cabinet to her eyes, her lingerie had dried. She grabbed the garments and transferred the clothes from the washer to the dryer. They'd be ready in about forty minutes.

Wearing just her bra and panties with a towel wrapped around her waist, Marie joined Paul in the kitchen. When he appeared a bit surprised at her state of undress, she said, "Relax. I wear less than this for weeks at a time around twenty strangers. It's part of my job. Think of it as a bathing suit top."

"Okay, sure," he said, fumbling with the lid on a jar of pickles. "A bathing suit it is." Of course, the fact that you could clearly see both nipples through the thin spandex, areola and all, didn't help bolster the illusion.

Marie pretended to pay no attention to his obviously-flustered state, just as he tried to keep it hidden from her.

"By the way, you look great," he said, then realized she probably thought he meant half naked. He wagged an extended index finger, tracing the shape of her head, "You're face, I mean. You look really pretty."

Marie grinned at his predicament. "Just my face?" she taunted. He was now in a no-win situation. Why not have some fun with it?

"No, you look great all over." His face reddened. "I just meant—"

She held up a hand. "It's okay. I'm just messing with you."

"Oh, that's good. I'm not usually this awkward around women. You seem to have that effect on me."

Marie grew serious. "You said you were a doctor, right?"

He nodded, setting the pickles down on the countertop.

"Great, how about patching up my shoulder?" She set the small first aid kit she's found in the "tub room" beside the pickles.

"I'm not that kind of doctor," he corrected, not wishing to give her the false impression that he was qualified to provide medical care.

"Well, since you're not going to be doing open heart surgery, there's really nothing for either of us to worry about. I'd do it myself, but it's kinda hard to reach the back hole, and wrapping it with one hand is a bitch. Just pour some of this hydrogen peroxide into both wounds, dab on a generous helping of the Neosporin here, and then wrap it all up nice and tight." She set the necessary items beside the kit and closed the lid.

"I can do that," he said reassuringly.

"Atta' boy," she said patting him on the shoulder. "You're having quite a superhero kind of day, aren't you?" She turned to the wall cabinets and opened one after another, finally asking, "Jesus, Paul, what kind of vacation is this? Don't you have *anything* to drink around this place?"

TWENTY-EIGHT

AS MARIE DID HER BEST to relax by the huge stone fireplace, making quick work of a second glass of the best port wine she'd ever tasted, Paul finished wrapping her wounded shoulder. They were both seated on the floor near the hearth, facing each other as he worked, the 1985 bottle of Dow's vintage port between them already half gone. Paul had built a fire with logs he'd gathered earlier in the week, and the place had become toasty warm in no time. The sweet smell of burning pine and the crackle-pop of the embers almost made her forget the hell that presently defined her life.

Paul had been gentle, even tender as he'd treated and bandaged her injury, but it had still hurt like hell, as if one of the glowing embers had gotten trapped under the tape as he worked. When he finally said, "All through," she let out a small sigh of relief and relaxed muscles that had been tensioned like springs for more than twenty minutes. She was so thankful that she was in such good physical condition. Three years of rowing a six-hundred pound boat and eleven hundred pounds of guests and gear for weeks on end had put her body in the best shape of her life. Even in the off season, rarely a day went by without her getting in four or five miles of hard jogging before sunup plus half an hour of free weights before bed. If not for this intense physical regimen, the fall from Eagle's Ridge would have killed her as surely as it had killed the bastard with her. Hoping to survive a suicidal plunge from a mountain had not been the initial driving motive for all her exercise, but it had turned out to be a really nice fringe benefit, she decided.

Still, whether in great shape or not, she hurt everywhere, and not just a nagging little hurt. This was real pain and she knew it would only be worse tomorrow, as battered muscles stiffened and damaged nerves inflamed. She had taken her four Advil, and they were helping, but she still ached all over. Nothing stronger could be found in the cabin.

"You okay?" he asked, putting down the adhesive tape and picking up his glass of port. He'd watched her face as he worked, trying hard to keep his eyes off her incredible breasts, and could see that she was still deeply troubled. She didn't have the kind of face that hid her feelings well.

"I miss her, Paul," she said, her voice quivering.

"Alex?"

"Yeah," she nodded, looking away. "She didn't deserve to die. I told her I'd protect her and I didn't. I let them kill her, just like—" She cut herself off and drained the rest of her glass. She held it out and he filled it again.

"It's not your fault," he assured her, though he knew at once it had been an anemic thing to say. It would change nothing in her mind or heart: she did feel responsible, and four words weren't going to alter that fact.

Marie sensed that Paul was about to enter his clinical psychologist mode again, rather than remain the really nice man who had been, for forty blissful minutes, just a man caring for her. She hadn't been with a man for more than three years, not since she'd earned the first bullet wound in her left arm. She fought back tears and forced the preaching little inner voice in her head to shut the hell up.

When the dryer buzzed, saving the day, she announced, "Clothes are dry," and rose swiftly to her feet. Her head became immediately light and she grabbed the mantel for support. Too much alcohol to drink was also something she hadn't done in more than three years.

He rose with her, taking her in his arms for support when he saw her become unstable. Rather than resist, she allowed him to hold her for a long moment. He felt strong and safe, and those were two very admirable traits in a man right now. When her mind cleared a bit, she said, "Not a great idea," and broke free from his arms, moving quickly to the dryer.

Paul knew when to press and when to retreat. Now was not the time to advance. "Ready to eat something?" he asked.

Marie pulled her jeans from the oven-warm bin and held them to her face. She loved the smell of clothes fresh from a dryer. "Sure, that would be great, Paul. Not too much, I'm kinda tired. I really need to sleep more than I need to eat."

"But you still need to eat," he insisted. "Just a grilled ham and Swiss on rye with a big old slice of dill pickle. You'll feel like a new woman."

"Promise?" she said, standing there with a tired, but also very sad look on her face. Before he could answer, she took her clothes and disappeared into the bedroom.

*   *   *

As they ate in relative silence, Marie's mind raced in a hundred frightening directions, spoiling what may have otherwise been the best ham and cheese she'd ever eaten. Paul sat at the granite bar, an overhang from the large kitchen peninsula that divided that room from the larger hearth room, and she sat again before the fire, allowing its warmth to ease the icy shiver she had felt since arriving. She knew the inner cold had nothing to do with the room's temperature, and that no fire could completely thaw the fear-induced chill, but at least it seemed to help.

"Perhaps it's about time we called the authorities, Marie," he said, biting his pickle slice in half. He had turned on his stool to face her. "We need to tell them about Alex and the man in the river. We need to tell them what the men tried to do to you. We need their help, don't you think?"

He knew without a doubt that the woman before the crackling fire would not act on his suggestion. The psychologist in him had decided, based upon all he'd heard and gathered since meeting Marie, that there were no bad guys following her—except in her mind. In all likelihood, Alex was either her best friend, or the "other woman," maybe both. The man in the river, he'd concluded, was either her husband or lover, or Alex's husband, in which case, Marie was the other woman. The problem played out well in his orderly mind either way it went; this whole tragedy was a love triangle gone awry.

The two main questions to be answered were: was Alex actually dead, and if so, at whose hand? And, who was the man in the water and who was responsible for *his* death? Perhaps Alex and the man had somehow been responsible for each other's deaths and Marie had only been a helpless witness, now suffering the psychological scars that such impotency of action often causes. Perhaps she'd attempted suicide afterward, explaining her being in the river. Maybe this had been a "lover's leap" ménage à trois and only Marie had survived, thanks to him, and was now doomed to face a lifetime of guilt and shame as a result.

If the latter, he owed her more than she could ever owe him for saving her life, because while he may have saved her physical form, he may have simultaneously condemned her spirit to suffer a slow and painful death.

That problem troubled him deeply.

He took a sip of the Diet Coke he'd fixed for them, figuring she'd had enough alcohol for one evening, and pondered a solution.

Marie looked up from her half-eaten sandwich. "Not now, Paul. I'm too tired to talk to anyone about any of this right now. Maybe in the morning." Of course, she had no intention of calling anyone in the morning, or even being at the cabin when the subject arose again—which it would. She had decided that while he showered, she would steal the keys to his car, pull the phone line from the wall, and buy herself a few hours of lead time before the cops could be alerted to the vehicle's theft. By then, she'd have reached one of her "safe spots," prearranged three years ago in the event something like this ever happened to her again.

The safe spots, as she thought of them, had been a paranoid defense, born out of primal fear and the desire to survive another round with the bad guys at all costs when it came. A part of her, the larger part, had never expected to need these resources, trying for years now to convince the smaller, deeply distrustful part, that her past was behind her and it would remain just that—the past. The bad guys she'd feared for so long were no longer interested in her.

The problem now was that the people she had been running and hiding from for thirty-six months had nothing whatsoever to do with Colonel Mustard and the Clue gang. These thugs had no idea who she was; all they wanted was the "item." They were, to her horrified amazement, a whole new batch of bad guys in her life. The absolute insanity of it all had the food on her stomach souring as soon as she swallowed.

She pushed the plate and half sandwich aside, pulling the sleeping bag tightly around her shoulders. Paul's sweatshirt, as warm as it was, didn't keep the chill away.

"We have to tell them about all of this, don't you think?" Paul pressed gently. He was trying to get her to stay connected with the events of the day without shutting down emotionally. He sat patiently on the stool, finishing the last of his sandwich.

Marie looked hard and thoughtfully up at him, as if deciding how to answer. Finally she said, "It was the icy water. That's why it was possible." It was as if a light had come on in the attic of her mind.

Accustomed to rapid changes of direction in their conversation, Paul was nonetheless unable to connect these dots. "Sorry," he said. "The icy water?"

"Exactly. I work as a whitewater guide. We've all heard lots of stories—we thought they were all urban legends—of people drowning in the cold waters in the mountains, or during winter months, and being revived even after an hour. The cold water apparently causes their bodies and brains to go into a kind of suspended state, neither alive nor dead, and the reduced need for oxygen keeps them from suffering permanent trauma." She took a sip of her Coke. "That's why you were able to bring me back. That's also why I'm not presently a hundred-twenty-five pound carrot."

"Carrot?" he said, his furrowed brow showing his puzzlement.

"Yeah, a vegetable, you know. Brain damaged."

"Oh, sure, a carrot. Got it."

"Thanks for that, by the way. Never cared much for carrots. I'm more of a green vegetable kind of girl," she said with a twisted smile. She may have been making light of the day's terror, but her fear still showed in the consistent tremor of her slender form beneath the covers.

In the soft glow of the fire, outlining one of the best faces he could remember seeing, he was glad he didn't yet have to tell her that she may not have entirely escaped that which she feared most. From what he could tell, while she may still be able to carry on a conversation and dress herself, she was not at all of sound mind.

For now, she appeared in no immediate danger, either physically or mentally, and that was enough. He'd get her to a hospital tomorrow, no matter how much she argued or fought back. It would be for her own good.

"Would you get me a pillow from the bedroom," Marie asked, her voice weary and as soft as an old woman's.

"You need to be in bed. Let me help you," he said, rising from the bar and coming to her.

"No, I want to sleep by the fire. I sleep by the fire all the time. It makes me feel safe. Would you just get me a pillow, please?"

He touched her cheek softly then left, returning shortly with a pair of the thick down pillows from the "shower room."

"One's fine," she said, taking the pillow and scrunching it up beneath her head. She was resting on her right side, her damaged left arm elevated.

"The other one is mine." She gave him a puzzled look. "Someone has to watch over you while you sleep." The warm smile seemed genuine enough and she returned it.

Before he had made a spot on the couch, she was sound asleep.

He looked at the phone on the wall by the refrigerator and tried to decide how long he should wait to make the call.

TWENTY-NINE

JAMES MERKETT AND HIS two teams of veteran soldiers were having no luck finding either the body of their man, who'd most recently gone by the absurd name of Witherspoon, or that of Marie Matthews. It was tedious and frustrating work, with patience and even tempers at a premium after six fruitless hours.

At 2:10 a.m. Monday morning, he pulled his cell phone from his pocket and called First Lieutenant Tom Pickard, the head of Echo Team. They had been sent into town the evening before to monitor any emergency facility where a drowning victim, alive or dead, might be taken.

"Sir," Pickard answered smartly.

"Status."

"Negative, sir."

"All of your team in constant contact with you?"

"On the top and six, sir," he said, indicating that he'd gotten calls from his team every thirty minutes, on the hour and half hour. "I repeat, negative."

"Thank you, Tom," Merkett said not wishing to use his rank on the phone. He closed the phone. He and Pickard were friends, had been for six years, and he trusted him with his life, as he did all of these men. If Tom said the woman had not turned up, then she was still out here.

He decided to split his remaining men into two teams again, instructing Delta to continue downriver for at least another five miles before breaking for the rendezvous point. He would take Charlie and go upriver to a spot a mile or more north of their original starting point. By then, it would be light anyway and their presence along the river would be much more difficult to conceal and nearly impossible to explain.

He cursed under his breath as Charlie Team followed him toward the road where the SUVs had been shadowing their progress along the bank. This was not going easy or well, but then, the whole plan had gotten a kink in it from the outset, hadn't it. He cursed Goodman as well, just for good measure.

"My calculations don't support either of the bodies being that close to the initial point of entry," Donald Shelton said, referring to the LED screen of his iPhone as he walked. "The speed of the current, along with—"

"Lieutenant!" Merkett barked. "Enough. We're going back to the point we started and then we're moving upriver from there. Hell, we can't do any worse than we've already done, right."

Shelton studied the small screen and looked unsure. "I suppose not, sir. I just don't understand what could have gone wrong with my figures."

"They're figures, Lieutenant, not real life. They're perfect and life is sticky and messy and unpredictable. Sometimes, numbers just don't work. Remember that."

"Yes, sir," Shelton said, pocketing his phone.

When they reached the two Suburbans, Merkett quickly told the drivers how the plans had changed. The driver of the lead vehicle nodded his understanding and continued to shadow Delta Team, while the trailing vehicle immediately made a U-turn in the dirt road, as tight as it was, and gathered Charlie Team for the ride north.

Half an hour later, using GPS to precisely guide their movements, the driver suddenly stopped at a point along the narrow back road. "Where we began, sir," he said, pointing in the direction of the river.

Merkett and the others bailed out and trekked double-time to the water's edge, a distance of less than a hundred yards. At some places along the Duchesne, the access road, if one existed, was within mere yards of the river, while at other times, a walk of more than a mile was required to reach water.

At once, they began the journey upriver, their powerful tactical flashlights scanning the edge and surface of the water for any sign of a body, no matter how insignificant. If they didn't find the corpses, someone else would, and that presented a whole other set of problems that he didn't want to consider at present. He'd already given the General bad intel, and though based on the best evidence at that moment, made him look like an incompetent fool. He didn't like being seen as an incompetent fool, and God help those responsible.

The terrain below their boots alternated between soft, wet sand, nearly rock-hard gravel, and gigantic boulders that took all their skill to climb over or work around. It was slow going, as it had been since shortly before twenty-one-hundred hours—nine p.m.

"Got something, sir," Kevin Branch announced, fifty feet ahead of the group. With the exception of his immediate superior, Sergeant Major Ron Phelps, Staff Sergeant Branch was the only enlisted man on Charlie Team. However, he was the best 'tracker' in the group. His skills had been put to good and frequent use in Iraq and Afghanistan, where he'd gained not only the interest of Colonel Merkett, but also his respect and trust.

Several of the team stood staring down at the white circle in the sand created by Branch's tactical LED flashlight. "What do you see?" Merkett asked, joining them.

"Matched set of footprints, sir. Extra-large. Waders would be my guess. Makes an average man appear to have a foot the size of Shaquille O'Neal," he explained.

272

"So what?" Shelton said. "You'd expect to see this all up and down the river."

"Sir, with all due respect, these are the first we've seen all night. The rains were really heavy last week and the river was up maybe two or three feet higher than now. Only went down in the last day or two. That means these were made Saturday or yesterday at the earliest. I'd say yesterday."

"Go ahead, Sergeant," Merkett said, studying the footprints.

"If you look carefully, sir, you'll see that the depressions heading into the water are shallow, but these here," he pointed his flashlight to his left, revealing identically-shaped prints that were far deeper in the sand, "the ones coming from the water, they indicate the man was carrying something really heavy, maybe half his weight or more."

"Could be our boy," Shelton said, referring to Witherspoon.

"Sir, I don't think so," Branch interjected.

"Why not, Sergeant," Merkett asked.

"Just like us, a man would have pulled another man out of the water by his arms or feet, but he'd have carried a woman's body out. Especially a looker like the Matthews woman. The deeper tracks say he had Matthews over his shoulder when he came out of the water."

"Good work, Staff Sergeant," Phelps said, patting him on the back.

Not finished yet, Branch said, "There's more, sir."

"Go ahead," Merkett said, intrigued.

He waved his flashlight around the area just up the bank from the initial footprints. "Someone has gone to considerable effort to eradicate the rest of the prints, all indication that they were even here. Probably used a limb pulled from a tree nearby, then tossed it into the river. Not a bad job, but not a great one, either." With nothing else to report at the water's edge, Branch moved up the hill toward the road, continuing to follow the tracks of the previous guests.

"Why would anyone do something like that," Shelton said. "What's to be gained?"

Merkett shook his head in controlled anger, as if denying what he knew to be true. "Time. It means the bitch is still alive, calling the shots, trying desperately to buy a little lead time on us. It's the only plausible explanation."

Just then, his phone rang: it was Delta Team. "Go ahead."

"Got one of the lost packages, sir," Nate Fisher reported, the relief evident in his tired voice. "It's the blue package. Still have no idea where the pink one is." The colors referred to those most often associated with newborn boys and girls. It meant they'd found Witherspoon's body.

"Good work, Nate. We've got information on the pink package. Join us at once half a mile north of the initial search point. You'll see the car."

Fisher said he'd be there in half an hour, maybe a little more, and ended the call.

"Colonel," Branch shouted from the road. He was standing in the glow of the headlights of their SUV. "Got something else."

Merkett and Shelton sprinted up the small grade to the Suburban and the rest of Charlie Team. Before he could speak, Branch pointed his flashlight at some clearly defined tire tracks twenty feet or so on the water's side of the dirt road. "Most likely the vehicle our Boy Scout used to drive the woman away," he said.

Merkett nodded in agreement.

Shelton immediately grabbed his digital camera and a tape measure from his equipment case in the back of the Suburban. "Sergeant, take this tape and precisely measure the tire width, wheelbase, and vehicle track." He handed the tape to Branch who immediately did as he was instructed. Then he snapped several close-up shots of the tire tread pattern. "I'll have the make and model for you in an hour, Colonel. After that, finding the owner will be a breeze."

Merkett nodded his approval, pulling his phone from his pocket. "We're done in town," he said to the leader of Echo Team.

"Get all your men back to the rendezvous point at once. We've got a live one on the run and not a lot of time before we get real cold and way behind."

*   *   *

The brightly painted Mardi Gras mask seemed to call to Marie from across the darkened room. Without conscious thought or decision, she glided toward it with the effortless grace of someone not bound to this earth by the laws of physics.

Within an otherwise midnight-black room, whose size she could not begin to guess, it appeared to be glowing, but try as she may, it was impossible to determine the font of the celestial illumination. Rather than having been under a spotlight, she soon came to understand that the mask was actually lit from within, as if it were its own source of power and energy.

"You're so beautiful," she said aloud, drawing ever closer.

When the mask was less than an arm's length from her, Marie reached for it, knowing instinctively that to touch it would be to gain some of its beauty and strength. As her fingers neared its smooth, porcelain surface, the mask began to move away from her, simultaneously rising to a point where its hollow eyes and empty smile were directly in line with those features in her own face. Again she reached for it, but could not make contact, the distance only inches and yet also infinite.

"Why can't I touch you?" she asked in a reverent whisper. As soon as she'd spoken the words, the bright colors of the mask began to swirl and coalesce, like a child's sidewalk drawing in a summer shower. "Don't go," she pleaded, and when the swirling ceased, the mask had become the face of Alexia Summers, its eyes still vacant, its mouth open wide and empty. The enigmatic smile seemed to be mocking her and Marie wanted to turn away, but instead, she reached out again, hoping to touch it at last.

When fingertips met cheek, the pain that exploded from her hand was like touching the glowing red eye of a stove, melting her fingers into the porcelain visage, her entire hand soon becoming one with the object. "Please don't," Marie beseeched, but the mask continued to consume more and more of her arm, having melted it up to the elbow by now. When she tried with all her might to pull away, a mocking laughter erupted from the empty mouth, growing in pitch and volume until she was sure her eardrums would burst. "Oh, God, please don't, Alex," she begged, but the satanic image only increased its torment in answer to her plea.

Suddenly, flames as intense as those from hell's own furnace shot from the empty sockets of both eyes, engulfing Marie's head in white-hot flames. She screamed as she'd never screamed in her life, thrashing at the conflagration with her free hand, begging for Alex to release her.

"It's okay, Marie," Paul said, pulling her flailing arms to her side and then wrapping his own tightly around her. "It was a nightmare, nothing more." Within his firm grip, she still struggled with the demons of the night while pleading for Alex to let her go. At last, as he pulled her ever tighter to him, rubbing her back and stroking her hair as she buried her face in his neck, she awoke. "It's okay, Marie, you're safe. It was a nightmare, nothing more. You're here, with me, and you're safe. Do you understand me, Marie?"

She nodded just enough for him to realize that she'd responded, but began to weep like a child. The shivering returned, more intensely than ever. She allowed him to continue to hold her as she wept, needing the solace of his embrace, the security of his arms.

As Paul brushed her hair and gently rubbed her back, he looked again at the phone. He could not put off making the call any longer. He would do it the moment he could get her to sleep.

He prayed that it wasn't already too late for her to make the long journey back to sanity.

THIRTY

THE BLACK SUBURBAN SAT on the dusty back road in tomblike silence, not far from the campsite where Charlie Team had found the tantalizing tire tracks, four of its five occupants sleeping as soundly as babies in their mother's arms. Only Donald Shelton, the middle of three passengers in the back seat, remained awake, attacking the technological problem that faced him with the same focus and ferocity with which his associates had battled the Taliban, Al-Qaeda and Isis.

When the pieces of the ether-based puzzle finally fell into place, he shouted, "HELL YES! GOT YOU!" at the top of his excited lungs, banging his fists down hard on his thighs and bringing four heavily-armed and highly-volatile killers to a state of siege awareness in the same tick of the clock. A pair of Beretta 9MM automatics were, in a second tick of that clock, thrust into opposite sides of his neck beneath his jaw, itchy fingers massaging hair triggers.

"Sorry, guys," he said meekly but otherwise not moving a muscle. "Guess you were sleeping, huh." The two men on opposite sides of him lowered their weapons and began to swear angrily.

"For Christ's sake, Shelton," Merkett grumbled from the front seat, waving his own pistol animatedly in the squint's fact, "this better be good. I swear, if you just won the damned Internet lottery, I'm going to shoot you between the eyes myself."

He may have been kidding.

"I didn't," Shelton said, eyes fixed on the muzzle of the Beretta, "but we did, sir." Though this recent discovery may have been heralded with a bit more fanfare than prudent, considering the present state of agitation among Charlie Team, he couldn't have been more proud if he'd just made a thousand-yard kill shot, which, of course, he had no skill for whatsoever. He used the Internet to "kill," and no one was better.

Merkett lowered his pistol and gave him a "go ahead" scowl.

Shelton inhaled deeply and began: "The tracks belong to a Range Rover Sport Limited Edition. Brand new. Only two-hundred-fifty of them were built for this model year, if you can believe that shit. It's Lucerne Green with Alpaca leather interior—not really from an alpaca, I'm pretty sure—and chrome alloy wheels." The balance of his initial breath was exhaled dramatically.

Make and model from tire size and vehicle track was possible, they all knew that much, but when the squint provided the Range Rover's interior and exterior colors, all of Charlie Team turned their eyes to the smallest member of their elite group. Donald Shelton could feel the respect in their rapt attention. "Finding the particular asshole who owns *our* Range Rover Sport Limited Edition was a short shot on a windless day," he said, adding a little Unit-speak to his report.

"Good work, Don," Merkett smiled. "What can you tell us about this this asshole, as you so aptly put it?"

Referring again to his laptop screen, Shelton continued to read from the notes he'd compiled. "Dr. Paul Anthony Burks. Not a real doctor, one of those pricks whose always trying to fix lousy marriages and screwed up kids. Lives and works in Sausalito, California. Divorced. Black hair but beginning to gray according to his

DMV photo. Blue eyes. Played football at Golden State. Turned forty-four last month. Born in San Francisco. No kids. Has a ton of money in the bank. Correct that," Shelton grinned wickedly, "*had* a ton of money in the bank. It's all being moved to the Unit's Cayman Islands account as we speak. Even if we don't kill him, he'll be too broke to buy his clothes at Goodwill." He knew of course that the good doctor was most certainly going to die. And soon.

Merkett smirked. Shelton just loved electronically 'appropriating' the funds of those who'd gotten in his way or had pissed him off, and then erasing all evidence of the transaction. He called it his specialty. He was probably a millionaire in his own right, all from appropriated funds, Merkett often considered, but as long as he didn't mess with the money that should rightfully go to the Unit—like the doctor's money—or bring undo attention to the Unit, he couldn't have cared less. "That all?" he asked, sensing that the coup de grâce, or killing blow, had been saved for last. It was simply Shelton's style.

"He's an avid outdoorsman. Applied for a fourteen-day trout fishing license a week ago in Truman. Gave the required local address as a residence not far from here, twenty minutes upriver." The computer geek rotated the laptop so the Colonel could see the full-screen photo of the structure in question taken from space and pulled from Google Earth. "See, it's some sort of cabin or small lodge. Totally isolated, a mile from anyone else. Hell, we could drop a Tomahawk on it and not one neighbor would lose a wink of sleep." He was not referring to the hatchet-like weapon often associated with Native American culture, but the military's premier satellite-guided strike missile. "I have the exact coordinates already downloaded so we should be able to drive right up to the front door."

Merkett stretched in the front seat, extending his legs fully into the foot well and raising his arms until they touched the headliner above the back seat. Several bones cracked loudly. He was getting too old for all this cloak and dagger crap, he thought. "Lock and load, boys," he said, indicating for the driver to head out at once in the direction Shelton had indicated. "It's time to pay Marie Matthews and the late Dr. Burks a little visit."

* * *

The five members of Charlie Team moved along the dusty scar of a road as quietly as vipers, acutely aware that only perfect silence would allow them to remain undetected. The moon, nearly full and directly overhead, coupled with the added illumination of more stars than you could count in a lifetime, had draped each of the black-clad warriors in an eerie cloak of gray-blue light. On a flat plain, they could have been seen for a mile with the naked eye, and that fact had fingers anxiously caressing the triggers of automatic weapons whose barrels remained fixed on the windows and doors of the small building directly ahead of them.

If there was any good news, it was that the road disappeared down a small grade just south of the cabin, and they had been in full view for only the last few seconds. Still, that was bad enough for men who'd spent their lives exploiting such blunders made by their country's enemies. They were under a "killing moon" and each knew it only too well. For even a novice shooter inside the cabin, they were sitting ducks.

Using the precise GPS coordinates that Donald Shelton had provided, they had stopped their Suburban well short of the cabin, electing to cover the remaining quarter mile on foot. Colonel Merkett had decided not to wait for Delta and Echo Teams to join them, believing the collective firepower of his immediate assets to be more than adequate to the task at hand.

With less than a full complement of troops, however—making rear and flanking cover impossible—stealth rather than overwhelming force was now the best means of ensuring a successful kill.

As they approached the south face of the cabin, less than fifty feet distant, Merkett held up a fisted hand, indicating for everyone to halt. All did so without a sound.

He studied the scene and made an immediate assessment, then using hand gestures only, deployed one if his men to the rear of the structure where he assumed at least one door led onto the wraparound deck that was visible on both the west and south faces. Two other men he directed to cover a pair of doors that led from rooms—probably bedrooms—on the south or facing end of the structure. If the couple were sleeping, and the complete absence of light issuing from cabin windows suggested that to be the case, then these were likely to be the rooms, or room, in which they would be found.

Motioning for Shelton to accompany him to the front door, he gave the 'go' signal and each man moved to his assigned assault point. All had previously been given explicit instructions to shoot anyone who offered the least resistance, without a word of warning and without hesitation. All would comply perfectly.

One thing that bothered Merkett as he approached the front door was the absence of the Range Rover, but with a small garage on the north end of the cabin, he decided that the vehicle was most likely behind its closed door. Perhaps the rich prick wanted to keep the dew off his new paint, he considered, with a sudden and intense desire to kick the prick's ass into the next zip code.

Peering in carefully through the front door, which was comprised of solid wood from the midpoint down, but contained nine panes of clear glass—three by three—above that, Merkett could just make out the form of a body in a sleeping bag by the fire, though he couldn't tell if it belonged to the man or the woman. Most likely the woman, he reasoned, with the doctor probably preferring a nice warm bed. However, there was a long couch between the kitchen and the fireplace, and if a person were asleep on it, they would be hidden from view. He studied the fire: a fresh log had recently been added, perhaps less than fifteen minutes ago based on its lack of consumption thus far. That meant at least one of them had recently been fully awake, and may still be. He touched a small transmitter on his belt and a tiny red LED illuminated for a split second on the similar device worn by each member of Charlie Team.

At once, all four doors were simultaneously breached with such ferocity that huge splinters of wood from fractured jambs flew through the air and struck interior walls like frightened birds. The collective shout to GET DOWN! GET DOWN! GET DOWN! was ear-splitting, and the prearranged single burst of automatic gunfire from Merkett's SOPMOD M4 assault rifle, directed at the ceiling nearest his point of entry, punctuated the moment in a way no words could possibly have matched.

Then, as quickly as the bedlam had begun, the cabin fell deathly silent, though gun barrels and laser pointers continued to sweep each room with chaotic frenzy. Even this searching ceased after a few seconds when it became obvious to everyone that the only people presently in this structure were the members of Charlie Team.

Merkett stepped deliberately to the sleeping bag and gave it a quick kick with his boot, exposing a thick down pillow beneath its folds. "SON OF A BITCH!" he shouted.

No Dr. Burks.

No Marie Matthews.

No damned Range Rover Sport Limited Edition in Lucerne Green with Alpaca interior.

And no video for certain.

"Lieutenant!" he barked, turning his angry, nearly black eyes, toward Donald Shelton. "I want you to put a full description of the doctor's car on the Internet, but provide no names and don't give the license number. Use one of those bullshit websites you created for this kind of crap. Offer a $10,000 cash no-questions-asked reward for information leading to its recovery. Say it's part of a divorce settlement property dispute that the worthless husband and his new blonde girlfriend have run off with despite having been awarded to the man's poor wife. Get the word out that the vehicle is most likely in Utah at present, so concentrate all searches there until further notice. Make damn sure everyone understands that no one is to interfere with the couple in any way, you understand me, no John Wayne bullshit or there won't be a penny in it for them. They're only to report the vehicle if spotted providing a license plate number. You'll use that for confirmation. Add any other clever twist you think will get the public—but not the cops—looking on our behalf."

"I'm on it, sir," Shelton said, turning toward the front door.

"Get back here, I'm not through with you yet," Merkett snapped, stopping Shelton in his tracks. "I also want to know who the hell Marie Matthews is, because she sure as shit isn't some two-bit doctor's lab assistant or part-time river guide. If she calls a kid she met in kindergarten, if she tries to borrow a dime from a third cousin twice removed on her step-uncle's side of the family, I want to know it before it happens. I want you to do what you do so well and put this bitch in a living hell with no place to turn until I can get my fingers around her scrawny little neck. Now go."

When Shelton had left the cabin, Merkett called the rest of his men to him. "Search the place thoroughly, though I don't expect we'll find a damned thing. We may get lucky and get some idea where they're headed, but I doubt that, too. If the bitch still has the video, and I'll bet a full pay grade she does, then she'll have it with her. When you're done, burn the place. The owner will not be returning to voice a complaint."

"Think she's a pro, Jim?" Mack Fuhrman asked as the others began to ransack the interior. The First Lieutenant was one of the Unit's two chopper pilots and a close friend of Merkett. Like the Colonel, he now understood that Marie Matthews was more than just a damn lucky and stubbornly resilient woman.

"Not the way you're thinking, Mack. She'd have called 'home' the moment she saw the video, and right now we'd have a shitstorm of feds after us that would make the hunt for Eric Rudolph look like an Easter egg hunt."

Eric Rudolph was the man responsible for the 1996 bombing at Olympic Park in Atlanta, and the subsequent and equally fatal bombing of an abortion clinic in North Carolina. The manhunt for him had been the largest of its kind ever conducted in the U.S.

The image knotted Merkett's stomach.

"Then she hasn't seen it yet. I say she has no idea what she's even got. There was little time at the clinic to download the video file, if any, and she hasn't exactly had a computer at her disposal in the meantime." Fuhrman waved his weapon around the room like a pointer, indicating no PC anywhere in the cabin.

Since Marie Matthews had been nearly naked in the clearing at Eagle's Ridge, they'd reached a consensus in subsequent conversations that they were no longer looking for a relatively huge cell phone—which could not possibly have been concealed within tight jeans and a skimpy bra—but were instead in search of a diminutive memory card, perhaps half the size of a dime. That, she could have hidden on her person, they reasoned, probably in her bra by the way she reacted at once when it was about to be removed.

Who was this very irritating woman? Merkett wondered. "I agree that she probably doesn't know what she's got, but given any time at all, she will, and when she does, it's all over. We cannot let that happen, Mack, even if we have to go totally overt."

Fuhrman knew that Merkett meant tossing aside the cloak of secrecy and conducting the hunt for Matthews aggressively and with prejudice. Once she realized what was on the video, she would race to the nearest TV station or highway patrol headquarters and life would be over for General Clayton Longmont, and the Unit he had so carefully and painstakingly assembled.

"It's not going to come to that, Jim. I give you my word that every man in this outfit is willing to lay down his life for this cause, and there's no way on earth a lone woman and a divorce doctor can survive against that kind of dedication and firepower." Fuhrman put his hand on Merkett's shoulder. "We'll find them, Colonel, and when we do, we'll kill them where they stand."

THIRTY-ONE

THEY HAD DRIVEN NONSTOP since three a.m., when the nightmare that had awakened Marie had also made the thought of additional sleep impossible. Now, finally stopped at a high point along a remote fire access road that provided an unobstructed 360-degree view of the county for miles in each direction, Paul snored softly, his face pressed firmly against the driver's side glass. Marie, as awake as if it were noon instead of 5:45 Monday morning, spent half her time studying the topographical map of the area she'd found in the SUV's glove box, and the other half watching for any vehicle approaching within five miles of their location.

Shortly after the nightmare, when her shivering and weeping had finally subsided, Marie had informed Paul that she had to leave the cabin at once—on foot if necessary. The feeling of impending danger that had told her to flee had been part premonition, part claustrophobia, and part good old fashioned paranoia.

Though he'd argued vehemently at first, when he realized that the only way to prevent her from leaving would have involved physically restraining her—a thought that not only didn't appeal to him, but one he wasn't sure he could actually accomplish without assistance—Paul reluctantly agreed to flee from the cabin with her and act as chauffeur, though where they were headed she couldn't say and appeared to him to be anyone's guess. In her insistence they depart at once, he had been allowed to take only the clothes on his back.

As they drove, Marie had continually looked behind them, and after an hour of unexpected and inexplicable turns dictated by her, following every goat path and dirt bike trail in Duchesne County, had finally satisfied herself that they had not been followed.

Paul had found it all in character—a character he was more convinced than ever was suffering from delusional paranoia, a common side effect of severe hypoxia, or oxygen deprivation, compounded by her rather extensive physical injuries.

Despite the relatively low risk of hanging out with a 'crazy' person, in his professional opinion, the roller coaster adventure in which he now found himself fully immersed, even if driven by a manic personality, represented the absolute antithesis of the regimented life he normally lived. Since leaving the cabin, he'd made up his mind to play along with her tale of imaginary bad guys chasing them, up to a point at least, since the benefits were not only completely out-of-character nonstop action, but also the close company of a beautiful and increasingly desirable woman.

Thus far, all things considered, it was shaping up to be the best damn vacation of his life.

"Wake up, Paul," Marie said, repeatedly poking his right shoulder with her finger.

"What is it?" he mumbled, using the back of his left hand to wipe a small rivulet of drool from the corner of his mouth. When his eyes finally focused, though squinting almost closed in the early morning light that poured in through her side window, he could see that she was pointing to a spot on the map spread across her lap.

"I need to go here. Now."

He leaned closer. "Dinosaur National Park?" he asked incredulously.

She looked at her index finger's position on the map, then moved it half an inch to the left. "No, Vernal."

"Okay, what's in Vernal at this hour?" He stretched and yawned, rubbing the sleep from his eyes.

"I need to go to church. I need to see a priest."

* * *

"She doesn't exist, sir," Shelton announced from the back seat of the Suburban. They had almost reached the small airstrip where their two Twin-Huey's sat, the other teams already there waiting as instructed.

Merkett turned in his seat, facing the computer expert. "What?" he said in an eerily flat tone.

"Let me rephrase that, sir. Marie Ann Matthews does exist, sort of, but she didn't exist prior to thirty-six months ago. Not a single tidbit of history, not the tiniest morsel of her childhood exists. And before you even ask, yes, there are tens of thousands of Marie Matthews out there, a couple of hundred in Utah alone, but our particular little lady is a ghost."

"Told you she was a pro," Fuhrman said.

Merkett silenced him with single raised finger. "Maybe you're wrong," he said, addressing Shelton.

The squint gave him the look.

"Okay, if not wrong, then maybe you overlooked something. Surely she has a Social Security Number, some kind of credit history. She had a job, she owned a Honda, for Christ's sake," Merkett said, neck deep in waters far less familiar or comfortable to him than combat. He excelled at killing anything he could see, but could barely wade through a day's e-mail without deleting at least one message he'd intended to reply to.

Shelton shook his head. "No credit cards in her name, no credit history, and we'll get to her work in a moment. As for the car, it appears she paid cash for it. I wrote the VIN down before we torched it and the records indicate it was on the Ken Garff Honda used car lot in Orem, Utah, thirty-six months ago. Then gone, sold to Marie Ann Matthews of Truman, Utah, but with no lien attached."

"How much?" Merkett asked.

"It was only three months old at the time, and pretty well loaded. Went for eighteen grand."

"I know you've already been in her bank records, where'd she get that kind of cash?"

"That's another thing that really bothers me, sir," Shelton said, continually punching buttons on his laptop as they drove. "She made a grand a week on the river, but that was only fourteen or fifteen weeks a year at best, and she wasn't paid for off weeks, so let's call it ten grand to be conservative. Then, Cameron paid her about four hundred a week at the clinic, so we'll call that another fourteen grand or so, bringing her annual income before taxes to twenty-five grand at best."

Merkett nodded. He'd done the math as Shelton spoke and agreed with the figure. "Your point?"

"None of it's in the bank, not one penny, saving or checking. In fact, she doesn't have a bank account of any kind that I can see. She had about two grand on her when we caught her at the clinic, and she lived virtually for free at the Summers' home, didn't have squat for personal possessions, you know, jewelry or plasma TVs and that kind of shit, so I'd guess that whatever she did have burned up with the house."

"Maybe she sent it home to her white-haired old mother," Ron Phelps suggested. "I used to send money home to my mom when she was alive, God rest her soul."

Again, Shelton shook his head. "This ghost doesn't have a mother, I'm telling you. She doesn't exist, her mother doesn't exist, and now anything that could point us to her past is up in flames. That may not have been such a good move, in hindsight." Merkett narrowed his eyes. "Of course, it was probably way better than risking the video being found," he added quickly.

"Way better," Merkett said coldly. He wasn't upset with Shelton, but the news of this woman's identity, or rather lack of identity, had him seeing red.

"How about the IRS? What's her history there? No one can escape those bastards," Fuhrman asked, his mind racing.

"This just keeps getting better and better," Shelton said sarcastically. "Filed short form for the last three years—no chance of getting audited that way—but her SSN didn't exist before that point. Can't speak about earlier since I can only go back as far as her bullshit identity allows me to at this point."

"How's that possible?" Kevin Branch asked. "You get your SSN practically at birth. She was, what, thirty-three?"

"Thirty-two," Shelton said.

"Great, so unless she's only been employed for the last ten percent of her life, where's her previous work history?"

"The IRS strictly goes by what's filed each year," Shelton said stoically. "They don't exactly call you and tell you that you're only three years old, you can't possibly be making twenty-five grand. They only check to see if your claim of income matches your employer's W2s or 1099s, and if you've paid the appropriate tax based on that income."

Merkett held up a hand to silence the wrangling. "Okay, she had a fake driver's license, a fake SSN, and no bank account. Who does that and why? Think people. I need answers."

"Witness protection," Phelps said.

Merkett considered the possibility. *Could be*, he thought, though it didn't really fit what he knew of the woman so far. Secreted witnesses under federal protection still had easy access to the U.S. Marshals Service whenever they felt it necessary. It was heavily discouraged for budgetary reasons if nothing else—always requiring immediate and costly relocation of the witness—but when a valuable witness's life was at stake, help was just a phone call away. He shook his head.

"Someone on the run, then, probably from the law. Perhaps Matthews was a bank robber or some shit like that," Branch suggested.

That thought actually intrigued Merkett, though the very idea of a wanted fugitive choosing to live in the same house as a veteran homicide detective seemed not only bold, but outright suicidal. He thought of the saving move she'd made at the cliff's edge and the words "bold" and "suicidal" appeared in flashing neon before his mind's eye.

"She's CIA," Fuhrman insisted, still convinced the woman was a pro.

"She's not a damned spook, Mack, how many times do I have to say it. She's on her own, running scared. There was a phone in the cabin and she didn't make a single call from it. If she had backup, she'd have called in the cavalry the moment she got near a phone. She didn't: QED, she's a loner."

For the remainder of the ride to the remote airstrip, not another word was said about Marie Ann Matthews, or whatever her real name was, but she was on everyone's mind.

THIRTY-TWO

THE SMALL CATHOLIC CHURCH of St. Michael's still sat contentedly, if a tad weary-looking, on West 100 Street and Main in Vernal, having been at that same location for more than eighty years. A recently-applied coat of gleaming white paint, closely-cropped grass, and colorful plantings lent an inviting and bucolic air to the urban setting, beckoning parishioners and visitors alike to enter without regard for formality. It had been the church's complete lack of pretense that had first drawn Marie to it more than three years ago.

Now, with so much time having passed since her last visit, she wasn't sure that same hand of welcome would be extended. She had not exactly been one of the 'faithful' since first coming to St. Michael's back then, having consistently failed to attend even the two services each year when virtually every Christian, regardless of denomination, sang hymns and gave thanks: Easter and Christmas.

"Is this the place?" Paul asked, pulling to the curb in front of St. Michael's. He left the engine running. Her directions since leaving their vantage point on the fire road had been specific and succinct, though she'd barely spoken otherwise. He could sense her becoming ever more withdrawn and introspective.

For the longest time after they'd stopped, Marie sat staring through the side glass at the narthex, with its massive oak doors rising to nearly twice her height. It reminded her of the first time she'd gone to church with her parents, as a very young girl, her small hands in theirs, standing before a pair of similar doors. Then, she stood but a fourth of their height and the awe-inspiring sight had taken her breath away. No great cathedral of Europe could have been so large or imposing, and she was certain at that moment that God Himself must live within her parent's church.

It felt like another life entirely, and it felt like yesterday.

Where had her faith gone? she wondered. A knot formed in her throat. "Yes, this is it. I'll only be a few minutes." With that, she reached for the door handle.

"Hey, hold on, Marie," Paul said, taking her arm and staying her exit. "We're in this together, remember. Where you go, I go." His expression was concerned but not demanding.

"Not this time. This I need to do alone."

"I'll sit ten pews away; you won't even know I'm there."

She shook her head. "Listen to me, Paul, I need you to stay here. You cannot come with me or after me, understand?" He didn't respond but only studied her with those psychologist's eyes of his. They made her feel a bit like a bug under a microscope. "Don't look at me like that, Paul. It makes me feel like you think I'm crazy or something. Promise me you'll stay here until I get back." She put her hand on his hand, squeezed it warmly, then removed it from her arm.

"Ten minutes," he said touching his watch face.

"Until I get back," she said, standing in the half-closed door.

"Twenty minutes," he pressed.

"Maybe twenty," she said, then closed the door and moved slowly toward the huge oak doors.

Once through the narthex, standing beside the holy water font near the last pew, Marie's eyes fought to adjust to the abrupt change from the June morning outside. The nave seemed at first to be as dark as a closet, but it was always like that in older Catholic churches, she thought, with their high stained-glass windows and the general lack of artificial lighting. In a moment, the irises opened enough for her to see that she was the only person within, though this at once troubled her more than if she'd stumbled in during a High Holy Mass.

She looked at her watch but saw only the back of her wrist. "Damn," she said, then put her hand to her mouth. "Sorry, God. Really. Bad habit I need to break, I know. Sorry."

When a sound interrupted her plea for forgiveness, she turned her eyes toward the chancel. A young boy, perhaps eleven or twelve, was removing two small crystal decanters from the altar. He hadn't seen her yet.

"Hello," she called out in a church voice, not much above a whisper. He turned and stared in her direction.

"Yes, ma'am. Something you need?" He approached the chancel railing.

Marie immediately hurried down the central aisle, through the long nave, until she was standing on the other side of the railing, just a few feet from the young boy. He was cherub-faced with large, dark eyes and a shock of short blonde hair. Bleached. Like hers, she thought, though it suited his olive complexion well. When she reached him, he repeated, "Is there something you need, ma'am?"

She smiled warmly at him. "I need to see Father Edwards. Is he around?"

The boy gave her a puzzled look. "I've only been an altar boy for a year and I've never heard of a priest by that name at St. Michael's. Are you sure you have the right name? We have a Father Gary." He studied her expression and could see that the news had not pleased her. "Would you like me to get Father Gary for you, ma'am?"

Marie stood at the altar in complete disbelief. She had met Father Edwards when she'd stumbled upon St. Michaels in June, three years ago, and he had been as much help—no, far more help, than she could have hoped for. He'd been the answer to a prayer.

Now, he was gone, and there was no one else who could help.

"Do you know where I could reach Father Edwards?" she asked, but realized as soon as she'd asked, that the pleasant young man would have no idea. He hadn't even heard of the former pastor.

As expected, he shook his head. "Sorry, ma'am." With that, he turned toward the sanctuary with his decanters of water and wine.

Marie paced slowly down the center aisle toward the narthex, her hope of getting the help she so desperately needed at this moment dashed. Why hadn't she come back to see Father Edwards even once in all the months? At least that way, he could have been able to tell her that he was leaving. She could have made other arrangements. Now, she was so totally screwed that for the first time since this insanity began, she'd lost hope. There was no longer any chance of reaching any of her "safe spots" without the kindly priest who'd taken so much on faith back then.

She thought about screaming and cursing out loud, railing at the heavens for having let her down—yet again—but instead just dropped her shoulders and slumped into the last pew. She knelt and lowered her head to the back of the pew in front, resting her forehead against folded hands. "Oh, God, I needed Father Edwards' help. You know that. Why have you taken him from me? I'm not asking for you to make all this go away. I understand it's my burden to bear for some insane reason. It's just that I can't possibly win if you keep throwing obstacles in my way. Can't you just give me a little break, for once? Just don't fight me, please, that's all I ask."

It was a feeble prayer, she knew, poorly worded and not one likely to be answered or even heard, but it had been from her heart. She stood and turned toward the aisle to leave.

"Marie Matthews?" the man's voice asked.

Startled, Marie stepped back defensively and tried to locate the origin of the voice, then to put a face with the voice. In the shadows of the space behind the last pew, near the stairs leading to the choir loft, a lone man stood quietly, hands clasped at his waist. He was dressed in all black, from head to foot, and seemed to be trying to find the same recognition in her face that she sought.

"I'm Father Gary. The boy you spoke with said you were look-ing for Father Edwards. You are Marie Matthews, aren't you?"

When he took a step toward her, she could see that he was wearing a traditional cassock, the common garb of Catholic priests, and not the dreaded night gear of the Colonel and his men. He was a short man about seventy, maybe seventy-five, with a slender build and penetrating gray eyes. His smile, however, told her at once that he meant her no harm, even if he had scared the crap out of her.

"Yes, I'm Marie Matthews," she said timidly. "But how would you know that?"

The man motioned for her to sit and joined her in the last pew. She took her seat, allowing him ample room to sit comfortably while facing her. "Before he left, Father Edwards told me that one day, perhaps in a week, perhaps not for many years, a very attractive young woman matching your description exactly, would ask for him."

"Where did Father Edwards go?" she asked.

"We all get reassigned from time to time. It was just his time. He's at a small church in El Salvador, in Central America. He'd always wanted to return since serving his novitiate there. The Bishop finally granted him his wish."

"You said he told you about me."

"He did, but not very much, I'm afraid. Just enough to keep me alert in case you did come calling." He put his hand on hers, pressing gently. "He said you were a deeply troubled young woman, but there was nothing to fear from you. He said you were a good person but that you were running."

The words startled Marie and her expression told him so.

He smiled even more warmly. "Not from the authorities or from your responsibilities, he assured me, but from yourself. He told me that when you came seeking him some day, I was to extend to you the same courtesies and confidences he would if he were still here. I want you to know that I'm prepared to do just that."

"No questions asked," she said in a child's voice.

"No questions asked," he assured her.

"But why? You don't know me."

"Because Father Edwards and I deal in acceptance and trust, Marie. May I call you Marie?" She put her hand on his and smiled. "Those are the foundation blocks of our faith. Perhaps that faith and whatever help I can offer will be the answer to your prayer."

"You heard?"

He grinned broadly. "This old church is drafty in the winter and a bit warm in August, but it has excellent acoustics. Now, I suppose you'd like to see your box." With that, he rose and moved toward the sanctuary.

She followed in pleased but stunned silence.

As Marie sat in a pew in the center of the nave, certain that she was still alone in the small church, she fingered the combination tumblers on the ornate wooden jewelry box in her lap. She remembered the six-digit combination from heart—her father's initials and her mother's maiden name initials as they would appear on a telephone keypad—and entered it quickly, rolling each polished brass dial into place with the alignment line. When all six dials were correctly positioned, she pressed the small brass latch and the box lid raised a fraction of an inch as the locking hook moved free.

Fearing the box may have somehow been opened over the many months, she hesitated before raising the lid. When she finally pushed it back, everything was just as she'd left it. Filling the entire inner space of the 10x5x3 inch hand-carved jewelry box was a solid block of soft foam which she'd fashioned herself to allow not even the slightest movement within the box. She couldn't risk shaking of the box to either reveal the contents, or worse, make a jumble of them.

Cut into the foam were six slots, an inch or so apart, running front to back but using only three of the five inches that were possible, an inch of cushioning foam all around.

Pressing her fingers into the foam on either side of the first slot, she withdrew a small key, a tiny slip of paper, a plastic-coated driver's license, and a Social Security card. Holding the four items to her heart for a second, she looked toward the cross above the altar and whispered, "Thank you, God."

Quickly, she withdrew the identical four items from the second slot, though neither this license nor Social Security card bore any resemblance in name, address, or number to the first she'd removed, and neither set contained the name Marie Matthews anywhere on them.

She closed the box, scrambled the combination, and stuffed the retrieved items quickly in her jeans pockets, one set in the left front, one in the right.

Moving with a sense of urgency nagging at her again, she hurried to the sanctuary where Father Gary was sitting patiently, working on his sermon for the coming Sunday. He looked up as she entered. When he saw the incredible transformation in her demeanor and the relieved expression on her face, he smiled and said, "Apparently prayers still get answered, even in these troubling times."

Marie sat near him and laid the box on the table beside his notes. "You have been so kind, so trusting. I give you my word that I'm not—"

Before she could finish, he put a finger to her lips. "There's no need for that, my child. Your eyes tell me that you are, as Father Edwards so aptly put it, a good woman. That's enough for me. I suppose you'll be needing this again in the future?" He indicated the intricately-carved wooden box.

She nodded. "I'd like to think I wouldn't, but it seems I have a knack for getting myself into messes that require this kind of help."

"Then it will be waiting for you when you call upon us again. And if it be God's will that I leave St. Michael's, though at my age that will more likely be to meet my Maker than my new congregation,

I will pass along your secret to the one who succeeds me. On that you have my solemn oath."

She shook her head in wonder. "Aren't you the least bit curious what's in here?" she asked, putting her hand on the box.

He leaned toward her and put his finger to his own lips this time. "It's a secret. And secrets are meant to be kept," he whispered, then leaned back with the broad smile of his proudly displayed.

"You're a very good man," she said, a tear rimming her eyes.

"And you deserve to be free of whatever's troubling you. May that be God's will, and soon."

She thanked him again and headed back to meet Paul.

At least now, she had something with which to fight.

* * *

Unlike the hectic driving they'd done since three in the morning, almost six hours earlier, the trip from St. Michael's to their next stop was a short two blocks. At a booth in a coffee shop at the corner of N. Vernal Avenue and W. Main Street, Paul and Marie sat eating hash browns and scrambled eggs, with thick slices of hickory-smoked bacon and coffee strong and hot enough to strip paint.

It tasted heavenly.

She'd eaten at this same small diner only once before, on an almost identical trip thirty-six months earlier, and just as then, she sat in the booth, eating hash browns and counting off minutes in her head. In ten more, the Grand Valley National Bank, directly across the street, would open for business.

"You late for an appointment?" Paul asked, the roof of his mouth still smarting from the large gulp of coffee-lava he'd just swallowed. He had noticed her surreptitiously watching the clock on the wall behind him; he'd seen it when they arrived.

So far, she had steadfastly refused to say a word about her visit to St. Michael's, except that it had made her feel much better. Now, as she put a forkful of eggs into her mouth, she indicated with a shrug that she couldn't answer with her mouth full. When it was obvious by his consistent stare that he wasn't going to let it pass, she chewed fast, swallowed, and said, "Just waiting for the bank to open. I need some traveling money."

He blew across his cup, trying to get the coffee's temperature down from four figures to a more drinkable level. "Going somewhere?"

Again the shrug and again he remained a statue of silent defiance.

"You're probably pretty good at your job, aren't you?" she said, rather than answering the question.

"Not bad."

"What exactly is it that you do? Counsel people going through a divorce and that kind of stuff?"

"And that kind of stuff," he said, taking a brave sip.

Still too hot. He blew some more.

"Well, I'm not married, so there you go." She raised both hands in a gesture of mock victory.

"Ever married?" he asked, watching her eyes especially close. When they twitched, he knew the answer. Now, would she tell him what he already knew?

Marie bit into one of the large pieces of extra-crispy bacon and thought about the question before answering. Finally she said, "Marriage is not all it's cracked up to be, is it." It wasn't a question.

"So you were married."

"Once. It didn't take."

"You didn't take to him, he didn't take to you, or you didn't take to the idea of marriage?"

"Why not 'he didn't take to the idea of marriage'?" she asked, dropping the bacon into the plate.

"Okay, sorry, why didn't he take to the idea of marriage?" Paul set his cup beside his plate and made a tent of his arms, elbows resting on the table.

Marie tossed her napkin into the center of her mostly finished plate and scooted to her left, out of the booth. "Bank's open. Be right back."

As he was about to speak, she held up one finger to indicate that she was going to do this alone, too. He picked up his coffee again and said to her back as she disappeared through the door, "I'll be right here when you come back," though he let the last of the sentence drift off into a whisper. He looked at the waitress who had also seen Marie leave. "It's okay," he assured her, "she wanted to be in line early. The first ten people to open a checking account today get a free toaster."

"Really?" the waitress said, eyes wide, studying the bank with renewed interest. She could use a new toaster.

Inside the bank, Marie walked directly up to the pleasant-looking man at the third desk, bypassing the women in the first two desks. She'd always done much better with men at everything and she needed this to go perfectly smooth.

"Good morning," he said, rising to shake her hand. "How can we be of assistance to you today?"

"I need to get into my safe deposit box, please." She sat in one of the leather chairs opposite his plain, very businesslike desk.

He smiled as if she'd just told him she would be depositing a million bucks. "Excellent. Name, please." He turned his keyboard to more squarely face the position of his chair. With the bank having been open only forty-five seconds, he hadn't fully settled in for the day.

Without hesitation, Marie answered, "Vickie Brennan," then slid her driver's license and Social Security card across the desk for his approval.

Efficiently, the bank officer—Jack Tabor, Vice President, according to the brass and fake-walnut name plate beside his flat-panel monitor—entered her name into the system, and almost at once picked up the two required forms of I.D. When he had verified to his satisfaction that the woman on the Utah driver's license and the very attractive woman across from him were one and the same, he smiled his best banking smile. "You have your key?"

She held the small brass key up and smiled back. At that moment, she realized that the key around her neck, the one from the clinic that now hung between her breasts on four strands of dental floss, was also a key to someone's safe deposit box.

When she seemed frozen in place, her mind a thousand miles away, the bank officer asked, "Is everything alright?"

Marie forced herself back to the moment and the man across from her. "Certainly. Just remembered I hadn't dropped off my husband's dry cleaning. He's going to kill me. Will this take long?" It was limp and she knew it, but the man seemed totally satisfied with her explanation.

"A quick signature on the activity card and we're done." He slid the small yellowish card across to her and she signed in the space indicated. Then, holding it to the PC screen to match her penmanship to the signature on the screen, he again smiled. "If you'll come this way, please."

Marie thanked him and rose from her chair, putting her I.D. back in her left front pocket. Now she wished she'd thought to bring a large purse with her, but she didn't normally carry a purse, wouldn't have had one with her if she had, and there'd been no place to buy one in Vernal before the bank opened. She'd have to improvise.

Jack Tabor led her into the vault area where a large antechamber housed a full wall of safe deposit boxes of various sizes at one end. Marie took a quick glance at the number on her key and visually matched it to the corresponding box on the wall. She now remembered having accessed this particular box only once before, as she had the other eight, but acted as if she did it all the time. Of course, the activity card would indicate that she'd only been here that one other time, but who gave a damn? This was a bank, not FBI Headquarters. People didn't have to answer for eccentric behavior. Besides, she'd paid for all nine boxes at nine different banks—all independent from each other and spread across three states—for ten years in advance. They could think of her anyway they cared, as long as they granted her access to her box whenever she wanted it.

Like now.

When the two keys had been inserted into their respective locks and turned, the one she'd brought and the bank's master key, Jack Tabor told her she could take all the time she needed. There was even a small privacy booth—he pointed to the phone-booth-sized room adjacent to the wall of boxes—where she could peruse the contents of her box without the fear of prying eyes.

"Thanks," she said demurely as he pulled the smallest of the boxes from the middle of the rack and handed it to her. It hadn't felt too heavy for her to handle on her own, he thought, and he was used to owners—or rather renters—being very skittish about the contents of their boxes.

"I'll be just a step away if you need anything else, Ms. Brennan."

She smiled and entered the privacy room as he held its door for her.

Once inside, Marie checked to see if the door had a lock, which it did not. "Damn," she said, then apologized to the ceiling. She decided that it was highly unlikely that the very efficient Mr. Tabor would allow another box holder to attempt to use this room until she'd vacated it, but she was still as nervous as if she were pulling off a robbery. Sweat trickled down her back and beneath her arms, though it was quite cool in the almost refrigerated bank.

She took a deep breath and raised the lid on the elongated metal box, letting it rest against the wall that formed the back of the small table on which it sat. She smiled at the contents, having not seen the familiar faces for many years. It meant she now had the power to move about with relative ease and without having to depend on outside help.

Relative ease at least compared to her present circumstances.

Stacked in tightly-wrapped packets, one hundred to a bundle, was a huge pile of wrinkled and faded U.S. currency. She took a quick inventory: five bundles of tens; five bundles of twenties; three bundles of fifties; two bundles of hundreds—Hamilton, Jackson, Grant, and good old Ben Franklin, all staring back at her, all anxious to be free of their metal prison.

Or so she imagined, the thought amusing her.

God knows she would be after three years in solitary confinement.

With care, they would all fit in the waistband of her jeans and Paul's oversized sweatshirt, which she'd worn since her shower Sunday night, would conceal everything perfectly. *Hell, it practically hung to mid-thigh*, she thought. It had been the reason she had not elected to take one of the smaller t-shirts when he'd offered it to her.

She worked quickly, evenly distributing the fifteen half-inch thick stacks of money around her waist, making certain all were exactly halfway down her pants, halfway above the waistline. That way, she reasoned, she wouldn't have to deal with Ben Franklin taking a joy ride down her pant leg as she crossed the marble floor of the bank.

Whether her money or not, whether she could prove it or not, it would look so much like a heist that the guard by the front door would probably shoot her where she stood.

The money stayed in place and she told the bank officer that she was through with her box, it was empty and she would no longer be requiring its use.

He looked at his screen. "But you paid for seven more years. In advance."

"I know, but things change, don't they. Thank you again."

"Where shall we send the refund check? I don't see an address on file for you, Ms. Brennan." The thought of his records not being perfect appeared to fluster the man.

"You keep it," Marie said as she turned to leave. "Take your wife to dinner."

THIRTY-THREE

MORE FRUSTRATED THAN EITHER of them had been in their collective memory, Colonel Merkett and his chief squint—supposedly the Unit's resident computer genius—sat staring at the seventeen-inch LCD screen of Shelton's laptop. It was as blank as the history of the woman they were seeking. His genius was failing them.

They were in the small tin hangar of the remote airstrip, ten miles northeast of Truman and miles from any home or business, with no air conditioning, no coffee, no food to eat, and no idea whatsoever who, or rather what, the former Marie Matthews was.

"She had help, professional help," Shelton repeated for the third time in an hour. Merkett had not agreed earlier and it was clear he didn't agree still.

"Bullshit, Don. I repeat, where's the cavalry? Where is even *one* U.S. Marshal racing to her rescue? If the most likely scenario we've come up with so far is that she's in the Federal Witness Protection Program, then she had a contact number, a designated marshal she could call in an extreme emergency. Why didn't she? There was a damn phone two feet away, and if she was scared enough of us to jump off a mountain for Christ's sake, I'd say she considered the situation pretty extreme. I'm not buying any of it. There's another explanation we haven't come up with yet."

Shelton nodded his agreement, but in his mind he firmly believed that the kind of disappearing act that this woman had pulled off could only be accomplished with such finesse if she'd had help of the most professional, and therefore, the most costly, kind. Whether from the government or private sector, the documents Marie Matthews had on her for the last three years were good enough to pass as genuine, under even the closest scrutiny.

"Any word on the Range Rover yet?" Merkett asked. "Surely by now, someone has spotted the damned thing."

"It's only been a few hours, Colonel. It's not yet noon on the first day. Ten grand is one hell of a grand prize for just keeping your friggin eyes open. It'll be spotted; we need to give it a little time, that's all."

Merkett pounded his fist on the old wooden table and shoved his chair back. "Time is the one thing we're damn short on, Lieutenant."

While Shelton pecked away, the rest of the Unit slept uneasily in the cramped bays of the two Huey choppers or were busy sitting on whatever they could scrounge up or overturn, cleaning weapons but clearly bored. Not a word had been exchanged among them in an hour. Each knew when to interject a suggestion or comment, and when not to. Until their Colonel worked out the Matthews' problem, or the squint found her pretty little ass hiding somewhere in cyberspace, anything that was said would only exacerbate the tension that was already palpable within the dusty building.

At least with a roof, such as it was, keeping the sweltering June sun off their heads, they weren't frying like worms on a blacktop road, even if the cramped temporary quarters had become a sauna. It was better than still being in Afghanistan or Iraq, though they much preferred the action of combat to the monotony of waiting.

Merkett wiped the sweat from his brow with a sleeve. They had successfully traced her driver's license number in the state DMV records, hoping to gain some small foothold on the woman's past, but it had led to a dead end—literally. The number was real enough, and it had belonged to a Marie Ann Matthews of St. George, Utah, but she had died in an auto accident in Oklahoma the same week the new Marie Matthews was 'born' in her place. Apparently the DMV didn't care that they had deceased drivers motoring about the state.

The SSN she'd used when filing her last three federal tax returns had also belonged to that same Marie Matthews of St. George, and apparently, just like the Utah Department of Motor Vehicles, the IRS didn't care if they continued to get tax revenue from a corpse. Experts at getting blood from turnips, it probably seemed normal to them.

Perhaps, Shelton reasoned, neither organization realized the real Marie Matthews had died, or maybe the woman who'd assumed her identity had informed them that the report of her demise had been greatly exaggerated, and that she was living proof of that error. Whichever the case, it had apparently been easier to slip into the dead woman's life and continue it in Truman than it would have been to slip into a pair of her shoes.

All subsequent Internet searches, through a dozen state and federal databases, had yielded no greater connection between the real Marie Matthews, dead three years now, and their current fugitive of the same name, than random selection. Evidently, the woman they now sought had merely chosen a name from the obituaries whose age and description she closely resembled, and had walked away a new woman.

But walked away from where? Who the hell had she been before that moment? The problem plagued Shelton like a rash.

He would get to the bottom of it one way or another.

With nothing concrete about her life prior to that moment to go on, there was literally no place left to begin a search. In the U.S. alone, there were at present more than 12,375,000 women who, because of similar ethnicity and age range—three years either side of Matthews' assumed age of thirty-two—could be a candidate for the woman running around with their damned video. If she were Canadian or European, that number could easily double.

Merkett paced the dirt floor while Shelton pecked mindlessly at his keyboard. Then, in a moment of inspiration, he yelled out, "Facial recognition software!"

Merkett turned to him, hoping this would prove to be another one of those epiphanic moments his evil little Cyber Ranger was so famous for. "Explain," he said brusquely.

"Every face is unique, just like fingerprints. It's the underlying premise of the counter-terrorist identification algorithms being used at all our borders." He fingered the keys like a madman as he talked.

"I'm with you," Merkett nodded, moving toward the table where the powerful laptop sat, its high-speed wireless Internet connection extending from its left side and linking them to the entire world beyond the hot, dusty shed. "So, we take the current Utah DMV photo we have of Matthews..."

Shelton looked at him quizzically.

"Look, I know it offends you, but we'll continue to call her that until you can give me her real name, okay."

Shelton conceded the small point: it *wasn't* her name, and not knowing it pissed him off, but keeping it Matthews for now was better than assigning her an unpronounceable symbol like the musician Prince had done.

"Then you'll run that face against what?" Merkett asked, unsure of the next step.

"All DMV photos from three to, say, five years back, across all fifty states. For starters, at least. If she existed in any one of them, we should be able to nail her in a couple of hours. Dammit! I should have thought of it right off," he said in a moment of sincere derision. He didn't make mistakes, not when it came to computers and data.

"Hours!" Merkett barked. "Why so damned long?"

Donald Shelton folded his hands on the table, a testy expression on his face. "Colonel, not once in all the time we've worked together have I asked you why it took so long to capture a terrorist or take an objective, have I?"

Merkett threw up his hands defensively. "Okay, okay. I admit I don't know shit about what you do, how you do it, or why in hell it takes so long." He gave him a hard look. "Just remember, my friend, that every minute we waste is another nail in our coffins." With a sweep of his hand, he indicated everyone in the tin shed.

*　　*　　*

"Time to go shopping," Marie announced when she'd rejoined Paul in the booth of the small diner. She had been gone only fifteen minutes, but it had seemed like hours to him. Again, she had a cheery, even giddy, look about her.

Bipolar disorder, he silently diagnosed. Undoubtedly, and acute, but also cute as hell. It would be a shame to lock her away somewhere, or medicate her to the point where she lost the spark he found so exciting. Perhaps he'd take her on as a full-time private patient, let her stay at his place, but just as quickly as the idea formed, the oversight ethics committee assembled before his mind's eye, threatening the revocation of his license for unprofessional conduct.

An outpatient living on her own would be much better.

Close by, though. Close enough to see every day.

"And, just what is it that we're shopping for this fine June morning?" he asked. He could barely await the response.

"Well for starters, I need a backpack."

Not what he'd expected, but that he'd been caught totally off-guard again was exactly what he'd expected. "So, we're going camping now?" he asked.

The plates had been cleared and he was nursing a second cup of coffee, this one with an almost completely melted ice cube floating in it.

"Nope. Just hate purses, that's all. You ready?" She slid to the edge of the booth.

"You hate purses. Did one offend you once? Maybe eat your phone or something like that?" he jabbed playfully.

"Nope. They just keep going out of style long before they're worn out, and they never hold the kind of stuff I like to carry. They cost too much, have to be coordinated with your outfit every day—you guys wouldn't understand stuff like that—and are just begging to be snatched by every lowlife on a bike or jerk-wad cruising a crowded mall. They're dumb." She slid from the booth less than a minute after she'd retaken her seat and headed for the door. "Did you pay the check?" she asked looking back.

As usual, Paul was several steps behind. "Yep. You owe me six bucks. By the way, where are we doing this shopping?"

"Grand Junction," Marie said, disappearing through the door and out into the morning. Shading her eyes from the intense Utah sun, she made a mental note to buy some good sunglasses when they reached the city. As long as she went anywhere that Colonel Sanders wouldn't be looking for her, based on nothing more than intuition, then Grand Junction was as good a choice as any. Besides, she knew the town.

Once inside the SUV, Paul fastened his seat belt and said, "I can't just go running off to Colorado, Marie, and neither can you. I hate to overstate the obvious, but we left a dead guy back there—in case you forgot—and I still don't have any idea who he is. Care to shed some light on that for me?"

"Can't," she shrugged, studying the map, then, "Okay, make a right here and we'll head southeast on US-40 for about half an hour to Dinosaur—yes, that's actually the name of the town," she said, anticipating his question, "then we'll go southeast on US-64 to Rangely. Head due south on Highway 139 for about an hour to I-70 near Loma. From there, Grand Junction is only about ten minutes east. We're heading for the Mesa Mall right off the

Interstate. Exit-26." She seemed pleased with her succinct directions and folded the map.

She was ready to go.

"That's not an acceptable answer, Marie. 'Can't' isn't an answer, it's a cop out. Let's start with something simple: how did you and that man happen to fall into the Duchesne River? This is serious. I need to know or we're not moving one inch from here, and we're certainly not going all the way to Grand Junction, Colorado, on a shopping spree." He held the ignition key defiantly in his hand and waved it as a warning that he meant what he said.

Marie turned toward him with an expression that had lost all its charm from a moment ago. "You bet your ass this is serious, Paul. It's deadly serious. I have some really bad men—no, let me amend that—'we' have some really bad men after us and if they catch us, they're going to kill us. Not like in the movies dead where you get up afterward and go for a latte, but dead like in the morgue dead. Dead like that asshole in the water dead. Our only hope of surviving is to get to a large city where the likelihood of being tripped over will be significantly less than it is presently on these two-lane highways out in the middle of nowhere." She snatched the key from his hand and jammed it into the ignition, then turned it clockwise until the engine started. "And, we didn't *fall* into the river," she added with a frown. "I pushed the bastard in to kill him and to keep them from killing me. Now, either drive me to Grand Junction or I'll find my own way."

She folded her arms resolutely and faced the road ahead.

* * *

The mall was crowded for a Monday afternoon, Marie thought, and she welcomed the company of other people, even if all were unknown to her. After the relative isolation she'd experienced for the last twenty-four hours, the busy throng felt ten times it's actual size. It was almost a carnival atmosphere as hundreds of kids, recently released from school for the summer, roamed in constantly-texting mini-herds or followed non-working moms around the maze of stores with "oh my God" looks on their faces. Everywhere, there could be heard a cacophony of giggles, shouts, keyboard tapping, and screeching 'Heelys,' those annoying tennis shoes with skate wheels in the heels that made kids look like they were immune to the laws of physics that adults were forced to obey.

Perhaps they were.

At one end of the mall, in the anchor spot, an REI superstore was unusually busy. The premier outdoor outfitter was a veritable playground for anyone interested in canoeing, kayaking, boating, fishing, hunting, camping, or, in Marie's case, surviving to see another sunrise.

As she clicked off the items she'd compiled in her head during the three-hour drive from Vernal, putting each into the buggy she'd gotten just inside the front door when they entered, Paul asked for the fifth time what she was going to do with *that*.

Just like before, she'd ignored him.

And, just like before, he'd allowed her to ignore him as he continued to try to determine if she had completely lost her marbles, was treatably bipolar, was merely eccentric and suffering from post-traumatic stress disorder—like a war veteran—or was a wily criminal-murderer who had somehow used him to affect her getaway from a neighboring state.

It was enough to make him crazy and he loved every minute of it.

Of course, the fact that he'd seen her naked—twice—and her magnificent shape and spectacular tan lines were indelibly etched in his mind, helped to keep his interest piqued.

He'd decided he was going to sleep with her, even if it meant legal trouble, though he doubted it would come to that. He hoped not, at least. After all, he hadn't done anything wrong, and he could always say that he hadn't even seen the dead man, only the woman whom he saved in a Herculean effort. Who were the authorities more likely to believe?

"That should just about do it," she announced after forty minutes of non-stop shopping, flitting from one department in the huge store to another, like a bee darting from flower to flower in search of pollen.

Paul recognized everything, or almost everything, that Marie had purchased, though understanding the function of each item had done little to explained its intended use in their current situation. The backpack he'd expected. A few new items of casual clothing made sense, of course, but why had she needed a four-hundred-dollar handheld, weatherproof Garmin GPS? And, what on earth was she going to do with a handful of mixed-meal MREs, those historically inedible meals-ready-to-eat that the military was so fond of? Why a canteen, for Pete's sake?

It was time to sit this young lady down and have the talk they'd needed to have for eighteen hours, before the man's body was discovered—Alex's, too, if she were in fact a real person, and was, in fact, also dead—and that discovery led to his arrest and conviction as an accomplice after the fact.

The dichotomous internal dilemma he kept experiencing had *him* feeling bipolar. On the one hand, he could stay on the run and probably get to sleep with the beautiful woman, to hell with the consequences. On the other hand, he could call a screeching halt to all the running around, or running away—he was confused—and get to the bottom of all the intrigue, bring the law into the equation, find out who the dead guy was, and maybe, though very doubtfully, still get to sleep with the beautiful woman.

Not an easy decision, he thought. Why couldn't she have been ugly or old—or both. The decision would be considerably easier then.

He needed his own couch.

Paul grabbed Marie's arm as she pushed the half-filled buggy toward the checkout counter. "We need to talk, Marie. This minute. I'm a licensed therapist and I face serious consequences, both legally and professionally, when it comes to dead bodies known to me and yet unreported by me. I'm not going to be put off by your charm one more time. We're talking about this right now or I'm finding the closest cop and busting this whole game of yours wide open. It is all a game to you, isn't it?"

Needing anything but a confrontation with authorities at this moment, Marie said, "So, you find me charming, do you?" She batted her eyes mockingly, flashing her best smile. "That's good, because I find you to be the perfect man at the perfect time in my life. And part of your splendid perfection is your saintly patience. Now be a good boy and push the buggy to the checkout counter while I go to the ladies room."

Realizing that he'd been beaten yet again by a gorgeous face, a great set of boobs, a killer body, and more pure animal charm than he'd seen in a lifetime of other women, he nodded agreeably. "Over lunch. We're going to talk over lunch or we're going to stay right here until we do." He made his most unwavering face.

As she moved toward the restrooms, she turned and said, "Yes, daddy," then winked seductively.

THIRTY-FOUR

LIEUTENANT DONALD SHELTON HASTILY read the e-mail he'd just received, then stood and shouted across the hangar, "Colonel, they've been spotted in Grand Junction, Colorado!" Everyone rose to his feet as if called to action stations. "Just got an Internet hit from some guy named Glen Turner who was taking a big client to lunch. Spotted the Range Rover getting off I-70 at Exit-26. He was in the left-hand lane and almost wrecked his car trying to follow them. He provided the correct tag number of the Range Rover, so it's definitely our boy and girl, sir. Finally lost them at Mesa Mall." He looked at his watch. "The lead is about an hour old now; Turner said he couldn't get rid of his big client as quickly as he'd hoped. Wants to know if he's gonna get the ten grand."

Merkett stood between Shelton and Captain Nate Fisher, stroking his stubbled chin. With a full day's growth, he was looking rough around the edges.

It fit his mood.

"What the hell is she doing at a shopping mall in Colorado?" he said to no one in particular.

"Whatever it is, in a city that size, she now has all the access she needs to download the data from the memory card. She'll be able to watch the video in any of a thousand places," Shelton said, his frustrated anger at a boiling point. No matter how long it took, he had sworn to find the identity of this bitch and destroy her life, and the lives of everyone she cared about along with her.

"Not good, Colonel," Fisher said stoically. "Worst case scenario. What do you want us to do?"

Merkett clasped his hands behind his back and paced slowly across the hangar floor, then turned and strolled back. He seemed more resigned to his fate than either concerned or angry. Finally, he said, "Okay, if she watches the video, and we have to assume she will the first chance she gets, she'll have the information in the hands of the feds within five minutes. I sure as hell would in her position." All nodded in agreement; it was clearly her best defense. He addressed Shelton. "I assume there's no way to know when or where she actually downloads the video?" The squint shook his head. "Hell, it won't matter at that point anyway," Merkett said resolutely. "We're all dead meat the moment she pops that memory card in a computer."

Again, Merkett paced, his mind going full tilt. The video that Marec Vanover shot—or at least the one that they all feared had been shot, since there was no way of actually knowing without seeing the damned thing—had been recorded during a clandestine meeting at the ranch where General Clayton Longmont had outlined in full detail the timetable, principle players, and strategic locations chosen for Operation Evil Wind. Within a few hours, Vanover had vanished from the ranch, a meeting with senator Goodman had been conducted, money had exchanged hands, and Vanover had vanished a second time, only this time from the face of the earth.

Later that day, Goodman's plane was brought down, killing everyone on board. It should have been "problem solved." The hitch that could not have been foreseen was that Goodman wasn't onboard at the time of the crash.

Now, nine months later, this elite, highly-decorated corps of men sat in a hot, dusty hangar in northern Utah, awaiting a fate they appeared to no longer have any voice in controlling.

When the FBI and Homeland Security got their hands on the video and its most unlikely cast of characters, there would be such a swarm of cops and feds at the ranch, that it would make Waco and Ruby Ridge look like small family gatherings.

A dozen pairs of eyes watched in silent anticipation of Merkett's next words, all realizing that the great risk they'd all taken, their beloved country's very future at stake, had probably just blown up in their faces. Soon, they would all be hunted down like dogs. At this point, they would do anything, risk anything, and kill anyone, rather than have "Traitor" engraved on their tombstones.

The worst thing about secrets as classified as theirs was that when everyone who knew the real truth had been killed, only public perception remained, and history would judge them all based on that perception, and nothing more. Truth would not matter; it seldom did.

Merkett stopped between his senior officers, his mind working feverishly. He turned to Shelton. "Don, how long, worst case, would it take to download that video, watch it, and then transmit it to FBI headquarters in D.C.?"

Shelton made a quick checklist in his mind. "Once she has a PC or a Mac and a card reader that will accept that particular memory card, all of which is available at any computer store in the city, plus most libraries and schools, she's good to go. Let's say half a minute to copy the file, though she can also access it directly from the card. Then ten seconds to open it and launch the media viewer, however long the video lasts to watch it, but I previously determined that to be around twenty-five minutes, and then two or three minutes to transmit it over the Internet to anyone in the world she chooses." He did the math. "Just under half an hour, Colonel. That means this conversation could all be a moot point by more than thirty minutes now."

"Exactly, Don. You're exactly right," he said with inexplicable excitement illuminating his dark eyes.

Shelton may have been "right," but he was also as confused as hell.

Merkett looked at Lieutenants Mack Fuhrman and Tom Pickard, the two chopper pilots and the men charged with maintaining contact with the rest of the Unit at the ranch. "Our radios are still working fine, correct gentlemen?"

"Absolutely, Colonel. Both A-Okay," they agreed at once.

"And we all have cell phones that are still working, right?" Merkett said. He pulled his from his pocket, noted the three bars of service even in this remote location, and turned it to face his men.

This time, though a dozen men stared back and nodded, none had connected the dots. Suddenly, Sergeant Major Ron Phelps began to see the picture Merkett was trying to paint. "Why so quiet, right, sir? Why haven't we heard a peep from the ranch?"

Merkett gave a wicked and knowing smile. "If the shit has already hit the fan, they wouldn't come at us with a stealthy strike team crawling on their bellies, hoping not to break a single dry twig, they'd send the fucking Marines and every Fed with a gun west of the Mississippi!"

All now began to see the point being made, and the mood immediately elevated. "That's right," Nate Fisher said. "This would go overt so damned fast it'd look like a fuckin' war zone."

Branch chimed in: "It'd be the lead story on every TV station in the country—hell, the world!—within minutes."

Shelton added the final straw: "The fact that we're all still here means the bitch hasn't seen the video yet."

"But why?" Phelps asked. "She had to know that we were after the damned memory card for the data contained on it, even if she didn't know what that data was, so why not try to find out the first chance she got? Why drive hundreds of miles, to a mall, for Christ's sake, when she could have gone to the closest public library last night? This morning anyway?"

This time, Merkett didn't just smile, he grinned broadly, his straight, white teeth gleaming against his leathery skin. "Because she doesn't *have* the video, that's why."

It suddenly made perfect sense to him.

"She sure as shit didn't have the cell phone on her," Shelton said resolutely. "She was half naked at the cliff and—"

"I agree, Don, she didn't," Merkett interrupted. "But I'll bet a pay grade she doesn't have anything on her that is self-explanatory, self-directing."

"I don't understand, sir," Branch said.

Merkett took his original chair near the old table and propped his feet up. "Let's look at this whole scenario from a totally different perspective, boys. Vanover sells his phone or memory card to Goodman—doesn't really matter for the purpose of this conversation—and Goodman then watches the video he shot. He realizes immediately that he has his hands on the most explosive intel of his career, an item of world-shaking value. He's compelled to act on that intel at once, being the kind of man he is. Or *was*." Everyone grinned. "Other men might have tried to profit from the video, but not Boy Scout Goodman. That explains his call to Wagner, and his emergency trip to D.C. to meet with the Senate Intelligence Committee.

"Wagner, in turn, alerts Clark Corello, his lackey, of the emergency meeting later that day with the most influential member of the Democratic party, to begin the necessary arrangements, but doesn't tell him anything about the video, other than that a mystery video exists and that it's hotter than the sun itself according to Goodman. We already know that neither of them knew anything of the video's actual contents or they would have acted on that knowledge the second Goodman died, if for no other reason than to cover their own butts.

"Corello secretly alerts General Longmont of the emergency meeting with Goodman, having been on the General's 'information gathering' payroll for more than a year prior to that point. The General's call to me, as we all know, resulted in his plane being brought down before Goodman could set foot in D.C. Unfortunately, no plan is perfect and this one took a nasty turn for the worst when Goodman wasn't onboard at the moment of impact."

His team had gathered around the table where the laptop and Merkett sat. Their collective expression was one of agreement with the timeline and the known facts thus far.

"Okay," Merkett continued, "that much we already know. Now for the new perspective I mentioned. What if Goodman didn't bring the cell phone or memory card with him on the plane, but instead stashed it somewhere he felt would be totally safe before he left California, at least until the Senate Intelligence Committee could outline the best course of action. I imagine that wouldn't have taken very long after his soulful and detailed account of the video. It probably would have only been a matter of minutes before they had the head of every agency under Homeland Security behind closed doors plotting our total annihilation with extreme prejudice."

"The committee wouldn't have risked letting one man retrieve the video," Mack Fuhrman surmised. "Would have sent a large cadre of feds for it. Goodman would have stayed to grandstand in front of the cameras while it all went down. Skipper Goodman, the great savior of the country. Coming soon to a White House near you."

"I agree," Merkett said, chuckling at Fuhrman's humor. "That means he would have had to tell them where the video was so they could retrieve it, which logically means it's locked away somewhere."

"So," Nate Fisher pondered, "he probably gave them the combination to his safe."

"Not likely a combination and definitely not a safe in his home," Shelton said. "We turned up nothing at the Goodman mansion even after a protracted search, and Ritchie Frye, Goodman's bodyguard, told us back then that the senator went straight from his meeting with Vanover to the Santa Barbara Airport where he kept his plane. No stops along the way. Didn't even go to his bedroom or the head before departing."

Within days of the crash, the Unit had put someone inside the Goodman mansion, on the household staff, with explicit orders to find the cell phone and/or its memory card, but to do so in absolute secrecy. In the succeeding months, that operative, in her role as a housemaid, had been through every square inch of the massive estate, including both wall safes, which were old-style combination units, but had turned up nothing.

"Then a key," Fisher suggested.

The Colonel nodded as he thought, again kneading his chin between his thumb and forefinger. "That'd be my bet. It fits all the pieces of the puzzle as we're beginning to understand them. Also, a key would have been as easily concealed on Matthews' person as a small memory card. As freaked out as she got when I threatened to cut off her bra and jeans, I'd bet it was either in there or in her panties, and though my hardware is a bit different than hers, the latter still seems a bit uncomfortable to my way of thinking. I'm going with the bra. Besides, that's been a favorite hidey-hole of women since Mata Hari. Not very original, but pretty effective up to a point."

Merkett stood again and stretched, feeling much better than he'd felt in months, despite the hot, dusty, cramped tin shed in which he now found himself and his team. "We've been given a great and rare gift, men." He turned to face his loyal team of soldiers. "The gift of time. One of the most precious commodities known to man. Now, we have to honor that unexpected gift with decisive action. We need to find this very annoying young woman, whoever the hell she is, before she puts that key into a lock and our necks are once again on the chopping block."

"Colonel, we can't exactly go running around Grand Junction in a pair of Hueys without drawing a hell of a lot of unwanted attention," Mack Fuhrman said. "So far, we've operated under cover of night, but this is the middle of a friggin' weekday."

"We'll use the Suburbans exclusively for now, splitting into three teams again. You gentlemen," he said, pointing toward the two pilots, "will head to different staging points between here and Goodman's private airstrip, somewhere low-key and remote, but readily accessible. Don will tell you exactly where when he and I work out the details. You'll wait for us there, fully-fueled and ready to go at a moment's notice in case we need to cover a lot of ground in a hurry. When we locate her, and we *will*, we'll have to ambush her and disappear before the local Barneys even know we were there. That will most likely mean an air strike or at the very least, an air evac."

Merkett moved to the table and threw open a huge map of the western United States, spreading it out to its full width. He stabbed a rigid finger at Grand Junction, Colorado. "We know where she is at this moment, or was sixty-five minutes ago, but not where she'll be an hour from now. The best I can make out from what she's done so far is that she has no idea we're on to the Range Rover and the good doctor. If she did, the clever little bitch would have ditched him and his fancy ride first thing. That gives us the edge." He pulled at his stubbled chin as he continued to work out the details of the mission in his mind. He'd done this a thousand times in combat; this was no different just because it was on American soil.

"How do you explain their sudden departure from the cabin at three in the morning, sir?" Branch said. "That kind of unexpected behavior usually indicates awareness of a predator's presence, the knowledge or belief that you're in imminent danger."

"More likely just the *fear* of it," Merkett said. "It would be logical for her to go all paranoid and shit with that cabin being in the immediate vicinity of the last place she saw us. Don't forget, we're the men who just killed her best friend and who tried to kill her. As soon as she was able to travel again, maybe with a little food in her, she probably just got skittish and bolted. Just bad timing for us, nothing more."

He looked at his men as he'd done many times before, making eye contact with each in turn. He wanted them to understand what he was thinking and what would be expected of them. He knew they'd follow orders no matter what and with no questions asked, but being in on the mission at the core level, whenever possible or prudent, always created greater unity and a sense of 'ownership' of the mission by all involved. "Listen, men, I don't really know what got her moving at that hour, but it wasn't our arrival and it wasn't a call to or from the place. I'd say it was just some more of her dumbass good luck, and we've all seen it a thousand times: luck always runs out. Only skill and training can be counted on when it comes to surviving. Her hours are numbered."

He continued to study the map, then turned to his squad leaders. "Mount up, boys. I want Delta Team to head due west to Provo. That will block her northern escape route through Salt Lake City. Echo Team, follow them to I-15 then go south to where it meets I-70; that will cut off her western route. I'll take Charlie Team to Grand Junction. If we don't intercept her there, we'll proceed south to Durango, sealing off her southernmost route. There's no telling where this illogical bitch will go next. Stay in constant communication by cell phone. Lieutenant Shelton will coordinate all search efforts; he'll let us all know the moment anyone spots the Range Rover." He turned to Shelton. "Raise the reward to fifty-thousand, Don. Let's ramp this thing up and get some real eyes on the road. You go with Mack in his chopper and keep doing all that computer shit you do so well. We're gonna need every trick you can throw our way if we're gonna catch this wily bitch before she can get to wherever it is she's heading."

"Where *is* she heading, Colonel?" Ron Phelps asked. "Any idea?"

"Sure, Ron, toward the lock that key fits."

"And where's that?"

"No idea, but you can bet it's within a few minutes of Goodman's home. He had almost no time at all between Vanover's departure from the mansion and his limo ride to the airport. Frye said they made no stops en route after leaving the home. That means he had to leave and return without anyone even knowing he was gone in that short time span. That means damn close by."

"But, sir, 'close by' isn't exactly a known target. Hell, the state's largest city could be considered 'close by'. That lock could be anywhere."

"No, it couldn't, that's my point. Frye distinctly told us when he called that Vanover arrived and left within half an hour, and Goodman left for the airport within ten minutes of that. Assuming the worst, that would mean a four minute drive somewhere, two minutes to be in and out, and four minutes back. Frye admitted that he didn't have his eyes on the man during that ten minute period. He could have slipped out and back in without his knowledge and we have to assume he did somehow since the phone or memory card were not found in the residence. Given traffic congestion at that time of day, the hiding place has to be within a mile or two of the mansion."

Phelps was still not convinced. "But where, that still leaves hundreds of potential places where you could hide something as small as a cell phone. How the hell is she going to find that one place when we have no idea how to find it?"

Merkett had wondered the same thing. "One of two things is going on here: either she has this supposed key and was probably provided with some clue as to the location of the lock it fits when she first took possession; or, she has nothing at all and is only running simply because we killed her friend and everyone else around her. I'd love to think the latter because we could just go back to the ranch and get on with our work. I cannot, however, accept that theory and survival instinct tells me that she isn't running *from* us as much as she's running *toward* something. She probably assumes that uncovering the key's secret will magically end all this and allow her to live out her remaining days in peace and harmony."

Most nodded their agreement with this theory. Some remained silent, perhaps skeptical, perhaps just working on theories of their own. Whether they reached the same or a different conclusion, all would do exactly as ordered by Merkett.

"A bank," Shelton said. "It's a safe deposit box key and he stashed Vanover's phone at a bank. Totally safe, easily accessible. Smart move."

Merkett nodded. "I agree. Most likely a bank. That means she can't do a thing until she gets to that location, and we have to prevent that at all cost. The fall back plan will be that we identify the most logical bank, or banks, and stake them out. That's your job, Don. Find out every bank Goodman did business with and pinpoint every branch within three miles of the mansion. Once we have the probable locations, we wait for her to arrive and grab her the second she exits the building with the video."

He clapped his hands together loudly. "Hit it, boys. We have a lot of ground to cover and the day isn't getting any longer. We need to find her while it's still daylight, because this will get exponentially harder when the sun goes down."

Within five minutes, two Hueys and three Suburbans had departed the small airstrip. Their mission: find the Range Rover, kill the occupants, disappear back to the ranch.

All were ready to do whatever it took to end this quickly.

THIRTY-FIVE

HE KUNG PAO CHICKEN in the food court was actually pretty good for mall grub, Marie thought, following up a mouthful of the tasty rice with a generous swallow of Diet Coke. A Tsingtao Beer would have tasted better, she decided, but since the mall wasn't big on serving alcoholic beverages in a food court normally populated by teens, pre-teens, and image-conscious mothers with strollers, she was forced to settle for the soda.

In REI's restroom, Marie had rearranged the money in her jeans' waistband, double checking to ensure that a stack of bills wasn't going to suddenly drop onto the floor as she walked, or poke out of her pants like a flag the first time she bent over. She had also withdrawn several bills of each denomination, about a thousand bucks in all, and had stuffed that "spending money" into her left front pants pocket along with her new I.D. The second set of I.D., which had been in the front right pocket, had been transferred to her right boot, between her sock and the boot's inner liner. It was safer there; no chance of accidentally pulling it out or losing it.

It was essential that Paul not see the information contained on either this new driver's license or Social Security Card if she had to present identification for any reason. Trying to explain who Vickie

Brennan was would be even more difficult than trying to explain what had happened thus far, and that was bordering on the Twilight Zone. Because she would be paying cash for all her purchases, the likelihood of I.D. being required was slim. So far, he hadn't suspected that she'd gotten more money from the bank in Vernal than was necessary to tide her over for a few days. He certainly didn't realize that she had fifty grand under his borrowed sweatshirt. She'd transfer all her purchases and the cash to her backpack in the motel room this evening, eliminating the potential problem.

"We're talking now, remember?" Paul said, interrupting her dreams of ice-cold beer and hidden cash. She gave him a tired look. "I don't want to hear it, Marie. We had a deal."

"Can't it wait until we stop for the night? I'm sore all over, as tired as hell, and I need a shower. It wouldn't be asking too much to wait just a little longer, would it?" She batted her eyes at him, but when she realized he wasn't buying it this time said, "Fine. What do you want to talk about?" She pushed her half-eaten meal away to punctuate her disapproval with yet another uninvited interrogation.

On the other hand, she supposed he had every right to something of an explanation that made sense.

Too bad she didn't have one to offer.

"For starters, let's get to the dead man. Who was he, or at the very least, what did he have to do with you?" He had barely touched his Moo Goo Gai Pan and he sipped on his own soda with indifference.

She looked around furtively to ensure that they were not too close to curious ears at neighboring tables. With loud and mostly obnoxious children running around everywhere, crying babies in strollers, and shopping bags and purses to watch out for, the adults, mostly women, had too much on their own minds to be worried about her conversation.

"All I know is what I've already told you. There's no sense in repeating everything just for the sake of conversation. Short and sweet, he shot my best friend, then shot me, so I pushed him into the river to even the score. He happened to be holding onto me at the time, so logically, we both ended up going over the edge. I have no idea who, or even what, the other men were. Maybe Feds for all I know. Satisfied?"

She sipped her drink.

"You're serious about this, aren't you?" As hard as it was to swallow, he was beginning to think she may not be crazy but actually on the level. He wrestled madly with the thought as it tried to gain a foothold within the logic of his mind.

"Yep. As serious as a heart attack."

"Okay, here's a simple question: why?"

"Why as serious as a heart attack?"

"No, dammit, why you two?"

"Wrong place at the wrong time, I guess. Simple as that." It was lame and she knew it.

He shook his head. "If we were talking about just you and Alex, I might buy that. But what about the six or eight other people you say these men killed?" He played back the question for mental review and scoffed at his own words. Who was he kidding? This woman, as gorgeous as she may be, was a classic paranoid schizophrenic. Completely delusional. He was letting his interest in her physically cloud his professional assessment. How would he be treating her if she had just stumbled onto his couch, perhaps the referral from a friend, with such an absurd story?

"Can't say," she shrugged, sipping her Coke.

It had become her classic response, but it was, in truth, a genuine answer. She did not know what this was all about, except that it probably centered around Skipper Goodman and his damned key. This single brass key hanging around her neck meant nothing out of context, and even in the context of all she suspected, was as thin a thread on which to base her suspicions as any she could have imagined.

As he processed her standard "non-answer," Marie said, "I would really like to reach Nevada by dinnertime, Paul. We've got a lot of driving to do if we're gonna make that."

Great, he thought, still no acceptable answers and off again, this time headed for yet another state. "What's in Nevada?" he asked. His tone sounded more weary than upset.

Not physically weary so much as emotionally spent.

She sensed his mood at once.

"Paul," she said sitting beside him and taking his arm in hers. "I am eternally grateful to you for saving my life. You are entitled to answers and I will try my very best to come up with them for you. I have a lot going through my mind right now and way more confusion than certainty. Can you understand that?" He allowed a half smile. "When we stop for the night, we'll open a bottle of wine— you didn't know I brought a couple from the cabin, did you?" His smile widened. "Then we'll talk until you are completely satisfied with this whole situation. I'm not crazy, Paul. I know you've been thinking that, but of course, all crazy people think they're the least crazy people in the world, don't they?" The smile was now wide and his body language said he would patiently wait until evening for answers.

Marie was a student of body language, especially men's, and though she hated playing anyone merely to get something she wanted, also realized there were times when the stakes were just too damn high not to use whatever tools God had given her.

This was one of those times. There were deaths to avenge. Very bad people had to be uncovered and made to pay. Colonel 'whoever' and his scary band of thugs could not be allowed to kill innocent people and just walk away. If she had to flirt with her temporary chauffeur to get closer to the solution, to the truth, he'd simply have to get over it.

No one said life was going to be easy or fair, she reminded herself.

It certainly had not been for her in many, many years.

"Where in Nevada?" he asked as he stood and took their Styrofoam plates to the trash container.

* * *

Despite their best efforts to reach the next state to the west, driving like a pair of bank robbers from the 1930s seeking shelter from the law that crossing a state line provided during that era, several vehicle accidents along I-70 had slowed their progress, allowing them to only get as far as Salina, Utah, by dusk.

They'd spoken little en route, Marie glued to her map and Paul processing every word she'd uttered since pulling her from the river. It wasn't a tense atmosphere as much as it was one of emotional weariness on the part of both travelers. They each needed space, and since physical proximity was a fact, mental space was all that could be granted for the moment.

"There's a Roadway Inn about a mile ahead," she finally announced, having just read the Interstate sign detailing the motel options at the upcoming exit. She was exhausted and ready for bed. Her mind ached almost as much as her body and her body ached like hell.

"What's wrong with the Holiday Inn?" he asked, having read the same huge green notice.

"It's too far off the Interstate. No sense in having to backtrack in the morning."

"It's a mile further," he grumbled. "I like Holiday Inns when I travel."

He eased the Range Rover onto the exit leading to all motels. "The Roadway Inn looks fine," she said, pleased by its attractive exterior and recent construction, but also noting the large and busy truck stop across the exit, within walking distance. She was careful to keep her eyes on their sleeping accommodations, and not on her planned escape route while he showered in the morning.

It was time to leave Paul and make it the rest of the way on her own. Too many questions, too few answers.

Besides, the longer they stayed together, the greater the likelihood of his becoming embroiled in a situation from which he had neither the means nor the skills to extricate himself. If she left him, here and now, the charming, if persistently-nosey, therapist might just make it out of this thing alive.

She prayed that would be the case, and while she had no tangible evidence to support her fears of having been somehow tracked by the horrid Colonel and his men, knew they probably had the means with which to do just that if given enough time.

Time: so long her enemy.

How much was left?

She couldn't even begin to guess.

By separating, however, time would again be on her side, at least momentarily, and if Paul were no longer in her company, he might not even appear on their radar. It was clear they wanted her and the "item." They probably didn't even know there was a Paul at this point.

It was definitely time to leave him before she cost the life of the man who'd saved hers. She was bone tired of people dying because of her.

"It looks alright, I guess. Kinda busy," he said, surprised by the number of vehicles already in the parking lot. He stopped the SUV beneath the two-story port cochere that sheltered the front doors and registration, then reached for the door handle.

"I'll get it," she said, exiting the vehicle before he knew what had happened. She scurried around the front of the SUV and came to his window. "Why don't you just wait right here and I'll check us in. Then we can settle in for the night, order a pizza, open a bottle of wine, and have that little chat I promised."

In truth, Marie couldn't risk Paul paying for the room with a credit card, which he surely would, knowing that their exact whereabouts could be pinpointed in a second if such a blunder were made. However, sharing this concern with him would take as much explanation as all the other items she'd been avoiding— maybe more.

It was easier and safer to just check them in herself and pay in cash.

Paul knew better than to argue with her, already being halfway to the front door, so he just sat beneath the awning and waited for her to return. *God, she had a cute butt*, he thought.

"Hello," Marie said in an upbeat tone when she neared the registration desk. A pleasant-looking young woman, perhaps in her early twenties, smiled back. Her nametag bore the logo of the motel chain as well as her first name. "I'd like a room for my husband and me, Claire," she said, adding the girl's name. "Two queen beds if possible. He has a bad back and sleeps much better if I don't keep bumping into him all night."

She gave a wide and genuine smile.

Claire tapped a few keys dutifully, but quickly received the same answer she'd gotten from three previous requests for rooms with two beds: there weren't any. "I'm sorry, ma'am, but we only have kings left. All non-smoking. Would you like me to check in town?"

"No, a king non-smoking will be fine," she said without hesitation. "I'll give him a sleeping pill." Another disarming smile.

She presented her driver's license, paid for one night in cash, and joined Paul out front with a single keycard in hand. In two minutes, he'd parked the Range Rover and they had collected their meager belongings. When he offered to carry everything, she said "no" without explanation.

Her independence hadn't surprised him, though it did make him feel ungentlemanly letting her carry everything, as little as it may have been.

If Claire found it odd or suspicious that Mrs. Brennan hurried across the lobby with no luggage, just three plastic shopping bags and a backpack, while her husband carried a bottle of wine in each hand, she didn't show it.

THIRTY-SIX

NOTING THE KING-SIZED bed the moment he entered the room, Paul Burks could not have been more thrilled. It was all he could do to hide the Cheshire Cat grin on his face, but he somehow managed to appear as though he had no thoughts in his head other than a nice quiet dinner followed by a good night of platonic rest. The images of her naked body in the glow of the camp light played like an R-rated drive-in movie in his mind.

He had to call his best friend and bring him up to speed.

Marie dropped her bags and backpack on the foot of the bed and fell across it on her back, careful to keep the long sweatshirt from rising above her beltline. It was a quick gesture that Paul didn't appear to even notice.

"Pretty good size room," he said, dropping into one of the chairs flanking the small round table by the bed. He studied the tall, slender woman ten feet away and wished he could just take her now. Perhaps, he considered for a moment, that was the message she was trying to send by lying there like that.

He began to rise when she sat up quickly.

"I'm going to wash this mop I used to call hair," she announced, untying the laces of her hiking boots, "and then I'm going to brush my teeth. I bought us both toothbrushes at the mall." She dug through one of the plastic bags and came out sporting a pair of Reach toothbrushes and two tubes of Crest.

"Thanks," he said, furtively running his tongue along the front of his teeth. They could use a good brushing before—he didn't allow his mind to finish forming the image.

All in good time, he smiled within.

Marie rose and transferred all her possessions to the small bathroom. When she leaned back through the open doorway, she said, "I'll be a few minutes. Want to grab us some ice and a couple of sodas? Maybe look in the room directory for a Pizza Hut nearby? But don't order until I get out. I don't know what I want yet."

In reality, she didn't want him using one of his credit cards over the phone, on the slim chance they were being monitored for activity by the men who'd tried to kill her. With his marching orders delivered, she closed and quietly locked the bathroom door.

Paul rose at once and grabbed the ice bucket from the dresser. Then, taking with him the plastic key she'd left on the bed, exited the room and returned to the elevator. He made his way to the ground level, turned left, and headed straight for the ice and vending machines, softly whistling an old Beatles tune that had popped into his head. He smiled when he saw the pay phone he'd spotted earlier.

Reece Davies answered on the fourth ring, just as Paul was about to hang up. "Hello," he said impatiently. He had been heading out the door to meet some friends for dinner nearby when the phone began to ring.

"You're not going to believe this shit," Paul said excitedly. He hadn't needed to introduce himself to his best friend of twenty years.

"You actually caught a fish this trip," Davies joked. It was normal behavior among the friends to answer each other in the absurd. It was Davies' cabin that Paul had been borrowing in Truman. His friend had found it on the Internet a few years earlier and had bought it sight unseen. About the only one in his large group of friends who had not stayed a single night in it thus far was Davies, himself.

"Yep, a mermaid." Paul checked his watch. He needed to be back in the room in five minutes.

Davies was intrigued. "Like Daryl Hannah in *Splash*?" he said, referring to the movie of that name where she played just such a creature caught by Tom Hanks. He dropped into a chair in his den. If this was a typical Paul Burks call, it would take awhile; he might as well get comfortable.

"Exactly, only way better built and just as naked."

When his highly-regimented and somewhat uptight psychologist friend sounded like an eighth-grader with a crush on a high school cheerleader, Davies pressed for details. "Okay, Paul, you've got my attention. Let's have it all."

Over the next ten minutes, talking non-stop and as fast as one of those guys reading the automobile ad disclaimers on TV, Paul Burks recounted every detail of the last twenty-four hours, paying particular attention to the parts where he saw her beautiful naked body not once, but twice.

He completely lost track of time.

"So, what about this dead guy?" Davies asked. It was the obvious question that had not been answered to his satisfaction during the hastily-told story. "Could spell trouble with a capital 'T' when it all comes down."

"Nah, I'll just tell them that I never saw the other body, being too involved in saving the girl's life. They'll buy it; probably pin a medal on me."

"Her story will conflict with yours," Davies warned.

"That's okay. I can always say that while she told me about another body, I never actually saw one. I'll say that I assumed she was delusional from her extended hypoxia and gave it no credence. Of course they'll believe me over her."

It was said with absolute certainty.

Davies chewed on his friend's explanation for a moment and then asked, "So, when are you going to sleep with her?"

"Did I mention that she just checked us into one motel room with a king-sized bed? Even paid for the room herself. In fact, she's paid for everything. In cash, no less. I'm telling you, other than being as nutty as a fruitcake, this is one fascinating woman. If I were a betting man, I'd say it was going to happen in the next couple of hours." He looked at his watch and suddenly realized that fifteen minutes had passed. She would be pissed if he were still gone, and he would have some serious explaining to do. No way could he tell her about this phone call. "Oh, man, I gotta go now or I'm in a world of shit. Talk to you tomorrow. I'll let you know how things went."

"I want all the sordid details," Davies insisted, "pictures, too," but he was speaking to a line that had already gone dead.

*   *   *

"You still there?" Marie asked from the bathroom when she'd finished toweling her hair dry. Receiving no reply, she opened the door and peered into the room. Paul was not where she had last seen him, in the chair by the bed. Not pleased, she stepped out into the room.

"Hello," he said, laying the motel area guide in his lap. He had taken a spot on the bed that was not visible from the bathroom and was absorbed in hunting for pizza delivery.

"Oh, sorry. I didn't see you," Marie said, the towel draped over her shoulders but otherwise nude. She pulled it around her quickly but without ceremony. "Get the ice?" she asked casually.

Silently admiring her freshly-scrubbed beauty, and realizing for the first time in the full light of the motel room that she wasn't a natural blonde—a redhead, in fact—he pointed to the ice bucket and Dr. Peppers on the small table.

That makes three times, he thought.

"Ice is probably half melted by now, though. Want me to get some fresh?"

Not so much embarrassed as mildly annoyed at having once again managed to find herself completely naked in front of the man, she said, "No, it'll be fine."

She returned to the bathroom, closing the door behind her.

When she had dressed, including new lingerie bought from the Victoria's Secret in the mall, she carefully packed all of her world into her backpack, including most of the cash, and rejoined Paul in the bedroom. She was wearing khaki cargo shorts with an emerald-colored pullover. Summer weight but comfortable rather than sexy. Her trusty hiking boots were still on the floor near the foot of the bed, right where she'd left them earlier.

She tossed her bag on the bed again and flopped down beside it, then snatched the motel guide from his hands. "I'll order the pizza while you grab a shower. When you're through, the food will be here. Then we'll eat, open a bottle of wine, and I'll talk about everything that's happened, as promised, until you fall sound asleep from boredom."

"Unlike you, I don't have clean clothes," he said. "You did all the shopping and the thought never crossed my mind." He stood and walked over to where she was sitting at the foot of the bed.

"No problem. You won't be needing any clean clothes until morning, and we can deal with it then." It was a lie, but one she knew would send him into the bathroom without hesitation. She punctuated that lie by taking his hand and kissing his fingertips seductively.

"Be right back," he said, stripping off his shirt while simultaneously using the opposite foot to remove both shoes. "Don't go anywhere."

Marie smiled and began thumbing through the motel guide again. "I'll be right here," she assured him.

By the time the shower had been running for less than a minute, she had donned her boots and had slipped from the room.

*   *   *

Once again, Donald Shelton's magic had served the Unit well. A second Internet lead at around five p.m. had placed the Range Rover in a long line of stalled traffic, waiting for an accident to be cleared from the west-bound lane of I-70, about twenty miles west of Grand Junction. It was clear to Merkett that the couple was again on the move, this time heading west—just as he'd predicted.

Now, as Merkett and his team raced west along the Interstate, his cell phone rang for a second time since leaving the airstrip north of Truman. Again, it was Shelton.

"Got an exact location, sir," he said, referring to his laptop screen. "I was monitoring a series of most-frequently-called numbers I'd been able to pull from the doctor's call history when one of them got a hit. Seems a friend of his named Reece Davies just got a call from a payphone at the Roadway Inn near Salina, Utah. It's right on the Interstate, you can't miss it."

"Any idea who this Davies is?"

"His name appeared on the title of the cabin in Truman."

"Good work, Don. Keep at it."

When Merkett hung up, he turned to Staff Sergeant Branch in the back seat. "Grab those silencers from the back, will you Sergeant." When each of the team had been issued a noise suppressor for his Beretta or assault rifle, Merkett said, "No time to change into civvies, so we go in like Homeland Security. No one is going to get in the way of armed soldiers of the United States Army, but I want to be in and out in five. Understood?"

Each of the other three men nodded silently as the Suburban approached the exit. They could clearly see the motel a mile ahead on the right.

*   *   *

Paul finished showering in record time and wrapped a towel around his waist, then stepped from the bathroom, anxious to claim his prize. It took only a second to realize that not only was Marie gone, but so was her backpack and all her belongings.

"SON OF A BITCH!" he shouted as he threw on his pants.

At the truck stop across the Interstate, Marie carefully searched the various eighteen-wheelers for one with an unlocked door. In her first five tries, she'd struck out.

The massive transfer trucks, lined up in neat parallel rows with their cargo doors facing the small restaurant that serviced the steady stream of long-distance drivers, had all been left running. Some because they were hauling fruit or vegetables that required constant refrigeration, which meant running the huge diesel engines non-stop; and others because their owners didn't want to return from dinner to find their overnight accommodations—the large attached sleeper cabs that provided all the comforts of home—hot and uninviting.

As she continued to try every opening, both cab doors and sleeper doors, her frustration mounted. All were locked, which made perfect sense considering all you had to do to steal one of these expensive monsters if the engine was left running was to drop in behind the wheel and throw it in gear. She had wanted to be gone by now, well on her way, but the only progress she'd made toward that goal so far was to work up a healthy sweat hoofing it across the expressway from the motel to the truck stop.

She spotted one toward the end, closest to the motel, that didn't appear to have smoke issuing from its exhausts. As she reached for the handle on the passenger's side, a man grabbed her by the arm.

Without hesitation, Marie shot her elbow back with lightning speed, striking the man in the chin and throat with an intensity that knocked him off his feet.

When she turned to run, Paul called out to her. "Jesus Christ, Marie, what the hell'd you hit me for?"

As surprised to hear her name as she had been to have the man's hand on her arm a moment earlier, she fought to bring his features, hidden in the deep shadows between the huge trailers, into focus.

"Paul?" she said, half recognizing his prone form on the asphalt. His car keys lay on the ground beside him.

"Who'd you think it was? For Christ's sake, Marie, you could have broken my damn jaw!" As he got to his feet, he was clearly not a happy camper.

"What the hell are you doing here?" she asked angrily.

"No, what the hell are *you* doing here? Now, that's the real question." He rubbed his battered face and spat out a mouthful of blood. "Imagine my surprise when I finish my shower and find you gone. Not exactly the deal we made, huh."

"I have no time for any of this, Paul. I sincerely thank you for all you've done for me, but I gotta be on my way. Please, just leave. Go back to the motel and get some sleep. You can call the cops in the morning and tell them anything you like, but just let me be on my way."

He stepped up to her and put a hand firmly on each shoulder. When she winced at the contact with her left shoulder, he made an apologetic face and lowered his hands to envelop hers. "Marie, I don't know what's going on but I do know that you need serious psychological help. All this running around and intrigue, the bad guys chasing you, dead people all around you, it's all symptomatic of some deeply seated psychosis. Come with me now, we'll go to the closest treatment center and I swear on my life, I'll get you the finest care money can buy."

As he spoke, Marie's eyes widened at the frightening sight that filled them. It couldn't be, not here, not now. But it was. She pulled her hands from Paul's and taking him by the shoulders, spun him around to face the motel. As he was about to turn and physically restrain her, he too saw the huge black Suburban pull to a screeching stop in the same spot they had occupied only an hour earlier.

Beneath the motel's port cochere, four doors were flung open and four armed men, all dressed in black and all with automatic weapons drawn and ready, bolted across the walkway and disappeared through the front doors.

"So you think I need to see a shrink because I'm making all this shit up, eh?" she seethed, standing beside him. They were watching the action across the street from the opening between the cab and cargo trailer of the big rig. "Maybe you also think the men with the machine guns heading through the front door of the motel, in search of us I might add, would also benefit from a long chat with a shrink, since they're obviously trapped within the same delusional dream as I."

Paul was so shocked by the sight that he was unable to speak. Fear like he had never known swept over him and his knees felt like they could no longer support him. He wanted to run, but couldn't pry his eyes from the black Suburban a hundred yards north of them.

Marie suddenly spotted the Range Rover near the entrance to the truck stop diner and realized, thankfully, that Paul had brought the vehicle with him, using the overpass, instead of crossing the Interstate on foot as she had.

With a pressing need to get the hell away from there, and with the armed men momentarily preoccupied with the siege of their motel room, she grabbed the keys off the pavement that Paul had dropped when she'd decked him and darted for his SUV. "Move your ass if you want to live!" she shouted as she ran.

As she dove behind the wheel of his Range Rover and started the engine, he stood with a confused and dazed look on his face at the open driver's door. "Passenger side, now!" she shouted, pulling her door closed. Through the open window she said, "I swear to God, Paul, if you say one damn word, I'll leave you where you stand."

THIRTY-SEVEN

MARIE EASED THE RANGE Rover from the truck stop to avoid drawing unwanted attention to the vehicle, then took the westbound on-ramp, keeping the rows of big rigs between them and the motel. Once on the Interstate, she nailed the throttle and the SUV responded without complaint. In less than half a mile, she was going thirty miles an hour over the posted speed of seventy, spending half her time watching the road ahead, the other half glued to the mirror.

It wasn't necessary: Paul had not taken his eyes off the back glass since practically falling into the passenger seat.

"Obviously they know about you and what kind of car we're driving. That complicates things," she groaned, swerving quickly into the left lane and then back into the right to narrowly avoid first ramming the guy in front of her and then the truck eighty feet ahead of him in the left lane. For some inexplicable reason, the jerk was going fifty—twenty under the speed limit. As she shot around him, she could see him attempting to dial a number on his cell phone, his face illuminated by the eerie green glow. If she hadn't already been a hundred feet past him when she processed the absurd image, she would have given him a piece of her mind.

341

"What I'd like to know is how." Knowing meant that she could avoid giving them similar information in the future.

The future. The thought of even a single tomorrow seemed preposterous at the moment.

"WHO ARE THOSE MEN!" Paul shouted, his anger clearly directed at her. He was either winded from his sprint to the car or he was hyperventilating.

"You don't have to yell, Paul. I'm sitting right here," she said calmly, softening her own voice in an effort to lower the emotional level that was rapidly escalating within her distraught passenger. Marie knew they had to get off the Interstate, and quickly. A five-minute head start on these bastards would not be worth beans the moment they discovered the motel room empty. Worse, they would learn that she'd registered under the name of Vickie Brennan. *Thank God for the second set of I.D.*, she thought. *Probably not getting back to St. Michael's anytime soon.*

"Don't tell me not to yell!" he continued to shout, though with a bit less ferocity.

She fully understood his anxiety and fear. She remembered being in his shoes, a little more than three years ago. It had been a horrifying moment, just as this must be for Paul. It was a feeling she wouldn't wish on anyone.

He took a deep and calming breath. "Who are those men and what do they want with you? Please."

As she scanned the highway for any alternate road that might lead to safety, at least relative to staying on this arrow-straight path to ultimate capture, she thought of the best way to answer his question without telling him anything that would compromise her in any way.

"As I've tried to tell you several times, I don't know who they are, and quite honestly, I have no idea what they want with me. It may be that—"

"That's BULLSHIT, Marie, and you know it!" he interrupted. The yelling was back.

She held up a hand. "You need to calm down, Paul. Seriously. You're going to have a heart attack and that's not going to help either one of us."

It had not been what he wanted to hear, and the unintelligible cursing and ranting that persisted for the next five minutes, without respite, made her want to throw him from the vehicle. Finally, with a clear stretch of road ahead, she reached between the seats and pulled a bottle of water from her backpack. When she handed it to him, she was surprised that he didn't use it as a missile and nail her alongside the head with it. *Probably a good thing we're going as fast as we are,* she thought.

He unscrewed the plastic top and drank like a man who'd been digging ditches all day.

When he tried to speak again, his voice was raspy and nearly gone. He took another long sip. "Will you please tell me anything that will help me make sense of this insanity?"

It had been more a plea than a question.

She squeezed his knee reassuringly and started to speak at the precise moment they passed the kind of road she'd been praying for. Braking the heavy SUV with all the power in her right leg, she practically stood it on its front grill. Luckily, there were no vehicles behind them as they decelerated from just over a hundred to just under thirty in less than five seconds. With Paul practically cleaved in half by his shoulder strap, unable to do anything but gasp in disbelief and clutch the dash with both hands, Marie tested the Range Rover even further by throwing it into a hard left turn, into the median, while they were still at speed.

Rising onto its two right wheels in an ear-splitting shriek of tires and groaning metal, she was certain she'd overestimated the capability of the expensive import and had doomed them to cartwheel across the center divider like an empty beer can tossed from a pickup.

Amazingly, the vehicle held, leaving the pavement and entering the dust, sand, and scrub grass of the center strip with as much bouncing and bucking as a Brahma bull that didn't wish to be ridden.

Dumb luck far more than skillful driving prevented them from becoming mangled bits of flesh and steel, narrowly missing the front grill of an oncoming eighteen-wheeler as they bolted across the two eastbound lanes of the Interstate and then down the southern slope.

The eighty-thousand-pound truck was all air horns and smoking tires as its driver did a masterful job of keeping the British SUV from becoming a hood ornament while not rolling his own rig in the process.

In another minute, I-70 was a memory in the rearview mirror.

For the next half hour, Marie and Paul followed the fire road south, driving at breakneck speeds until the road had become little more than a scratch in the desert landscape.

Finally, at the point where even that pitiful path disappeared into a stream, she stopped the car. Crossing any body of water without knowing its width and, more importantly, its depth, especially at night, was foolish, often suicidal. The headlights of the Range Rover, as good as they were, failed to illuminate the far side, as if they'd just reached the bank of a great lake. She replayed the map contours that she'd studied all day in her mind, yet could think of no such body of water within fifty miles of their present, or more correctly, their most likely location.

It didn't matter until morning, she decided. For now, they were safe. Headlights approaching from the north could be seen for miles, providing ample warning.

Daylight would bring another set of problems altogether, but she'd deal with them as they arose.

"Please, God, only one crisis at a time," she said in silent prayer.

* * *

It had taken Merkett and Nate Fisher less than a minute to reach the room and determine that they had, once again, been outfoxed.

Sergeant major Ron Phelps had been left in the lobby to watch that entrance and to keep the charming and cooperative Claire calm and off the phone. The fourth man, Staff Sergeant Kevin Branch, had been ordered to locate the Range Rover and to prevent it from leaving the parking lot at all cost.

Without having to be asked twice, Claire had given the men with the huge guns and the Homeland Security I.D. the couple's room number and had quickly coded a second electronic room key for their use. There'd been no mistaking who they were after: she had immediately recognized the picture of the woman they had shoved in her face, and told them so. What had surprised her was their repeatedly referring to her as Marie Matthews.

Having returned to the lobby empty handed, Merkett stood before the cowering desk clerk, his weapon in its holster. As he was about to address her, Branch came in through the motel's rear entrance, hurried down the long hall past the elevators and vending machines, and approached the Colonel.

"Not here, sir," he reported. He had run full tilt around the building, covering both front and rear parking areas, and was barely breathing hard.

Merkett nodded and turned his attention back to the desk clerk. "Thank you for your help earlier, Claire. Unfortunately, neither of the suspects we're seeking appears to be in your establishment at present. Can you please tell me how long ago they may have left?" He rested his thick arms on the desk, fingers interlaced. He tried to produce a pleasant, non-threatening smile but his mood made it nearly impossible.

His scruffy face and dusty condition of his clothes didn't help.

"I never saw the woman leave, but I may have seen the man run through the lobby a few minutes ago. I was doing my nightly report and he was in such a hurry that I didn't get a real good look at his face, but I'm pretty sure it was the same man who came in with Mrs. Brennan earlier." She alternated her concerned stare between the other three men and the man questioning her.

This was going to be a night to remember.

"You mean Marie Matthews?"

"The picture you showed me was the same lady who checked in using a Utah driver's license with the name Vickie Brennan on it. That's all I know."

"Brennan. Not Matthews?" he repeated, as if the concept were not easy to grasp.

She nodded and smiled as sincerely as she could in the midst of an armed assault on her workplace.

Realizing there was nothing left to do here that wouldn't exponentially increase the risk of their encountering the authorities, Merkett signaled for his men to head for the car. It would take the frightened Claire several minutes to regain her wits and report her recent hair-raising encounter to her boss, who would most certainly and immediately call a buddy with the local sheriff's office wanting to know what the hell had just happened at his motel.

It was time to go.

THIRTY-EIGHT

AS SOON AS MARIE switched off the headlights and killed the engine, soft blue gray light from a full moon directly overhead spilled in through the windshield and sunroof, illuminating the interior enough to allow them to talk without their conversation being in complete darkness. The alternative, switching on the overhead map lamps, was completely out of the question. She knew that even the smallest glow in a desertscape otherwise devoid of artificial light would stand out like a signal fire for miles in all directions. She'd seen it many times on the river, as a lone hiker, a mile above their campground, made his or her way along the ridge, guided by a single flashlight.

It had appeared to be the brightest star in the night sky.

Now, in this temporary sanctuary in the middle of nowhere, the image seemed like a lifetime ago.

She felt her pulse and was not shocked to discover it elevated to the point where a massive stroke at any moment wouldn't surprise her. She took in several deep breaths and exhaled them very slowly, hoping to bring her heart rate back down into double digits; preferably back to normal.

Paul was faring much worse. He actually appeared to be freezing, so intense were the tremors that rocked his entire body. While no longer the sweltering day it had been earlier, the desert had not yet given up its accumulated warmth, and was not the cause of his shaking. She knew the true origin of his shaking: fear.

Unbridled, undiluted terror.

She extended her right hand to his shoulder to steady him and to reassure him that they were safe for the moment, but for a man whose entire life had been one continuous feast of safe moments, now receiving that same assurance of security one pitiful morsel at a time provided no comfort at all.

She would try anyway. As she squeezed affectionately, she said, "Paul, we're safe now. There's no way they could have followed us here."

He turned to her with panic and disbelief contorting his face. "What have you done?"

"What have *I* done!" she snapped, having not anticipated being blamed for their predicament. "I haven't done a damn thing. You think I brought this on myself? On us? You think I chose any of this shit? You think I like being chased to hell and back by assholes with automatic weapons? Are you crazy or something?" She realized that she'd balled her hands into tight fists and was brandishing them like a prizefighter.

She told herself to relax, that anger would be counterproductive.

It was no use; the fists remained taut and whatever progress she'd made at reducing her heart rate had been reversed.

"Well, you sure as hell did something, whether you ever intend to tell me or not. Normal people don't incur the wrath of armed gunmen."

"So, I'm not normal? Is that your professional evaluation?"

He nodded. "I think you're as crazy as a loon."

"What a wonderfully warm bedside manner you've got there, Doctor Burks. Must bring you lots of referral business." She unscrewed the cap on the water and took a swallow, wiping her mouth afterward with the back of her hand. "I suppose I'm crazy because I'm just imagining all this shit. Well, hell, I certainly hope that's true, because I'd love to take a Prozac and have it all go away."

He glared at her for what seemed an hour then said, "Prozac is for depression."

"Well since all this depresses the living shit out of me, I'd say dispense 'em if you got 'em, doc." She held out an open hand mockingly.

His angry stare continued as he pondered his fate in the coming hours. Clearly, the crazy woman across from him, regardless of how she'd gotten into this mess, was far more adept at surviving situations like this than he could ever hope to be. An alliance, at least until he could reach the authorities, was probably his best move at present. "Listen, we're in this together, whether we want to be or not. We need to pool our resources and figure a way out that doesn't involve getting killed."

She sat there shaking her head.

"What the hell does that mean? We don't need to pool our resources or there's no way out without dying?"

"Both," she said flatly. "This is something I have to do on my own from here on, and if I'm not successful, I and a lot of other people are going to die."

"There you go! How do you know that? What makes you say things like that? What the hell is going on, Marie?" His trembling had not abated and his voice was still as scratchy as an old man's.

"All I know is this, whatever these men want from me, they will stop at nothing to get it. That can only mean one of two things: either a lot of money's at stake, or someone's ass is on the line. Probably both." She began to feel the chill of the desert night creeping into the vehicle. It was going to be cold in a few hours.

Paul felt as if he would vomit at any moment. It was mostly the fear, but also the roller coaster rocket ride along the dirt road for the last twenty-five miles.

"I feel nauseous," he said, fumbling with his seat belt. "When I get back, you're telling me everything you know and then I'm driving the both of us straight to the nearest sheriff's office. We'll let them sort all this shit out."

He exited the vehicle, slamming the door behind him.

Marie watched as he moved to the rear of the vehicle and then get swallowed up by the velvet darkness of the barren landscape.

Despite his insistence, which she fully understood and was in complete sympathy with, she wasn't going to tell him anything that might get him killed, and which would certainly get her killed. And, she sure as hell wasn't going to any damn sheriff's office until she had put the key around her neck into the lock it was intended to fit.

The secret, and therefore the answer to this nightmare, lay beyond that lock.

The only way out of her hellhole was straight through the center of it, just like getting sober or quitting drugs. No end run, no easy out.

Guts, brains, hard work, and a whole lot of luck.

She could count on the first three, especially when her life depended on it.

What frightened her the most was running out of luck.

It could be as fickle as fate itself.

She looked toward her backpack and knew what she had to do.

He would not understand or ever forgive her, but if she acted quickly, he just might live to complain to her about it one day.

She prayed she was doing the correct thing, but right or wrong, it was the only move left on the board.

*　*　*

"Who in god's name is Vickie Brennan?" Merkett shouted into his cell phone. The Suburban was traveling west on I-70 at well above the posted speed, but not so fast as to instantly bring every cop in the county down on them. In a pinch, their Homeland Security identification would do.

If an officer stopped them and got too pushy or inquisitive, they'd simply kill him and be on their way.

"No idea, sir," was all Donald Shelton could say. He hammered at his keyboard while his cell phone remained on speaker mode. There was no one around to hear but Mack Fuhrman; they were in the middle of the Nevada desert, miles from the nearest town. Fortunately, even this remote location, adjacent to an Interstate highway, had cell service almost every mile of the way. "There's no record of anyone by that name, fitting Matthews' general description anyway, in the Utah DMV. I also checked neighboring states."

"Who is this bitch?" Merkett growled. "First, she's a dead woman and now she's a ghost. What's up with that facial recognition search of yours? You wanted hours and you've had way more time than that. You have anything for me or not?"

Shelton had dreaded having this conversation, hoping the Colonel would simply forget about the nationwide DMV database search he'd begun back at Truman. He pulled in a deep breath and braced himself for the angry response his report would surely elicit. "Got a number of hits that were ninety-eight percent or above, sir."

"What the hell does that mean?"

He could tell the Colonel was pissed and he hadn't even delivered the bad news yet. He continued: "Unless the facial recognition software rates a possible candidate match at ninety-eight percent or higher, it rejects it. There were six in the national DMV search registering that degree of probability, going back no more than five years. Four of the women were easily culled for one reason or another, mostly because of height or some other physical factor. One had a prosthetic leg, for instance. As expected, Marie Matthews of Truman, Utah, was number two of six, scoring a perfect one-hundred-percent match."

"So, who was number one? She'll be the person we're after, right?"

"Marie Matthews of St. George, Utah, also with a one-hundred-percent facial match."

"I'm confused," Merkett said. "How can both of them score a perfect match? I thought this damned software was designed to find the one person in a million who was unique, like fingerprints or DNA."

"It is, sir, and it can only return a result like this for one reason."

"And that is?" His patience had grown thin.

"Because they're the same woman?" Shelton said, waiting for the phone to explode in front of him.

Merkett puzzled with the squint's words for a long moment, then said, "Are you telling me that the original Marie Matthews didn't die back then, and that we're chasing the same person?"

"No, sir, she died alright. In Oklahoma, just like the initial search indicated. To be certain, I cross-checked the medical records and police reports, then checked them again."

"So what are you saying, dammit!"

"What I'm saying is that our Marie Matthews merely used the other woman's DMV photo as her own. I only got to look at her for a minute or so, and the light wasn't all that great in the clearing at the river, but she could have easily passed for the dead woman."

"So she used not only the woman's identity, but her actual photo? What if she got stopped for speeding? That's a hell of a risk."

"Not if they look almost alike. You know as well as I do that civil servants don't look at licenses for exact matches. They look for a general appearance match, whether the license is expired, whether there are any outstanding wants or warrants, but not whether the nose is a quarter of an inch longer or shorter on the actual person than in their license photo. Apparently, she chose the deceased Marie Matthews not only because of the similarity in age and race, but also because she looked like her twin. Or almost, anyway. It's brilliant, actually. Totally screws anyone attempting a search like we just ran. You simply get handed your own question as the answer. You've got to hand it to her, sir, she's one wily-ass bitch."

Perhaps, upon honest reflection, his professed admiration for the woman's guile and cunning had been a bit over the top, but whether that had been the trigger, or the woman's ability to vex a saint, the next three minutes of angry monologue from the boss featured some of the most creative combinations of expletives Shelton had heard in his military career.

By the time the Colonel had hung up, it was clear he wanted his computer genius to find the bitch and her running companion by morning or the Unit would be looking for a new computer genius.

*   *   *

Paul leaned in wearily through the passenger's window and asked Marie to please hand him the open bottle of Aquafina. She quickly obliged and he took a generous gulp, swirled it around in his mouth, and then spat it out beside the SUV.

Marie prayed he wouldn't rinse and spit a second time, no matter how vile the taste in his mouth—it was the last of the bottled water. She still had the canteen she'd filled earlier, but that wouldn't do. She watched in silent anticipation as he emptied the remainder of the bottle into his mouth, held it there for what seemed eternity, and then finally swallowed.

Thank, God, she thought, letting out a deep sigh.

Paul threw the empty bottle into the rear compartment and sank into the passenger's seat. He looked like he'd been whipped.

"Feeling a little better?" she asked taking his left hand in hers.

He only nodded faintly, his mind still trying to get a grip on all that had happened. He turned in his seat and leaned uncomfortably against the door, drawing his left leg up and under his right. "I think I deserve to know why someone is trying to kill me." His voice was again that of a therapist, though course and scratchy.

"You do, and I'm going to tell you everything," she said, pressing his hand firmly between hers. Marie knew that if she began at the river and slowly, monotonously, recounted the events of the last full day, it would be like a familiar nursery rhyme to a weary child. The two sleeping pills she'd dissolved in the water bottle, as he threw up somewhere in the desert behind the vehicle, while not of prescription strength, would nonetheless have him out like a light within ten or fifteen minutes.

It was mean, deceitful, and unfair of her. She knew it only too well and wasn't proud that it had come down to this. On the other hand, if Paul did exactly as she would instruct him, and didn't go running to the cops like a scared rabbit at first light, he might actually make it out of this alive.

It redefined "long-shot" to be sure, but it was better than no shot at all. She hadn't asked for any of this, and in the end, it was the Colonel and whomever he answered to who were to blame.

Not her.

She kept telling herself that, and yet it helped little.

Innocence was no shield against tragedy, no defense against oppression. Doing nothing meant death, and so these men had given her no choice but to lay down and die or spit in their faces. She had chosen to go out swinging, and she thanked God for having been through this hell before. Not being a naive lamb awaiting the slaughter provided a measure of comfort.

Not much, but some.

The vivid image of Alex lying murdered at the edge of the small woods, having never harmed a soul in her short life, rekindled Marie's need to even the score. She didn't care if it meant her life. If that were the price, she'd pay it without tears, without complaint.

But not until she had made them all pay.

Trying to run with Paul like an albatross around her neck would only turn her very slim chance of success into guaranteed failure.

On her own, at least there *was* a chance.

She reached across the gulf between them and touched her hand gently to his cheek, then slowly began to retell the story.

THIRTY-NINE

DONALD SHELTON HAD NOT taken the Colonel's warning lightly. He knew well that James Merkett would not tolerate excuses and detested failure with a passion that bordered on psychosis. It was a defining trait that made men like him such effective combat leaders, though that same intolerance would prevent such men as he from keeping corporate jobs longer than five minutes. Shelton respected his Colonel, but he also feared him, and of the two, Merkett would much have preferred the latter in his subordinates if given the choice. The price McGhee had paid for merely leaving his post to buy a carton of cigarettes was still fresh in his mind.

He had no intention of sharing his fate.

For hours, the self-professed Cyber Ranger hacked and searched, looking everywhere he could imagine, deep into every possible database, for the one clue that might lead him to the true identity of Marie Matthews, or at the very least, her present whereabouts.

There had not been a single reliable lead on the Range Rover since twenty-two-hundred hours—ten p.m.—more than six hours ago, despite the astronomical sum being offered on the Internet.

Sightings had occurred as far north as Canada and as far south as Key West, but none had been able to provide the defining piece of the puzzle: a correct tag number.

As he scrutinized the financial records of the woman's last three years, as skimpy as they were, he could not put his finger on a single anomaly. Not one item that might indicate who she had been in her former life, or who in the hell the Vickie Brennan was under whose name she had registered at the Roadway Inn in Salina, Utah.

As fatigue set in and he found himself covering the same ground three and four times without realizing it until he'd wasted half an hour, he stood and stretched, then slid the crew bay door back on the Huey and jumped to the ground. The pilot, Mack Fuhrman, was near the tail rotor smoking one of his last cigarettes. Having spent most of his military career flying one chopper or another, though most often in Hueys—in and out of combat zones on three continents—the veteran pilot didn't handle the monotony of endless waiting as well as the squint.

"Wish I smoked," Shelton said stepping up beside him. Ahead, in the east, the slightest glimmer of light had begun to color the sky at the horizon. "From what I can tell, it helps at times like this."

"Sun will be up in another twenty or twenty-five minutes," Fuhrman said. "Any luck so far?"

Shelton shook his head.

"Glad that's you at the keyboard and not me."

"Why's that?" he asked, though he knew.

"Hell, I'd be bored shitless, that's why. I don't know how you do it."

"Like you, it's my job. Just got pretty good at it along the way."

"Yeah, well you're the best damn squint I've ever known." He pointed a gnarled finger at Shelton's nose. "Let me remind you again, if you ever come after me the way you went after that congressman who cut you off in traffic, I'll have any one of a dozen of my closest friends cut your balls off and stuff 'em down your throat."

356

They'd had this good-natured talk before, and while Shelton knew it to be, as it always had been, just bravado among friends—fellow warriors—he also knew the man meant every word. Brute force, or at least the fear of it, was what kept the world in balance.

Without it, anarchy would reign supreme.

"No worries, you don't make enough money for me to come after you."

"Yeah, well I drive like a maniac, so I'm just liable to run you into a curb someday. If I do, remind me to kill you afterward."

"Oh, sure, I'll put that note in my phone so I don't forget."

Fuhrman chuckled then dropped his cigarette to the ground, crushing it with his boot. "What are you gonna try now?"

"All out of ideas, Mack. They've vanished into thin air and no one has seen shit in hours. It's like they fell off the face of the earth. One thing's for sure, they're not on any road with traffic. For fifty grand these days, people would turn in their mothers."

Again the pilot seemed amused. He moved to the crew bay and sat on the floor, legs dangling above the starboard skid. "Too bad the damn thing doesn't have a GPS tracker on it, like a FedEx truck. We could drive right up beside 'em and pop 'em before they even saw us coming."

Shelton pondered the pilot's words for a moment then climbed back into the bay, taking the seat that was still warm. He placed his laptop across his thighs and began typing and fingering the trackpad at a frenetic pace.

Puzzled by the unexpected surge of energy in the man he would have sworn, only seconds before, was about to drop, Fuhrman said, "Sudden flash of brilliance, Don?"

"No, something you said."

He finally relocated the exact entry in the doctor's financial records that Fuhrman's comment had tied a thin thread to, and began pursuing that delicate fiber of information to its source. Inside of a minute, he produced a smile that spanned his entire face.

"The son of a bitch had a LoJack system installed on his pretty new SUV on the fifth of this month. I saw the service record hours ago and figured it was a different radio or maybe a DVD system for the back seat. Never even considered LoJack. Damn!"

"That's one of those little electronic devices that tells the cops where your car is when it's stolen, right?"

"Yep. And it's going to tell *us* where they've been hiding all this time. All I have to do now," he said, typing like he was in a contest for most keystrokes per minute, "is take a peek into LoJack's database."

Forty minutes later, with sweat pouring from his brow and the coordinates of the Range Rover's present location in hand, Shelton pointed to an area map displayed on the LCD screen and said with a sadistic grin, "There you are, my little beauty. Time for your wake-up call."

*   *   *

When the morning sun finally rose behind Mt. Dutton, the highest peak to the east, the light that poured into Paul Burks' SUV hit him like a polar tsunami instead of a warming stream of amber-hued photons. He shot up in his seat, banging his head on the upper door frame, as disoriented as if he'd just awakened on Venus.

Looking all about him for any clue that would place him in a familiar and recognizable place on his own planet, and not in the midst of some Venusian desert, his eyes were drawn to a single sheet of paper lying in the driver's seat. When he grabbed the paper, he saw two thick stacks of currency lying beneath it. He dropped the sheet of paper and took the money, one stack in each hand. The brown paper bands that encircled each said $10,000 in block letters—twenty grand in all. He fanned each stack to be sure and saw that each note was, indeed, a one-hundred-dollar bill.

"What the hell?"

He reached for the sheet of paper again. When it seemed vaguely familiar, he realized it was a page torn from the 'notes' section in the back of his Range Rover's owner's manual.

Someone had written a lengthy note across both sides in hastily-scribbled longhand.

He knew at once, of course, that Marie had been the author.

Crushing the sheet within an angry fist, he bolted from the car, searching in every direction for her, yelling her name at the top of his lungs. By the time he'd shouted her name only twice, he understood that she wouldn't have heard him if he'd fired a canon. Wherever she'd gone, whenever she'd left, it had been hours ago—probably right after she'd drugged him.

"YOU BITCH!" he yelled toward the rising sun, though the east was no more likely to have been her route of escape than any other point on the compass.

"Oh, shit!" he said, afraid she'd taken the keys. He yanked open the driver's door and leaned across the seat, feeling to the right of the steering column. His key ring dangled from the ignition.

Thank God, he thought, at least I wouldn't have to walk back to the Interstate—wherever the hell that is.

He studied the craggy road at the rear of the SUV, little more than a prairie dog path at this point, and then turned to the opposite direction, to the east. Perhaps eighty feet ahead lay a small stream, fifty or sixty feet across, and from the appearance of the water that flowed anemically alongside basketball-sized boulders, was currently only six or eight inches deep. Most likely, in another day or two, it would again be a dry streambed.

They had certainly not come that way last night. The stream, such as it was, had most likely been the reason Marie had finally stopped throwing them around the outback like a Baja racer.

He rubbed eyes not fully awake, then realized he still had the crumpled paper in his fist. He flattened it across the hood of the car with a few quick hand passes, then flipped it over to where the letter began:

Paul,

Please forgive me for not giving you the answers you wanted and deserve, but I have no answers to give. I am truly sorry for having put something in your water to make you sleep, but I needed to be able to leave without a confrontation. While we both need to live, I have something vital to do as well, and if I get caught before I have a chance to succeed, I fear many lost lives will be the cost of my failure.

None of this is fair, I know, but the moment you pulled me from the river, your destiny was linked with mine by the cruelest twist of fate. If either of us is to survive, it will only be by going our separate ways. Perhaps, they, whoever they are, will turn their attention from you as they focus on finding me. I hope so with all my heart.

While I cannot tell you why any of this insanity is happening, you must believe me when I tell you the one thing I know beyond question: If you want to live, you must disappear. I can't say for how long. I'm not crazy, Paul, I know what I'm talking about. I do not know who these men are, by name or association, but I know these men only too well. They will not stop until they get what they want and they will kill everyone who gets in their way. They will feel no remorse. Your life depends on you believing what I say.

I beg you, do not go home or anywhere else that can be connected with you. Contact no one from your past and do not seek help from the authorities—they cannot protect you from the bastards who are after me, and now you.

I know it's far too little, but I've left you what cash I can spare. Under no circumstances are you to use a credit card of any kind. Leave your vehicle and just walk away. It will lead them straight to you. Do not stay here. Go quickly, the moment you finish reading this.

Make no mistakes, Paul. Leave no trail. It's a nearly impossible task to require of someone, but to do otherwise will mean your life and the lives of everyone you contact for help.

There's nothing else I can say except thank you for saving my life. I'm sorry I cannot do the same for you—only you can do that now.

Marie

"Screw that," he said, wadding the sheet into an even tighter knot than before. "And screw you, Marie Matthews." Enraged, he flung the ball of paper out into the desert, then jammed the cash onto his Dockers' pockets and climbed in behind the wheel. He was going straight to the authorities and have this crazy bitch arrested, but there was no sense in them knowing about the money.

Then, after she'd been charged with every possible criminal offense he could encourage the District Attorney to pursue, he'd have her committed to an institution for the criminally insane. Not one of those cushy country clubs where celebrities got sent, but an under-funded state-run hellhole where the only thing that got taken from an inmate faster than the last semblance of sanity was their dignity.

He started the SUV and maneuvered it carefully to avoid getting stuck, then retraced the route they'd taken last night. Though initially the road wasn't a real road in fact, barely more than a single set of tire tracks in the dust, it proved to be an easy matter making his way back the way they'd come.

Within a few miles, driving much more responsibly than she had on the previous trip, the fire road was once again beneath his tires. He was pretty certain the Interstate lay ahead, perhaps twenty or thirty miles.

He had no way of knowing for sure but continuing north seemed to make the most sense.

To his immense satisfaction, after applying years of professional training, as well as logical and deductive reasoning, to his own bruised psyche and perilous predicament, he'd been able to completely set aside his unfounded fears of the previous night.

After all, he'd only seen their world as she'd painted it, as she'd wanted him to see it.

There was no truth in her words, only lies upon lies.

It was stupid, a freshman mistake.

He reminded himself to be far less accepting of a pretty face in the future.

Reason dictated that the men at the motel were only after her, not him. She was probably wanted for some heinous offense, most likely the first-degree murder of the man she'd already admitted killing; maybe even the murder of that Alex woman, as well.

To his mind, Marie Matthews was nothing but a deranged individual, capable of anything, including homicide.

He wished now that he'd kept the note she'd written, to help prove intent and premeditation, but in the end, his professional testimony would be far more damning.

He began to rehearse his version of the events of the last thirty-six hours as he made his way steadily toward I-70. He needed to be certain that whatever he said when he finally reached the authorities, it would paint him in the best possible light, even heroically, and the woman he'd saved from drowning as little more than a dangerous nutcase. He would have to be careful, though, to avoid any implication in her crimes as an accomplice "after the fact."

The fear that he'd believed to be a thing of the past, a brief spell of anxiety and nothing more, suddenly stuck in his throat like a fist. A quarter mile ahead, a dusty, dark Suburban sat squarely in his path, three men dressed in matching black leaning against its massive chrome grill as cool as cucumbers. A fourth man, whom he'd not seen at first, was seated behind the wheel.

When the air was repeatedly broken by a deep thump, thump, thump—like a monstrous kettle drum—his eyes were drawn to the sky. Perhaps two hundred feet above the Suburban, and a hundred yards to its rear, a huge helicopter, painted desert camouflage from nose to tail, hovered like some giant killer wasp. If he'd had an ounce of fluid in his body, he'd have pissed himself where he sat.

Paul eased his vehicle to within a few yards of the Suburban and switched off the engine.

In a blinding storm of dust and sand, the Huey set down in the middle of the narrow road, directly beneath the spot it had been hovering.

Within a few seconds, the manmade cloud began to settle, the rotor blades of the Huey now thrumming with a dull whoop, whoop, whoop as their speed continued to drop.

As Paul was about to exit the car to begin presenting his carefully-prepared speech, he suddenly realized that during the few seconds he'd been unable to see, two of the men had taken up positions opposite and slightly behind both front doors of his SUV, their weapons drawn and aimed squarely at his head.

His stomach tied itself into knots.

"Please step out of the vehicle, sir," the man on his side ordered. "Keep your hands clearly visible at all times. Any sudden movement on your part will be deemed an act of aggression and we will respond to it accordingly."

Amazed that his muscles still yielded to commands from a brain that had turned to jelly, Paul opened his door using the outside handle and stepped to the ground beside the Range Rover—hands apart and raised, palms open and facing forward—exactly as instructed.

His heart hammered against his ribs like horses galloping across a wooden bridge.

The man on the right quickly swept the vehicle, then indicated to Merkett with a simple hand gesture that the woman was gone.

"Good morning, Doctor Burks," the third man said as he stared indifferently at Paul. He had not moved from his original position. "So kind of you to join us. We have so much to talk about, and not much time, I'm afraid."

FORTY

I T WAS JUST PAST midnight when Marie exited the Range
Rover. She'd written the warning note to Paul, had left him
what cash she could spare, then had methodically plotted the
best possible course to I-15 while he snored softly in the passenger's seat. Her handheld GPS told her that the Interstate highway,
which ran north-south through Utah, was just over fifteen miles
due west as the crow flies. Unfortunately, she wasn't a crow, or any
other creature possessing the gift of flight, and the distance on
foot, carefully avoiding the many gullies and circumventing hills—
short mountains was more like it—would be closer to twenty.

Maybe twenty-two.

Grueling, but doable.

She had begun quickly, wishing to put as much distance
between the SUV and herself as possible, but within two hours,
clouds had blocked out the moon and the grayish light that had lit
her way—as faint as it may have been—had become nothing more
than velvet emptiness. Now, with knees scraped and palms raw
from having stumbled in the darkness more times than she could
count, her initial frenetic pace had become a dull routine of step
and pray, step and pray.

If she continued to make steady progress—though tortuously slow—didn't fall into a deep crevasse and shatter both legs, and was lucky enough to cross the remaining stretch of foreboding desert without stepping directly on top of a rattlesnake, she might still reach her intended destination by first light.

A hell of a lot of 'ifs' over which she had little or no control.

As the crusty soil gave way underfoot, leaving in her wake a perfectly preserved trail of footprints, she could just make out an occasional silhouette of the approaching horizon, though how far distant it lay was impossible to estimate.

Even as the first rays of morning began to add subtle dimension to the moonscape before her, allowing for a greatly increased pace with less fear of finding the Lost Dutchman's Mine—headfirst—she knew it was also a curse. If she could see then she could be seen. Even a piss poor sniper could pick her off at a thousand yards on this mostly flat terrain, and being the only human within miles, the only moving object that extended perpendicular to the earth more than a few inches, could do so with impunity.

Marie stopped and activated her GPS for the tenth time. Within a few seconds, the state-of-the-art device had acquired more than enough satellites for the accuracy indicator to display nine feet, meaning she knew at once, to within that dimension, her exact position on the planet. The digital map currently shown on the tiny LCD screen—the one she'd chosen as her "base map" while still in the Range Rover—portrayed in three dimensions the prevailing topography. Not only did she know precisely where she was, but also what the ground around, and more importantly, ahead of her, looked like.

At least in very broad detail.

Her pack, though only twenty pounds or so with everything she possessed inside it, cut painfully into her right shoulder. Because of her injured left arm, she'd decided not to subject it to the torment of sharing the load. It was probably a wise decision, though her right shoulder would heartily disagree at present.

"Let's go, girl," she said aloud to help encourage muscles that were beginning to balk with each step. She dropped the GPS into her baggy left front pocket, rubbed sore and chaffed palms together for a moment, than set off at a jog toward the small cleft in the upcoming ridge.

The western sky was still the pale purple hue of an old bruise but beginning to lighten with each step.

Time was running out.

The display had shown the approaching divide to be a manageable climb with easily traversable terrain before and after. At just over a mile away, it presented the last major obstacle between her current position and the Interstate, but topo maps could be deceiving. They were great for an overview of an area, but failed to indicate things like boulders in your path the size of apartment buildings, or skyscraper-deep slits in the earth that no mountain lion could span.

Steadily she moved west, keeping at a full jog, but just as relentlessly, the sun in the eastern sky brought the full light of morning to the landscape. The sweat poured from her body with each step; her clothes were saturated and there was no water left to replenish what she'd lost. She'd taken the last swallow from her canteen an hour ago. Cramps began to stitch her sides and the backs of both legs.

"Keep going, dammit!" she screamed as she fell again, reawakening painful injuries to knees and palms, and causing her left shoulder to claw at raw nerves like fingers on a chalkboard.

When the Interstate finally came into view, now only two miles west across an open plane, her shadow had become clearly visible. With each footprint that slammed into the dust, the ghost on the ground ahead grew a shade darker, a millimeter shorter.

She prayed that no high-powered round would find the back of her skull as one had found Alex's.

* * *

Paul Burks could feel the warmth from his SUV's engine in the small of his back as he was roughly pulled from his driver's door and shoved against the Range Rover's grill. On each side of him stood men with guns, huge guns, though he had no clue as to their make or caliber. All he knew was that these men looked displeased with him, probably more so because of the woman's departure some time during the night.

"Doctor Paul Anthony Burks, clinical psychologist from Sausalito, California," the man who'd remained by the Suburban said as if reading his tombstone. It sent chills down Paul's spine. "You had quite a busy Monday. I'd love to hear all about it."

It was evident to Paul that whoever he was, this man was clearly in charge. Time to assert himself and get this situation on a more even keel. After all, while they may know his name, these men obviously didn't realize who they were dealing with.

"And just who might you be? Would you care to show me some identification?"

There, that went well, he thought. Authoritative. Manly.

The crack to the side of his head came from the right before he'd gotten the last syllable across his lips, dropping him to his hands and knees in the dusty road. His right hand went to the impact spot and when he withdrew it to have a look, found his fingers to be reddened with blood.

The men who flanked him took an arm each and jerked him to his feet, then shoved him against the hood of his car for the second time. Bright flashes of light came and went like fireflies in his brain.

"Who the hell do you think—"

This time, the butt of an assault rifle was thrust into his solar plexus, in the precise spot that will drop a grown man like a sack of corn.

Again he found himself eating dirt and again he was yanked to his feet and thrown against the hot grill.

"I can do this all day long, doctor Burks. Can you?" Merkett asked.

No, he couldn't, he understood with the fear of death now far more prevalent in his mind than the desire to sue these bastards for civil rights violations. "Wait! Just wait," he said in a pleading tone, his palms held up and outward in a gesture of surrender. "I haven't done anything. I don't deserve any of this. I'm not who you want. This isn't fair."

The five men around him grinned in amusement, a short, lightly-built man from the helicopter having just joined the other four from the Suburban.

"He thinks this has something to do with fair play and rules," the smallest member of the group chuckled, barely able to contain outright laughter.

The other men increased their grins to sniggers. All except the man in the middle. He only narrowed his eyes and his face grew as hard as stone.

Paul knew at that moment Marie had been right. Whatever she'd done, whether criminal or not, the men pursuing her were definitely not the good guys.

They were playing for keeps, winner take all.

Jesus! What the hell had he gotten himself into?

"I have done nothing to you, broken no laws," he pleaded, trying his best to display some semblance of manliness in his demeanor and voice. "All I did was pull a drowning woman from the river and revive her. I would think you'd be pleased I saved her. I mean, that way, you can still deal with her anyway you like. She's no good to you dead, right?" His head throbbed and he rubbed it to calm the ache that was only growing worse by the minute.

Merkett leaned toward Paul, placing his face just inches away. Instinctively, Paul wanted to climb onto the hood, but managed to only lean a few inches back. "That's the rub, doc. You see, we didn't want her alive. Hell, if the crazy bitch hadn't jumped off the damn cliff, taking one of my men with her, she'd be dead and gone a day and a half ago, and we'd be back, well, let's just say, where we came from with all of this unpleasant and distracting shit long behind us. So, while you may have had the best of intentions, your heroic deed spoiled our plans." He resumed his comfortable position against the hood of his own vehicle. "Now, since no good deed ever goes unpunished, as they say, you're going to tell us all there is to know about your time spent with the woman. Everything." His right hand went to the butt of his pistol. "Or, we'll simply kill you where you stand."

Paul felt his legs wobble and he knew they could all see him shaking like a child. He didn't believe these men would actually kill him, though the threat certainly felt real enough. This wasn't some third-world country or foreign battle zone. This was Utah, for God's sake. America. Shit like this just didn't happen in America.

He'd tell them all about the woman and they'd let him go. He reminded himself that it was her they were after. They had to be tough with him to make him understand the seriousness of their quest.

When he got free of these thugs, he'd go straight to the Attorney General of California and lodge a formal complaint. Someone was going to pay for treating him like a common criminal when he'd done nothing at all.

In the meantime, he'd play their game. "I'll tell you everything, I swear," Paul said in his most sincere voice. "What exactly do you want to know?"

Merkett grinned. "Excellent. I love cooperation. Let's begin with the key." While he didn't know for sure there was a key—it had only been a logical deduction given what they *did* know—he'd have bet money on it.

"The key? Yes, there was a key," Paul confirmed quickly.

"Was?"

"No, she still has a key with her. I'm sure it's the one you want. I only meant that there *was* a key on her when I pulled her from the river. It was stuffed in her bra but fell out when I was doing CPR."

Merkett looked at Shelton and the two men nodded furtively to each other.

"Where is the key now?" Shelton asked.

"Around her neck the last time I saw her. She fastened a lanyard of sorts—from dental floss of all things. She tried to tell me the key was nothing, to not even think about it anymore, so I knew it was important to her. She said it only had sentimental value, but she almost went ballistic when she first came around and couldn't put her hands on it."

"What exactly can you tell me about this key?"

Paul thought for a moment. "It was solid brass and smooth, no grooves or teeth like a house key. Kinda looked like a safe deposit box key more than anything else. I have a box at my bank and the keys are almost identical, come to think of it."

Over the next half hour, Paul kept his word and told Merkett and his men everything the woman had done, every item she'd purchased at the mall after her visit to the bank, every place they'd driven together.

Well, not everything entirely.

He hadn't told them about her visit to St. Michael's or about the twenty-thousand-dollars stuffed in his pockets.

The former he'd kept to himself because Marie's need for spiritual replenishment, or a burning desire to confess her sins, or for whatever she'd sought an audience with the Lord in a house of worship, would be, in his opinion, the last thing this man wanted to hear right now.

The latter he'd kept to himself out of pure greed. Screw the woman and keep the cash, he'd decided.

A win-win scenario.

"Is that everything?" Merkett said when Paul had finally finished speaking. His attention to detail had pleased the Colonel.

"Yes, that's all. As you can see, I've done nothing wrong. I don't deserve your anger in any way." His head still hurt but he no longer thought much about it. His primary concern now was whether or not he'd gotten himself off the hook with these men.

Merkett looked at Shelton who in turn looked at Captain Nate Fisher. Fisher nodded agreeably, as did the two men standing beside the Range Rover.

Shelton turned back to Merkett and shrugged indifferently.

"Well, Doctor Burks, it appears my men believe you have been straight with me, and because of that, I have good news for you."

"Oh, thank you," Paul said, lowering his head and placing his hands on wobbly knees. He was determined not to vomit in front of these men, though it took all his willpower to keep his stomach in check.

When he raised his head to ask if he were now free to go, he saw the flash of a 9MM Beretta only inches from his face.

It would be the last image he'd ever see.

"That good news," Merkett said, holstering his weapon, "is that your death will now be quick and painless."

He indicated for his men to deposit his body in the brush a few yards to the south of the road and take the Range Rover. They'd abandon it somewhere en route and burn it. That way, it would look like the woman had taken it after killing the psychologist, or at the very least, that he'd been the victim of a random carjacking and robbery.

Either would work for them, Merkett reasoned. The woman wouldn't be alive to provide a contradictory version of the events.

When Ron Phelps and Kevin Branch had dumped Paul's body in a shallow depression concealed by a scruffy growth of desert hackberry, the Sergeant Major knelt and rifled through the doctor's pockets while Branch removed his expensive watch. They knew no thief would leave valuables on a corpse, so neither could they if the scene were to 'read' correctly with the local cops.

When Phelps dug his hand into the front left pocket, he withdrew the first stack of hundreds. Immediately searching the other front pocket, he produced its twin, and held both high for the Colonel to see.

"Sir," he shouted across the short distance that separated them. "It appears that our deceased doctor, here, may not have told us everything he knew."

FORTY-ONE

THE DISTINCTIVE SOUND OF rotor blades from the Huey UH-1N broke the morning air like distant thunder, and Marie knew at once that she would not make the last quarter mile to the small truck stop without being spotted. She cursed angrily but dropped at once into a shallow gully, the remnant of some long-ago stream. While she could not yet see the helicopter, she could tell by the increasing intensity of its sound that it was not far off and closing rapidly.

Her only hope now was to disappear.

Trying not to disturb the soil any more than necessary—while still doing what must be done—she lay flat on her back and used both arms to sweep the uppermost sand and loose gravel across her legs and torso, not so much in the hopes of covering them fully—though that would be ideal—as to greatly reduce the contrast between her coloration and form and that of the natural surroundings. In a best case scenario, she would appear to be nothing more than a small mound of dirt or a partially-hidden tree limb.

The rotors thumped threateningly as she worked. The men chasing her were close now and only a few hundred feet overhead. Continued movement and disturbance of the soil would only do more harm than good. With a last generous heap of dust and sand across her face and hair, she pressed herself into the earth, hoping to present as low a profile as possible against the otherwise flat ground around her.

She held her breath and prayed.

Onboard, Merkett and Fisher had joined Shelton and Fuhrman. The Unit's best tracker, Kevin Branch, had determined, based on the items the Matthews' woman had purchased in Grand Junction, that she'd gone overland on foot with the intention of making her way toward I-15, across the hilly and broken ground to the south of them. Based on the information he'd gleaned from the topographical map in the Suburban, he'd also determined that there was only one manageable route she could have chosen. Any other path would have led her either deeper into the desert or back toward I-70—the point from which she'd run so hard the night before.

Neither were logical moves in his opinion.

Merkett concurred and had taken to the air.

At five hundred feet, they could sweep a large section of ground along that proposed pathway and the woman would be virtually impossible to miss.

"How much longer to the Interstate?" Merkett asked over the headset, his eyes never leaving the ground below them.

"Five minutes, sir," Fuhrman said. "There's a small truck stop along I-15 that's in a direct line with her assumed starting point last night. Nothing but highway for miles either side of that. It's her best shot at catching a ride."

Merkett nodded but did not answer.

As the helicopter moved at a fast clip across the scruffy terrain, all four men kept their eyes peeled for any sign of the woman. Branch had been right, given her height and the relative flatness of the prevailing terrain, she would stand out like a signpost.

Still, with only an estimate of her departure time, and a best guess as to the speed she'd make over ground, actually spotting her, even from the air, before she reached the truck stop, was a long shot.

"What's that?" Phelps shouted into his mike, pointing out the port side of the chopper. Fuhrman, on the same side of the craft, turned his head fully to the left and immediately spotted a dust cloud rising from the ground, like a lion wrestling with a gazelle on the Serengeti.

"Take us down for a closer look," Merkett barked. The Pilot had already responded to the dusty phantasm by reducing their airspeed. Now, he put the craft into a steep dive and quickly cut their altitude by eighty percent.

At only one hundred feet, they would practically be able to pat the woman on her head. They would be able to reach out and touch her with one of their long guns, in any case.

Ron Phelps flipped off the safety on his Heckler & Koch MP5 SD3, a fully-suppressed version of the automatic rifle carried by the military as well as many SWAT Teams, and trained his sights on the center of the small dust devil.

When they were only about sixty yards northeast of it, he gently massaged the trigger, and was just about to fire when a Kit fox suddenly dropped the black-tailed jackrabbit he had finally run to ground and took off in a direction that didn't include an incredibly frightening monster thundering overhead.

"Son of a bitch!" Phelps swore into his mike. "Sorry, sir, just a damn coyote."

Merkett reengaged the safety on his own weapon. "Set us down at the truck stop, Mack," he shouted.

Marie watched in horror as the huge military helicopter—just like the ones she'd seen on television during the extensive coverage of all the wars that plagued so much of the planet so much of the time—hovered not two hundred feet from her makeshift grave. She had seen the large black man in the open crew bay point his weapon at the ground, and had expected to be riddled with bullets at any second. She remembered him from the clearing at Eagle's Ridge.

Then, to her amazement, the craft suddenly lifted into the air and hastened in the direction she'd been heading.

Spitting dust and sand, she elevated her head and shoulders just enough to see the chopper land four hundred yards west at the edge of the parking lot of the only truck stop—the only stop of any kind—for thirty miles in either direction.

She lowered her head and squeezed her eyes tightly shut. Her heart pounded at twice the rate it even when she'd been jogging earlier.

"That's just great," she seethed. "Mind if I call you Colonel asshole from now on, you worthless bastard!" Despite her moment of angry release, Marie knew she was trapped—at least for now. Even the slightest movement by her at such a short distance from the men seeking her would beg for attention like a neon sign on a city street.

"How the hell did you find me so quickly?" she mumbled, then knew instinctively that Paul was dead. They had found him—though how she couldn't even imagine—and he had told them everything.

From the Range Rover's position last night to the only truck stop within miles was a straight line on a map. She'd done the same thing just before midnight when planning the shortest and best route to safety. She had not counted on the moon hiding most of the night behind a thick blanket of clouds. If not for that, she would have quickly hitched a ride and would have been long gone an hour ago.

"Shit!" she cursed, realizing her note intended to save Paul had probably led them directly to her. "So much for good deeds."

Just when she was certain things couldn't get any worse, she felt something brush across her right foot.

Raising her head slightly again, half expecting to see some benign horned toad scurrying across the sand, a Great Basin rattlesnake, one of the most deadly vipers in the Desert Southwest, moved slowly up her leg. Like some creature from the depths of hell itself, its bifurcated tongue probing and darting in and out, left and right, constantly searching for something to eat or the presence of a threat, it slithered steadily upward.

Marie froze, half out of pure, undiluted terror and half because she knew that any movement on her part would be seen as a threat to a creature so primal that it only lived to eat, make little snakes, and defend itself. The fact that it hadn't needed to evolve appreciably for forty million years proved that it had all three of its most basic survival instincts honed to perfection.

If Marie wasn't food, then she was a threat.

Simple as that.

Part of her training for the transportation of paying guests down the state's many rivers included an extensive course on the various poisonous snakes, lizards, and insects that might be encountered en route. In her mind, it was supposed to be theoretical knowledge for hypothetical situations, not a primer on how to survive a personal encounter.

She tried to remember anything that might help. What she recalled most vividly was that while a bite from this particular viper might not be fatal if treated with the proper anti-venom within half an hour of being injected, if left untreated, she would soon suffer violent cramps and muscle spasms, accompanied by intense and relentless pain. The site of the injection and all the surrounding tissue would swell to unbearable proportions, splitting skin and muscle alike as the body tried to allow for the rapid increase in size. As far as the affected tissue was concerned, it would be like going from conception to nine months pregnant in mere hours—her body simply wouldn't adapt before destroying itself completely. If that weren't enough, the venom would also attack her nervous system while simultaneously destroying the lining of her arteries and blood vessels, effectively causing her to drown in her own blood.

If bitten, her only prayer of making a hospital in time would be the damned helicopter—the very thing that would also guarantee she'd never see a hospital until she had a tag on her toe.

Very carefully, she eased her head flat against the ground again and tried to regulate her breathing and heart rate, though it would have been easier if she'd been running a marathon.

Using every ounce of willpower, she forced her body to be still, as still as a corpse.

Though her eyes remained tightly closed, her mind trying to put her anywhere but where she was, she felt the viper reach her stomach, though she could also feel it still crossing her right foot and down the entire length of that leg. That meant it had to be at least five feet long, allowing for the natural curve of its body that permitted movement. It was also surprisingly heavy, perhaps fifteen or twenty pounds, as much as a two-year-old child.

The thought nauseated her.

While she didn't care much for wasps, and spiders were not on her list of favorite creatures, she'd never had a phobia about snakes.

She knew she wouldn't be able to say the same thing tomorrow.

With one very slow and even inhalation, Marie sucked in her last breath and locked it in her throat. She knew that she could hold it for up to a minute, seventy-five seconds on the outside. When she had to finally exhale, if the satanic creature maintained its current pace, they would literally be face to face.

She didn't even want to think about that moment.

The serpent's head moved side to side between her breasts, then its tongue tickled the underside of her chin, sending a wave of panic through Marie that screamed for her to grab the damned thing with both hands and choke the life out of it.

Or throw it as far as possible and run like hell in the opposite direction.

Not only would she not be quick enough, she knew—vipers such as this struck with the speed of a bullet—but any success in ridding herself of the beast would only bring the men in the chopper down on her before she could take a single breath.

Marie knew that at any second she should expect to feel inch-long fangs burst through the flesh of her face, the worst possible place to be bitten other than the neck, as the constantly-searching head of the creature crested her chin line and moved with maniacal slowness across her cheek, eyelid, brow, and forehead.

Against her chest, the full girth and weight of its body pressed her breasts apart and down, then followed the head up and over her chin, face, and brow as the dead air in her lungs became impossible to hold.

Just a few more seconds, please God, her mind begged, pleading for the strength to hold on a little longer.

Finally, when she could contain her breath no more she heard the faintest sound of the rattler at the end of its long body as it passed less than an inch from her right ear. Five agonizing seconds later, she could feel the serpent on her skin no more and the stale air spewed forth from her throat and mouth like a burst balloon.

Risking detection from the men she had been able to clearly see moments before, she rose on one elbow and looked quickly behind her. She wouldn't have been surprised to have been struck by the viper, or to have a bullet suddenly smash her skull, but neither happened. The snake continued its slow journey eastward and the men had not begun firing.

Back into her prone position she lay, her stomach dancing painfully, knotting and twitching as if the creature were now inside her.

Perhaps the fact that she had been partially covered with dirt prevented the viper from taking more of an interest in her, possibly considering her to be nothing more than another minor obstacle in its journey toward the burrow of a field mouse.

She had no idea why she had not been bitten, it was enough that she had survived the encounter.

For fifty, dry, hot, agonizing minutes Marie lay in that same position, without moving a muscle, though constantly dreading the thought of another encounter with a snake, even a garter snake. She knew the men wouldn't wait indefinitely for her at the truck stop, if not because their heavily-armed presence in a military helicopter would have a lot of people asking a lot of questions they would probably rather not answer, then because they would eventually come to realize that instead of beating her there, they had arrived too late.

At that point, they would race to the next most logical place to intercept her. So far, they'd been batting a thousand, their timing off by only minutes. Her luck would not continue.

"But where are they going next?" she whispered to the flat blue sky above. "How can they have any idea where I'm heading when *I* have no idea?"

For the first time, Marie realized that she'd only been running away from the Colonel and his men since finding the key.

Now, she had to start running toward... *toward what?* she wondered.

She eased her right hand to a spot between her breasts and felt for the key. It was still there, suspended by the new lanyard she'd bought at the mall in Grand Junction.

Had Paul told them about the key? Of course he had.

She knew this beyond question.

"Okay, Colonel whoever-the-hell you-are, you've got friends in high places. Well so do I, and it's about time we found out which one of us is smarter."

FORTY-TWO

THE NEED FOR WATER had become far more intense than Marie would have imagined after only a few hours without it. Her tongue felt twice its normal size in her mouth and she no longer had enough saliva to moisten her lips. They were beginning to crack and bleed under the intense Utah sun. The human body could endure days without food, but would begin to shut down completely within twenty-four hours if denied liquid. She thought of the many warnings she'd given her river guests each day of a trip: "Be sure to drink a full pint of water or Gatorade every hour. You dehydrate faster in the desert than you can imagine. There's no excuse for anyone dying on my watch when all you want to drink is an arm's length away."

"An arm's length away," she repeated. Just like the truck stop. Only it might as well have been on another planet.

As the morning sun continued to rise behind her, quickly pushing the temperature to ninety-five in the shade, she felt a pressing need to sleep. She was so tired, so completely without the energy to move even a finger. Her eyelids weighed ten pounds each.

If she could just get to her backpack, she could at least put on her sunglasses. That would provide some small measure of relief. But it was at her feet, and that would require sitting up fully, exposing herself to them. Besides, she didn't have the energy to reach for it.

Maybe after she slept for just a little while, a few blessed, restful minutes. "Just five," she promised herself in a voice too soft to be heard except in her mind. Her eyes felt so heavy.

* * *

"Wake up, Marie," she said aloud to a sky the color of aluminum and completely devoid of clouds. "You sleep, you die."

Gently raising her head to see what the Colonel was up to, she was certain her eyes beheld an all-to-common phenomenon of the desert, a mirage, those impish, shifting shapes created by heat and atmosphere roiling off the scorched earth. She repeatedly closed both eyes and blinked to clear away the dust and sand, then strained to make sense of the scene to the west.

It was gone, alright. No mirage.

But it couldn't be. She would certainly have heard it leave.

Despite her inability to comprehend how it had occurred, the helicopter of death was nowhere to be seen.

Had she slept without knowing it? What time was it? She pulled the cheap wristwatch she'd bought to her face and blew away the dust obscuring its dial: 11:15. She'd been in her makeshift grave for more than four and a half hours, though she would have sworn it had been no longer than a single hour.

No wonder she was dying of thirst and her lips felt like they would crack if she moved them even slightly. When she tried to moisten them with her tongue, it felt like two pieces of sandpaper rubbing together.

She needed liquid and she needed it soon. Another hour and the Colonel wouldn't need to kill her—the sun would do that for him.

Carefully she studied the truck stop, looking for any sign of someone from the helicopter having been left behind. That would be a smart move on their part, she considered. These seemed to be smart men, even if she did want them all dead. They would do something like that. She would have.

After ten minutes of straining to see anything that might spell instant death, any break in the pattern of normal activity as she imagined it would be, she decided the need for liquids had finally outweighed the risk of capture.

Against one man, she might stand a chance, especially if she could gain any benefit of surprise.

Against the Utah sun with nothing to drink, her fate was sealed.

Reenergized by the thought of splashing cold water in her face, and of a huge bottle of green tea or Gatorade removing the dust from her mouth and throat, Marie rose painfully and slowly to her knees, careful not to stir the talc-fine dust that had partially covered her body more than absolutely necessary.

As she considered her actions over the next few minutes, she was sure the Colonel had passed her DMV photo around the truck stop, trying to ascertain if anyone had seen the woman they were after. It was the only photo she could imagine him having access to, though nothing he did at this point would surprise her.

She also felt sure that Paul had told them what she'd been wearing the last time he saw her. A thirties-something woman with long, wavy blonde hair, wearing khaki cargo shorts, an emerald top, and hauling around a yellow and black North Face backpack, would make for a pretty easy target. A near-sighted grandmother could spot her a mile away.

She unzipped the backpack and rifled through its contents, grateful now that she'd bought more than one change of clothes. Dressing on her back to reduce her silhouette against the horizon— still uncomfortable at being so close to the busy truck stop—she removed her shorts and top. Rolling them tightly to conserve space, she stuffed them in the backpack and pulled on a pair of black shorts, also cargo-style with lots of pockets. Her new top was red, the twin of the green pullover she'd just removed.

When she'd transferred her cash and I.D. to her new pockets, she pushed her dust mop hairdo inside a new 49'ers ball cap.

With her backpack across her right shoulder, she stood slowly and moved warily toward the small oasis, brushing the remaining dust from her clothes as she walked, again careful to do so with as little visual fanfare as possible. She needed to look like she'd stepped from one of the many vehicles in the parking lot, not like someone who'd been buried in the desert for the last half day.

* * *

Colonel Merkett gathered all of his men together in the desert near Scipio, Utah, along Interstate-15, ninety miles north of the point where they'd hoped to intercept Matthews and recover the key. They'd shown her picture to every person working at the truck stop, but had gotten nothing at all in the form of a lead. Not one person had seen anyone matching her general description, or anyone hitchhiking with a backpack—male or female—for that matter.

Catching a lift from strangers wasn't the thrilling and economical travel mode it had once been. Today, the person behind the wheel was as likely to be a deranged serial killer as the person thumbing a ride.

Apparently, Merkett surmised, either she'd managed to catch a ride before anyone had the opportunity to see her, or she had not come that direction in the first place. Given her very limited options from the point on the map the doctor had indicated they'd spent the previous night—fifteen miles south of where they'd caught up with him—the truck stop was still the most likely scenario.

They'd missed her—again. No sense crying over un-spilled blood. Now they had to get to where she was heading before she got there.

With both choppers on the ground as well as all three Suburbans, miles from prying eyes, Merkett spread a map across the hood of his SUV. "The last place we know Matthews to have been is here." He pointed to the spot Paul Burks had indicated on the map. "Sergeant Branch feels certain she headed for this truck stop here. I agree." Again, he touched the point along I-15 where chopper-1 had spent an hour earlier in the morning. "I don't know how she did it, but somehow she hoofed it across twenty miles of desert at a pace that would put any one of us to shame, and she did it in total darkness." He regarded each man in turn. "Make no mistake, boys, this is one wily and driven bitch."

"Where's she heading now, Colonel?" Tom Pickard asked. He was the pilot of chopper-2.

"We have to assume she'll try to put that key in its lock as soon as possible. That means within two miles of Goodman's mansion, near Santa Barbara, California. We're all heading there now by chopper. We'll clean the cars thoroughly then leave them where they sit. There's no way she'll beat our time going by road, so we should arrive at least half a day ahead of her. That'll give us plenty of time to get new transportation and find the best place to stake out every location the senator would have used. Don has already made a list of banks in the area where Goodman had a safe deposit box. There are only four, plus the mansion, itself—we have to assume she might go there—so that means we'll split into two-man teams: a driver and one on the ground, with the pilots staying with the choppers and Don staying at the computer. If he can pare down the branches by even one, we'll add a man on the ground at the mansion plus one of the banks."

"What if she goes by air as well?" Nate Fisher asked.

"She won't. Too risky. She has to know we'd anticipate such an obvious move, and so far, she hasn't proven to be inept. I don't expect her to go brain dead at this stage of the game. If anything, she'll ramp it up a notch, just like anyone when they're in the Red Zone."

He was referring to the last few yards on a football field that had to be crossed for a touchdown.

Every man nodded.

"I don't understand why she doesn't go to the first cop she sees and tell him everything. That'd be my move," one of the men said.

Merkett had thought a great deal about the man's question, puzzling in his head why she wouldn't do just that. With a deep, contemplative breath, he said, "I don't think so. I believe she feels we're operating in an official capacity and are willing to kill anyone between us and the key, which is true. Either she doesn't want to be responsible for any more innocent lives being lost, which is a bit noble to my mind, or she wants to put an end to this herself. Maybe both. Remember, we killed everyone she knew or loved looking for that damned video. She's not about to put it into the hands of some Barney and hope he somehow brings us down.

"She also has to realize that once she shows up with the key and her fantastic story, and the cops—whoever they are—connect all the dots in Truman, they aren't simply going to let her drop the thing off and be on her way. She'll be held, probably as a suspect, which means she'll be stuck in a six-by-six cell while they sort it all out. That won't happen overnight. She's not going to risk being anywhere that we can walk in, show our creds, and leave with her.

"I don't know who this woman is, but she isn't stupid and she isn't a quitter. She'll see this through to the end if it means dying in the process, and she's going to do it her way."

"I agree, Colonel," Shelton said. While he had sworn a solemn oath to destroy Matthews before this was over—for him, at least—the squint had also come to respect her drive and determination. "She's going straight for the lock."

Merkett slapped his hands together, bringing all eyes on him. "This is our last shot at her, gentlemen. We fail and the mission fails. If that happens, we will have let down the country we've all bled for, that so many of our closest friends have died for. Are we going to let that happen?"

"NO SIR!" came the collective yell, shouted like some primordial war chant.

"Okay, I want everyone into civvies now, except Lieutenants Fuhrman and Pickard. It's best they remain in uniform in the Hueys. The rest of us will need to blend into the landscape like we were born there."

"When we spot her?" Phelps asked.

"She probably won't be looking for anyone in civilian clothes, but don't spook her by getting in her space. Give her plenty of comfort room. We need her to get into the bank, retrieve the video, and leave, all nice and easy. When she hits the street again, we take her down."

"If she resists?" Branch asked.

"Oh, she'll resist, alright," Merkett assured them. "Use your knife to cut her throat or a silenced pistol shot to the head, then throw her dead ass in your car and get the hell out of there. Understand this: even if you have to unload a full magazine from a long gun in front of a hundred witnesses to bring her down, she is not to get out of your sight once she's left the bank. Whoever messes this one up will not have to wait for the feds to take him down. You'll answer to me."

All nodded that they understood what was expected of them, and what the cost of failure would be.

FORTY-THREE

FORTUNATELY FOR MARIE, THE truck stop was on the northbound side of the Interstate, which meant she didn't have to cross four lanes of highway and the center median to reach it. She could approach the main building from the rear, across the back parking lot, where the fewest number of eyes would be watching her every move. Perhaps, if she were lucky, she could slip in without being seen and blend in with the other tourists.

She didn't count on her luck holding out much longer, but crossed her fingers anyway.

When her hiking boots touched asphalt, she stopped to reassess her situation. Out front, a steady stream of summer tourists heading for I-70 or Salt Lake City pulled in, filled tanks, grabbed a bag of pork rinds and a Coke or two, and went on their way. No sense in loitering in a place as desolate and devoid of all historical and visual interest as this.

The diesel pumps were along the north side of the truck stop, to her right, allowing for the greatest number of big rigs to be in line for refueling at any one time without blocking quicker moving car traffic. Filling one of those hungry beasts didn't happen in two or three minutes as it did with passenger cars, generally requiring more than a quarter of an hour, depending upon tank capacity. Two hundred gallons was not uncommon.

At times, during the forty or fifty minutes she'd kept her eye on the helicopter after first seeking the shelter of her dusty ravine, a line of eighteen-wheelers had stretched around the building, almost blocking it from view. Currently, there were only two; one filling at each of the side-by-side pumps.

She set her backpack behind a small cluster of Prince's Plume that had been planted at the southeast corner of the property. Standing three feet tall, their delicate yellow flowers seemed completely out of place, with the hostile moon-like environment at their backs and a sea of frying-pan-hot pavement in their faces.

As she kicked a small clump of dry mulch across the pack for added camouflage, she prayed that no one would discover it before she could return, but she knew its distinctive coloration would be instantly recognizable to anyone watching for a woman with a backpack, even if she had managed to change her appearance somewhat.

Fortunately, neither of the big rig drivers looked in her direction as she made her way around the south end of the building.

The blast of refrigerated air that spilled out from the glass door when she entered the small convenience store took her breath away, almost removing her cap. She gave it a quick tug, pulling it low across her brow, and made her way straight for the restrooms.

Thankfully, this one-horse truck stop was not large enough, or consumer-friendly enough, to have more than one stall in either of the bathrooms. Once inside, Marie locked the door and ran the cold water, filling a double handful and burying her face in her palms.

It felt like Heaven, even as it stung her chapped lips.

For two full minutes, she repeated the routine of emptying her palms and refilling them with fresh water, then submerging her hot, sweaty, and unbelievably filthy face in the life-giving liquid until it no longer felt cool. Finally, she pulled a handful of paper from the wall dispenser, moistened the small stack completely, and used the damp towels to scrub the dust from her face, neck, and arms as best she could. She would need a long hot shower to get truly clean, but for now, she could once again pass for human, and not some creature from the dust bowls of Mars.

With cap in place, sunglasses still hiding her eyes, Marie reentered the store in search of something to drink.

She found just what she had been dreaming of since awakening from her long and unexpected slumber in the desert: a sixteen-ounce bottle of AriZona Green Tea with ginseng and honey. She grabbed five of them, filling both arms; they were as cold as ice against her bare skin, and she cradled them like a baby.

At the register, she paid for the drinks as well as two bananas that she grabbed from the small produce stand beside the checkout area. The place was fairly busy, with eight or ten vehicles either at one of the four pumps or parked in one of the spaces in front of the convenience store. Inside, three couples perused both sides of the snack aisle and a small circular sunglasses display, while a family of five tried to decide whether to go with the medium fountain drinks or not. They weren't sure if the larger size would fit the cup holders in their minivan.

As far as she could tell, no one in the place, neither customer nor employee, paid any special attention to her. There were the occasional side stares she always got from men—young and old alike—who didn't think she was looking, or that their wives were looking, but even the few she noticed were quick glances and hardly worth a second thought.

She breathed a deep sigh of relief as she sat at one of the small tables in the corner.

Inside of five minutes, both bananas were nothing but peels and two of the five bottles of ginseng tea were empty. She would use the remaining three, still in the flimsy plastic bag, to refill her canteen when she retrieved her pack.

As she kept a wary eye on everyone in the place, her interest in their actions kept hidden behind her dark glasses, she spotted a pay phone on the wall beside an old pinball machine. The game no longer worked, or at least it was no longer plugged into the wall outlet, and the phone had seen better days, but none of that matter. It had reminded her of a small display she'd seen behind the checkout counter.

The nice young boy at the register, the same one who'd waited on her earlier, had been pleased to sell her one of the 'no-contract' cellular phones that came pre-loaded with sixty 'anytime' minutes. It would be more than enough. After she'd made her one call, probably taking no more than eight or ten minutes, she'd drop it in the trash along with the empty bottles and banana peels.

She thought about buying a second 'burner' phone but as the thought formed, realized that there was no one left in her life to call. It was like a punch to the gut.

Taking a long steadying breath, Marie thanked the clerk and returned to her table in the corner, then dialed the number from memory.

It was answered on the second ring.

Not recognizing the caller-ID displayed on her phone, the woman at the other end simply answered, "Hello," in a monotone voice, her finger already on the END button. She got a lot of weird calls at all hours of the day. This was probably just one more.

Her mobile number wasn't published, and only a small handful of her closest friends and business associates knew it, but that didn't keep idiots from punching in seven digits and connecting to her by accident. Also, for reasons unknown to her, she'd apparently made some 'Top Ten Call Me Every Day And Maybe I'll Finally Relent and Give You Some Money For Your Favorite Charity' list. She had nothing against charities, but some groups had gotten almost militant with their fundraising tactics.

"Hey, girl," Marie said, knowing the other woman would recognize her voice at once. Before she had time to respond, Marie added, "I'm in a bit of a mess and I could really use your help."

The understanding that these two old friends had, going back more than three years now, was that no names were ever to be used over the phone, and that only Marie would do the calling. Never to the other woman's work, never to her home, only to her private cell phone.

"Sure, what can I do?" she said, but couldn't contain her excitement at hearing the familiar voice after nearly a year. "Oh, my God, how are you, where have you been? It's been so long since you called, I was beginning to think something bad had happened to you."

Marie couldn't help smiling. Her oldest living friend had that effect on her. One day, who knew when, they would meet over dinner at a nice restaurant, somewhere in the Midwest, or New Orleans, perhaps. She'd really like that. "I'm so sorry I can't talk about any of that right now. I'll call again real soon, I promise. Right now, I need information, the kind you can get like no one else I know."

"Sure, just tell me what you want."

"Who knows Robert Wayne Goodman better than anyone else? Someone who would know his habits, his secrets."

"Skipper Goodman? Jesus, girl! What the hell are you into?"

"Deep shit, as usual. This time, though, I just stepped in it. I didn't have a thing to do with it being there in the first place."

"Yeah, well shit doesn't care how you got it on you. It's still shit."

Marie chuckled. "Tell me about it."

"Goodman has been the biggest story on the news for more than a week now. You knew they finally found his body, right? In Utah, near the town of Truman, wherever the hell that is."

Because Marie had told her friend nothing specific about her life since they'd parted company thirty-six months ago—in an effort to keep them both safe—she had no idea that Marie actually lived in Utah, more or less Truman.

Or rather, *had* lived there until two days ago.

"Yeah, I know. What I don't know is who, better than anyone else alive, can tell me about him. Subtle things, real in-depth stuff."

"I'm afraid to ask why you want this, because I know you won't tell me and also because you might."

"I won't," Marie assured her. She kept her attention on the convenience store, but she might as well have been another broken pinball game for all the attention she was getting.

"Give me a few minutes to do some quick digging. I'll be right back. You okay to hang on?"

"Yeah, I'm good for the moment. Can't say how things will be ten minutes from now. Let's just say the situation is fluid," Marie added stoically.

"Could be your theme song. You should be used to it by now." She heard the other woman let out a subdued chuckle. "Don't worry, I'll be quick." With that, Marie heard the phone being laid on a hard surface and her friend's fingers begin tearing at a keyboard. As promised, she was back on the line in less than five minutes. "Blaine Howard McAllan, professor of political science at U. C. Berkeley. He's supposed to be the leading authority on Goodman, even wrote an authorized biography on him that was about to go to print when the senator's body was found. Now, the buzz is that the book is getting a new ending that may or may not be finished before he heads off to the land of furry hats and vodka."

"What's that supposed to mean?"

"Supposedly McAllan will be leaving any day on a six-month sabbatical to Moscow to study post-Communist Russian politics or some such crap. Probably going for a third PhD."

"He already has *two*?"

"Yep. Did his last thesis on Goodman."

"He sounds like my man. California-Berkeley, right?"

"Uh, huh. Now I want you to listen carefully to what I'm about to say, okay?"

"Always." Marie checked her watch. Her bag had been left unattended, with thirty grand stuffed inside, for nearly half an hour. As much as she loved her friend, she hoped this wouldn't be one of her long-winded 'quit looking for trouble' speeches.

Her friend paused for dramatic effect, something she often did, then said in a flat and ominous tone, "I obviously don't know what this is all about, but you need to be extremely careful. You're treading on dangerous ground. No surprise there, huh? Some very big dogs in D.C. got snuffed within hours of Goodman's body being found. Professional hits according to my source inside Homeland. That means the gloves are off, anyone is fair game. If whoever this is will take down a high-ranking congressman and his chief of staff, then no one is safe. If you're going to San Francisco in search of this Professor McAllan, be sure you don't leave your heart there, as the song goes, or any other vital body parts."

"Thanks, I'll do my best. Sorry, but I really gotta go."

"Before you do, you know who is doing great. Just thought you would like to know."

"Thanks, that means so much to me. And thanks again for being there when we both needed you most.," Marie said sincerely, a fist in her throat.

"When will I hear from you again?"

"Can't say, but whether the next few days go as planned or end up like the last few, my guess is that you'll hear from me, or *about* me, sooner than you think."

Before her friend could respond, Marie ended the call and gathered up her mess. She tossed everything in the receptacle by the door, phone included. With her plastic bag and three bottles of green tea, she returned to the far corner of the parking lot to retrieve her backpack.

Fortunately, it had not been disturbed.

Just then, a new Freightliner pulled to the diesel pumps and the driver jumped out whistling an old Eagles song. She was a large woman, almost as wide as she was tall, but had a face that seemed straight out of a Norman Rockwell painting.

Best of all, her rig had "Bay City Transfer and Storage—San Francisco, California," emblazoned on both sides and across the cargo doors in letters three feet tall.

The sight brought an instant smile to Marie's lips.

PART 3:
RETRIBUTION

"... and if you wrong us
shall we not seek revenge?"

William Shakespeare
(1564–1616)

FORTY-FOUR

MARIE STOOD AT THE window of her sixth-floor hotel room overlooking the Berkeley campus. More importantly, her room provided a clear view of Barrows Hall, home to the political science department—and home to Dr. Blaine Howard McAllan, knower of all things related to Skipper Goodman.

Or so she prayed.

If this man couldn't tell her what she needed to know, no one could. She would collect all of her remaining cash, spread out across three states, then flee to Mexico, her tail between her legs.

Alex would just have to understand that sometimes the good guys didn't finish first. Sometimes life punched you in the gut and there wasn't a damned thing you could do about it but extend your middle finger, for all the good that did.

The thought of losing to these bastards sickened her. She wanted them to pay for what they'd done, but she was also a realist. In the end, what the hell could she possibly hope to do against the Colonel and his squad of killers? Did she actually think she could beat them?

Then something her father had said to her shortly after her sixteenth birthday, when she had asked him why we'd gone to war with Iraq after they invaded Kuwait, since both countries were so far away and of so little interest to her and her friends. He looked her squarely in the eye and said, "Remember, the only thing necessary for evil to triumph, is for good people to do nothing at all. It's a hell of a lot easier to remove a cancer when you first discover it, than to wait until it has spread."

She later came to understand that the words had not all been his, having heard them used many times by many different people over the years, but they had expressed succinctly how her father had felt, and how he'd lived his own life.

They had never made much sense to her until now.

God, why couldn't he be here to help me through this, she thought with a twinge in her heart.

She went to her bag and emptied the contents onto the comforter, separating things that needed washing from items that were still somewhat clean. Though she was exhausted from the long ride and needed a shower and some sleep, she knew she had to prepare for the important day ahead before resting. It was now 1:30 Wednesday morning and from what the night clerk had told her when she registered, most classes on campus wouldn't begin until eight at the earliest.

She stripped out of her clothes, including her underwear, and took everything to the sink, along with the dusty shorts and top she'd removed in the desert. She washed everything thoroughly by hand, then rinsed in clean water and hung to dry. With only shampoo and body wash as laundry detergent, it was a makeshift job at best. In the morning, she'd give the outer garments a quick press with the iron before carefully returning them to her backpack.

As she stood in front of the full-length mirror on the back of the bathroom door, she was surprised she didn't look far worse than she did. At least she didn't look as bad as she felt. Her stark tan line, pale skin against an even, warm brown, almost appeared to be a white bikini, with some obvious exceptions.

She gently pulled the tape from her left shoulder and studied the bullet entry carefully, concerned that infection may have begun to set in. If it had, she'd soon be racked with fever and would be on her back in an emergency room within a day, whether she liked the idea or not. Alternately, she could ignore the infection and be on a morgue table in three days.

Neither thought pleased her.

By twisting her head and torso in an unnaturally contorted position, she was just able to see the exit hole in the mirror as well. Though angry-looking and puckered, like its twin in front, and still large enough to push a pencil through, neither wound bled nor did they show any telltale sign of infection. Paul had done an admirable job patching her up.

The thought of him lying dead in a field somewhere was a sucker punch to the gut, and she clutched the sink for support.

After a dizzying moment filled with weak knees and shaky hands, Marie popped four Advil into her mouth and washed them down with water from the tap. She was grateful to be alive, considering all that had happened, and said a silent "thank you" to the older couple at the truck stop who had come to her rescue.

Doreen Kennedy and her husband Earl co-owned and co-piloted the eighteen-wheeler that had transported Marie to within twenty miles of the Berkeley campus.

When she'd told them of her plight—a clever concoction of lies that explained her meager possessions and haggard appearance—they had been more than happy to lend a helping hand to the attractive, but troubled, young woman who reminded them so much of their own daughter. The fact that Marie had offered them five hundred bucks for the ride hadn't hurt matters, though it had almost been enough to make them worry they were transporting a fugitive.

Sensing the angst in their expressions when she handed Doreen the cash, she reassured them both that she only wanted to get as far away from her wife-beating, no-count husband as possible, and Oakland, California, was the last place on earth he would look for her. She'd left him their small house and everything in it and she'd taken nothing but the clothes on her back and what little money they had in the bank.

Doreen had said that Earl wouldn't get off that easy if he ever laid a hand on her.

Earl had not disagreed.

At just past eleven Tuesday morning, they had reentered I-15 heading south through Las Vegas and then west to Barstow, California. At Barstow, they took California Highway-58 to Lost Hills, west of Bakersfield, then north along I-5 to I-580 and finally to Oakland. From there, Marie had caught a cab to her hotel near the Berkeley campus, having taken the cabby's recommendation.

The exhausting drive, a distance of 768 miles, had taken fourteen hours with one stop for dinner just outside Barstow where I-15 and CA-58 joined.

After a shower hot enough to boil a lobster, Marie redressed her shoulder injury, applying more peroxide and Neosporin before wrapping it in a clean bandage, all courtesy of the mall pharmacy in Grand Junction.

The pain no longer radiated from her elbow to the middle of her back, but had localized in the immediate area of the wound. Even her mobility had returned to an acceptable level, except when she tried to reach overhead. Since she didn't intend to do much of that, she didn't concern herself with the pain it caused.

To say that the bed felt like a little slice of paradise was an understatement, all the more heavenly considering she hadn't slept longer than a few hours since Saturday night in Moab.

Within thirty seconds, she was deep in a dreamless asleep.

*   *   *

Blaine McAllan parked his Montego Blue BMW convertible on Bancroft Way, locked it with the remote, then strolled along the sidewalk toward Barrows Hall, briefcase in one hand, Apple PowerBook in the other. He had back-to-back classes beginning in forty-five minutes, followed by his normal Wednesday lunch with the dean of the Political Science department.

With his office just two minutes away, he walked casually, enjoying the mild June morning.

"Professor McAllan?" someone called out softly. He hadn't noticed anyone since leaving his car, but that wasn't unusual. After a decade of teaching, with tens of thousands of students on campus even during summer term, he'd almost become immune to their presence except when face to face in the classroom. It was akin to growing deaf to a grandfather clock in your own home. The gong, gong, gong at three in the morning would drive your houseguests up the wall while you slept like a baby.

"Yes," he said, turning toward the woman's voice. He was pleasantly surprised to see a tall, very attractive blonde in her early thirties standing in the shade of a massive Blackwood Acacia tree, just beside the walkway. "How may I help you?"

Marie stepped from the shadows and removed her sunglasses. "Do you have a few moments to talk about Robert Wayne Goodman with me?"

While his authority on the former politician was well known around campus, and he was constantly bombarded with questions about the famous man, those doing the inquiring were typically between eighteen and twenty, starry-eyed kids barely out of high school who dreamed of walking in the senator's footsteps one day.

Though this woman could easily have been a student—their ages during any given semester ranging from sixteen to eighty— he got the feeling she wanted something more than help with a term paper.

"Well, I have class in a few minutes, so—"

"I know," Marie interrupted, glancing at her watch and then at a piece of paper on which she'd hastily scribbled some notes, only half of which made any sense to her. "Forty-three minutes to be precise. International Relations at ten and Comparative Politics at eleven, whatever the hell those are."

She scrunched up her nose as she read. "After that, you're scheduled to have lunch with Dean Mumford at Le Cheval." She pointed behind him; the restaurant was less than a hundred yards from where his BMW sat parked.

In the hour she had since speaking with his assistant, Yao Honghui, Marie had scoped out McAllan's office—from the outside, at least—as well as the restaurant he'd chosen for lunch, trying to decide on the best location for an initial meeting. In the end, she had decided to simply 'ambush' him as he walked to class.

The professor regarded her warily but didn't comment. Instead, he tried to determine the woman's motive for wanting to meet with him. *Probably just another reporter*, he decided, trying to hide his disdain.

She returned his quiet stare with her most disarming smile. "I talked to your graduate assistant earlier. Told him it was a matter of life and death that I speak with you as soon as possible. He gave me your entire day's agenda. Even told me where you normally park. Good thing I'm not a hit man. Or hit *woman*, huh."

Humor often helped, but it hadn't seemed to work in this case. His expression remained impassive, even disapproving.

She had no way of knowing that the only thing this man hated more than reporters, were reporters who thought they were funny.

He nodded almost imperceptibly. "Yes, good thing, indeed. And you are...?"

Marie extended her hand. "Carol Palmer. Nice to meet you, Dr. McAllan."

The name she'd given him matched her new I.D., the second set she'd retrieved from her jewelry box at St. Michael's. Vickie Brennan had been left in the desert somewhere between the Range

Rover and the truck stop. With the Colonel knowing every move she'd made since Sunday evening, she could hardly continue being either Vickie Brennan or Marie Matthews.

She prayed she wouldn't accidentally refer to herself by all three names in the same conversation, though it wouldn't surprise her in the least if she did.

He wedged his laptop under his left arm and shook hands with her. "Likewise." The response sounded more sincere than it was.

As he was about to say something else, Marie cut the distance between them in half and said in her most sincere voice, her eyes locked on his, "Is there somewhere we can talk, Professor McAllan? It really is a matter of life and death."

Taken aback by the woman's persistent candor and unwavering eye contact, he said, "I don't really know what I could possibly tell you about Skipper Goodman that could be of such importance, but I actually do have class to prepare for. Now may not be the best moment for a lengthy discussion, I'm afraid. Perhaps some other time."

He extended his hand again, this time to bid her goodbye, but she did not offer hers in return.

Instead, Marie squeezed her eyes tightly shut, silently praying that her next move would not be a brief prelude to her last. On the long drive from Utah, she'd decided to tell McAllan, assuming he hadn't yet left for Moscow, everything that had transpired over the last few days—in particular, everything she knew or suspected about the key. The only way she could possibly expect to find the answers she wanted was to trust someone and pray for the best, and this man was her last hope.

This was not the time for being coy or aloof.

When she opened her eyes again, he was still standing opposite her, though it was clear his initial curiosity was long gone and all he wanted was to be rid of the very odd woman standing a bit too close.

She grasped the lanyard around her neck and withdrew the small brass key from beneath her blouse, practically shoving it in his face. "Senator Goodman had this clutched in his fist in a death grip when he died on that mountain in Utah. It was obvious from his remains that he wanted to be certain the very first thing anyone saw when they eventually found him was *this*. Since his body's discovery ten days ago, everyone who has come near this damned thing has died—murdered to be precise. At least eleven people so far. Totally innocent people who did nothing more than to have the misfortune of being in the wrong place at the wrong time. One of them was my very best friend, and I watched her die. They shot her in the back of the head. They also shot me, but I managed to escape by jumping off a cliff. Took one of the bastards with me, I'm happy to say."

She took a slow, stuttering breath, determined to finish her prepared speech. "Now, I'm the only one left. If you don't help me learn what the hell this key is all about—because it sure as hell has everything to do with Goodman—then all of them, including me, will have died for nothing."

Tears coursed down her cheeks as she spoke and she wiped them away with the back of her hand.

McAllan studied the key for a long moment. "I would have thought, if what you say is true, that the first place you would have gone was the police."

"I can't, that's all I can say right now."

He looked carefully into her eyes, saying nothing but taking in everything. Then he pulled his cell phone from his pocket and quickly punched in a number.

Marie slid the key back between her breasts and turned to leave, certain she had just made the biggest mistake of her life.

Probably the last mistake she would ever make.

As the phone rang, McAllan grabbed her arm to stop her. "Yao," he said, when his graduate assistant answered, "I'm going to need you to cover my two morning classes. Also, please tell Dean

Mumford that today isn't a good time for us to have lunch. I just remembered that I have a prior commitment. A very important one."

When he'd returned the phone to his pocket, he said, "Le Cheval has really great Vietnamese cuisine, and I already have my regular booth reserved. Would you care to join me for an early lunch?"

Again he extended his hand to her, only this time Marie accepted it warmly.

FORTY-FIVE

UNLIKE THE OTHER MEN in the Unit, Donald Shelton reveled in "down time." He could sit for days on end before a computer screen, hacking his way through one firewall after another, piercing the veil of secrecy surrounding the most secure databases and Internet sites in the world. Though he'd made a small personal fortune at this game—cleverly tucked away in Switzerland and the Cayman Islands—he would have been assassinated in an instant for a fraction of his net worth if any of the governments or agencies he'd violated had the slightest clue he'd breeched their so-called impenetrable security.

That thought didn't bother him in the least.

If he were a mere artist at getting in, then he was Michelangelo, himself, at rummaging around and getting out undetected.

What did bother him, however, was his inability to put his hands on the woman known to the Unit as Marie Matthews. Despite having to call her something other than "that irritating bitch whore," he knew Matthews wasn't her real name, and that irked him even more.

Finally able to work his magic in peace, no longer having to endure the less than ideal conditions that traveling across three states in a crowded helicopter presented, he was actually making progress—albeit much slower than he would have liked.

Given the timetable of Goodman's final morning—which, before boarding the plane, Ritchie Frye had assured Colonel Merkett was accurate to the minute—his search of possible bank locations where the video would likely have been stashed had been narrowed down to just four.

The problem was that each represented a separate financial institution, not merely a different branch of the same bank. That meant four separate and unique databases—each with its own firewall structure and security, each with different password levels and layers of encryption.

In short, every step it took to crack one had to be repeated in painstaking quadruplicate.

Despite the daunting task, two and a half hours of nonstop hacking finally yielded a breech at the most likely of the four banks. He'd previously ranked them by their proximity to the mansion, from closest, or most likely, to farthest away, or least likely. Unfortunately, as he quickly scrolled through the bank's database for the day of the crash, he could find no activity of any kind related to Robert Wayne Goodman.

He cursed under his breath and moved on to the next bank in line. Maybe he'd have better luck with this one.

* * *

Le Cheval sat comfortably on the corner of Bowditch Street and Bancroft Way in Berkeley, across from the Hearst Memorial Gymnasium and Aquatic Center that was part of the main campus. A favorite restaurant of locals and students alike, its Craftsman-style exterior with its wisteria-covered pergolas was complemented by a warm and welcoming interior, with cozy nooks that invited discrete conversation.

The seclusion suited Marie perfectly.

When they'd been seated, Blaine scooted much closer to Marie than she was initially comfortable with, and it caused her to lean away reflexively.

He raised his hands to signal his benign intent. "Sorry. Not making a move on you, just wanted to have a closer look at that key. That is, if you don't mind." He leaned back against the padded booth to give her a few more inches of comfort room.

"Please, don't apologize. I shouldn't be so jumpy. It's just the last few days been very strange." She withdrew the key but kept the lanyard securely around her neck.

When he realized she wasn't going to actually hand it to him, he took it gently in his hand, squinting to read the writing on the side facing him. He was forced to use the table candle to make the numbers legible. "Twenty-two," he said. "Probably the box number."

"I agree." She produced her own key and placed them alongside each other. "I have a similar box, and while the keys aren't twins, they are close enough to be family. See, mine has the number nineteen on it."

She turned both keys over. "Mine is blank on the back side, but Goodman's has some sort of symbol on it. I don't recognize it, but it would be fantastic if it were somehow connected to the bank where this box is located."

Blaine studied the odd symbol carefully, then set his Power-Book on the table and raised the screen. It was already on, so the LCD illuminated at once, having just awakened from sleep mode. He did a quick web search—the restaurant offered free Wi-Fi, one of the reasons it was such a popular hangout—and turned the screen to face the woman he knew as Carol Palmer. "Pacific States Banking and Reserve. They have branches from Baja to Seattle."

Marie could hardly believe her good fortune. If the key had been a 'blank' like hers, it could have literally fit any box at any branch of any bank in America. A needle in a haystack would be an understatement.

More excited than she'd been in days, she said, "How do we pinpoint the branch where this box is located?"

Blaine closed the lid on the laptop and leaned back against the booth again. His expression grew quite serious. "Carol—may I call you that?"

Hell, why not, Marie thought. It'll help me remember who I'm supposed to be this week. She simply nodded her approval.

He took a thoughtful breath. "Carol, I need you to start at the beginning, when Skipper's body was found, and go real slow from there, eventually getting to the place where you and I are sitting in a restaurant in Berkeley. I'll admit that you knocked me over back there with a story that sounds truly fantastic, and before we proceed, I need a little more background and detail." He folded his hands on the table. "Take all the time you need."

She looked around to be sure they were alone. Blaine had already told the waitress that they wanted to take a few minutes before ordering. She took the hint and disappeared, reading more into the rendezvous than the facts supported, but she'd seen McAllan in here many times before, and often in the company of an attractive young woman.

Though Marie had rehearsed in the hotel room everything she was going to say to Professor McAllan, it all seemed to jumble together now. She took a long drink from her water glass and tried to gather her thoughts.

"For the last three years, I lived in Truman, Utah, with my best friend, Alex—actually it's Alexia but no one ever calls her that—and her father, Ty Summers. He was the sheriff of Duchesne County."

Blaine held up a hand. "You said 'lived' and 'was'—both past tense. You don't live there anymore? Summers is no longer the sheriff?"

Marie didn't want to have to deal with a constant stream of interruptions as she waded through the entire story, so she said, "Professor McAllan, I—"

"Please call me Blaine."

"Okay, Blaine. I think everything will be clear when I've finished telling you what I know."

"My bad," he said apologetically.

She recollected her thoughts and began again. "I don't know exactly how Goodman's body got discovered or where, but from what I was able to determine, four college kids from BYU were hiking the trails north of town. It's a pretty popular spot this time of year. I guess they must have stumbled over him. Apparently, they called the local sheriff's office to report it and Ty went out to collect the body. He did that all the time. People were always getting lost in the mountains and dying of one thing or another, usually hypothermia, sometimes an animal attack or snake bite."

Blaine's expression reflected his discomfort at the thought.

"Anyway, Goodman's body ended up at the local coroner's office, where I worked for three years. Will—Doctor Cameron, I mean—was one of only a few doctors in the small town, and he was also the coroner, or Medical Examiner. I never have gotten those two straight. Ty must have taken the body there sometime Saturday afternoon, the day it was found."

She took another sip of water. "Alex—Ty's daughter—and I were both river guides for Great Western Expeditions, a white-water rafting company based in Moab. We worked two weeks on and one week off all summer. We were on the Green River in Desolation Canyon with a large group when Goodman was found and didn't even know about it until we returned to Truman the following Sunday, eight days later. By then, Ty and Will had been murdered. Both were made to look like accidents, of course, but they were murdered, believe me."

Blaine sat impassively, taking in everything.

Over the next half hour, Marie recounted in detail everything that had transpired since arriving in Truman three days ago. She left out nothing except the trip to St. Michael's and the money she'd gotten from the bank. She had lied and said that the money she'd taken from her apartment hadn't been found by the men at the cliff's edge.

It was a harmless fabrication that didn't impact the facts of the story in any way, or the likelihood of finding out about the key.

Some things she had to keep to herself.

Like her life before Truman.

When she'd finished talking, almost like magic the waitress reappeared. Blaine took the liberty of ordering for them both.

"Carol, why not just go to the FBI with all this?" he asked. "I know you said you couldn't earlier, but that's not a satisfactory answer. They could locate the box that key belongs to in a heartbeat and you'd be totally off the hook. Case closed. Easier for you, better for everyone." It made perfect sense to him.

Marie stuffed the key back inside her blouse. "I'm going to tell you something that has nothing to do with any of this, but when I'm finished, maybe you'll understand." Her hands began to tremble and she interlocked her fingers in her lap to steady them. "Three years ago, I witnessed a horrible crime, a murder, and went to the cops with what I'd seen. Turns out, the cops were the bad guys, as were a whole bunch of other people normally on the side of law and order. Before it was all done, everyone I knew or loved had been killed. I even got shot—same damn arm, too."

She pulled the left shoulder of her top to the side, exposing the medical wrapping.

He winced at the sight. He'd never been shot, let alone twice.

"Oh, yeah, I just remembered something I was told yesterday: two high-ranking politicians were murdered in D.C. the same day Goodman was found, though I don't know who they were. My friend said their murders were professionally done."

This time, Blaine's expression grew dark. "J.D. Wagner and Clark Corello," he said softly. This time, he looked around to be sure they were still of no interest to anyone else in the restaurant. "He was the Chairman of the Senate Intelligence Committee and Corello was his chief factotum."

Marie gave him an odd look.

"Flunky. Gopher."

"Oh," she said, then added, "You think Wagner knew about the key?"

Their food arrived and the waitress asked all the normal questions about how the food looked, if they wanted anything else, then disappeared when Blaine told her all they wanted was privacy.

Marie looked at hers but her appetite had disappeared, despite having only grabbed a single Danish and a cup of black coffee on her way through the lobby at eight a.m.

Blaine said, "Can't say, but since I don't believe in coincidences, I'd bet my aunt's cat he knew something about something, Goodman-wise, and that knowledge got him killed."

Marie grinned. "I hate coincidences, too. They never feel quite right, do they?"

"No, they don't," he said with the first warm smile she had seen him display since meeting.

Blaine McAllan was exceedingly handsome with light brown hair and green eyes the color of jade. At thirty-four and just over six feet tall, he was still as slim as he'd been in college, though not by chance. He maintained his build and stayed in peak condition through a strict daily regimen of running and exercise.

He took a spoonful of his Tom Yam Goong—hot and sour soup—followed by a second, then a third. It was especially good today. Finally, he set his spoon beside the bowl and said, "Okay, out here we've got a renegade Colonel and a group of at least a dozen armed men, probably soldiers of some kind, flying around the country in a Huey killing everyone they meet. Back east, we've got hired assassins knocking off high-ranking politicians and their high-profile assistants with impunity. We've got a dead presidential candidate who left us a single safe deposit box key as the only clue tying all of this together." He took a moment to think, then said, "Did I forget anything?"

Marie shook her head, but then thought about it. "Maybe one important thing."

"And that is...?"

"Someone well placed is pulling our Colonel's strings, putting water on all the fires he starts before anyone even smells smoke. I'll bet your aunt's cat it's the same person who had Wagner and his flunky killed, as well as Skipper Goodman. That's the son of a bitch we really want."

This time Blaine smiled. "My aunt is a dog lover. She wouldn't own a cat."

"But you said..." She didn't finish, but found herself grinning from ear to ear, just as he was. She liked this man's humor and his "cut to the chase" mindset. Better still, he hadn't stared at her boobs even once, and she'd been watching. *Probably second nature after teaching for a decade*, she thought. "How's the soup?" she asked, sliding her bowl closer.

For twenty minutes, they both ate in silence, replaying their conversation and trying to comprehend all its implications. One thing Blaine knew for certain: the key was too hot to hold onto for very long. The sooner it got put into the appropriate lock, or into someone else's hands, the better he'd like it.

When the waitress had cleared the table, he asked for the check.

"Oh, please, allow me to get it. It's the least I can do," Marie said.

"Why? You don't owe me anything, certainly not lunch."

"Then let's just say I'd like to buy you lunch. I haven't bought a man lunch in a very long time." Suddenly, she regretted her words; they might well be taken wrong and she hated being misunderstood. Or worse, pitied.

"In that case, I accept. Thank you," Blaine said sincerely.

Marie withdrew enough for the meal and a generous tip and placed the cash inside the black leather holder that contained the bill. The waitress returned, thanked them, and assured them they could stay as long as they liked. Then she vanished for the last time.

Marie leaned back comfortably in the booth. "Ever been married?"

Blaine rested his elbows on the table and folded his hands. "No. Engaged once. It was a long time ago, though."

Before he could ask her the same question, she said, "What happened?"

Blaine looked into the distance, focusing on a spot somewhere beyond the restaurant that only his mind's eye could see. "We met our senior year and fell in love immediately. She was the most beautiful thing I'd ever seen at the time, smart, rich, the whole enchilada. I kept telling her that she was too good for me, then one day, I came home to the apartment we shared and all that was left was a note saying that she agreed."

He rolled his head side to side and his bones cracked from the tension of the last hour.

"It was for the best," he said.

"How can you say that?"

"Because nothing can keep two people together if they weren't meant to be together, just like nothing can keep two people apart if they're destined to share their lives."

Marie thought about his words and about her life to this point. She nodded in agreement, though with an inner sadness she hoped he didn't see.

"So, what do we do next?" she asked. "I have no idea where Colonel Mustard is at the moment"—Blaine chuckled at her joke—"but he has never been too far from this thing"—she touched the key between her breasts—"and he's not likely to be far away right now. If he came storming in this minute, guns blazing, I wouldn't be the least bit surprised."

Though Marie didn't turn toward the door they'd entered an hour earlier, Blaine did, and was immensely pleased to find Le Cheval devoid of ruthless killers at present.

"We know the key fits Box-22 in some branch of the Pacific States Banking and Reserve, but there are at least six hundred of them across three states. It could be any one of them." It seemed an insurmountable task to him.

Marie said, "I disagree, Blaine. In fact, I don't think the number of possible branches will be greater than two or three once we get to looking at the most logical places. I mean, they can't be like Starbucks with one on every corner, can they?"

"They're all over the tristate area, but, no, they're not on every corner," he said, though not following her thought process. He didn't understand how she'd just whittled down six hundred branches to a fraction of that number.

"Great! That makes it a lot easier."

"I need a little elaboration here. Why can't it be in any branch in the PSBR network?"

"Simple, I think. I don't know exactly how things went down, but here's my theory: Goodman gets some kind of information that exists in the real world. Not like an e-mail or a phone call. You know, something like photographs or documents. Real stuff."

He nodded that he was following her.

"Okay, he locks this stuff away in a box at some branch of the Pacific States Banking and Reserve, then gets on his plane and BAM!—down it goes killing everyone onboard, including him. Problem solved. Only he and the mysterious stuff aren't blown to bits like everyone thinks."

Blaine grimaced at her descriptive explanation.

"Sorry, I get carried away," she said.

"Go ahead, I'm following you so far."

Marie took another long drink of water. "When his body is finally found ten days ago, the risk of the stuff being on him is too frightening a thought for the Colonel and the people pulling his strings to deal with, so they begin killing everyone who comes near the body."

"Only, he doesn't have this stuff, whatever it is, on him at the time of the crash," Blaine said, leaning toward her and putting his hand on her knee. "He stashed it for safe keeping before the flight.

All he had with him was that key." He realized he was squeezing her leg and pulled back his hand.

"Right," she said. "And since I'd bet your aunt's cat he didn't have that stuff for more than a few hours before booking it to D.C., maybe even a few minutes, he would have had to stash it in a branch that was really close by. That's why I said it won't be but one of two or three at most. Now all we have to do is figure out where he was when he got his hands on the stuff."

Blaine said, "I wonder what this stuff, as we keep calling it, is all about. Whatever it is, it has to be unbelievably explosive and damaging for so many to have been killed to keep it quiet."

"Money," Marie said. "It's always about the cash."

Blaine held up a finger. "Perhaps. Maybe even likely, but I study politics and politicians for a living, and while money may be the most common factor in cases like this, don't underestimate the power of old fashioned patriotism or religious fervor. More crimes against humanity have been perpetrated in the name of blind devotion to a country, cause, or deity than for all the gold ever mined."

Marie thought about his words and shook her head. She didn't buy it. "I'm going with greed."

"What, you don't believe in causes?"

"Absolutely I do." She gave him a look of incredulity. "You don't think I'm doing all this shit for a gold pot at the end of the rainbow, do you? Nobody's gonna write me a check or pin a medal on me at the end of the day if I *somehow* manage to live through this nightmare. In fact, I fully expect to be thrown into prison after this is done for any number of offenses, federal and local, so there's your blind devotion to a cause up front and personal."

Despite her words, she didn't look or sound bitter, merely resigned to a fate she was certain had already been written and was completely inescapable.

"Then why do it?" he asked. This time, he put his hand on her knee and kept it there.

"For Alex more than anything, I guess. I promised her I'd keep her safe and those bastards made me break that promise. I'll be damned if I'll break my second promise to her."

"What was that?"

"To make them pay for her death, and the deaths of Ty and Will. All the others, too. People just like you and me who just wanted to live their lives and didn't give a shit about money or agendas or lofty ideals." She stared at him with such intensity in her deep brown eyes that for a moment, he thought he felt heat emanating from them.

Blaine raised his hand and put it gently against her cheek.

She reached up and put her hand on his. "Thank you for helping me, Blaine."

"I haven't done anything yet, but I know just the person who can give us the information we need, and I'll bet my aunt's cat"—he gave her a slow wink—"she'll be more than eager to help. But first, we have to go for a little ride."

They both smiled at his words, but they also knew things were about to get really ugly.

FORTY-SIX

WHEN THE SECOND BANK in his list of four candidates yielded absolutely no activity at any of the boxes held by Goodman, Donald Shelton pushed away from his computer and finally lit the cigar he'd been chewing on for the better part of an hour. He was frustrated, tired, and pissed. The good news, if there was any, was that the video, whether on the memory card alone or still in Vanover's cell phone, had to be at one of the last two banks.

For a moment, he seriously considered emptying the man's accounts—every cent—and then disappearing to the Cayman Islands or perhaps Fiji, but realized that this man had extremely powerful and dangerous friends—even in death—and he would eventually be caught.

It just wasn't worth the gamble when there was so much money out there that didn't bear such potential liability.

No, he'd restrict his financial plundering to those who'd offended the Unit or him personally, but who also didn't possess friends powerful enough to cause any trouble.

"Ordinary people, little people," he said to his cigar as he gave it a long draw. The thought brought a smile back to his face and reenergized his tired muscles.

It was time to see what was behind door number-three.

* * *

"There's no way in hell Colonel pecker-head won't be watching the mansion," Marie said as they drove at a brisk clip down College Avenue, heading for I-880 and finally US-101 South at San Jose. "That's the first place I'd expect to find my dumb ass if I were the Colonel, which is why I'm not going anywhere near the place."

Blaine chuckled at her new name for the nameless man. "That's exactly right," he affirmed. "We'll get a hotel room. Two actually," he corrected before she could comment, "and after we've gotten you safely out of sight, I'll go on to the mansion alone."

He changed lanes to go around a slower moving vehicle and accelerated to well above the posted speed when he'd cleared it. Santa Barbara was three hundred thirty-five miles to the south, a drive of five hours and forty minutes with good traffic.

Of course, there was never good traffic on US-101, even at three in the morning, and this was the middle of a work day. Blaine looked at the digital clock on the car's onboard GPS: a few minutes before noon. The trip would most likely take seven or eight hours, possibly longer, putting them in Santa Barbara long after the banks had closed.

After leaving Le Cheval, they had swung by her hotel so Marie could grab her backpack and checkout, but had mutually agreed to buy whatever he might need on the road instead of wasting time stopping by his home. Her hotel, only a block from the restaurant, wasn't out of the way and had consumed less than five minutes. Blaine's home was twenty miles in the opposite direction and would have taken an hour.

"How do you know she'll even be there tonight? Maybe she'll be off doing whatever it is billionaire widows do on Wednesday nights. What if she's at church, or out buying a professional football team or something?"

Blaine couldn't help laughing at Marie's bizarre sense of humor, especially when he knew she had the weight of the world on her shoulders. "Are you always this upbeat with everything crashing down around you? I'm not trying to be bleak, just stating the obvious."

Marie thought about his words for a brief moment, just as she had pondered her situation for the last several days, then said, "Well, since it happens so often, I'd be suicidal if I couldn't laugh a little. No matter what people do to you, it's always up to you how you let it affect you in the end. Abe Lincoln said that most folks are about as happy as they set their minds to be. I guess that pretty much says it for me."

Amazed at her resilience, he lifted his cell phone from the dash and handed it to her. "Touch CONTACTS, then scroll down and you'll find her information under 'G.'"

In a few seconds, Marie had located the many numbers for Marguerite Goodman. She studied the display. "Marguerite. I guess she used to be Maggie before she had a billion dollars."

"Actually, Marguerite is the one with the money. She's a La Fontaine. Old European money. Her family owns most of the coastline where her home is located, plus ten miles in both directions for as many miles inland. The landholdings go back four generations, before Santa Barbara was even a dream."

"Oh. My bad. Not used to old money. Not used to new money, either, for that matter." She turned the display toward him. "What now, captain?"

"Just touch the number opposite Home," he said, keeping his eyes on the road. At eighty-five, she was grateful his mind was on driving and not on dinking with the phone buttons, like half the people they passed.

When she touched the number, she immediately heard the radio—which had been playing softly in the background—fall silent and a phone begin to ring in the car's speakers.

"I have my cell phone linked to my car's radio by Bluetooth. Better than eating a semi while trying to dial," he said with a reassuring smile.

"Much," she said, putting the phone back in the center console.

Five minutes later, Blaine had spoken with Mrs. Goodman's personal assistant and had arranged a meeting with the matriarch of the Goodman estate for eight p.m.

"That was pretty quick," Marie said, surprised at how simple it had been to reach the wealthy widow. "Are all billionaires that easy to have a sit-down with? Maybe I should give old Warren or Bill a call and see if they want to do brunch or dinner sometime." She caressed the wood dash sensuously with her fingertips. "I believe I could spend a billion dollars," she said mockingly.

Blaine grinned. "I don't think most billionaires would be quite so easy to approach, even for a beautiful woman like you. I could be wrong, of course." He gave her a playful wink.

Marie said, "So, does this chummy relationship with the widow Goodman have something to do with the book you're doing on her late hubby?"

At first surprised, Blaine quickly realized that the reason he'd been chosen by her in the first place was because of his extensive knowledge of Robert Wayne Goodman. She had to have known about the book he was writing. "I see you've done your homework."

"Yep. Like to know as much as I can before I jump into a fire. Doesn't always work out, as you can tell, but it's a good plan to have, anyway." She shifted in her seat and brought her left leg up under her right.

"The family was extremely helpful as I compiled the book, often working with me for days at a time after the accident. They told me that they trusted me to portray Skipper in a good and fair light."

"Why?" Marie asked. "That's a pretty tall assumption."

"I worked on his first congressional campaign. They knew me from back then and also knew I was a devout Goodman supporter."

"Oh, I see. So they basically gave you the kind of unfettered access biography writers dream of getting, but seldom do."

"Pretty much. Anyway, that was back in the fall. Not much contact since then. Until a few days ago, I thought I had all there was to have on the man, at least for a first book on him. Was just about to write the closing chapter when his body was found and everyone suddenly realized that the crash had not been an accident."

He gave his passenger a long stare, as lengthy as he could risk while still maintaining their current speed. There was something incredibly familiar about her and it nagged at a half-formed memory in his mind, but he couldn't quite put his finger on it. Letting the thought pass for now, he turned his head back to the road. "Then you showed up this morning and the new ending I thought I had perfectly outlined in my mind, and was just about to write, went straight to hell."

"Sorry. None of this was my idea."

"Yeah, I know," he said, squeezing her left knee. "Maybe we'll get through this together with no more problems."

"Wanna bet," she said in a sardonic whisper that only the passenger glass heard.

*　*　*

The problem with door number three was that it was exactly like the two preceding it, yielding nothing of value other than one more place the damned video wasn't.

Donald Shelton cracked the knuckles of his very tired fingers and closed the lid on his laptop. Merkett was coming toward him at a quick pace and he wasn't going to be pleased with the bad news he was about to receive. Still, as Edison once said, "I may have learned one way to make an electric light, but in the process, I also learned ten thousand ways *not* to make one." Maybe his boss would take solace in that ideology.

Probably not, Shelton reconsidered.

"What do you have for me?" the Colonel said with an extremely stern look on his face.

"Has to be in the last bank," the squint said with as much confidence as he could muster.

Merkett didn't look so sure. "Have you thought this thing out carefully, Don? Are we overlooking anything, anything at all?"

Shelton drew in a calming breath. "I've gone back over Frye's phone conversation with you the morning of the crash. The timeline is explicit and finite. Goodman had only ten minutes at most that were unaccounted for from the time Vanover left the estate to the time he and Frye headed for the airport. No stops along the way. Even driving like a maniac, he could have only reached the four banks I've already outlined. There wasn't enough time to go anywhere else. The next closest bank he did business with would have required more than twenty-five minutes round trip. There wasn't time."

"Why not some other bank, then, one he didn't usually bank with?"

"The only banks within four minutes' drive, five minutes at most, are these here." He pointed to the list of four, on which three had already been scratched through in red pen.

Merkett dropped heavily into the chair beside Shelton. "Well, finish what you're doing then pack up. We have to get back to the ranch ASAP."

"What about the key? The woman?" Shelton asked.

"Won't matter in a few days," Merkett said, his expression weary. The reality of what he and the Unit were about to finally bring to culmination, after millions of dollars and months of careful planning, was gnawing at him with all its fury. There could be no mistakes now. There was no turning back.

They were about to become the greatest patriots of all time, or the most reviled traitors in U.S. history. It all hinged on whether or not that infernal video ever reared its ugly head.

"What's going on, Colonel?" Shelton asked.

Merkett folded his arms and stared off into space for a long moment. "Just got off the phone with the General. Whether we find the video or not, he's decided it's our best bet to roll the dice and advance the timetable. I agree, given all that's happened over the last ten days. Too many loose ends—one is bound to trip us up if we don't act now."

Shelton leaned forward and found himself speaking in a whisper, despite being nowhere an 'outsider' could overhear them. "Advance it by how much, sir?"

Merkett stood and arched his back to loosen stiff muscles. He'd been sitting too long these last few days. He looked down at Shelton. "The operation will go down exactly as planned, with one notable exception: instead of late October, all targets will be taken out this Saturday. The world, as thousands of people currently know it, is going to come to an end"—he studied his watch and did a quick calculation—"in just under sixty-eight hours."

Shelton understood this fact and the thought of innocent lives being taken didn't bother him in the least. "What about the Matthews woman?" he asked, his tone concerned and angry. He had no intention of turning his back on the meddlesome bitch at this point.

"If we don't catch her in the next few hours, we'll have to deal with her afterward. Whether it's today, tomorrow, or next week, that pesky little whore is going to die, as sure as I'm standing here."

The computer man raised his laptop screen, a new sense of determination in his soul. "If it's all the same to you, sir, I'd prefer she die today."

Merkett put his hand on the programmer's shoulder and gave him a cold look. "So would I, Lieutenant. Do what you can to make that happen while I bring the rest of the team up to speed. We've got a lot to accomplish in very little time."

* * *

The Hotel Mar Monte on Cabrillo Boulevard was the closest inn to the Goodman mansion that Blaine was familiar with, yet still far enough away to keep Carol safe from anyone who might be watching the estate. Situated directly on the ocean with the mountains at its back, it's turn-of-the-century Mission-style architecture made it look more like a beautiful white postcard than a place where people actually slept and ate.

He'd stayed at the exquisite inn on many occasions in the months following the crash of Skipper Goodman's plane, though he had not been back since the beginning of the year.

As he and Marie crossed the vast lobby, the desk clerk remembered him at once. "Good evening, Professor McAllan. Welcome back to the Hotel Mar Monte. How long will you be staying with us this time?"

Blaine shook the man's hand. "Hello, Juan. Good to see you, too." He put his arm around Marie's waist. "This is my friend and associate, Carol Palmer. We'll be needing two rooms for just one night. Can you make them adjoining? We have a lot of work to do."

Juan tapped a few keys and studied his monitor. "Still working on that book or yours?" he said as he found two rooms that met the professor's requirements. Before Blaine could answer the question, he added, "Ah, yes, two adjoining rooms. I'm afraid, however, that all of our Oceanside rooms are taken for this evening. Will that be okay?"

Since it was too late to do any sightseeing this evening, and they would most likely check out right after breakfast—as soon as the banks opened on Thursday—he accepted the rooms with a grateful smile.

Marie had previously thought of warning Blaine about using a credit card, but weighed the likelihood of anyone knowing she was even with him in the first place and decided it was a calculated risk worth taking. Besides, paying cash for a room in this ritzy place would probably set off more bells than a fire alarm.

They moved quickly to their rooms, instinctively locking the doors behind them. Marie was the first to knock on the adjoining door.

Blaine opened it at once.

"So, I guess you're off to see Mrs. Goodman," she said. They had stopped en route and Blaine had purchased a few items of clothing and some toiletries. He squeezed out some toothpaste onto his brand new toothbrush as she talked. "How far away is the place?"

"Just down the coast a bit. You can walk there in ten minutes or less, no problem." He brushed and rinsed.

"A little close, don't you think?" she said, concerned that the Colonel might have his men all over the area.

"Listen, there are a half dozen really great hotels within a mile of the mansion, plus a dozen lesser establishments within two or three. He can't cover everything, so he'll most likely concentrate his men on the main gate to the home. It's the only point you absolutely have to cross if you're going to pay the family a visit. Since there's no way in hell he'll be looking for me, we're fine."

He could tell she was still nervous about the whole thing and put his arms around her tenderly. "Carol, we talked about this and it's a good gamble. As safe a bet as we can make, but if you don't think I should go, then—"

"No, you should go," she said, cutting off his words and also pushing away from him. She'd almost forgotten that her name was currently Carol Palmer. Damn! she hated all this subterfuge. Perhaps she should tell him everything, and not just the fact that she hadn't told him about Marie Matthews or Vickie Brennan. Everything, going back more than three years. Get it all on the table. No more lies.

As she was about to speak, he said, "Well, I'm off then. See you soon, I hope."

"What is that supposed to mean, you hope?" she asked. Everything was suddenly making her jumpy.

"Sorry, I didn't mean it like that," he said, taking her hands in his. They felt clammy all of a sudden. "I only meant I hope I'll see you shortly, as opposed to a couple of hours from now. That way, we can still have dinner together. They've got a great restaurant with a view of the Pacific that's to die for."

Let's hope not, she thought.

"I'd like that. Be careful, Blaine. Remember, watch out for anyone following you after you leave the mansion."

"I know, I know," he assured her, remembering her hour-long speech in the car covering that topic in detail.

When Blaine had left the room, she relocked her side of the adjoining door and double-checked both locks on the outer door as well. Confident that she was safe—at least for now—and would be alone for an hour or more, she listened for a sound she hadn't heard in days.

She could hear the huge bathtub calling her name.

FORTY-SEVEN

WHEN THE LAST BANK in his short list was finally cracked, as the other three before it, this one showed not the slightest activity for the entire day Skipper Goodman's plane went down—the entire month, for that matter. At that moment, Donald Shelton knew he'd been following the wrong path for the better part of a full day. It wasn't that his concept was flawed, rather that he'd simply gone right when he should have gone left. Goodman hiding the phone had been a logical direction to follow, the most logical. That was the right turn he'd taken. He now understood that in order to find the phone, and the video, he had to figure out who represented the theoretical left turn that he'd missed.

Rather than infuriate him, the problem intrigued him. There *was* a key, that much had been determined to a high degree of certainty, and that specific key was most likely to a safe deposit box at a bank near the Goodman mansion in Santa Barbara. If Goodman had the key on him when he died, then there were only a few minutes between Vanover leaving the mansion and the ride to the airport.

Whatever had happened to the video, had happened in that very brief time span. But what?

"Okay, you old fox, you pulled a fast one on us, didn't you," Shelton said to his screen as he toyed with the problem in his brain. "Who would you have trusted with that information? How did they hide the phone at a bank and still hand you the key before takeoff?"

He pulled up the full transcript of the conversation with Merkett and Frye before the plane left Santa Barbara Airport, reading every line and word more carefully than ever.

Suddenly it was staring him squarely in the eye.

"Oh, you sly son of a bitch. I got you this time, though," he said as he popped his knuckles and prepared to hack into yet another bank.

*   *   *

The Goodman estate lay resplendently, though not pompously, on twenty incredibly manicured acres along Channel Drive in Santa Barbara, near the Montecito Country Club. It held a commanding view of the Pacific, without a single manmade object impeding its breathtaking panorama. Built in 1911 by Marguerite's grandfather for the then lofty sum of a quarter of a million dollars, the property today was conservatively worth more than two hundred and fifty times that amount.

Of course, the family would never sell, not for ten times that sum. They would never need the money such a sale would bring, and the thought of their beloved family estate in the hands of strangers was unthinkable.

The first time Blaine McAllan passed through the huge stone wall and massive iron gates that looked like they'd been borrowed from Buckingham Palace, the grounds and main house had left him breathless.

This evening was no different, perhaps even more stunning because it was the first time he'd seen the residence at night. As much care and expense had been put into lighting the grounds as had been spent on the plantings themselves. It was the kind of manor the staff of *Architectural Digest* might have dreamed up if given an unrestricted budget and limitless time.

When the armed guard at the main gate had admitted him, Blaine eased his BMW down the long cobbled drive. After a few hundred winding yards, he came to a stop before the colossal double main entrance doors, nearly as large as the gates through which he'd just passed. Again, the scene at night was completely different than the impression made under a cobalt-blue California sky, but equally as striking.

At more than forty-thousand square feet, the principal residence—one of five structures on the estate, but larger than all the others combined—was one of the finest examples of Tudor Revival architecture in North America. In fact, it had been featured over the years on not one, but three *Architectural Digest* covers, as well as other such publications too numerous to even begin to count.

It was a stunning property, and it well bespoke the power contained within its walls. Even with Skipper gone, Marguerite's family was a major political force to be reckoned with, much as the Kennedy family was back east. Soon, their son and daughter would make their own marks within the Democratic Party, and Blaine had already been tapped to help with both campaigns when the time came.

He stepped to the front doors and was greeted at once by Marguerite's butler. "Good evening, Doctor McAllan," he said in a thick British accent. The man and his wife, both from England, had been with the family for three decades.

"Good evening, Thomas. I believe I'm expected."

"Indeed you are, sir. If you'll please follow me."

With that, Thomas led Blaine to the first room on the left of the great entrance hall, referred to as the Walnut Room because of the lavish use of that wood in its flooring, ornate walls, cabinetry, and coffers. If the ceiling hadn't been more than thirty feet high, and the room at least six hundred square feet, the extensive use of such a dark wood would have been overwhelming, even claustrophobic. As it was, because of its immensity, the room felt warm and inviting.

When Thomas had left his guest with the assurance that Mrs. Goodman would be with him shortly, Blaine took a seat in one of the thickly-padded leather writing chairs. There were two of them, probably a hundred years old if they were a day, but in such fine condition that they could have been reproductions.

He knew they were not, the pair probably costing his annual salary at the university.

Skipper and his wife were not pretentious people, they could simply afford life's finer things, which they appreciated to the fullest. They didn't collect for the sake of accumulating trinkets or showing off their wealth, but because the items they bought suited their temperaments and personalities. Everything got used, much as items in ordinary homes do. Despite its grandeur and scale, this was first and foremost a home in which a family lived and loved.

He at once missed Skipper. In their months together on the campaign trail, they had become friends. He also missed the time they'd spent on his boat, the "La Margarita," a play on his wife's name. The boat, or rather motor yacht, was a one hundred forty-five foot Benetti, with a composite-hull and twin ocean-going diesel engines. It took to the sea like a craft a third its size took to a mill pond, with the ease of a skater on ice. Since he had become fully certified to pilot the yacht on his own—though he always kept a full crew on payroll year round and never took to the water without them—the press had dubbed him 'Skipper' and the name had stuck throughout the years.

"Blaine," came a pleasant and familiar voice from his right.

He turned at once in its direction.

Marguerite had just entered the room, arms outstretched with a warm smile on her face. Even at fifty-six, Marguerite Danielle La Fontaine-Goodman was a stunningly-beautiful woman, who

431

had benefited in every possible way from a lifetime of superb care, excellent nutrition, and limited worries.

Blaine stood and they embraced warmly.

"So gracious of you to see me on such short notice, Marguerite," he said. She took the writer's chair beside his.

"When you spoke with Eileen, you didn't give me any indication as to the nature of your visit, so I must assume it has something to do with the book." Eileen was Marguerite's personal assistant, the woman with whom Blaine had made the appointment.

Marguerite sat with an easy but elegant grace, as someone who'd entertained numerous dignitaries and heads of state over the years. Blaine thought her the most politically insightful woman he'd ever known, though she was pleased to be seen by most as someone only casually interested in politics. It disarmed them, and that was always to her advantage.

In the weeks following Skipper's disappearance and presumed death, she had provided Blaine with unfettered access as he worked on her husband's biography. She knew that he would never do anything to paint the man she loved and admired in a bad light, even though some of his book might contain moments the Goodman family—like all families—would rather forget.

Such was life in the public eye. She knew its highs and its lows.

Blaine took a deep breath. Since his call to Marguerite, he had considered many ways to begin this conversation, and in the end, all appeared fraught with pitfalls. Straight down the middle was the course he had chosen, right between the eyes.

"Marguerite, I have come across some information that may lead us to not only the reason Skipper was killed, but also those responsible." The fact that her husband's death was no longer being considered an accident was known to her, though she was trusting the FBI to keep her abreast of the progress of their investigation.

This news, however, came as a total surprise to her.

"I don't understand, Blaine. What kind of information?"

He could see a touch of uncharacteristic anxiety in her expression.

"Actually, I don't have the information as much as I believe I know where it may be hidden." He wished he'd chosen his words better when he saw her expression turn from worry to disbelief.

"Perhaps you can be a bit more specific."

"Of course. I recently met a woman who has in her possession a small key, one which belongs to a safe deposit box held at some branch of Pacific States Banking and Reserve. She found it at the clinic where Skipper's body was taken after it was found in the mountains."

"Yes, I sent our attorneys to Truman, Utah, to collect Bob's remains the moment I heard he'd been discovered. What do you mean she found it at the clinic? What does that have to do with Skipper?"

"This woman worked for several years as an assistant to the doctor who received Skipper's body. She says that while he performed no procedures on your husband, he did make a few x-rays. She suggests the reason may have been simply because Bob was such a famous person and he couldn't pass up such an opportunity."

"Doctor Cameron, I believe?" she said, remembering what her attorneys had reported upon arrival back in Santa Barbara.

"That's correct."

"I received no word of any x-rays. Are you sure of this?"

"Yes, positive. As it turns out, that may have been a very fortuitous thing."

"How so?"

"Without an x-ray of Skipper's left hand, the presence of the key he was holding would have remained unknown to us. The men who were looking for it would have simply taken it and none of us would be any the wiser."

"What men?" she asked, alarmed by his words. She knew conspiracies, large and small, were facts of life—and death—in the world of politics, but she had never been party to one, at least to her knowledge. She wondered if this is how Jackie Kennedy must have felt in the days after November 22, 1963. "Why would anyone be looking for anything my husband might have had with him? Does this have something to do with the crash?" She knotted her hands together nervously.

Blaine reached across and put his hand on hers. "It is my belief, Marguerite, that on the day Skipper's plane went down, someone came to visit him, and that person left him some important information. Exactly what that information is, I have no idea. What I suspect is that Skipper knew the value, or rather, the destructive nature, of the information and concealed it in the safe deposit box before leaving for D.C. Apparently, he didn't trust it being with him, and it seems he was right."

Marguerite remembered the morning well. She'd played her last moments with her husband over and over in her head until the images had become threadbare. "There was a man that day, a very strange and troubled man. He came to the main gate and asked for Bob. Within a few minutes, he'd been allowed in, and Bob met him on the front steps. Shortly thereafter, they moved in here." She indicated the Walnut Room. "Approximately half an hour later, Bob ran to the office, but came back after only a few minutes, carrying a package. I assumed it belonged to the man, because Bob gave it to him and the man left at once. I told the FBI all of this after the crash, but they didn't give it any credence. Told me it was coincidental."

"It wasn't," Blaine said with conviction.

"What did this man have to do with the crash?" she asked, her hands trembling.

"Probably nothing other than the information he gave Skipper was likely the reason for the crash."

"My God," she said, her hands to her face. "Where is this information now? Does the FBI know of this?"

"To answer the second question, no, the FBI knows nothing of any of this. Everything has come to light in the last seventy-two hours, and the woman who brought the key to me has been on the run the whole time."

"Where is this key?"

"With the woman."

"And she is…?"

"At the Hotel Mar Monte on Cabrillo, just up the coast. I thought it best to keep her away from here as we both suspect your home is being watched by the men looking for the key."

Marguerite Goodman's expression grew stern. "We need to call the FBI at once. Whoever these men are, I will see that they pay for Bob's death if it takes my last penny."

"I agree, Marguerite, but first we need to find the information and determine if the FBI is implicated in this in any way."

This concept had never crossed the woman's mind and the thought seemed to horrify her. "You think that's possible?"

"Considering all the people these men have killed, and the apparent impunity with which they've acted so far, I'd say that some agency, or some individual, with great influence is behind their actions. I don't wish to bring anyone in until I can rule them out as a co-conspirator. To do otherwise would only invite disaster."

"Absolutely. I agree completely." She seemed to be analyzing everything that had been said in the last twenty minutes. Finally, she said, "How can I help you find this information?"

It was exactly what Blaine had hoped she would say and he said a silent prayer of thanks. "The key had the Pacific States Banking and Reserve logo on it, box twenty-two, but I have no idea which branch. We suspect it will be near your home, here, but even that is little more than an educated guess based on a number of assumptions."

"You want to know at which branch of that bank Bob held safe deposit box number twenty-two?"

"Yes, thank you."

Marguerite stood. "I'll be a few minutes in the office. He was incredibly organized about these things, but we have so much of this kind of information. I'll hurry." She walked toward the door. "You know your way to the kitchen, Blaine. Grab something to drink. We have every make of beer imaginable as well as all kinds of soft drinks. I'll join you there as quickly as I can."

With that, the woman practically sprinted across the foyer toward the ground-floor office.

Blaine wound his way to the back of the home, a distance of nearly two hundred feet, finding the kitchen on his first try. He was pleased he'd remembered the route after all these months, and hadn't had to call out for Thomas to rescue him.

Eileen, Marguerite's secretary and Thomas' wife, was seated at a granite bar the size of a handball court. She was watching CNN and appeared to be finishing the last of her dinner.

When Blaine appeared, she rose at once, embarrassed to be seen eating in the presence of a house guest. Quickly realizing that the man was someone she'd seen on many occasions, and a friend of the family, she was greatly relieved.

"Oh, sir," she said in an accent much thicker than her husband's. "You gave me quite a start. Thomas didn't tell me there was anyone in the house." She looked at the clock on the wall above one set of stainless sinks. "But then, I had forgotten that I made your appointment with the Madam for this evening. Please forgive me."

She began clearing her dishes from the bar.

"Hello, Eileen. Didn't mean to barge in on you like this. Please, finish eating and don't pay me any mind at all."

The woman stopped what she was doing and gave him a mischievous look. "You think it will be alright, sir?"

"Absolutely. Just point me toward a cold beer and I'll join you."

With that, she returned her plate to the bar and dashed to the leftmost of the three massive refrigerators to retrieve his beer. "If my memory serves me, Master Blaine, you prefer a Guinness Stout."

"That I do," he said, accepting the beer and a huge frosted mug.

When Eileen had determined that he needed nothing else, she returned to her dinner. "Should I leave the TV on for you. It makes no difference to me. It's not like there's anything I can do about the news, is there?"

Blaine chuckled at her straightforward but motherly manner. "It's fine. Just leave it."

For the next few minutes, the news droned on about gun violence, a roller coaster stock market, the price of gas, and increasingly tighter flight restrictions. Nothing new on any of those fronts, just the same old news.

All bad.

As he was finishing his Guinness, he was intrigued by a report from Truman, Utah. The CNN field reporter was about to interview the acting sheriff, Doug Rozier, about some very strange occurrences in the town where Skipper Goodman had been brought after being found in the mountains north of there.

Over the next five minutes, everything he knew about Carol Palmer was turned upside down.

FORTY-EIGHT

JAMES MERKETT WAS EXTREMELY pleased with
the news his squint had just delivered. In fact, it was fair to
say it was the best news he'd gotten in months. He unrolled
the detailed map of Santa Barbara and found the location Shelton
had given him at once. With the tip of his knife, he pointed to
the address, a branch of Pacific States Banking and Reserve at the
corner of La Cadena and Quinientos, just under three miles west
of the Goodman Estate. Box-22 at that location, the one containing Marec Vanover's damned video, was held not in Goodman's
name as they'd assumed, but in the name of his personal assistant,
Angel Britt.

He looked at each man in turn, then said, "The bank opens
at nine a.m. sharp. Lieutenant Shelton assures me that there has
been no activity on Britt's safe deposit box since the morning of
the crash. On that morning, she accessed it less than ten minutes
after Vanover left the estate, then joined Goodman at the airport
for the flight to D.C. Frye never picked up on it because he hadn't
realized Britt was at Goodman's home that morning. Apparently,
she came in through the servant's entrance, that's the best we can
figure. It makes no difference at this point. What we do know is

that the video is there and we have to assume the Matthews woman will eventually head there as well."

"How will she know to look at that branch, sir? How can she possibly know about Angel Britt?" Sergeant Branch asked.

"The same way we did. The FBI created a detailed timeline of Goodman's last morning and it will not be hard to get her hands on a copy. Hell, she can get it online using any computer or smart phone in the country."

"But, we have to assume she'll need someone like Lieutenant Shelton in order to get into the box, correct?" Ron Phelps said.

Donald Shelton stepped in. "That's correct, since the box is in Angel Britt's name, and she died on the plane. Thank god she had no family or that box would have been opened months ago. Now, it will take a court order to gain access unless Matthews manages to change the owner's information in their database. However, that's not a deal breaker considering there's no shortage of qualified hackers in the state."

"Won't that cost her plenty?" Nate Fisher asked.

"You bet," Shelton said. "But considering we found twenty grand on the shrink, all in cash, we have to assume she gave him only a portion of the money she had. Now, where she got that money is anyone's guess, but it's more than safe to assume the good doctor wasn't entirely forthcoming with us, and it's also not a stretch of the imagination to assume she kept the lion's share for her own use. She'll have enough money to hire this hacker."

Everyone seemed to be digesting the information with mixed feelings. They were pleased the box containing the video had been located, but they were worried, down to the man, that the woman was still out there with the only key.

Merkett sensed their concern and spoke up. "Men, whether she shows up at that branch today, tomorrow, or a week from now, we'll grab her. Don will constantly monitor the activity at that branch and will alert us the moment the information on Britt's box is changed. It's a safe bet that the woman will attempt to use the key shortly thereafter. When she does, we pounce. I'm leaving three of you here to intercept her, and the rest of us are going to start preparing for the big day." He looked at Phelps. "Sergeant major, take Branch and Woodard and get that worrisome bitch the moment she makes her move, however long that takes. Nothing else matters, understood."

"You can count on it, sir," Phelps said.

"You think she'll still attempt to retrieve whatever's in the box after Saturday," Fisher asked. "Why not just give it to the FBI at that point?"

"First, it's my belief she won't automatically connect the dots between Saturday's events and the key. And second, I sincerely believe this woman doesn't trust anyone, not even the FBI. Until she can see whatever is inside that safe deposit box, and make her own determination as to whom it implicates and exonerates, she'll trust no one but herself. And that paranoia of hers is the very thing that's gonna allow us to take her down."

* * *

When Marguerite rejoined Blaine in the kitchen, Eileen had already finished dinner and had retired for the evening. Thomas had stopped by to assure the professor that he would see him out when he and the Madam had finished their business. Blaine had thanked him, but told him he needn't bother. With that, Thomas had also bid him a good evening and had left to join his wife.

Marguerite took a stool beside Blaine, a puzzled look on her face.

"What?" he asked, sensing something was amiss.

"Are you certain of the bank where this mysterious box resides?" she asked.

"Yes, their logo is quite distinctive."

"In that case, I fear you've been given some bad information. I don't know what game this woman of yours is playing, but Bob had no safe deposit boxes at any branch within the entire Pacific

States chain. To be certain, I phoned our business manager at his home and he verified it."

Blaine was astounded, but considering what he'd just seen on the news, not entirely surprised.

Now, to gracefully exit without causing Mrs. Goodman to think he'd completely lost his mind.

Or worse, that he was part of some scheme.

"I'm so sorry, Marguerite. I really thought I was on to something important. Never in a million years would I have disturbed you with this matter if I had not been convinced of its authenticity."

She touched his arm. "Blaine, I think you and I know each other well enough to leave that unsaid, but thank you anyway. I suggest you find out what this woman is up to before she puts you in some situation that cannot be resolved with a simple apology."

She stood and motioned toward the front of the home. In his mind, it was a polite way of saying, "Beat it, bub, you've caused enough trouble for one day."

Blaine and Marguerite embraced at the front door and she assured him that he need not hesitate to call her anytime he needed her assistance in any way. They were friends, and that's all that mattered.

He thanked her and left, his tail between his legs, but also with a burning desire to ring the neck of Carol Palmer, or Marie Matthews, or whatever the hell her real name was.

FORTY-NINE

MARIE FINISHED HER BATH and searched for something clean to wear. With only three casual outfits to her name, her choice had been severely limited from the outset, but when desert dust, rattlesnakes, sweat, and three days on the run were factored in, she might as well have been a homeless bum with a bag of rags for a wardrobe.

At least I have clean underwear, she thought, hanging everything across the shower rod to dry. Both bras and both pairs of panties had been thoroughly rinsed in the basin, as had her boot socks, using the last of the small bottle of Woolite she'd purchased earlier. They would be dry by morning.

The shorts and tops, despite having been "camp washed" in hair shampoo the previous evening, were not exactly spotless. She wished she could send them out to the cleaners, or at the very least, that the hotel had a laundry room, but not this place. Perhaps if they were staying at a Motel 6. The swankier the place, the less you could do for yourself.

Resigned to the fact that they were presently as clean as they were going to be for the foreseeable future, she folded her meager belongings and placed them on the dresser. She'd give the cargo shorts and summer-weight tops a thorough ironing in the morning. *Not exactly ideal, but presentable*, she decided.

Wearing only the robe supplied by the hotel, Marie stretched out on the king-size bed and tried to make sense of everything that had happened over the last three and a half days. Despite having slept well last night, at the hotel near the campus, she was still exhausted.

Within a minute, she was snoring softly.

It wasn't until the banging on the heavy wooden door became loud enough to have been heard in the lobby that she awakened. At first disoriented, she sat bolt upright in the bed and looked quickly around the room as if she had somehow been magically transported there with no recollection of the journey. When she heard a familiar voice practically shouting for her to answer, she stood and quickly opened the door adjoining their rooms.

"I've been knocking for five minutes, dammit!" Blaine said angrily as he moved past her and into her room.

"Excuse the hell out of me, professor," she said indignantly. "I must have fallen asleep." She walked past him and dropped into one of the thickly padded chairs beside the window. In daylight, the room would have had a splendid view of the mountains, but for now, the heavy curtains were pulled tight and the view was nonexistent.

Blaine remained standing, his eyes fixed on the woman.

"What's got your shorts in a wad all of a sudden?" she barked back, matching his tone. "When you left here, we were on the same page, or so I thought."

"Yeah, well things change."

"Apparently they do," she said, folding her arms defensively across her chest. "Care to elaborate or shall we just glare at each other for the rest of the night?"

"How about this for starters: just who the hell are you, because I know for damn certain you're not Carol Palmer, and the sheriff of Duchesne County is damn certain you're not Marie Matthews?"

Now, he folded his arms across *his* chest. The glaring intensified.

She knew it would eventually come to this, though she hadn't planned on the truth having to come out under the present circumstances. She had planned on telling Blaine everything before he'd left for Goodman's, only she hadn't gotten the chance.

No, she corrected herself, *I didn't take the chance when I had it.* She knew she could have told him before he left, but had chickened out. She had opted for later, but later had unexpectedly become *now.*

She cursed herself for having to deal with all the lies she'd been caught in under less than idyllic conditions. She was on the defensive now instead of being able to control the flow of information at a pace of her choosing. What exactly had triggered his abrupt mood change she didn't know, but she assumed he'd most likely seen, read, or heard something about the fiasco in Truman on Sunday. Considering the Goodman tie-in, it had certainly made the news—probably "front page" nationally—and she along with it.

She softened her demeanor considerably as she began, hoping to bring his tone down to match hers. "Blaine, please sit down and I'll tell you everything. I owe you that after all you've done. Please." She motioned to the bed.

"You're damned right you do!" he shouted, but then lowered his voice when he realized how much louder he sounded now. "And why in hell should I believe a word you're about to say when you've done nothing but lie up to this point?"

He remained standing, his posture still clearly defensive.

She didn't blame him for the way he felt. She'd have felt exactly the same in his shoes. However, she was unwilling to accept his last comment without rebuttal and chose her words carefully. "I only lied about my *name*," she said indignantly, trying to regain a little of the offensive. "Other things I simply *omitted* for the moment."

"Omitted? Is that your version of honesty?"

"Not telling you everything right off the bat is not lying. Except for my name, everything I did tell you was absolutely true."

"Yeah? How about the key," he said resolutely.

"What about the key?" she said in a confused tone. There could be no misunderstanding about the key. Every single thing she knew about it, he now knew about it.

"That *key*," he said in an exaggerated tone, "did not belong to Goodman. His wife verified it beyond question. Skipper didn't even have a safe deposit box with PSBR. At *any* branch."

She couldn't believe what she was hearing. It had to be his. It was, quite literally, the key to the whole puzzle. If it weren't Goodman's, then none of this made any sense at all, and she would die, most certainly along with Blaine now, and for nothing. Never knowing who. Never knowing why. Never knowing a damn thing more than she knew at this very moment, which was precisely nothing at all.

The thought knotted her stomach and her expression clearly reflected her utter sense of defeat.

"Ah, ha," he taunted, noting her increasingly pale demeanor. "It's not much fun getting caught in a lie, is it?"

She turned away but couldn't hide her tears. She wasn't afraid of dying, but she was desperately afraid of dying for nothing. And Alex; there would be no keeping the second promise to her now. Her death, too, would be absolutely meaningless. And worse, unavenged.

When Blaine saw the tears streaming down her face, he suddenly felt like a complete jerk for having been so hard, so hateful. He sat on the edge of the bed closest to her chair.

"Hey, look, I'm sorry, really. I didn't mean to be so cruel, it's not like me. I just feel so lost and lied to, like a pawn in some game I don't even understand."

"Oh, really? Tell me about it," she said in a broken voice.

He touched her knee. "Won't you just tell me what this is all about? I promise not to yell anymore. Maybe we can still work through this together."

Together. She liked the sound of that. She wiped away the tears with the sleeve of her robe and faced him again. "No more yelling, you promise?"

He held up his hand like a Boy Scout. "I swear."

Her breathing still shuttered and she turned her face away for a full minute before facing him again. "Remember I told you I witnessed a murder a few years ago?"

Blaine nodded.

"Well, it wasn't just some street shooting, you know, gang-bangers acting like fools. It was a mob assassination. Mario Giacano paid some thug named Joey Ray Griffin to kill a beautiful young woman the old mobster was sleeping with back in Nashville, a woman named Donna Stanton. Turns out he was in collusion with the governor and—"

"HOLY SHIT!" Blaine exclaimed, cleaving her words in half as he sprung to his feet. "I thought I recognized you first thing this morning, though your blonde hair threw me off. You're Kasey Riteman, the psychic who brought down the governor of Tennessee, along with his assistant, a handful of crooked cops, and Mario Antonio Giacano, the mob king himself. Son of a bitch! For semester after semester during my Modern Democracy lectures, I used Kasey as an example of what one good person can do against corrupt government. Kasey was my hero, for god's sake. Kasey *is* my hero."

His former anger and distrust had suddenly been replaced by something akin to awe and reverence.

Or, at the very least, profound admiration.

He shook his head in disbelief.

She pulled her long legs under her and tucked her robe tightly around them, suddenly quite cold.

"Blaine," she said, "you have my name right, it is Kasey Riteman, but I'm not a psychic."

"Sure you are," he said with certainty.

"No, I'm not, and I think I ought to know," she said.

He stared at her with a confused look on his face.

"After having watched that beautiful, young woman die so violently, so horribly—"

"Donna Stanton," Blaine interjected.

Kasey nodded solemnly. "I was afraid, more afraid than you can possibly imagine. Pretending I was a psychic was merely a ruse I concocted to keep from having to testify as a material witness. It was so carefully thought out that I was positive it couldn't fail. I'd get the bastard who killed Stanton and no one would ever come after me for turning him in. No actual witness to kill or coerce, just some weirdo psychic. It was perfect. Couldn't fail." She shook her head softly back and forth as a tear formed. "But you know what they say about perfect plans. In the end, I got everyone killed: my best friend, my ex-husband, a couple of cops—including one really good cop I had fallen in love with—and God only knows how many others. Even some poor dumb runaway kid whose only mistake was that she had hitched a ride on one of the killer's bikes at a restaurant where they'd met an hour earlier. It was one of the most horrible things I've ever seen. It was *all* horrible. And it was all my fault."

Blaine instinctively knew that attempting to say anything comforting at the moment would be a futile gesture. There were no healing words for what Kasey was feeling.

She wiped her eyes again with both sleeves as the tears continued to flow. "Oh, I came out of it great, the networks and magazines were throwing money at me like rice at a wedding. For a dumbass, poor-as-dirt steakhouse waitress with bill collectors coming out of every closet and a sleazy boss trying to nail me every time I got within fifty feet of him, it was all pretty hard to pass up. But, as I painfully discovered, it was also real hard to deal with the longer it went on. I made a lot of bad decisions and everyone else paid the price for *my* poor choices."

Blaine knelt beside her and put his arms across her legs. "Kasey, you didn't do anything wrong. You can't rewrite history so that it somehow makes you out to be the bad guy in all this. You didn't kill anyone." She gave him a look that told him he knew better. "Okay, maybe you did kill *one* person, but he deserved it if anyone on the planet has ever deserved killing. All you did was try to bring a little justice to a murdered woman without getting yourself killed in the process. Hell, I doubt if one person in a thousand would have done any better and the rest of us would have done nothing. You got them all, everyone involved, including that scumbag Griffin. I remember the case like it was yesterday. You were most definitely the good guy in this scenario, don't ever think otherwise. So what if you got paid." He touched her cheek softly. "And you're certainly no dumbass, not by a long shot, and you're definitely no coward. In fact, I think you're about the bravest person I've ever known, Kasey."

It was so good to finally hear her own name again after all the years of being someone else, but it also carried a huge weight with it.

She took Blaine's hands in hers. "There's more, I'm afraid. As long as I'm being completely honest, you need to know everything."

He nodded his head as if he knew there had to be more.

"When everything had pretty much settled down in Nashville, I was on my way out to Hollywood to work with TriStar Pictures. They were going to do a movie about all the stuff that happened and I was hired to be a 'consultant.' Unbelievable, huh."

He gave her a warm smile. "I gather you never made it to 'la la land.'"

She took a deep breath and looked away from him for a moment. "I understand they did just fine without me, big hit and all." She stared at a spot on the wall to her right, the old images haunting her again. "Didn't really need to see it."

He nodded his understanding. "Was a great movie. Honestly. They got it pretty close. Won a Golden Globe, I think."

She just shrugged indifferently.

"Apparently the Giacano family didn't take kindly to my putting the Don behind bars for the rest of his days, and the damned movie didn't help their vile dispositions, as you might imagine." After a long pause, she made direct eye contact with Blaine and took a slow, deep breath. "They ordered a hit on me. A hundred grand, so I was told."

That news was like a fist in his gut. "Jesus, Kasey, you're not serious?" He knew at once she was dead serious. He stammered as he tried to form his next thoughts. "What, uh, I mean, how did you find out about the hit? The contract? I mean, most people with the mob after them like that simply vanish or end up in a river."

She could tell he was racking his brain for a solution and took his hand. "The one good cop who had been part of the whole insane puzzle back in Nashville—the one who survived, anyway—called me on my cell phone the moment he got wind of it. I was somewhere in Oklahoma at the time in my shiny new yellow Mustang convertible, bought with some of the blood money I'd been paid."

Blaine started to speak, to correct her, but knew it would do no good. He could see the pain in her eyes brought on by the decisions she had made back then, decisions she would have to live with the rest of her days. He touched her hand affectionately.

Kasey allowed the faintest of smiles to form on her lips.

"A friend of his with the FBI in Chicago got a tip from an undercover cop, or something like that. Anyway, he called to tell me I'd better totally disappear for the rest of my life, or it'd be a very short one with an ending I wouldn't like. He gave me the name of a guy in Dallas who specialized in world-class fake I.D., passports, that kind of stuff, and suggested I call him. I sold my car at the first Ford dealer I came to. Got a pretty nice price for it and then paid cash for something far less conspicuous—a plain white Honda. Would have been kinda hard to hide from the bad guys driving around in an electric banana." Blaine chuckled. "My greatest regret was, and still is, that I had to send my beautiful Sam to live with a friend in Nashville, the reporter that I had worked with from the beginning. She moved to New York a few months after that. Sam hates cold weather."

"Sam?" Blaine questioned.

Before he could even formulate a full thought about the unfamiliar name, Kasey said, "My cat. My best buddy."

"Oh," Blaine nodded, silently grateful that it hadn't been her son. He immediately felt a sense of shame for his selfish thought.

"I knew I couldn't cut and run at a moment's notice if I had to think about Sam, and it would have also given the mob one more identifying marker they could use in tracking me down." She raised her chin defiantly. "I could accept them killing me for the things I'd done, but there was no way in hell I was going to get my precious Sam killed in the process."

Her next words seemed less certain. "When this is all over, I'm going to drive to New York and get him. I'm going to take him someplace warm where he can lie in the sun all day and get as fat as an old toad."

Blaine could only smile at her colorful words. "Then what did you do?" he asked.

"After I put Sam on a plane in Oklahoma City, I located the guy in Dallas. That's how I went from Kasey René Riteman to Marie Ann Matthews. I chose her from the choices he offered me because we looked almost identical except for her being a blonde," Kasey twirled a length of her yellow curls in her fingers, "and me a natural redhead. Anyway, I thought if one set of fake I.D. was good, seven would be even better."

"Seven?" he said surprised. "Why so many?"

"Didn't know how many times I'd have to move around in the years that followed and I knew the guy in Dallas wouldn't always be at my beck and call. Just seemed to be the right number some-how. Good thing; I've been through three of them in the last four days alone."

"I understand that kind of top-notch work is really expensive."

"Yep, cost more than five grand each, but what the hell. I had the money and it bought some badly needed peace of mind."

Kasey shuddered as if a cold wind had just blown across bare skin. "How was I to know Skipper Goodman would end up being found right in my back yard? What are the odds of that, huh? Talk about suck for luck."

Blaine believed every word of her story, but at the same time, could scarcely believe such an insane tale could be true. It was like a dozen bad dreams colliding at one time in the middle of a mind-numbing nightmare.

Kasey looked at him as if she expected him to have an answer, the way a child looks at its father sometimes.

She was anything but a child, and far from helpless, but at this moment, in this hotel room on the other side of the world she'd always known, she felt as vulnerable as a little girl.

He looked into the brownest eyes he'd ever seen—soft, warm, yet so filled with pain and sadness. Without even being aware he'd moved toward her, their lips met in a long, full kiss.

When they parted, Kasey put her hands on his shoulders, holding him at bay. "What was that for?" she asked. She'd been caught totally off guard by the kiss, and having been the only one she'd felt in the past thirty-six months, still reeled from its effect on her.

"Didn't even know I was going to kiss you," he said. "Just sort of happened, I guess."

"Well, okay," she said, fumbling for the right words. "Just warn me before you do anything like that again. Okay?"

"Okay," he agreed, easing toward her. "I guess I should warn you then, I'm pretty sure it's about to happen again."

This time, Kasey kissed him back.

FIFTY

KASEY RITEMAN PACED THE floor of her hotel room, trying to understand why Skipper Goodman would have wanted whoever found him to immediately turn their attention to the key clutched in his fist—if that key had nothing to do with his life or his death. It made no sense at all. She stopped every few cycles of wall-to-wall pacing to sip on her tea or nibble on her BLT. Their beautiful dinner by the ocean had become cold sandwiches and sodas delivered by room service.

Blaine sat at his laptop, surfing the Internet like a man possessed. He had told her every word of the meeting with Marguerite Goodman, including her resolve to see the men responsible for Skipper's death burn in hell if it took her last cent. Kasey liked the woman at once.

Once their lips had met that first time, they had kissed passionately until Kasey's head swooned like she'd had too much to drink. It would have only taken a moment's lapse in willpower for them to have wound up in bed, but she was determined not to make that mistake this time.

Not that she considered love and sex a mistake, conceptually, anyway, and she sincerely hoped to experience both again—before she was too old to appreciate them—but tonight was not the night. The Five-Star hotel on the beach certainly provided the right atmosphere, and the handsome, kind, and sensitive man working at his laptop was as desirable as any she'd known in years—or ever, for that matter—but mixing romance and bullets had been disastrous the last time, and she was determined to learn from the errors she'd made.

"Any luck?" she asked, stopping behind him and putting her arms around his neck. Just because she wasn't going to sleep with him, yet, anyway, didn't mean she couldn't enjoy feeling his body against hers.

Blaine rubbed her forearms, then returned to his search. He typed for a few more seconds, then shouted, "Got it!"

Kasey took a seat on the bed and tucked her long legs beneath her, yoga-style. "Got what?" she said.

He read the screen for a moment, then turned to tell her what he'd discovered. When he took her all in, he couldn't help noticing that her robe was no longer as tightly closed as it had been earlier in the evening. The striking contrast between her tan skin and the pale white of her breasts left him speechless.

Kasey looked down and realized she was showing a bit more cleavage than might be prudent with all that lay ahead of them. Amused by his open-mouthed gaze, she slowly narrowed the gap in her robe and said, "You were saying?"

Blaine forced himself to make eye contact again, though he would have given a month's pay to see the rest of the hidden tan line. Looking back at the screen to refresh his mind, he said, "I know who owns the key, or rather, who owns the box your key fits. And I even know how Skipper ended up with it."

He had Kasey's undivided attention.

"On that last day, Skipper and Angel Britt had an appointment to meet at the mansion at 8:30 in the morning to go over some upcoming campaign issues. Angel was his personal assistant for years and a lovely woman, one of the best," Blaine explained.

"Around 9:30, some man—he never gave his name and the FBI was never able to ID him—showed up at the front gate and told the guard that he needed to speak with Senator Goodman."

Blaine swiveled his chair, slipped off his shoes, and put his legs on the bed beside her. Kasey looked at his feet, then pinched her nose and made a sour face. As he was about to move them, she smiled broadly and rested her arm across his legs. She shook her head to make sure he knew she was only having a little fun at his expense.

He was amazed that she could keep a sense of humor with so many people trying to kill her. He was sure he would not be half as brave.

"Anyway," he continued, "just showing up at the mansion and wanting to talk with anyone inside will normally get you about as far as showing up at the White House gates with the same request. However, this man gave a note to the guard and told him that if he gave it to his boss, he was sure the senator would want to speak with him at once.

"The guard told the FBI that the note was a single sheet of paper folded twice, and while he didn't read it, he did open it and examine it thoroughly before passing it along. The guard said he was positive it wasn't dangerous in any way or he would have held it for the FBI instead of giving it to his boss."

"And they were never able to identify this man?" she asked. "Didn't they have cameras at the gate?"

"Sure, several of them, but even though they had clear pictures of him, he wasn't in any database anywhere, and the note never resurfaced. Goodman apparently took it with him."

"What about fingerprints at the guard gate, or anything he touched in the home?"

"Same thing, zilch. It was like the guy was a ghost."

"That must have caused a bit of heartburn at the FBI after the plane went down," she said.

"More than you can imagine, but no one could ever connect the man's visit with the accident—or what was considered an accident at the time."

"I wonder if he used to be one of the Colonel's men?" she said half to herself.

"Just what I was thinking. And he sold Skipper something the Colonel wanted back, maybe something to do with the Colonel, himself. Or better still, his puppet master."

"What do you mean sold?" she asked.

"Marguerite told the FBI that her husband met with this man in the den, and then about half an hour into their meeting, hurried to his office and then back again, only this time carrying a large package. It was never proven, because she never knew how much money Skipper kept in the house, but I'll bet my aunt's cat that he gave the man a bundle of cash as payment."

"You and that damned cat again," she said with a smirk. "It makes perfect sense, though. This guy gets some bad juju on the Colonel or his boss and sells it to Goodman, then skips to who-knows-where. Maybe he got cold feet about something they were planning, or saw dollar signs and decided to go for the cash—that'd be my bet, by the way."

"Yeah, I know, a cynic to the end."

"Not a cynic, just a realist. Money's the root of bad shit every time."

"You don't like money?" he taunted.

"Love it, just not what people are all too often willing to do for it. I've been guilty of that myself."

"What about conscience or morals? Maybe this guy couldn't deal with whatever was about to go down and decided to help stop it? Isn't that a possibility?"

Kasey leaned back on her elbows. "Listen, we can get into a long and fiery debate about the myriad causes of evil in the world some other time. If you're right, Skipper brought the man a sack of holy cards, and I'll bet your aunt's friggin' cat that ain't the way it went down. That bag was full of greenbacks."

Blaine thought about her words and had to agree. At least this deal appeared to be all about the money.

"Okay, I'll concede the point for now," he said. "But what in hell did he bring Goodman? What could be worth all these lives?"

"Something really heavy, you can be sure of that, and if we ever find the safe deposit box, we'll probably know. So, let's get back to the key. You were explaining to me about Angel Britt's role in all of this." She took the final bite of her BLT.

"The thing I was looking up on the Internet was the timeline of that morning. I'd read it many times, but that was months ago. It took me a few minutes to locate my copy in the university archives."

Kasey's expression told him that she was aging as he rambled but was getting no wiser in the process.

"Sorry. What I remembered was that Angel met the plane at Santa Barbara Airport about twenty minutes after everyone else had boarded. Since she was at the mansion when this man came, even though she wasn't in on their private meeting—according to Marguerite's testimony—she could have ridden to the airport in the limo, like she always did. The only reason she came late was because she took whatever this man had sold to Goodman and stashed it someplace no one would logically look, in her *own* safe deposit box. It makes perfect sense."

Kasey thought about it for a bit then said, "I agree. So, how do we find out where Angel hid, whatever the hell it is?"

Blaine moved to the bed and sat with his back against the headboard. She laid her legs across his. "That's only half the problem. The real issue is how to get into the box once we locate it."

"We need a world-class hacker," she said, as if ordering a pizza.

"You have any idea how hard it is to find someone with those skills, someone not already on the FBI watch list? It's not like getting someone to create you a website."

"Yep, I know, but either we hand what we have over to the authorities and pray they aren't in on it, or that they will believe a woman already wanted in Utah for any number of offenses, real or imagined, or we find ourselves a Houdini of cyberspace and keep our fate in our own hands for a little longer. My gut tells me to keep doing what I've been doing. It's kept me alive this long."

Blaine looked at the clock beside the bed: midnight. Not much could be done before first light.

"We both need some sleep," he said. "Set your alarm for 6:30 and plan on being out of the room by seven. We'll grab a bite and then I'll call Yao. I guarantee he'll know someone."

Kasey looked at him a little askew. "You may be able to get ready in thirty minutes, but I'm a girl, remember? I'll be ready to go at seven sharp, but don't be surprised if you hear me rummaging around over here at 5:30."

Blaine winced. "Just don't rummage too loud, please."

FIFTY-ONE

THE LIGHTS CAME ON at exactly four in the morning, just as they had every morning for the past nine months. Each man not wishing to be soaked by a freezing blast from the two-inch fire hose in the jailer's hands stood in silent attention at the foot of his bed. It wasn't wearing damp clothes all day that these men detested so much as it was having to sleep in a wet bed for the four or five days it took to dry after a thorough soaking.

For that reason, if for no other, there had been only one instance of "sleeping in" among all five prisoners during the last three months. Remarkable when you considered these men were not permitted to sleep more than a few hours a day: from midnight to four. The rest of the time, they were either being interrogated, subjected to a plethora of bloodless tortures, or forced to stand for hours on end, even while eating, while bombarded with a continuous stream of Americana: movies, music, and media.

If anyone sat or tried to sleep when they were supposed to be standing, they would get an immediate jolt from their electronic shock collars. When activated, which was virtually any time other than while they were permitted to sleep, the collars were set to administer 20,000 volts the moment the subject moved even a few degrees off vertical. The shock was equivalent to grabbing a sparkplug. It wouldn't do any permanent harm, but it would get your attention in a hurry.

No talking was permitted at morning reveille, except by the jailer who acted as their wakeup call. He loved to talk, to taunt, to ridicule, to deride. He considered it his duty to begin each of their days off right, lest they grow soft and complacent. Knowing that they were going to die shortly was not good enough for this man. He had to be certain their lives were as miserable as possible, right up to the very minute of their deaths.

The short, stocky man, the educated one, who still bore a scar on the side of his head earned the day of his capture in Afghanistan, immediately sensed that something had changed about their routine. This alarmed him more than anything done in recent months. In truth, life had become almost tolerable in the prison lately; unlike during the first months after their arrival in the States.

It was as boring in the tiny cells as was humanly imaginable, and not one had seen the slightest glimpse of the sky or ray of sunlight since their arrival, but at least they weren't being starved, and none of the physical abuse had been half as severe as it would have been for the American soldiers had the situation been reversed.

For these small blessings, he thanked Allah every day.

This morning, however, he had the sense that their stay in the American prison was about to come to an end. He knew they were going to be used as pawns in some great game, but how? Where?

And, as he'd asked a million times, when?

He didn't have to wait long for at least a partial answer to his questions. As the five mujahedeens watched in silent rage, the jailer withdrew a gas mask from a small locker beside the fire hose and pulled the straps tight across his head.

* * *

Having slept fitfully most of the night, Blaine awakened at 5:45 with a slight pain in his head and a terrific hunger in his belly. His one BLT at eleven last night had worn off hours ago, and he was ready to eat a horse, saddle and all. He opened his side of the double dividing doors, put his ear to the other door, and listened carefully.

He could hear the sound of water running in the shower.

As he was about to knock, the door suddenly flew open.

"This doesn't mean I'm going to be ready to leave by 6:15," Kasey said, a toothbrush in her hand. When she saw his completely puzzled expression, she said, "I saw your light come on under the door and heard you open your side."

Kasey was again clad in the hotel robe, her long blonde hair a tangle of curls and knotted waves. She looked wonderful, he thought.

Blaine was wearing only his boxers. "Sorry," he said. "Didn't expect you to be standing right there."

She studied him from foot to head, intentionally moving her gaze slowly up his six-foot-two-inch, one hundred ninety pound frame. She liked what she saw.

"Nice legs. You run?"

Feeling more naked than he actually was, he stuttered, "Yeah, uh, every morning I can. Try to get in about five or six miles at a good clip. You?"

"Yep. Pretty much the same. A little free weights at night."

"Same here." In his mind, he could picture her doing bench presses or bicep curls, the sweat trickling down between her breasts.

Needing desperately to get his mind off her body, he asked, "Are you as hungry as I am?"

"Famished," she said, pushing the door fully open between their rooms.

"Want to order room service again?"

"Sure. Get me one of everything on the breakfast menu. More if you plan to eat, too." She gave him a wink then disappeared into the bathroom, closing the door behind her.

As Kasey showered, Blaine ordered scrambled eggs, bacon, French Toast, mixed fruit, orange juice—two of everything—plus a pot of coffee. By the time she was drying her hair, the food was waiting on the table in his room.

He tapped lightly on her bathroom door and said, "Breakfast is ready. I thought we'd eat at my place this morning."

She switched off the noisy dryer, stuck her head through a crack in the door, and smiled. "Okay, be right there."

Blaine returned to his room and took the chair with its back to the window, giving her the full view of the mountains as the morning sun just began to color them. When she entered the room wearing only her bra and panties, he almost stopped breathing. He couldn't remember the last time he'd seen a more stunning woman. She was as brown as a gingerbread cookie with hair the color of flaxen and teeth so white they seemed to glow from within.

"Sorry," she said, indicating her scant wardrobe with a casual wave of her hand. "The hair dryer made me too hot to get dressed yet. Hope you don't mind."

She could tell by his expression that he didn't mind at all.

"Uh, no," he said.

"Wow! Fantastic view. I'll bet the sunsets are spectacular." She moved next to him and took in the full view.

"They are," he said, then realized he was staring at her and not the mountains. "Food's hot."

He took his seat, determined to keep his eyes on his food.

It wasn't easy, but she hadn't intended it to be.

Kasey kissed him on the back of the neck and then took the chair opposite him. "Thanks again for all your help. I couldn't do this without you."

He managed full eye contact, to his amazement. "Sure, no problem. I only hope it will be enough, soon enough."

"Yeah, me, too." There was melancholy in her voice.

They tore through the food, barely taking time to breathe, more or less continue their conversation.

Finally, when he could no longer feel the pangs of hunger gnawing at his stomach, Blaine said, "When I couldn't sleep last night, I got to thinking about the person we need to get into the bank's database. I seem to remember a Berkeley student a few years back who was a phenom when it came to hacking. It was rumored that he found his way inside every federal database, including the CIA and the FBI. The only one that supposedly gave him any trouble was the NSA, though he supposedly got into that one before he disappeared."

"May have been the *reason* he disappeared," Kasey said. "Those folks don't screw around and they have the brightest and best minds onboard at all times. However good he may have been, they probably had ten on the payroll twice as good. If he got in, they would have known it for sure and they wouldn't have looked kindly on it."

"I don't think he disappeared in that regard, I mean, they didn't kill him or anything sinister like that. He just fell off the map all of a sudden. If he still exists, he's the guy for us."

"Think Yao will know this guy?"

"If not, he'll know someone who does." He looked at the clock by his bed. "He'll be up in a few minutes. I'll give him a call and start the ball rolling."

"I still need to iron my clothes and then pack," she said. "I'll be ready in half an hour."

She pushed away from the table and strolled toward her room, her normally flat stomach wonderfully full and poking out a bit. She put both hands on it and pressed. "So full."

"Me, too," he echoed, his eyes missing nothing despite his most valiant effort to keep from ogling.

Kasey knew she'd teased the poor man as long as she dared without risking more complications at the moment than either of them could afford. She had to keep her mind in the game, as athletes say, and Blaine was distracting her.

A lot.

Apparently, she was having the same effect on him, and she loved the way his inability to look away made her feel.

It had been so long since she'd made love. So many months since she'd felt the warmth of a caring man against her body. She squeezed her eyes shut and thought about the work ahead. "Half an hour," she repeated, then turned to leave.

"I'll be ready," he said, watching her every move as she passed the end of the bed.

Straighten up, Kasey, she silently admonished herself, realizing that his eyes were still glued to her. *There'll be time for all of this if you don't get yourself killed first.*

"Yeah, and if you die first?" she mumbled in frustration as she disappeared into her own room. She had ironing to do and a man to get off her mind.

* * *

Yao Honghui was the perfect graduate assistant. Not only had he taken over all of Blaine's classes—since he hadn't heard anything from the professor in over a day—but he'd also came up with the name and address of the phenom hacker within five minutes of Blaine's call. The young man, Terry Leigh, lived less than half an hour south of Santa Barbara, in the town of Ventura.

Blaine had apologized profusely to Yao, stating only that something had come up unexpectedly regarding his book on Senator Goodman and he had to see it through, no matter how long it took. Yao had told him to do what he had to do. He had it covered. To his credit, he hadn't even asked how the hacker was related to the book, and for having to neither lie nor explain, Blaine was grateful.

The drive down had been horrific, as are most commutes in the greater Los Angeles area today—one continuous traffic jam. Instead of a highway, the 101 more aptly resembled a five-lane parking lot that stretched as far as the eye could see in both directions. Only motorcycles could make any progress, which seemed of no concern to some drivers while others would have shot them on the spot if they could have successfully escaped after pulling the trigger.

Escape was the problem. There was no escape.

What should have been a half hour drive became two before they finally made the turn onto West Prospect, Leigh's street.

It was now past nine Thursday morning and the banks had been open for more than forty minutes. Kasey could feel the clock ticking in her brain. The closer they got to the end of the maze, the more rapidly the hands of the clock seemed to move, as if they would fly off the face before she could reach the final exit.

She put her hand on Blaine's knee and squeezed.

"What is it?" he said, as he pulled to the curb in front of Leigh's bungalow.

"Just scared, I guess."

"Why? This guy's not gonna hurt you."

"It's not that. I don't know what it is exactly. I just have this sudden overwhelming sense of dread, like it's all going to go south before we even know it's happening and we'll be powerless to stop it." Her hand was trembling.

Blaine put his hand on hers. "Kasey, listen to me. There's no way they can know about the key or the box, and they sure as hell can't know about Angel. We'll get in, grab the information, and get out. Then, when we've figured out what to do with it, we'll take the next step. Okay?"

She nodded, but she wasn't convinced. Only too well she remembered how quickly everything had gone to hell in a hand basket back in Nashville. Just when everything seemed to be going in her favor, it all blew up in her face.

"Let's just get this over with," she said. "I had a pretty good life, such as it was, and I'd kinda like to get back to some semblance of it as soon as possible."

No sooner had she said the words than she knew that was impossible. Alex was dead. Ty was dead. Will Cameron was dead. Where she lived and worked had been burned to the ground, consuming not only her few possessions, but also her livelihood. Worst of all, her identity had been blown. She could no longer be Marie Matthews, and she sure as hell couldn't show up as someone else, so going back to either Truman or the river was now out of the question. Losing her beloved work on the river suddenly seemed the hardest loss of all. It had helped redefine her, purge her of her past. It had been incredibly peaceful in a world so devoid of calm and solitude. Somehow, working anywhere else seemed intolerable now.

Maybe it will be best for me if this doesn't end well after all, she thought, the sheer weight of the losses she had already suffered crushing her spirit and making the thought of a meaningful future seem as unlikely as beating the colonel and all of his men in hand-to-hand combat.

"Hey," Blaine said, squeezing her hand. "You still here?"

For a moment, he'd lost her to some faraway place.

"Yeah. Just daydreaming, sorry." She grabbed her door handle.

Blaine followed her up the steps to the front door of Leigh's home.

Just as they were about to knock, the door opened.

"Was expecting you sooner, Dr. McAllan," Leigh said. "Must have gotten bagged on the 101. Traffic's a bitch this time of day. I never go out before ten at the earliest. And you are?" His eyes had turned to Kasey.

Blaine and Kasey looked at each other in silent amazement. "How'd you know we were coming to see you?" Blaine asked, avoiding the other man's request for an introduction to his traveling companion.

Kasey found herself amused by the odd exchange.

"Still have lots of friends at UCB, Professor. Not many people ask about me anymore, so when the head of the Poly-Sci department makes an inquiry, including wanting to know my home address, it doesn't take high-order math to figure out that I'm about to be paid a visit." He looked at Kasey again. "And you are?" he repeated, hand extended this time, a wide smile spanning his face.

Blaine quickly introduced Kasey as Carol Palmer and they shook hands cordially. No sense confusing the young man any more than necessary. Since he was going to be working with her under that identity, why not from the outset?

"Welcome Carol. Won't you both come in?" he said warmly.

As Blaine and Kasey followed, Leigh led them across the living room, through the formal dining room and kitchen, and into a casual, but elegantly-appointed, back sitting room. It had once been a screened porch, but was now more of a loggia, though the breezes still found their way through the walls of open windows.

They were surprised to find the home not only neat and clean, but immaculate. Spectacular. Right out of *Better Homes and Gardens*. Not the cyber-geek rat-hole either of them had expected.

"You have a beautiful home," Kasey said. "So..."

Leigh smiled. "So unexpected from a nerd like me."

Though neither answered, their expressions told him he was right on the money.

"Not my doing, I confess. I got married a year ago. Shirley—that's my wife—is an interior decorator. Does this for a living, so naturally..." He extended both arms in a grand sweeping gesture, encompassing the entire room.

"Naturally," Blaine said with a nod of approval.

"She does incredible work," Kasey said, taking the chair Leigh indicated. Blaine sat to her left and Leigh opposite them both. A small coffee table made from the trunk of a gnarled and twisted hemlock tree and polished to a glass-like shine sat low and between them. On it was a coffee pot and three cups, along with cream, sugar, and a plethora of sweeteners, both artificial and natural.

Again, both Blaine and Kasey were left speechless.

Leigh poured himself a cup of some very aromatic brew and then added a touch of cream.

Kasey followed suit, then Blaine.

When they were all comfortably seated with coffee in hand, Leigh said, "So, who do you need me to crack, Professor McAllan?"

OVER THE NEXT FIFTEEN minutes, Blaine and Kasey told Terry Leigh only as much as they had previously agreed would be prudent. He didn't have to know much of the back story in order to do the work required, and the less he knew, the better for all of them. They had decided to leave out the part where bad guys with guns were killing everyone in their path. Only the part about the key having belonged to Skipper Goodman, and its probable connection to his death, had been left intact.

When the conversation reached the part where they had realized it was Angel Britt's box they were after, and not one of Skipper Goodman's, there was little left to tell.

The master programmer had listened intently, taking in everything without interrupting once. Finally, he said, "That's a hell of a story, Dr. McAllan, ma'am, but it sounds to me like you need the FBI's help more than mine. I imagine they'd be more than a little curious about the content of that box, especially considering Skipper being in possession of its key at the end."

"You won't help us?" Kasey asked, the disappointment evident in her voice and expression.

Leigh stood and took their empty cups to the sink. "Even if I wanted to, which I don't, I could go to jail for doing what you're asking. Hell, you could go to jail just for asking." He ran water over the dirty cups and wiped his hands with a paper towel.

"I thought you were the hacker from hell," Blaine said, remembering Leigh's nickname around campus. "I thought you hated the establishment and this would be right up your alley. Why the sudden rush of conscience?"

Leigh rejoined them in the loggia. "I was far more urban legend than fact, Dr. McAllan—"

"Blaine, please."

"Okay, if you like. Anyway, my reputation as an anti-establishment kook suited my needs, and my ego I'll have to admit, so there was no reason to set anyone straight."

"What do you mean, 'set them straight'?" Kasey asked.

He sat again, comfortably reclined in the thickly-padded chair he'd just left. "All the time I was hacking into those government databases, I was on the payroll."

"I don't understand," Blaine said.

"I was paid by the government to hack everything I could and then help them develop ways to make it harder for someone else to do the same. Paid pretty well, too, or so it seemed at the time. Just because everyone at UCB thought I was some radical hacker who hated authority and the government didn't make it true. In fact, I've created a sweet little business doing the same thing for private industry. They pay way better and aren't nearly as uptight."

He smiled at the admission but got no smile in return.

Kasey stood and went to one of the huge windows, her mind trying to decide what to do now. They were running out of time, she knew it as surely as she knew anything.

She turned to Leigh. "I haven't been completely honest with you, Terry."

"Kasey, don't," Blaine interrupted. "It's not necessary. We'll find someone else."

"Who's Kasey?" Leigh asked.

"Let's just leave," Blaine said, standing and taking her hand. He turned to the former student. "Thanks for your time. I would consider it a personal favor if you kept our conversation between us, at least for the next few days."

He turned to leave, pulling Kasey's hand.

She stood her ground.

"Who's Kasey?" Leigh repeated, now thoroughly confused.

"I am," she said. "That's only a small part of what we didn't tell you. My name is Kasey Riteman, not Carol Palmer. I've been running from at least a dozen armed assassins for more than four straight days now, and if you don't help us get into Angel's safe deposit box, so that we can find out what this is all about, Blaine and I will be the twelfth and thirteenth people killed who have touched this damned thing since last Sunday." She pulled the key from beneath her blouse and held it for him to see. "My best friend, her father, even four dumb, innocent kids from BYU who did nothing more than stumble across Goodman's body are all dead at the hands of these men. Whatever is hidden in that box is worth a lot to them, and they don't care who they have to kill to keep it a secret.

"We came here to get your help because you're supposed to be the best there is, and because you were supposed to care about things other than money at one time. Apparently, we were wrong. I don't particularly cherish the thought of them killing me before I even know the reason why, but if you can live with your role in helping them accomplish that, good for you."

She moved toward the kitchen, following Blaine's lead this time, but turned back to Leigh as she reached the doorway. "You were right about one thing, Terry—you are far more legend than reality."

As she and Blaine reached the dining room, he called to them. "Hey, wait a minute. Hang on." He ran to them. "That's a lot of really heavy shit to put on someone all at once. It takes me a minute to kinda digest things, you know. Sure, I'll help you. Just tell me what you need exactly."

* * *

Terry Leigh was the best they'd ever seen, possibly the best on the planet today, they thought. To Blaine's immense satisfaction, the basement of the immaculate home where Leigh ran his cyber business was the messiest programmer's hive imaginable, sporting no fewer than eight huge LCD displays, each hooked up to multi-processor, RAM-laden, multi-drive PCs that spoke to the Internet at ten times the normal speed. With reams of paper, miles of wire, and electronic component carcasses strewn around the eight-hundred-square-foot space like a garage sale after a tornado, it was exactly the environment befitting the best hacker he'd ever had the pleasure to witness in operation.

In less than twenty minutes, Leigh had not only located the branch where Angel Britt kept Box-22, but had cracked the bank's security and substituted her information, photo, and signature for Carol Palmer's, matching the driver's license and Social Security card in Kasey's possession to the letter.

"Helps to have created their security in the first place," Leigh admitted when they had commented on the ease with which he'd hacked the bank's database. "Regardless of my motives, I'd be fired and probably imprisoned for doing this, so I made doubly sure no one would ever know I'd even been in there. All you have to do now is walk in, sign your name, and get the goods."

Blaine shook his hand warmly.

Kasey gave him a kiss on both cheeks. "What I said earlier, it wasn't true. No urban legend will ever live up to your reality. Thank you, Terry." She reached into one of her pockets and pulled out a thick stack of bills totaling more than twenty thousand dollars. "I want you to have this," she said, putting the money in his hands.

Leigh pushed it back just as quickly. "Don't want it and won't take it. Just let me know what you find in that box. Maybe not right away, maybe not next year, but someday. I don't think I could go forever without knowing." He gave them both a big smile, but then his expression grew extremely serious. "One thing you need to know."

"What's that?" Blaine asked.

Kasey stuffed the bills back in her pocket and turned her attention to Leigh.

"Someone has been poking around looking for Angel's box. Been all over the site in the last twenty-four hours. I should have caught it earlier, but that particular branch is way low on my threat level spreadsheet and I haven't put in any automatic alarms yet. You know, the things that alert me when someone is dinking with my code. Guess I'll have to fix that right away, huh."

"Any idea who it was?" Kasey asked. This information raised the threat level significantly. If they knew about Angel's box, they would be waiting for her the moment she set foot in the bank. She felt her palms grow instantly moist.

"I could possibly find out if I looked hard and long, but maybe not even then if they really don't want me finding them. If this guy is a pro, he'll destroy the path at some point to such a degree that there won't be any getting beyond it. My guess is that he *is* a pro, most likely one of the punk-ass bastards who's trying to stop you before you surface with that information. Even the most heavily armed forces today keep one of my type around."

He gave them a self-deprecating look and shrugged his shoulders. "Who'd have ever thought computers could be as dangerous as guns?"

FIFTY-THREE

THE BMW MOVED IN sync with the traffic heading north along the 101. At nearly forty miles an hour, the return to Santa Barbara was four times faster than the opposite trip earlier in the day, Blaine and Kasey sat in silence, each trying to come up with an acceptable solution to the dilemma facing them. Overhead, the sky had clouded a bit, and there was the smell of rain in the air. The temperature was seventy-four degrees, mild for mid-June even along the coast, but a breeze off the sea made it seem much cooler than it was.

The chill in the air wasn't the reason for Kasey's shivering.

She understood only too well that if the Colonel and his men knew of the particular branch where Angel had stashed the information—and it only made sense that they were the ones who'd been poking around the bank's database earlier—they could concentrate their forces in such a way that her escape from the bank would be virtually impossible.

Just thinking about it made Kasey's guts knot up like a snake whose head had just been crushed.

So damn close and yet so far away.

Why can't it just be easy for once? she thought.

"If we only knew who the information implicated," she said, "we could decide whether or not to call in the FBI. Maybe we should roll the dice and call them anyway. I don't generally think of myself as a coward, but I'm not too keen on committing suicide."

Blaine looked at her, touched her face affectionately, then brought his eyes back to the road. "I told you, you're the bravest person I've ever known."

"Craziest, you mean." She looked hard at him. "What do *you* think about going to the cops with the key?"

Blaine took a deep breath and let it out in a controlled, thoughtful exhalation. "We've talked about this, Kasey. The first thing they're going to do is bring you in for questioning. Hell, they might even take you back to Truman in the midst of it all. Assuming they eventually believe you, they'll still need a search warrant signed by a judge to get into Angel's safe deposit box. All of this will take hours, days maybe. The weekend is upon us, meaning nothing can possibly occur before Monday at the earliest.

"Given all that's happened thus far, and the speed with which the Colonel and his band of armed thugs have been approaching things, I'd bet hesitation like that will leave us a day late and a dollar short. I wouldn't put it past the bastards to nuke the place before they'd see the information fall into the hands of the Feds."

Kasey considered his words and couldn't find fault with anything he'd said. It didn't make hearing it any easier, but at least it narrowed their options. She wasn't going to get a lot more innocent people killed just because she had the last minute jitters.

"I'm going in," she said resolutely.

"Then I'm going in with you," he said with equal determination.

"No, they're looking for me, not you. There's no sense in you getting caught up in this anymore than you already have. Besides—"

"That's it!" he said with a yelp of excitement.

"That's what?"

"They're not looking for me. I can go in several minutes before you and they'll never even connect us."

"What if they stop me before I go in?"

"They won't. They want the information back in their hands and you're the only one who can do that for them."

"Not if they have the key. They can do the same thing we just did and substitute their information for mine, I mean Carol Palmer's. Whatever. This shit confuses the hell out of me. I'm thinking it out way too much. I need to get in, grab it, and try to get out again. Maybe my luck will last just a little bit longer."

She knew it wouldn't even as she said it.

"That's not necessary," he insisted. "You can retrieve the information and we'll examine it together. Then, depending upon what it says, we can either call the FBI directly from the bank, or I can leave with it and give it to, well, whomever is appropriate at that point. You can remain in the bank until I get back with help, even if I have to hire some private bodyguard types. In the meantime, you'll be perfectly safe in the bank."

Kasey sniggered. "What am I supposed to do in the bank for an hour while you round up the cavalry, open a dozen checking accounts?"

He tried to look at her as he drove, but traffic was too erratic to allow even a brief lapse in concentration. "I'm glad you still have your sense of humor," he said with a chuckle, "but it won't come to that, I'm sure. Most likely, the feds won't be involved in any of this and we'll simply call them from the bank. They'll come rescue us both and that'll be that. It'll be in their court then. You might even get a medal," he added with a grin.

"I don't want a medal. I want my life back."

"I know you do. This will work. I can feel it."

"I don't know," Kasey said. "All good plans have a way of unraveling when it's least opportune. I don't know why this time should be any different."

"Because they don't know about me. You said it yourself. That's the edge we have." He squeezed her knee affectionately. "It really is our best shot. All we have to do is get into the bank. The rest will be simple. Trust me."

She gave him a sincere, if troubled, smile. "I do trust you, Blaine. Even if this all turns to shit, which it probably will, I want you to know that your help means everything to me."

"Then you're gonna owe me big time," he said as they took the exit that led to the bank.

"And I'll be more than happy to pay up if we don't die first," she said, her stomach still dancing wildly.

*   *   *

Blaine parked his car as close to the front of the branch as possible, locked the door with his remote, then strolled casually toward the front door, hands in his pockets, looking to all the world like any other customer of Pacific States Banking and Reserve. He was careful not to appear vigilant or unduly interested in anyone outside the bank; Kasey had warned him about that.

He soon discovered that was about as easy as not humming a song to yourself once it got stuck in your brain. Everyone on the street seemed to be hiding a machine gun under his or her clothes, just waiting for the right moment to pull it out and blast him to hell. It was as if he had a huge three-ring target painted on his chest and back.

The forty yards from the car to the bank's front door was the longest walk of his life. He finally made it inside without being massacred on the street, to his immense satisfaction. Now, it was Kasey's turn; a much dicier proposition.

To minimize her exposure time on the street, they had decided she would arrive by hired car, with the driver dropping her immediately in front of the bank. All she had to do was cover the twenty feet from the car to the door—six steps at most.

Once inside the bank, Blaine was pleased to find the midday traffic unusually busy, with no less than fifteen customers at the various teller windows or in hushed consultation with some loan officer. In his mind, it was highly unlikely that the Colonel would be stupid enough to try anything with a crowd of witnesses like this.

Then he said a silent prayer to make it so.

He took a seat to await the next available bank officer and checked his watch. She would arrive in seven minutes.

It might as well have been seven hours as slowly as the hands on his watch counted off the ticks. At one point, he had to stare for several moments at the face to be certain the second had was, in fact, still moving.

After what felt like a full workday of waiting, though exactly on queue, one of the nondescript car-service vehicles pulled to the door, and Kasey stepped out, head held high, shoulders back. He hadn't walked from his car to the door half as bravely as she and the maniacs had no idea who he was. He was certain she'd been seen by the Colonel's men—though he hadn't yet seen anyone who, to his untrained eye, seemed to be a crazed killer—but thankfully, she cleared the front door without a bullet ripping off her head.

Her eyes quickly adjusted to the interior light and she saw Blaine signal her from his chair beside one of interior walls. Despite her own warning to Blaine, she found herself looking carefully at each customer in turn.

To her great relief, not one face registered with those she'd seen on the ridge near the clinic in Truman.

Of course, the Colonel could have a completely different batch of operatives for this occasion, but something told her she'd recognize them no matter who they were or how they were dressed.

As far as she could reasonably tell, the bank was clean. Unconsciously, she let out a deep sigh of relief. They were out there, alright, but at least she'd finally get a look at this damnable information, even if she died five minutes later.

At this point, it wouldn't matter. But for now, she could barely contain herself.

She was twenty feet from the answer.

"May I help you, sir?" the bank officer asked, turning his attention to Blaine, the next customer in line.

Blaine stood and Kasey joined him at the man's desk. "Yes, my sister and I would like to get into our safe deposit box. We need some papers for a family matter." He produced his friendliest smile.

"Certainly. The name on the account?"

Kasey handed the man her Carol Palmer driver's license.

He typed a few quick keystrokes and then glanced from the picture on the screen to the woman seated across from him. Satisfied, he pulled a sign-in sheet from his top drawer and placed it on the desk in front of her.

Without hesitation, Kasey signed the fake name as if she'd done it all her life. Because it was the same signature she'd given Terry Leigh earlier in the day, the one he'd uploaded to the bank's database, they matched perfectly.

"This way, please," the bank officer said. Neither she nor Blaine had thought to get his name.

When he'd led them to the safe deposit boxes, along two adjacent walls of a modest-size room at the back of the building, he produced his master key. Kasey withdrew her key, lanyard and all, and together they unlocked Box-22. Her heart was beating loud enough that she was certain he would ask her if she needed medical attention. To her, it sounded like an entire high-school drum corps practicing on hollow logs. Her legs felt like limp noodles and she just knew they'd fail her at any moment.

Sensing her anxiety, Blaine put his arm around her waist and pulled her to him.

The officer noticed the affectionate gesture but said nothing.

"Our father passed away earlier this week. I'm afraid she's still a bit overwhelmed by everything," Blaine said, increasing his grip on her. He could feel her trembling.

"Take all the time you like. My mother died last month and I know exactly what you're going through. Just let me know if there's anything I can do to help. I'll be right around the corner."

The very pleasant man touched Kasey on the arm as he left and mouthed "sorry."

Alone in the vault room, Blaine and Kasey stared at number-22, the gray metal box contained within just visible beyond its half-open stainless steel door. She took a deep breath and pushed the tiny door to the side, then withdrew the inner box, sliding it slowly and carefully toward her.

Once free of its confines, it slipped easily into her hands. To her surprise, it felt as if it contained nothing at all.

Oh, God no! she prayed. Don't let it be empty.

In a panic, she tilted it left then right. Within the box, something slid across the bottom before clanging against one side and then another.

At least it's not empty, she though with immeasurable relief.

Together they moved to the closest of the two mid-sized examination rooms and closed the door. Fortunately, the door contained a lock and Blaine engaged it. They sat at the chairs provided and Kasey laid the metal box between them.

"You ready?" she asked, her heart still thudding in her chest.

"Are *you* ready?" he echoed. "This is your baby, all the way."

"Not anymore. This is ours. Together."

She gave his arm a squeeze.

Without another word, she raised the metal lid and they peered inside.

FIFTY-FOUR

K ASEY COULD SCARCELY BELIEVE what she was seeing. She'd expected some thick folder with the words TOP SECRET stenciled across the top, or perhaps a bundle of weather-worn maps with the secret locations of weapons of mass destruction marked in blood. She reached into the metal box and withdrew a cell phone. Not content that this could possibly be everything, she turned the box upside down to spill out the vital secrets it refused to yield.

Nothing.

Just a cell phone.

She looked at Blaine, but his puzzled expression provided no answers.

"Turn it on," he suggested.

Kasey found the POWER button and gave it a solid press.

Not one LED awakened, not the slightest peep was heard.

"Dammit!" she swore, wanting to smash the thing against the block wall.

"I've got that same phone," Blaine said. "Hold it in for a full second."

479

Again, Kasey pressed the POWER button, holding it down for at least two seconds, but again, the display remained blank.

"Shit!" Blaine said. "I should have known. The battery is dead. This thing has been in here for more than nine months. I'm lucky if my battery lasts a full day."

"What'll we do?" Kasey asked, panic stricken that she had the answer in her hands and it might as well be a brick.

Blaine had already fished his own phone from his pocket and began to remove the internal battery. With a quick slip-pull of the plastic back, the white lithium-ion power pack fell into his hands.

Immediately, Kasey removed the depleted battery in a similar manner, then reinstalled Blaine's fully-charged cell. To keep things from getting scattered everywhere, he put the dead battery in his phone and reattached the back.

When she pressed the POWER button a third time, the screen illuminated at once and a confirming "ding" indicated that the phone was awakening from its long slumber.

She almost dropped it as her hands trembled.

With the screen's icon display fully populated, Blaine and she stared at it for the longest time, as if it would announce its importance to them without intervention.

It did not.

"Maybe it's an incriminating e-mail," he said.

She handed him the phone and he quickly accessed the e-mail account.

Empty.

Not even so much as the normal junk everyone gets on an hourly basis from discount pharmacies, porno sites, or friends passing along the latest cyber-humor.

Again, they both stared at the screen.

"A text message, then," she suggested.

Blaine looked in the SMS account.

Blank.

"Shit!" Kasey swore.

Blaine was silent but pensive. "Let's look at his contacts list. Maybe there will be something there that'll shed some light on this infernal mystery."

Kasey nodded and he called up the various names on the phone's internal database of contacts. There were dozens of them, but all simply said "Don" or "Nate" or "Jim" with a unique ten-digit number after each. Not a single last name in the entire lot.

"SHIT!" Kasey said much louder. First names wouldn't help a bit.

With a down motion of his hand, Blaine cautioned her to be a little less vocal.

"Sorry, but this pisses me off," she said, her voice much lower. "I practically get my ass shot off half a dozen times for some dude's personal phone." She clearly wasn't happy, but he could see that she was also deeply troubled.

As he was toying with the various icons on the home screen, he touched the one that looked like a small photograph of a mountain and the internal library of stored images appeared.

Once again, both of them turned their full attention to the small digital display.

Blaine touched the first thumbnail-sized image and its big brother filled the screen. It showed a ranch house of some kind with an impressive range of snow-capped mountains in the distant background. The structure appeared unusually large for a residence, with several out-buildings visible on either side of the main structure.

Perhaps it's one of those corporate retreats, Kasey thought.

She swiped her finger left to advance to the next image. It was a picture was of a burly man sitting in a desert-tan Hummer One, playfully giving the photographer the bird. His face was clearly visible.

"That's one of the men from Eagle's Ridge," she said excitedly.

"Where?" Blaine said.

"Remember when I pushed that asshole into the river back at the clinic, right after Alex was shot?" He nodded. "That point is called Eagle's Ridge."

"Oh."

Kasey gave the man a hard look. "Yep, he was standing to the left of the Colonel. I'm sure of it."

She immediately swiped left again: a better shot of the same man, this time talking on the two-way radio in the Hummer.

One by one, they scrolled through the entire image library until the list would advance no further. By the time they'd seen a hundred or more photos, she'd identified all dozen men from the ridge, along with Colonel butthead and the two killers in suits, only they hadn't been in business attire in the photos.

Blaine shook his head. "Lots of pretty pictures, but nothing incriminating. The FBI wouldn't give any of this a second look."

"WHAT!" Kasey barked. "These bastards are the ones running around the place like it's the Old West, shooting everyone in their way."

"I realize that, Kasey, but do any of the photos show that? As far as I can see, this is just a hunting lodge for a bunch of solider-types."

She couldn't believe she was hearing him correctly, but as his words began to cut through the emotion-filled anger and hatred, she knew he had told it just like it was, not as she wanted it to be. What she knew, she couldn't prove. What these pictures showed had nothing to do with what had happened to her or Alex.

Unfortunately, Blaine was right.

"Son of a bitch!" she swore.

"You were a sailor in a previous life, weren't you?" Blaine teased, hoping to restore a little calm. What they needed to do now was think, not have an aneurism.

At first, Kasey gave him a "screw you" look, but then had to smile. "Yeah, I know, I have a foul mouth. You certainly can't tell by my behavior recently, but before all of this shit—sorry, *stuff*—happened, I had almost broken the habit."

He grinned but then grew serious. "Well, you can pick up where you left off after all this is over. But for now, I don't need you going all ballistic on me. We need to think clearly. This guy had to have something that was worth Skipper purchasing, something the Colonel and his men are willing to kill for, and these pictures simply aren't it."

Kasey started to curse again but rolled the phone in her palm, staring at the icons. She squinted at a small one in the lower right corner of the home screen shaped like a short strip of 35MM film. "That's the video icon, right? Like movies and shit. Sorry, I'm trying, really."

He quickly recognized it. "Uh huh. You don't think..."

They both looked at each other hopefully, thinking the same thing.

Kasey touched the icon and a movie quickly appeared, the first frame frozen on the small screen. The digital display at the top put its record date as the day before Goodman's plane went down, and the time at 1:30 p.m. The display at the bottom said the running time was 28:13, just under half an hour.

It was obvious that the recording had been made with the phone on its side, and she had to orient the display ninety-degrees for the video to fill the entire screen. Blaine recognized the figure frozen in the center of the picture at once.

"Holy shit! That's General Longmont."

"Who?" she asked, knowing the answer wouldn't please her.

"Lieutenant General Clayton Longmont. He's the assistant theater commander for the Army's entire Mid-East campaign."

"What's he doing at this dude ranch?" she asked.

"I'll bet my aunt's cat we're looking at the Colonel's string-puller. If that's the case, this thing goes high and wide, just as you feared. Longmont is a real heavyweight, both militarily and politically."

Having been right about the colonel not acting on his own authority didn't alleviate her anxiety. If anything, her already exhausted heart thundered harder than ever.

With the little voice in her head screaming for her to throw the phone away and run like hell, Kasey pressed the PLAY button.

Longmont stood facing the camera, a whiteboard on his left, a wide-screen video display on his right. It was apparent that the person taking the video was trying desperately to keep that fact concealed. As the video ran, his fingers continuously and nervously blocked the tiny camera for entire seconds at a time. Every time they did, Kasey wanted to shout for him to move his damned hand.

It would have done little good.

For the next twenty-eight minutes and thirteen seconds, they sat in utter disbelief of every word and every frame of video they witnessed: General Longmont, with the aid of more than two dozen men under his direct command, had devised an elaborate, expensive, and ultra-violent plan designed to extend the war indefinitely. All it required was the capture at least three of the many wanted international terrorists hiding within Afghanistan and Iraq. When the five men currently in their custody had been taken prisoner near the northern Afghan border, it had been a windfall. Not only were they among the most currently sought after members of Isis, but their capture had been kept entirely within the Unit—as Longmont referred to his group of renegade soldiers.

Now, safely hidden away at the ranch—another Longmont euphemism—the five terrorists had become the unwilling linchpin in a plan that would ensure that the Mid-East war would continue, escalate in fact, for perhaps a decade or more. Five domestic targets had been chosen, some for their strategic value, others for the pure emotional toll their destruction would exact on the American public: the Golden Gate Bridge; Hoover Dam; the I-40 Mississippi River bridge at Memphis; the Brooklyn Bridge, and the Washington Monument. In the days just prior to the upcoming Presidential election, all five would simultaneously be destroyed by massive explosions in the same instant, reigning havoc on the American people such as they'd never known.

Their actions would also ensure that the Democratic candidate, Skipper Goodman, ardently campaigning for an immediate withdrawal of all U.S. troops, would be soundly defeated. There would be no time between the explosions and the election for "back-peddling" or "position shifting." Their hawkish candidate, who by then would have been warning the American people for months that a repeat of 9/11 was a very real threat, and not merely the imaginings of a few conspiracy-theory kooks, would win in a landslide.

Initial death toll, the General went on to say—mostly from the collapse of the dam and the subsequent flooding—would be between twenty and thirty thousand. An entirely acceptable number in his opinion, and far fewer civilian casualties than allied bombs had created in either Afghanistan or Iraq.

"The cost of war is the price of freedom," he kept repeating.

Five truck-style ambulances would be filled to overflowing with the military-grade explosives the Unit had smuggled into the country over the last year, and one of the five terrorists would be in the front seat of each vehicle. Alive and fully conscious, but restrained by Shiva—*whoever or whatever the hell she was*, they wondered—so no autopsy results could disprove their willing role in each bombing. One of the Unit's men would actually drive each emergency vehicle to its intended target site several minutes before its explosion, then set the detonation timer, exit the vehicle, and vanish from the scene with the aid of another Unit member in a following vehicle.

Because of their altered appearance and deliberate dress, all would be described by eyewitnesses near the scenes as men of Arab descent.

No doubt about it.

The entire time, Longmont was either scribbling numbers on the whiteboard with a marker, or images of the bomb sites were displayed on the video monitor, along with detailed maps noting predetermined routes of escape.

As the end of the video neared, Longmont took a seat on a stool at the head of the class. He told his men that the ambulances were currently at the ranch, the explosives had been installed along with the detonation timers, and the unwilling, bored, but otherwise healthy suicide bombers were impatiently enjoying the Unit's hospitality. An entire audience of men had laughed at the General's amusing quip, though none of their faces could be seen in the video.

He reminded them that they had brothers and sisters in Afghanistan and Iraq who were counting on them. Thousands had died already, and their deaths would have been in vain, as well as the security of the nation itself, if the war was not allowed to reach a satisfactory military conclusion, just like World War II. He told them that America didn't need another Vietnam or Korea.

Finally, Longmont grew more serious than he'd been in the previous twenty-seven minutes. He told them they were about to bring down the most powerful Democrat in the country, and he would deal severely with any man who broke the Unit's trust. There was no going back at this point, and there was no getting out of the Unit.

All shouted out that they were with him one-hundred percent as the video went black.

Kasey found it the most disturbing thing she'd ever seen, and was grateful she'd eaten hours ago. Even so, her stomach churned, as it had for days now.

Blaine simply sat speechless.

Finally, he mumbled, "Our own military killed the finest political mind and one of the best human beings this country has produced in the last three generations. And why? To keep an unjust war alive. It's insane." He sounded completely drained.

Kasey put an arm around his neck and turned his face toward her. "Not our military," she said firmly. "They're good men and good women, with effective and dedicated leadership. This Longmont fool and his Unit are renegades, as insane and outside the box as are suicide bombers to everyday Muslims." She made sure he was hearing her words, and he managed a faint smile as she continued to stare at him in questioning silence.

Finally, he nodded his agreement.

She needed him to stay with her emotionally as well as physically. She took a long breath and continued: "Blaine, there have always been nutcases running around spoiling things for the rest of the world, but it's the ninety-five percent of us who just want to raise families, eat junk food, and go to movies on Saturday night who've always brought their punk asses to justice. You want heroes, just look around you every day. The father who works two jobs so his family can have something better to live in than a rented slum. The mother who gets up every morning, fixes breakfast for her entire family, then walks her kids to school before working ten hours on her feet. The kid who says 'no' to drugs or joining a gang—they're the real heroes. These bastards don't deserve to live on the same planet with them, no matter how nobly they try to label their cause."

"Optimism at a time like this," he said shaking his head in wonder. "Where do you get your strength?"

"From not wanting these assholes to win, it's in my DNA, I guess. Now get your butt up and let's get this cell phone to the authorities. If this doesn't make them jump to attention like someone stuck a hot poker up their ass, we're all doomed."

They stood and unlocked the door to the small room, then moved slowly into the larger room with its walls of boxes. As Kasey was about to step onto the main floor of the bank, she caught a glimpse of a man standing outside the double glass front doors. It was the huge black man from the ledge, and fortunately, at that precise moment, he was looking to his right and not directly into the bank.

She threw out an arm and flattened Blaine against the closest wall, then ducked behind its leading edge and out of view of the front doors.

"What the hell?" he asked, startled by her sudden move.

"They're here," she said. "Remember the really big black guy from the video?"

He nodded.

"He's standing at the front door. Where there's one, there'll be more. Many more, probably. I gotta think."

With that, she moved deeper into the vault room, completely away from the doorway that led to the lobby and tellers.

She knew time was running out quickly. The clock on the wall told her that they'd been in the bank for over forty-five minutes. Anyone waiting outside would be climbing the wall by now, anxious to do anything other than wait another minute. She'd caught a glimpse of the lobby traffic and realized that at least twenty people were still inside. One wrong move on her part and she'd get them all killed.

On the other hand, a different wrong move could get thirty thousand people killed.

I don't want to have to do this! her mind shouted.

When a plan began to half form, she turned to Blaine. "Give me your phone."

"It's dead."

"Perfect."

"Now I'm confused as hell."

"I'm not going to call anyone. Go get the car. You need to walk out of the bank like you own the place, not like someone who just discovered the thugs between you and your BMW want to kill half of America—you included."

"That won't be easy. I don't exactly have a poker face."

"Then try harder. Fail and we die."

"Great. I always work better when I know my ass is on the line. Thanks for making that perfectly clear."

"Sorry, it is what it is. You prefer it sugar coated?"

"No."

"Didn't think so. You up to it?"

"What if they stop me?" he asked. "What'll I do then?"

"They won't. They don't even know you. They're looking for me, remember?" she said with less confidence than he would have liked.

"Why don't I simply go to one of those phones over there and call the FBI, just like we discussed?"

"Listen to me, Blaine, these guys are ready to pounce. I can feel it. They don't give a shit about the people in this bank. In fact, their chances of actually getting away will be improved by the sheer number of hostages they can grab in the process of coming after me and the video. By the time the Feds sort through our story and assemble a team powerful enough to deal with the men outside—remember, there could be a dozen of them—we'll all be dead and they'll be back at the ranch sipping on single-malt Scotch and smoking Cuban cigars in celebration of their great victory. We're on our own here, buddy boy. Now, get to the car and drive away nice and easy, then go around the block, double back, and pick me up behind the bank. I'll leave through the fire door. Just be ready to pick me up in exactly,"—she looked at the clock on the wall—"three minutes. Not one second longer. Once the fire door alarm goes off, the Colonel's men will be sprinting in my direction with guns draw. Are we clear on this? Three minutes."

Blaine checked the time on his wristwatch and nodded. "Sure, three minutes exactly. I'll be there. I promise."

"Great. When we're clear of the bank, we'll head straight for the feds."

He took a deep calming breath, exhaled slowly, and started to leave.

She pulled him to her and kissed him passionately on the lips. "Just in case," she said.

"Two minutes, fifty seconds," he said as he began his casual stroll down the center of the main floor. He knew beyond a doubt that he'd be dead before he set foot on the sidewalk.

Nervously, he fumbled with the BMW's keyless remote, anxious to put the bank behind him.

By the time he'd cleared half the distance to the front doors, Kasey had a slight change of plans, triggered by something Blaine had said earlier in the day. Still hidden behind her wall, she leaned out just enough to see the bank officer who'd helped her earlier.

She made a loud "psssst" sound to get his attention, and when he looked up, she beckoned him with a helpless expression.

No Madison Avenue billboard soliciting his help could have worked any better.

He rose at once to lend what assistance he could. "Yes, Ms. Palmer," he said warmly when he'd joined her in the vault room. "What can I do for you?"

Kasey produced her most winning smile and told him what she needed—and needed in less than two minutes.

FIFTY-FIVE

THE EMPLOYEE BREAK ROOM, coffee pot, and rear fire exit sat in a small concrete block room opposite the room containing the safe deposit boxes and viewing rooms. It was also located at the rear of the bank. The fire door led out to a narrow alley that backed other commercial buildings along La Quinientos Street. The street and alley both ran southwest to northeast through an attractive business section of Santa Barbara, only minutes from the highway. Kasey had noted the alley when the taxi had delivered her an hour ago.

The problem wasn't getting out the back door, even though that act would surely set off an alarm—it was getting across the wide expanse of open floor between the two rooms when that very expanse was clearly visible to anyone inside the bank. Also, anyone standing at the glass front doors.

She shoved the phone in her left Velcro-flap front pocket and studied the distance she had to cover. She wouldn't look to her right, toward the front, to see if she'd been spotted. That would consume precious seconds as well as bringing her suspicious movements to the attention of anyone who might otherwise not even notice her.

No, she would take a quick, but not too quick, stroll toward the break room, and when she was again concealed by the opposite wall, would bolt from the room like a scalded dog.

"It might work," she said under her breath.

She checked the wall clock and did a quick calculation. Blaine would just be pulling up in back.

Time to go.

With legs that once again felt less than fully stable, she made her move. What took, in actuality, less than three seconds to accomplish, seemed like it should have been measured on a calendar. Finally, when the far wall again blocked her from anyone in the main room, she headed straight for the metal fire door, its bright yellow band of caution tape marking the way like a beacon in the night.

Two bank employees—a young man and an older woman—enjoying their break called out in unison for her to stop, she wasn't allowed in there, but she kept moving as if they didn't exist.

The man shot to his feet and started after her, certain she had just robbed the place.

The woman began to yell for a manager.

Kasey hit the exit bar with the open palms of both hands and the door shot open. Just as she thought, a school bell began to toll angrily at the violation.

Disregarding it completely, she stepped into the alley.

No BMW.

No Blaine.

"Shit!" she cursed, looking up and down the alley.

The young man burst through the back door and seized her by the arm. "Ma'am. You'll have to come back inside with me—now!" he said with far more authority than he had. In fact, bank policy probably prohibited such individual acts of 'heroism' as they usually led to lawsuits or dead employees.

He wasn't kidding, however, and increased his hold on her arm.

Finally, the BMW appeared at the end of the alley and shot in her direction at a full gallop.

The young man persisted, doing his best to put Kasey into some sort of wrestling hold.

Now annoyed to the point where she no longer wished to simply get away from the wannabe Superman, but teach him a valuable lesson, she took the heel of her hand and thrust it beneath his chin, putting her full force behind the upwards punch. The boy dropped to the alley pavement like he'd been shot, unconscious but otherwise unhurt.

His bruised chin would heal much faster than his bruised ego.

The familiar Montego Blue BMW screeched to a stop several feet past the downed banker and the passenger door flew open. In a second, Kasey was around the back of the car and into the front seat.

The blood on the dash, upholstery, and windshield registered in her brain just as the lights went out.

The driver—the man from the Unit's surveillance team who looked the most like Blaine in overall appearance—mashed the accelerator to the floor and the German sports car shot away like a bullet.

When they made the right turn onto Salinas Street, the 101 lay just a quarter mile ahead. On their rear bumper, a black Suburban stayed as close as prudent considering the speed they were traveling.

Once safely away from the scene, they would back it down and blend in with traffic.

In the Suburban, Ron Phelps grabbed his cell phone and punched the top number on his speed dial. When it was answered on the first ring, he said, "Got them both, sir."

Merkett clenched his fist and wanted to shout for joy, but remained calm and focused. "The phone?"

No sooner had he asked the question than the man in the back seat of the BMW extracted the phone from the unconscious woman's pants pocket. Every member of the team had been thoroughly versed on the exact make and model of Marec Vanover's phone, so they would know it the moment it was located.

This was his phone alright.

He held the small device to the back window for visual verification and gave a thumb's up.

"Got it, too, sir," Phelps said with an audible sigh of relief.

"Excellent work, Sergeant Major."

"What do you want us to do with them, sir?"

Merkett thought about it for a moment. His first inclination was to simply kill them both and be done with it once and for all, but he wanted to meet this Marie Matthews and find out as much as he could about her in the time she had left. "Put them to sleep and bring them to me straight away. And, Sergeant..."

"Sir?"

"Destroy that goddamned phone and its memory card before you go another ten feet. Do I make myself perfectly clear?"

"It'll be history within the minute, sir. See you in San Francisco in a few hours."

"No screw ups, Sergeant. We're home free now."

"Count on us, sir."

With that, Phelps hung up then pressed another button on his speed dial. The man in the back seat of the BMW answered at once. "What's up, Sarge?"

"He wants them both alive for now, but we'll give 'em something to keep them out on the trip to Frisco."

"The phone?" Branch said.

"Destroy it most ricky tick," he said, meaning at once. "And be sure the memory card can never be read or used again. Clear?"

"Consider 'em toast," he said as he ended the call.

Branch pulled the small memory card from the phone and began braking it into unrecognizable pieces, using his teeth like cutting pliers. Each of the tiny fragments was tossed out the open rear window as they drove. When there was nothing left of the card, he carefully held the phone between his thumb and forefinger, then extended his hand just past the window frame, the clear blue sky as a backdrop. With the muzzle of his silenced 45-caliber Glock automatic pressed firmly against the center of the phone, he put his index finger on the trigger. "Fire in the hole," he said as he squeezed off a round, warning the driver not to freak out when he heard the shot, even as muffled as it would be. A single hollow-point bullet traveling at more than a thousand feet per second sent the electronic device into more pieces than had been used in its manufacture.

"Well, that's that," he said, pleased with himself. He studied the professor, in the seat to his left, to be certain the whack to his head hadn't killed him. He was bleeding freely from a two-inch gash above his right eye, but still breathing. Since the blood wasn't getting on him, he'd let it quit at its own pace. "How's the bitch?" he asked.

The driver had already slowed the BMW to match the speed of traffic on the 101, to minimize drawing unwanted attention. He studied his front seat guest. "Out like a light. Sounded like you might have cracked her skull, though."

"So what. When the Colonel finishes with her, that'll be the least of her worries."

The driver grinned as he thought of the reward they'd been promised for bringing the woman in, along with finding Vanover's phone. He'd already decided to keep the professor's car; it would just make the cash seem all that much sweeter.

"Probably need to transfer them to the Suburban as soon as possible," Branch said. "If we get stopped for any reason, this will end up in a shootout."

"Next exit," the driver said. He grabbed his phone to alert the Sergeant Major.

Under the cover of a small wooded park, Kasey and Blaine had been injected with a bolus dose of sodium thiopentalthan and transferred to the cargo hold of the Suburban, a heavy blanket covering them both. With the nearly black limo-tint on the rear windows of the SUV, they might as well have been invisible.

In five minutes, they were back on the 101 heading north at the posted speed limit. It would slow down considerably as the afternoon rush hour neared, but for now, they were making good time.

Phelps looked at the digital clock on his GPS display. At this pace, they would meet up with the rest of the Unit by midnight.

FIFTY-SIX

THE TOTAL ABSENCE OF light confused and disoriented Kascy; she wasn't sure if she was dead, blind, or buried alive. Instinctively, she sucked in a deep breath: there appeared to be plenty of air, so the third option seemed unlikely. That relieved her, but only for a brief moment. Simply not being trapped in an underground vault, doomed to a slow, suffocating death, didn't necessarily portend a rosy future. There were many ways to die, most of them painful.

Her head ached terribly, enough so to cause a touch of nausea.

All at once, the image of blood in the BMW, just before everything went black, filled her mind.

Oh, God! What had happened to Blaine?

She shouted his name. Then louder a second time.

No response, only absolute emptiness.

The thought of them having been separated, of him lying in a ditch somewhere, shot through the head, filled her with a sense of dread she hadn't felt in years. She didn't want him to be dead, even harmed.

This was all her fault.

Once again, she knew had gotten someone she cared about killed.

The old familiar guilt returned with a vengeance.

"DAMN YOU, YOU BASTARDS!" she screamed into the blackness, practically spitting the words.

When no sound returned, no rebuke or order to be silent, she slumped her head in despair. Whatever happened to her now didn't matter in the least. She only hoped it to be over quickly; she didn't want them to have the satisfaction of watching her suffer. She was tired of this shit—of these men and their war games. They were merchants of death, no matter how they tried to twist it so it would have a more politically correct tone.

These men killed because they loved killing. Simple as that.

As far as she was concerned, all the rest was nothing more than patriotic masturbation.

"Fine, have it your way. Kill me, you sons of bitches!" she shouted defiantly.

"Hey, what's all the yelling about?" Blaine asked in a voice that was soft and groggy. They had given him far more sodium thiopentalthan than Kasey and he was only now coming around.

"Oh, my God! You're alive!" Kasey said excitedly. In the complete absence of light, she still couldn't see him, but his voice told her that he was directly across from her, close, perhaps just beyond her reach.

Blaine coughed several times to clear his throat. It felt like he'd tried to swallow a huge cotton ball. His voice became stronger and he said, "Seems so. How are you?"

"I'm good," she assured him. "I saw the blood. I thought you were dead."

Blaine thought about what she'd said just as his injured brow began to awaken a few seconds after the rest of his body. He would rather it had stayed asleep because it hurt like hell. "I imagine that came from my head. I've got a burning pain above my right eye and I can feel what seems to be dried blood along the entire side of my face."

Blaine then blinked several times but couldn't get his eyes to clear. "Please tell me the lights are out."

"They are."

"That's good. The thought of being blind scares the shit out of me. Where are we?"

Kasey said, "I have no idea. The last thing I remember was seeing blood in your BMW, then I awoke here."

He tried to remember. "I left the bank and made it to my car. I used the remote to unlock the door." He fought to form the next image. "That's it. Just one big blank from that point. The next thing I remember is you yelling something about them killing you. Hey, what was that all about, anyway?"

"Just ready for this crap to be over with, that's all." Her voice didn't have the same resolve as before. Now, she had a reason to live. "Mostly just giving them some shit."

"Always remember that it ain't over until *you* quit. No fat lady, just an irrepressible determination to never give up."

"Sounds great in principle, but in case you haven't noticed, we're shackled like dogs in some black hole."

Blaine remembered the video. "Oh, shit, Kasey, where's the phone? Please don't tell me they got their hands on it."

Kasey had no idea what had become of the phone. She'd been knocked unconscious and the likelihood of it still being in her pocket was nil. With her hands bound, there was no way to check, however.

"I'm so sorry, Blaine. I put it in my pocket before I ran out of the bank. I have to assume they took it after cracking my skull."

He took a long, painful breath. Every muscle in his body ached and cramps were beginning to nag his legs. To prevent them from becoming agonizing knots, he needed to stretch out. Unfortunately, he couldn't move his feet more than two inches in any direction.

Like Kasey, they were shackled to the floor, his knees were bent, and his arms were secured to the vertical wall at his back in line with his head.

"It's okay. You did all you could. No one could have done more."

It didn't help. The very concept of Longmont and his thugs winning their deadly game was abhorrent. Inconceivable.

As she was about to express her regret again, her eyes seemed to burst in a white hot flash as bright as any noonday sun. With her hands unable to provide even a hint of shielding, all she could do was squeeze her lids tightly shut.

The intense illumination burned through them with ease and huge orange spots formed in her retinas like fireworks.

Opposite her, Blaine suffered a similar fate, the instantaneous arrival of a sea of light after hours of supreme blackness threw his irises into simultaneous spasm, and a headache like none he'd ever experienced exploded in his brain.

Very slowly, both of them were able to create tiny slits in their lids as the mind began to accept the change. Kasey could see that the surface on which she sat was some kind of shiny steel with a strange raised pattern to it. The more she studied it—still unable to raise her head toward the source of the light—the more she recognized it as the kind of non-slip metal used in emergency vehicles. The kind used in fire trucks and... "Oh, shit," she said in a shaky voice. "And in ambulances."

She forced her head to look around, despite the burning in her eyes that continued. Acceptance of the intense light was coming, but very, very slowly. When she saw Blaine's feet and legs, then his body and handsome face, she couldn't help smiling.

It made her feel wonderful that he was smiling right back at her.

Then her eyes beheld that which she had feared most, and she could tell from his sudden change in expression that Blaine had just comprehended their predicament as well. From floor to ceiling, and all around them, C-4 plastic explosive was stacked as full as a UPS truck on Christmas Eve. The light that had nearly blinded them seemed to be coming from some kind of high-intensity photographic lamp, but it was impossible, even with her eyes far more adjusted now, to tell for sure. All she knew was that the sun itself appeared to be six feet above them.

"Good morning, sleepyheads," came a voice she had heard only once before but recognized immediately.

"Fuck you, Colonel shithead!" she responded. "And fuck your sick band of sociopathic assholes!"

Blaine grimaced. "You really think it's the best idea to taunt the man with the detonator?"

"Screw him," she spat. "You think he's going to spare our lives just because I sweet talk him? I'd rather cut my own throat."

He nodded, then said to the headless voice, "What's with this damn light?"

With that, it was instantly black again.

"Oops, my bad," he said to himself.

"Oh, don't worry, just as soon as our eyes adjust to the dark, he'll zap us again. I think this sick bastard likes torturing people," Kasey said, certain she was beginning to understand the man.

Outside the vehicle, they both began to hear sounds of movement. Suddenly, the double side doors that were on Kasey's left and Blaine's right swung open wide.

The Colonel stood in the opening, hands on his hips.

"Actually, I'd like nothing better than to subject the two of you to a few months of combat interrogation, but,"—he looked at his watch—"you have a date with destiny and a bridge in twenty minutes."

Kasey remembered the video and realized she and Blaine were about to be driven the last few miles to the center of the Golden Gate Bridge and then turned into vapor. Despite being resigned to the idea of death—though not wishing for it—her heart still missed a beat.

She looked him squarely in the eye. "So, why the bullshit?" She looked up at the photo lamp.

"Just needed to know something, and you were kind enough to oblige in near record time." He produced a twisted grin.

"And that was...?"

The officer looked away, then back to her, as if not pleased with the admission he was about to make. He made certain that all of his men were out of earshot. "I had my men get rid of Vanover's phone before I had a chance to look at it. Stupid, I admit, and completely out of character, but I was so glad to finally have my hands on the damned thing that all I could think to do was destroy it at once. I could just imagine an unforeseen traffic accident between Santa Barbara and our base here and the cops getting possession of it."

Kasey gave him a look that said she had no idea what he was talking about.

He said, "I needed to know if you had the real phone on you, or had somehow pulled a fast one on me." He leaned toward her and got within inches of her face. "That really would be like you, you know."

She turned away.

Merkett stood. "What you told your sweetie, here, was enough to satisfy me. In the end, however, it really doesn't really matter. We're all prepared to die for our beliefs." Again, he leaned toward her. "How about you?" he said with hot breath that wafted across her skin.

Kasey had been generating as much saliva as possible within a mouth as dry as desert sand, and spat it squarely between his eyes.

Not a smart move, she immediately realized when he pulled his 9MM Beretta from its holster and pressed the barrel to her forehead. Fully understanding that she had no retreat other than to meekly turn her head away, Kasey met the muzzle squarely, a look that could kill burning in her eyes.

She could feel the tempered steel indenting her skin and knew a hollow point round would end her life at any moment.

Defiant to the end, she calmly said, "Go ahead, you worthless bastard. Show everyone here how almighty powerful you can be.

It must take a lot of guts to murder an unarmed, shackled woman. You're a hell of a man, Colonel."

Never once did she take her eyes from him.

Blaine remained silent, afraid anything he said would only escalate a situation that was already out of control. If he could have gotten to the Colonel, he would have ripped his head off. Even if he died trying, he would give his life to save Kasey's.

It was then that he realized he cared for her, more than he'd cared for anyone in his life, even his one-time fiancée. The blood formed at his wrists and ankles from the quiet strain he was exerting against his manacles.

Behind the Colonel, in her peripheral vision, Kasey saw three members of the Unit stop what they were doing and turn their attention toward the open doors of the ambulance.

The Colonel must have felt their presence.

"Back to work!" he barked, maintaining constant eye contact with the damnable woman.

She saw the men slowly turn and go about their duties. They may not approve of what he was doing, but they would offer no assistance. She hated them all the more for their cowardice.

It had become the ultimate game of poker, though Kasey knew she held only a pair of deuces to his royal flush. This was not a game she could win, she held no illusion about that, but she was determined to at least deny this prick the satisfaction of seeing her back down, even a single step.

After what seemed an eternity, he lowered his weapon. If Kasey hadn't already been seated, she would have dropped to her knees. She pulled in a slow and even breath through her nostrils, trying to keep her muscles from shaking visibly.

"I saw the same thing in your eyes Sunday night on that ridge," Merkett said. "You're not afraid to die. That's too bad. It takes all the fun out of killing someone when it no longer matters to them. I'll have to think of something else."

503

With that, he stuck the pistol in Blaine's chest and pulled the trigger. The explosion almost shattered her ear drums, but even as the deafening concussion began to fade, she heard herself screaming, "NO!"

It was already too late.

Blaine slumped to his left, away from the double doors. His arms drooped and his face fell limp against his chest. A trickle of blood formed at the corner of his mouth and red droplets began to stain his shirt.

When Merkett saw the pained expression on the woman's face, as shocked and horrified as any he'd seen on the many battlefields he'd trod, he grinned in total satisfaction. "I think that should do nicely," he said, holstering his weapon.

The pathetic, wheezing of lost hope issued from Kasey's parched throat like air escaping past the pinched neck of a balloon. She sounded like a wounded animal as she kept calling Blaine's name.

It was exactly the sound of abject despair he'd hoped to elicit.

As he slammed the doors, he also killed the overhead light, leaving her in total blackness once again.

Kasey couldn't even find the voice with which to curse the man, to call him the despicable coward that he was. With Blaine gone and her own death only minutes away, all she wanted to do was die. The sooner the better.

However, this son of a bitch had chosen to let her live. To live in eternal damnation with the knowledge that she had managed yet again to kill the only remaining person in her life who mattered.

"Oh, Blaine, sweet Blaine," she whispered pitifully in the darkness, tears streaming down her cheeks. "I'm so very sorry for getting you into this. I should have known it couldn't possibly end well. I had no right. Please forgive me, if you can find it in your heart."

She was sobbing bitterly as the vehicle lurched forward and sluggishly came up to traffic speed, slowed by more than a ton of deadly cargo.

Despite the complete absence of light, Kasey squeezed her eyes tightly shut and tried to recall how he felt against her. She could picture his broad shoulders and thick black hair, the way he looked in his boxers standing in the hotel doorway, and wished now that she had given in to her passion when she'd had the opportunity.

There would be no reprieve, no second chance.

Suddenly, what had *not* occurred hurt more than any tragedy that had befallen her during this week from hell.

So much of her life had been lived with regret born of rash behavior—the childish submission to meaningless relationships as she tried in vain to replace the love that had been stolen from her as a young girl.

Ironically, the last moments of her life would be spent bitterly regretting the one thing she had *not* done.

In a voice that only she could hear, she whispered, "It'll all be over soon, sweetheart. Then we can be together forever."

FIFTY-SEVEN

OR FIFTEEN SICKENING MINUTES, the ambulance laden with two thousand pounds of high explosives whooped and screamed its way through the San Francisco traffic, its rack of sirens blazing with earsplitting intensity. No citizen would block its route. Every cop would clear a path.

It was a perfect scenario if you wished to deliver a bomb with impunity.

The brightly-painted emergency vehicle hurried down Doyal Drive, past the Palace of Fine Arts, the National Cemetery, and the Presidio. At Fort Point, the ground gave way as the bridge which had spanned the bay since 1937 took its place. It wasn't just one of America's most recognizable landmarks and the most vital artery feeding the state's fourth largest city, it was the very heart of San Francisco.

General Clayton Longmont had chosen the site perfectly, not only for its tactical value, but more importantly for the emotional and spiritual toll it would exact on the people of California—the entire United States.

When Americans learned that Muslim extremists had once again visited upon them the horrors this Saturday would yield— all five bombings carried out with the same cold, calculating detachment that defined the very fall of the World Trade Center towers—there would be an outcry for the sands of the Middle East to be tuned into molten glass that would make the furor that followed 9/11 seem an angry whisper by comparison.

Nauseated by the constant curves and hills that define San Francisco and compounded by the vehicle's suicidal speed, Kasey was sure she'd vomit at any moment.

"Perfect," she said to the emptiness around her. Her stomach roiled and knotted and her mouth began to fill with the bitter taste of bile. "Just perfect."

Suddenly, the ambulance came to a screeching halt, slamming her painfully against the hard vertical surface to which her hands were shackled. She lowered her head instinctively, certain the dozens of heavy crates of meticulously-wired high explosives were about to come crashing down upon her.

Instead, she heard the sound of hammers banging angrily against the body of the ambulance. For what seemed an eternity, the incredibly loud hammering continued, and here and there, small stars of light began to appear in the steel walls of the vehicle. Sunlight streamed in like comet trails, stinging her eyes but providing welcomed illumination.

She hadn't wanted to die in the dark. It was silly, she knew, but she didn't think she could find her way in the next life if she left this one unable to see a thing.

Perhaps this was her penance, the cost of all her many failures.

"What's happening?" she said. Nothing made any sense.

Just as quickly as the hammering had begun, everything fell eerily silent.

"WHAT THE HELL'S HAPPENING?" she shouted at the top of her lungs, though she expected no answer other than a cataclysmic bang which only her disembodied spirit would ever hear. She'd seen explosions on TV and in the movies such as the one about to occur, and understood that she would go from a living, breathing organism to an inconsequential organic mist in a billionth of a second.

Everything she'd ever seen, thought, heard, or done just a pink vapor.

She closed her eyes and waited, her last breath locked in her throat.

When the side doors burst open, she almost pissed on herself. Like some inhumane torture in a repetitive laboratory experiment in hell, the intense light that instantly filled the small space blinded her as completely as had the blackness.

In a whisper this time, the will to fight almost gone, she said weakly, "Please tell me what's going on."

"Kasey Riteman?" a man's voice asked. It was deep and authoritative, but not one she recognized. It most definitely did not belong to the Colonel, a voice she would know and despise a hundred years from now.

Slowly, she tried to see the man's face through eye slits as thin as a sheet of paper. All she could make out was a black silhouette surrounded by intense blue.

"Are you Kasey Riteman?" the man asked again.

"Yes," she said hesitantly. "Is there any way you can help me? Please." Her heart felt as if it would burst.

"Over here!" the man shouted. "We've got a live one!"

She heard the sound of several people approaching the man at a run and forced her eyes to open wider. A few feet from her, this same man was holding his fingers against Blaine's throat.

"Leave him alone, you bastard!" she screamed, tugging at her restraints so she could hammer the stranger's face when she broke free.

The man looked toward the others who were running to meet him, though they were still only sounds in Kasey's ears. "We've got another live one!" he shouted again. When the others reached him he said, "I got a pulse on Dr. McAllan. It's very weak, I'm afraid."

Kasey's eyes were almost working properly now and she made out the figure of a man wearing a dark blue windbreaker, the capital letters "F-B-I" in bright yellow nearly six inches tall emblazoned on his chest.

"Please tell me what's happening," she pleaded. "Can't you just leave him alone? Where are you taking him?"

The man assisted in Blaine's removal then used the bolt cutters he'd been handed to cut through Kasey's restraints. Her arms fell to the heavy metal floor like they belonged to a rag doll instead of her.

Within a minute, they had released her from her ankle bonds as well and she was being led by both arms toward another ambulance, only this time, through a sea of heavily armed FBI agents and San Francisco SWAT Team members.

She tried to resist their attempts to hurry her from the scene, toward the waiting ambulance, but the men were the size of compact cars. She would be going exactly wherever they wanted her to go.

"Please," she said, "I need to know about Blaine. Tell me how he is. I can't leave here without knowing. Please," she repeated, her eyes swollen, red, and wet with tears.

"When we can ma'am, I give you my word," the man on her right said in a voice that was deep yet as soft as velvet. "I know he's heading for the care he desperately needs. He'll be in good hands. The best thing you can do right now, for everyone's sake, is come with us and help us sort all this out."

Not convinced Blaine was going to be okay, that he wasn't, in fact, already dead and they were simply withholding that information to keep her calm, she continued to pull against them. At the rear bumper of the second ambulance, she finally got them to stop. A third ambulance, which she hadn't noticed, pulled away quickly, its sirens wailing.

The sound made her jump as if a gun had just gone off behind her.

"Is that Blaine?" she asked, begging for answers.

The two men released their grip on her arms. Another man, this time in a business suit, appeared from her right. With a simple gesture of his hand, the two hulks took several steps back, though it was clear they intended to remain close by.

"Dr. McAllan is on his way to surgery even as we speak, Ms. Riteman."

She regarded him with an expression of confused concern.

He extended his hand. "I'm Michael Anderson, FBI Special Agent in charge."

"I'm in a lot of trouble, aren't I?" she said in the hoarse voice of a frightened child.

"On the contrary, Ms. Riteman. Thanks to you and Dr. McAllan, an untold number of lives were saved today, to say nothing of this beloved old bridge. You're a genuine hero." She had been taken by surprise by the use of her real name when the ambulance door had first been opened, bur remembered she had provided it to Marguerite Goodman in her hastily-scribbled note at the bank. In as few words as possible, it had been a desperate attempt to answer any questions she may have had about the mysterious woman with Dr. McAllan. Apparently, Marguerite had informed the FBI as well.

Kasey met his hand, still outstretched, and shook it weakly. Her arms, having been suspended above her head for most of a day, would barely move on their own.

He could see the pained expression on her face.

Anderson squeezed her hand tenderly. "He's going to get the best care money can buy, rest assured. There's nothing either you or I can do for him at the moment. You'll see him soon, I promise. Right now, we have far more questions than answers, and in a few hours, the entire country is going to be demanding those answers. So are the politicians and our military. At the moment, you seem to be the only person on earth who can provide those answers. Do you feel up to talking with us for a little while?"

His manner was professional but also quite pleasant, though it was clear from eyes as hard as stone that she would need to go with him and talk as long as they liked, whether she wanted to or not.

She understood his position completely.

There were probably a lot of really confused and angry people all over the country at the moment. Hell, *she* was confused, and she was certainly as angry as hell.

"Yes," she said in a tone that she wished had sounded stronger. She cleared her throat. "Before I do, though, I want to know where that bastard Colonel is. Did he get away somehow?"

Anderson shook his head. He looked back, toward the first ambulance, and raised his arm, index finger extended. "See for yourself."

Kasey turned her eyes in the direction he was indicating and suddenly realized what the hammering had been. The once-pristine emergency vehicle was now peppered with hundreds of penny-sized holes. Rivulets of water, antifreeze, and motor oil poured from beneath the hood, collecting in communal pools against the curb beside the right front tire, which, just like the left, was completely flat.

She immediately thought of the celebrated death car, the famous Ford V-8, that had been the last ride of Bonnie and Clyde, having seen the Warren Beatty-Faye Dunaway movie a dozen times.

As her eyes moved to the windshield, two men standing on the bullet-riddled front fenders were covering the entire front cab with a large yellow tarp, but just before the passenger compartment disappeared from view, she saw the bloody skull and torso of a man that she knew at once to be one of the captured terrorists, his glassy-eyed stare from the passenger's seat haunting and horrific.

However, it was the sight of Colonel James Merkett, with only half a head remaining, that brought up her stomach before she could do anything more than turn away. The FBI agent on her left had anticipated her reaction and managed to step aside before his shoes were ruined.

Anderson said, "I'm sorry about that, Ms. Riteman, but with all Colonel Merkett put you through, I thought there needed to be no doubt in your mind that he was no longer a threat to you or anyone else."

He took her arm to steady her.

She wiped her mouth with the back of her hand.

Fortunately, she hadn't eaten since Friday morning—more than thirty hours ago—and her moment of involuntary nausea was more sound than substance.

"Was that his name?" she said unsteadily.

"Yes, James Merkett. Come with us now and tell us all you know, then I'll answer every question you have. Deal?"

Kasey nodded. "I'm glad he's dead. He killed my best friend, Alex. He was responsible, anyway. A lot of other really good people, too. He was a scumbag." She allowed him to help her into the back of the ambulance where two attendants were waiting to put ice packs on her wrists and ankles, as well as get her anything else she might need.

The men who'd helped her to the ambulance piled in as well.

Anderson said, "Alexia Summers isn't dead, Ms. Riteman."

Kasey spun back toward him. "You're wrong. I saw her fall, felt the blood from the hole those bastards put in her head. She'd dead alright. I don't know why you—"

He raised a hand to stop her. "She was shot, yes, and she was in pretty bad shape for several days, critical in fact, but she's very much alive. In fact, my guys in Salt Lake City, where she's hospitalized, told me only this morning that she's being quite a pain in the butt. Something about demanding they tell her where her best friend Marie Matthews is or she isn't going to eat a bite until they do."

That sounded just like Alex, Kasey thought. She could be a real pistol at times.

Kasey burst into tears and slumped onto the gurney. "Thank you, Michael. You have no idea what that means to me."

He eased the left door shut but held the right one in his hand. "You're more than welcome Ms. Riteman, I—"

"Kasey," she said with the best smile she could find.

"Okay, Kasey. See you at the hospital shortly."

As he closed the remaining door, Kasey could already see the media gathering at the scene like vultures at a fresh carcass.

She dreaded the weeks to come.

Then, the thought of the Giacano family watching her celebrated image spill across channel after channel, seemed almost too much to bear. They would be coming for her and she had nowhere left to run.

"Oh, God, what have I done now?" she whispered as she lay back on the stretcher.

FIFTY-EIGHT

THE FEW MINUTES OF "casual conversation" with Michael Anderson had turned into two grueling days of nearly non-stop questioning. The only lengthy break had been the few hours she'd spent in surgery Saturday afternoon having the bullet wound to her arm properly repaired. Fortunately, it had only required a bit of serious cleaning inside and out, carefully trimming away the dead skin at the entry and exit holes, and two sets of stitches to close things up properly. The doctor assured her she would regain full use of it within a week or two and the scars would likely be minimal. She didn't care about the scars; they were reminders of how quickly life can end and how lucky she had been yet again. They would also remind her that such dumb luck wouldn't last forever.

Probably not even one more time.

During the lengthy "benign interrogation," Kasey had slept barely six hours in total, though she had managed to eat well and regularly thanks to Special Agent Anderson. To her delight and amazement, she had always been treated with the utmost respect, by every agency she met with, something for which she was more grateful than they could possibly know. She understood how easily it could have gone very differently for her.

When she wasn't answering the FBI's or some other agency's annoyingly repetitive questions, she had been at Blaine's side in ICU. Once, while he slept and she was sure he was stable, she had borrowed Michael Anderson's cell phone and had called her 'powerful' friend for the second time in a week, **Brandie Mueller,** senior political analyst for NBC in New York and weekend host of NBC Nightly News. Brandie was the woman who had told her about Wagner and Corello being killed in D.C., the same old friend who had asked her what hell-hole she had stepped into this time. The two had met when Brandie was still a news anchor at the NBC affiliate in Nashville and had been sought out by Kasey after she'd witnessed the mob assassination of Giacano's mistress, Donna Stanton. The nationally-syndicated story had propelled Mueller to the big time in the Big Apple and her new friend into perpetual hiding.

To say that Brandie had been relieved to hear her old friend still breathing, after seeing her on the network news, repeatedly being referred to as the 'victim' of a nearly-successful terrorist attack, would have been putting it mildly. To say that Brandie had been horrified when she also realized that her friend's Herculean efforts to remain hidden from Chicago mobsters were now all in vain— that she would likely be dead within days if not hours—would have been the understatement of the year.

"What the hell," Kasey had said indifferently after she'd reached Brandie on her private phone. "Ya gotta die sometime."

It had then taken the better part of an hour to convince Brandie that she was only kidding and had no intention of being outside the close company of a battalion of cops and feds until she had formulated a new 'escape plan,' one known only to her. The call ended with Kasey promising to call as soon as she landed in her new state or country.

Or on her new continent.

* * *

The FBI, Homeland Security, the Justice Department, the Army, and even the governors of five separate states had gotten in on the action. It seems no one was pleased with the idea of a small band of U.S. soldiers—regardless of their official military status—trying to start World War III, especially on American soil, and all parties were shocked, angered, and more than a little frightened at how close they had come to succeeding.

There had been no shortage of praise for both Kasey and Blaine, internally anyway, but as far as the public knew—or ever would know—they had nothing to do with anything. They were simply two hapless victims of a would-be terrorist act that had been thwarted by the tireless efforts and nearly limitless resources of the Department of Homeland Security and its many cooperating agencies.

Kasey had not minded the deception and had expressed no objection whatsoever. She knew the altered story was for the good of the country, a country still worth saving today as much as at any time in its history. Besides, the last thing she wanted when this was all over was to be famous again. She'd had a bellyful of fame last go-round. All she wanted was to go back to her beloved river with all of the insanity behind her.

And to see Blaine. She wanted that almost as much as the river.

"Maybe even more," she mouthed in silence, then let the thought evaporate; her heart and mind would reconcile the question one day soon. She knew hers wasn't the only heart in the equation. Maybe, at the end of the day, they would just go their separate ways. Having begun their time together tangled in a massive web of lies, and then sharing the near reality of being reduced to atoms by tons of high explosives, wasn't necessarily the best foundation upon which to build a long-term relationship.

She pushed the troubling images away for now and the river came back into focus in her mind's eye.

With all the publicity surrounding the events in Truman, Utah, she doubted the rafting company would welcome back a worker who had not only lied on her employment application, but who had also been linked to death, destruction, and mayhem across much of the west, to say nothing of being in the middle of a terrorist plot, "hapless victim" or not.

The press had been so consumed by the heroic intervention of Homeland Security and the FBI, and the near-Biblical disaster on the Golden Gate Bridge, that not even Truman's tiny newspaper had been the least bit interested in clearing the name of a woman who, as far as they were concerned, died in Oklahoma three years earlier. There was no Marie Matthews other than the rightful one—the dead one. No one cared about the crazy woman who'd claimed her identity.

The thought of her previous life in Truman having been destroyed, even if it were a life built on lies, troubled Kasey deeply. She still had enough money hidden away in her "safe spots" to live comfortably for years, so a roof over her head was not an issue. What gnawed at her heart and wracked her soul was the thought that she had no life to go back to, no future that didn't include hiding and running again.

No amount of money could correct that.

The Giacano family would be knocking on her proverbial door any day now, and they wouldn't be delivering a basket of fruit. Death was still out there waiting impatiently to claim her, always lurking in the shadows, always just behind the next door she opened. She could never ask Blaine to accept a life on the run, even if he said he wanted to be with her no matter what.

But, that was the real question, wasn't it, she considered, a small knot forming in her throat. *Would he even want to include her in his life?* She was glad she hadn't been afforded much time to dwell on such matters. It would have only made her feel worse than she did already.

The one bright note was that Alex was going to be okay, but even that was dulled somewhat by the thought that she could never see her again. That hurt almost as badly as when she'd believed she was dead, back at the edge of the woods by the clinic. She knew that the Giacano family, by way of their hired assassins, would use any means at their disposal to locate and kill their prey, and like Blaine, she could never—*would* never—put Alex in that kind of jeopardy.

*　*　*

Since its discovery on Thursday afternoon, Marec Vanover's video had been destroyed. Not by men from the Unit, as Merkett had thought before his death, but by those who understood the impact on, and long-term damage to, the average American psyche if the true story ever came to light.

Not even a single clandestine copy remained.

"You can't make a great country stronger by adding to the intense polarity that already tortured her soul," one congressman had said. Both sides knew this and it was to the credit of Democrats and Republicans alike that agreement on the subject had been swift and unanimous. The Unit's actions had not been about party politics, they were the selfish disregarding of the fundamental principles upon which America had been founded, and in which ninety-five percent of American still believed, regardless of political affiliation.

Immediately following its initial viewing, however, heads had begun to roll, beginning with that of Lieutenant General Clayton Longmont, who was taken into custody without warning or ceremony deep within the bowels of the Pentagon. He would not get a trial in the conventional sense of the word. His treasonous actions and egregious misuse of trust and power would be handled "internally," according to the Army.

Kasey hadn't asked what that meant and didn't really want to know. It was enough that his superiors had not condoned his actions and were taking every possible step to correct the damage he'd done.

All of the men from the Unit, in the five ambulances and the escape vehicles that accompanied them, as well as the few men who had remained at the ranch, had been swiftly killed. Death had seemed preferable to surrender in virtually every case.

In truth, it hadn't been an option.

Again, unanimous bipartisan agreement—from the few 'insiders' privy to the whole plot—came instantly and without objection from anyone. This was treason in the most heinous sense of the word and required a 'cure' that didn't include lawyers, courtrooms, and cameras.

The Army quickly determined that Longmont's insidious reach had been limited to the relatively few men he and Merkett had pulled from the 'fringes.' If not hidden away under his protective 'wing' for much of their military careers, the borderline personalities of these men, while perfect for the sociopathic agenda of the Unit, would have gotten them swift discharges from the regular Army.

Only Donald Shelton had been taken alive, found cowering in a corner of the computer room at the ranch, and he began singing like a trained parakeet the moment they placed the handcuffs on his wrists. At one point, early in his questioning, he had tried to buy immunity from prosecution with the promise of millions in personal wealth.

To his dismay, his millions were quickly found and confiscated, taken from him in the same manner by which he'd acquired them in the first place. Kasey hadn't bothered to ask if the money would be going back to its rightful owners. She knew the answer would only piss her off.

By 10:30 Monday evening, all the top brass had gone back to their respective offices and posts across the country. Only a handful of Anderson's best men remained on guard at the hospital, but they were accompanied by a dozen or more burley men from the San Francisco Police Department. It seems there had been no shortage of volunteers to stand watch over the two 'civilians' who'd almost lost their lives defending their beloved city.

Kasey was quite pleased, yet a bit surprised, to learn how many of the people she'd encountered since the bridge still believed in the idea of America as the world's last refuge of truth and safety—men and women ready to lay down their lives to protect what they considered the greatest country on earth.

* * *

After all the questioning had finally wrapped up, Kasey decided to tell Anderson about the contract on her, stating flatly that she was neither wanting nor willing to be put into the Witness Protection Program. The notion of being a notary public in Poughkeepsie for the rest of her life frightened her more than a bullet between the eyes. The senior agent had assured her that he would get right on it; nothing was going to happen to Blaine or her on his watch, not if he had to keep people on both of them 24/7/365.

As he left Monday evening, when only the two of them remained in the cramped room that had been home to her and an endless stream of answer-seekers for much of the last two days, he slipped her the twenty thousand dollars he had found on Merkett, the cash she'd left for Paul Burks. Told her it would be easier to just omit it from the report than to add it to the growing list of items being gathered relevant to the case. He fully understood that as time went on, the paperwork documenting the case in all its 'altered' depth would soon rival the current contents of the Library of Congress. It was her money, after all. His agency didn't need it but he knew she did or soon would.

The thought of Michael's endless protection, while comforting on the one hand, seemed hardly preferable to its alternative. As she would tell Brandie Mueller in her phone call the following day, she would escape their watchful eye at some point and begin yet another surreptitious life somewhere far, far away.

Anderson had sworn to protect Kasey until he could sort everything out and she genuinely believed he meant it as far as such things were within human capability. As long as she remained open to the idea of round-the-clock protection, she'd be safe enough. She and Michael had become friends of sorts, though she knew they wouldn't be exchanging Christmas cards next holiday season. Theirs was a relationship born of exigent circumstances, much as any tragedy welds fellow survivors at the hip—at least momentarily. When life returned to normal, as it always did, the underlying affection and respect might linger, but physical contact would fade as quickly as a photo left in the sun.

* * *

She stepped from the elevator on the ICU floor and walked quietly toward the room where Blaine had been moved Saturday evening following eight-hours of touch-and-go surgery to repair his fractured ribs, punctured lung, and damaged liver. While still a prisoner in the ambulance, though for only fifteen minutes after being shot, he'd lost more than half his total blood volume and had been within minutes of death when Merkett and his men had been stopped on the bridge.

Since then, he'd not regained consciousness, though his vital signs remained stable and continued to improve with each passing hour.

She waved at the nurses as she eased open his door, entering as quietly as a cat. She slipped into the reclining chair beside his bed, the one in which she'd slept both Saturday and Sunday evenings—for a few hours anyway—and fished among the stack of dog-eared magazines for one she hadn't read at least three times.

People, National Geographic, even *Field & Stream* were all ragged from use.

521

She settled on a three-month-old copy of *Cosmopolitan*.

"I like the hair," came a raspy voice to her right. It was barely above a whisper.

Kasey looked up immediately and dropped the magazine. She bolted from the chair, taking Blaine's hand in hers—the one without three intravenous lines originating from it.

"Oh, thank God," she wept, unable to control tears that appeared at once. She kissed the back of his hand. "I'm so sorry, Blaine. Can you ever forgive me?"

Her look was as pitiful as a beaten dog.

Groggy from having been out for more than two days, Blaine tried to blink away his confusion. "Uh, sorry, not really sure what you're talking about."

She put the back of his hand against her forehead, unable to look him in the eye. "I made Merkett shoot you. It's all my fault, I'm totally to blame. I was such an arrogant fool."

The tears increased.

Again, Blaine didn't know what to make of her words. "Slow down, Kasey. I think I need a little refresher course here."

He looked around, completely displaced.

"Let's start with where I am, and how I got here. The last thing I remember, we were both about to be blown to hell."

Kasey had already been warned by the doctors that Blaine would probably have no memory of being shot, perhaps even several minutes prior to that. Severe trauma has a way of protecting the mind from such horrors by blanking it completely, often leaving the victim at a total loss as to what had occurred.

She lowered his hand to the bed, keeping it sandwiched between hers. "That's right. Colonel Merkett, that was his name, James Merkett. Anyway, Merkett had us shackled in the back of the ambulance. You remember that, right?"

He nodded.

"He had us in the dark, then turned on that crazy light that almost blinded us. Remember that?"

He nodded again.

"Then he opened the side doors and I kinda got a little out of hand. I'm sure you remember that."

Blaine shook his head. That part he did not remember. "Define 'kinda got a little out of hand.'"

She shrugged sheepishly, like a kid who'd just been asked if she'd snuck a cookie before dinner. "He was being such an asshole and I simply was tired of it, that's all. May have cussed at him a little too much. Never did like guys like that."

"And..."

"You told me to cool it."

"I take it you didn't."

Kasey shook her head. "Nope. I spit in his face. I think that may have really pissed him off."

"Probably," Blaine agreed, so tired he could barely keep his eyes open. "That's not usually a favorite of crazed killers with inferiority complexes and really big guns. What did he do then?"

"You really don't remember?" she asked. Though she'd been warned this would likely happen, she found it hard to imagine. She sure as hell remembered each time she'd been shot.

"He shot you," Kasey said quickly to get it out before she had time to think about it or try to make it sound better than it was.

"He shot *me!* What the hell'd he shoot me? I didn't spit on him. Why didn't he shoot you instead?"

As Kasey thought about a suitable answer, she saw him smiling coyly at her. It was a weak smile, but his emerald eyes were bright and warm. "I'm glad you spat on the bastard," he said, raising his hand and gently stroking her cheek. "If you hadn't, I sure as hell would have."

She was truly grateful he didn't hate her for what she'd done and leaned across the bed to kiss him on the lips. She didn't kiss him passionately as she would have liked, but softly, like a mother kissing the forehead of a child.

The head ICU nurse entered the room as Kasey was leaning over Blaine and coughed in an exaggerated manner. "Interesting way to awaken the patient." Then to Blaine she said, "And I suppose you're Sleeping Beauty?"

He nodded with as much of a smile as he could muster. "Any chance of getting a big, fat cheeseburger around here? Maybe some fries or onion rings?"

Kasey chuckled but didn't tell him that had been her very meal an hour ago.

Instead of answering him, the nurse pulled a stethoscope from the side pocket of her teal scrubs and placed the microphone against one part of his chest after another. She stood erect, a pleased look on her face.

"Your lung is remarkably clear, Dr. McAllan. I imagine we can start you on clear broth by morning."

Not exactly a cheeseburger and fries. "Swell, I'll hold my breath," he moaned while wrinkling his nose. Despite his attempt at humor, he was fully aware that he was still a long way from being able to eat a Quarter Pounder without going into shock.

After checking a dozen instruments and noting their readings, then changing one of the drip bags hanging from the various stainless steel poles surrounding the bed, the nurse left. As she reached the door, she turned and addressed Kasey. "No sense in me telling you that you have to leave now so the patient can get some badly needed rest, I suppose?"

She shook her head. With her cadre of beefy and devoted bodyguards, the hospital administrator, himself, couldn't get her to leave.

"Don't go," he whispered, his eyes fighting to remain open.

The nurse gave them both a smile and left, pulling the door shut behind her.

"Don't worry, I put you in here, so it's only fair that I be right by your side until you can walk out of this place on your own."

A final smile crossed his lips and then he was gone.

She squeezed his hand but felt it go limp in hers. A quick glance at the monitors assured her that he had only drifted off to sleep. Still, her heart had skipped a beat.

When she saw him begin to snore as softly as a newborn, she sank into the recliner again and retrieved her magazine.

She said a silent prayer of thanks for her petition having been answered.

FIFTY-NINE

TUESDAY MORNING FOUND BLAINE McAllan a new man, though he was still days, perhaps even a week or more away from getting his Big Mac and fries. When Kasey returned from her shower—the ICU nurses had practically adopted her and allowed her to share their quarters as if she were staff—he was sitting up, his complexion almost normal. For days, he'd had the ashen gray hue of someone whose next stop was the undertaker. Now, his tan skin, though not the rich café-au-lait hue of Kasey's, looked healthy and vibrant again.

"Love your hair," he said for the second time as she entered the room.

She hadn't indicated that she'd even heard him when he'd commented yesterday.

Without responding, Kasey came quickly to him and kissed him on the lips, dropping yesterday's clothes on the recliner as she passed. She was wearing new blue jeans that looked like she'd had them forever and a black silk V-neck pullover—courtesy of Joyce Sylvester, one of the ICU nurses. Kasey had given her a bundle of cash as well as her sizes and Joyce had been kind enough to get her everything on her lengthy wish list from Walgreens, Victoria's Secret, and Nordstrom.

When Kasey had ordered her to buy two of everything she picked out, one for each of them, Joyce had initially refused. Kasey could be quite persuasive and ultimately got her way, as she often did when the outcome mattered to her. She wasn't going to let Joyce buy for her without a suitable reward for such kindness, and since she would have worn the same clothes for a month rather than leave Blaine's side for something as insignificant as clean socks, the cost had been cheap enough. The kindly, petite, brunette nurse had been ecstatic and it made Kasey's heart soar to see the delight in her eyes when Joyce returned with the spoils of shopping.

Her trusty hiking boots lay in a corner of Blaine's room, out of sight, temporarily replaced by a very comfortable pair of dressy sandals.

For the first time in ten days, she actually felt like a girl again.

"You look great," she said joyfully. She kissed him again and he kissed her back, this time with more of the passion they both felt.

As she stood beside the bed, his free hand again sandwiched between hers, he pointed at her head with the index finger of his tethered hand. "Tired of being a blonde? Aren't they supposed to have more fun?"

She had colored her hair the day before, during a long break in the questioning, and suddenly remembered that he'd mentioned it last night, but she'd been so grateful to see him awake and alive, that she'd ignored his comment then. "I have enough fun, thank you. Besides, I've been a blonde for so long, I've probably got brain damage from all the bleach." She turned full circle so he could see all of it. "Besides, this is my natural color. Thought it was about time I saw it again."

She knew that when she began her new life on the run, the color would have to change once more, but for now, while under police protection, it felt wonderful to see a familiar image looking back from the mirror.

"A redhead. Not surprised," he said with a twisted smile.

"I know all the redhead jokes, Dr. McAllan. I certainly hope you're referring to my temper." She gave him a stern look, though her eyes betrayed her.

"Well, you do have a rather short fuse."

"Rightfully so," she said defensively.

"And that mouth of yours." He clucked his tongue several times. "It's going to get you into real trouble one of these days."

"Real trouble! Listen, buddy boy, I don't know what you think comprises 'real trouble,' but if what we've just been through doesn't qualify, I better shoot myself right now. I've seen enough trouble to last three lifetimes, and, for your information, my *mouth* had nothing to do with any of it." She gave him a wide grin. "Still, I suppose it wouldn't hurt to clean up my act a little bit."

He indicated for her to come to him and again they kissed passionately, then he whispered as he held her to him, "You don't have to change a single thing on my account. Kasey René Riteman. I think you're perfect just as you are."

For a long moment, they remained in a warm embrace, staring into each other's eyes.

"Well, I see you're feeling much better," Michael Anderson said enthusiastically, entering the room ahead of two men in very expensive tailored suits and holding the door for them.

In the hall, through the full-height glass room divider that allowed ICU to keep a constant eye on Blaine—as well as all patients in Intensive Care—Blaine and Kasey could see a virtual squadron of suited men, all clones of the FBI bodyguards who'd been her shadow for three days. There now had to be more than two dozen armed men within fifty feet of Blaine and her.

It was enough to make one feel really important.

Or very, very paranoid.

Kasey naturally leaned toward the latter.

"Yes, thanks," Blaine said. He didn't recognize Anderson, but knew at once who the other two men were and practically sprang to attention in his bed.

Kasey noted his reaction and both eyebrows shot up at once. She knew something was about to happen.

"Glad to hear it," Anderson said after introducing himself to Blaine. "They just told me you're going to be transferred to a private room in a few hours. Seems you're finally out of danger. Excellent!"

The three men stood respectfully at the foot of the bed.

Anderson then said, "And a very good morning to you, Kasey."

"Thank you, Michael," Kasey said with a smile.

"We have some good news for you, Kasey," Anderson said. He turned slightly toward the man on his left. "I'd like you to meet Cabinet Secretary Martin Chekhov, Director of Homeland Security." As Kasey stared in disbelief, he turned toward the man on his right. "And this is Robert Mullins, my boss and the Director of the FBI."

Both men were in their early sixties, distinguished and fit, their individual and collective demeanors exuding authority and power.

It was enough to make Kasey extremely nervous and send her natural inclination toward paranoia into overdrive. She managed to keep her knees from knocking loud enough to be heard by all.

She had spoken with the FBI and DHS for three days, but to men of Anderson's status—field agents, guys who got things done. These two men were the highest ranking law enforcement officers in the country, perhaps the world. They *were* the FBI and the DHS.

She managed to utter, "Very pleased to meet you gentlemen," and extended her hand. In turn, they both shook it warmly.

With that, Anderson gave a faint nod to one of his men in the doorway and the curtain in Blaine's room was immediately pulled fully across the glass wall. The agent then exited without a word, closing the door behind him. Kasey had no doubt he had strict orders to prevent anyone from entering. She doubted the President could have gained admission without a gun battle in the hallway.

The room was now a makeshift sanctuary for the five of them. *Something is definitely about to happen*, Kasey thought.

Blaine managed to say, "May I ask what's going on, gentlemen?"

Anderson looked at Blaine, then turned fully to Kasey and said, "Thanks to the two of you, but most significantly Ms. Riteman, here,"—he turned back to Blaine, who nodded his complete agreement—"a terrible tragedy has been averted. In fact, you single-handedly prevented a series of atrocities, each the emotional, if not actual and financial equivalent of 9/11. It's safe to say you two saved not merely tens of thousands of lives, and hundreds of billions of dollars that would have had to come from a treasury already ravaged by a decade of war, historic mortgage nightmares, and gasoline prices that literally defy explanation, but perhaps even the country, itself. The very least we could do was try to show our appreciation in some meaningful way."

Kasey felt that she needed to sit, but grabbed the railing of the bed for support instead. Blaine sensed her disquiet and squeezed her hand.

FBI Director Mullins spoke up. "Kasey—may I call you that?" he asked politely, also making direct eye contact with her.

She nodded with a faint smile.

"During your many hours together since Saturday afternoon, you confided to Special Agent Anderson that you had some very bad men back east wishing you harm, and the notoriety currently surrounding the two of you was likely going to put you, perhaps even both of you, in mortal danger. Beyond question, Kasey, your life was going to be in jeopardy. Simply put, we could not permit that, so together with Cabinet Secretary Chekhov, we made the Giacano family an offer they couldn't refuse, if I can be forgiven an old movie cliché."

Kasey now knew she had to sit, regardless of the titles attached to these men. She slumped into her familiar chair beside Blaine's bed.

Secretary Chekhov spoke. "You see, Kasey, it just wouldn't be right for you to have risked everything to help your country—*our* country—and then have her turn her back on you. I'm afraid it's happened too often in recent years," he added apologetically. "We were determined that it was simply not going to happen this time. That would just be wrong."

Kasey nodded that she understood, though she clearly did not.

Chekhov continued. "Bob and I, along with a few 'friends,' met yesterday with all of the key figures of the Giacano crime syndicate and made them an offer. If they forgot you exist, totally and forever, we'd continue to treat them like the commonplace criminals and thugs they are, business as usual. If, however, you got so much as a hangnail before dying of old age, then my department, with the willing and able assistance of the FBI,"—he indicated Mullins and Anderson—"would seize every material asset they own, whether legally acquired or not, and would round up every one of them over the age of eighteen, male and female, for a long and hot stay at Gitmo. No sunscreen, no silk sheets, no fancy lawyers. Just the same rights as any other enemy combatant of this country—*none*."

Blaine asked in a tone he hoped didn't imply a lack of gratitude or disrespect, "But how, sir? The Giacano family had nothing to do with Longmont's insane plan."

Mullins grinned the kind of grin that comes from being able to bend the rules without having to worry about the consequences. "I can assure you that irrefutable evidence would suddenly come to light proving the Giacano family was behind this entire mess, from concept to bankrolling it. Hell, they know we've been itching to jail the whole lot of them for twenty years. The new laws give us virtually unlimited power when it comes to national security. The thought of being treated like Muslim extremists, instead of rich white guys with five-hundred-dollar-an-hour attorneys covering their spoiled asses and Armani suits scared the living shit out of them. They agreed at once and unconditionally. Even made the call to their 'hit squad' while we were sitting there ordering them to stand down and come home immediately." He looked at Kasey.

"You have nothing to worry about from that bunch ever again, I give you my solemn word."

"And you have mine as well, Kasey," Chekhov added, his firm expression not unlike the granite faces on Mount Rushmore.

Anderson smiled at her. "You can live your life as Kasey Riteman again. No more hiding, no more fear."

Chekhov took her hand and shook it again. "As we said earlier, Kasey, it was the very least we could do."

With that, the FBI Director and the Secretary of Homeland Security said their farewells, but not before Kasey had kissed both men on the cheek.

Anderson let them out and returned to the foot of the bed.

It was now his responsibility to let Kasey and Blaine know the rest of the story.

SIXTY

T HE DAYS FOLLOWING THE surprise visit by Mullins and Chekhov passed quickly for Blaine and Kasey. He was transferred to a private room, as promised, and his clear broth had become an indescribable and inedible concoction that lay limply along the food chain somewhere between baby food and oatmeal.

With Blaine's blessing, Kasey had a cot added to his room, to replace her trusty, if uncomfortable recliner from ICU, and had actually managed to sleep five or six hours a night. Always, of course, after he had finally drifted off and was breathing to her complete satisfaction.

On Friday, six days after their rescue from the ambulance, Blaine was doing well enough that Kasey told him she was going to Salt Lake City to see Alex. He'd completely understood, only expressing regret that he couldn't accompany her. She'd promised him that they would all get together soon over a long and private dinner and try to find some meaning within all the insanity. They would have to do it, however, without telling Alex a single truth about what had transpired since the clinic. That was the unequivocal and irreversible agreement they had made in exchange for getting Kasey's life back—no one could ever know any details of Longmont's plan or how close he'd come to achieving it.

Ever.

Anderson had been pleased to pass along their unconditional and unanimous consent to his boss who, in turn, had passed it along to Secretary Chekhov.

The more he thought about it, the more Blaine knew it actually was in the best interests of the country, even more so than the whole truth would have been in this particular case.

Democracy, like life, was always about compromise.

To Kasey's immense pleasure, Alex was due to be released from the hospital by the following weekend if her latest EEG and CAT Scan showed no lingering issues. Fortunately, the bullet that had struck Alex in the back of the head had pierced the skin and fractured the skull, but had not entered her brain. It hit at an oblique angle before exiting above her left ear. Kasey blamed her hard head for the miracle. In a twist of fate, had the damage been less severe, Alex would likely have remained conscious and would no doubt have been shot a second and fatal time when the men reached her body.

Her broken hand, the result of having been crushed by the man who shot her, was still aggravating her whenever she tried to make a fist. The physical therapist had assured Kasey, when she pressed her during a lengthy phone conversation, that it would be fine with a few more weeks of healing followed by intensive physical therapy. That Alex would be able to return to the river, where strong hands were a necessity, pleased Kasey immensely, though it also saddened her that she would never be able to join her. She doubted she would even be allowed on the river as a paying guest at this point.

Of course, she had promised to be at the hospital when Alex was discharged, to drive her to Joan Cameron's home where she'd be staying until her own home was rebuilt. Joan had insisted; she wouldn't have it any other way.

Doug Rozier had been at the hospital, too, as he had been every opportunity since he'd found Alex in the woods north of the clinic. He was the epitome of support for both women, and assured Kasey the entire town of Truman was behind her as well. He'd been given a plausible story about Kasey's subterfuge, as had Alex: Federal Witness Protection. She had been a vital part of the government's case against organized crime, having been an invaluable undercover asset for years, but had done her duty without complaint and was now free to resume a normal life.

He'd asked no questions after that, especially when it had been FBI Director, Robert Mullins, who'd personally made the call.

By Sunday, Kasey was again at Blaine's side in the hospital.

"Hello, stranger," she said, pleased to find him sitting at the small desk in the room. "Still working on your book?"

"Actually finished it while you were gone." They kissed once, then again more intensely.

She set her reliable North Face backpack on the floor beside her regular chair and dropped into it. The flight back to San Francisco had taken only an hour and Michael Anderson had picked her up at the airport, just as he'd dropped her off two days earlier.

"That's wonderful. I guess you found that ending you were looking for."

"Not the ending I'd initially expected, but a pretty hard one to beat. Couldn't have made up a crazier finish if I'd tried."

"How close to the truth did Anderson let you get?" she asked.

"Had him read the final version just before he went to pick you up at the airport. He said I pushed the envelope, as he expected I would, but he'd give it his blessing. At the end of the day, it tells the truth in spirit, doing justice to a great man trying to do the right thing for the country he loved, even if some of the details had to be amended."

She touched his face. "I know how much you hate amending the truth."

He nodded.

"Stick with me, you'll get used to it," she said with an impish wink.

Blaine pushed his chair back and turned fully to face Kasey. She put her legs across his and he rubbed them tenderly as he talked. She loved the way he made her feel.

"What now?" she asked.

"Have to find a publisher. Shouldn't be too hard since this will be the only authorized biography of Skipper Goodman in print. Marguerite has even offered to do the foreword."

"You do run in heady circles, Dr. McAllan. I need to hang with you more."

He chuckled but then decided to change the subject before they got distracted yet again. He'd wanted clarification on several nagging issues for days, but one thing after another had prevented him getting the answers he needed. He gave her one of his studious, professorial expressions and said, "I have some questions about the whole bridge rescue thing. You up for a few more questions on a topic I know you must be sick of by now?"

She leaned back comfortably. "Shoot."

"Bad choice of words," he said, feigning discomfort as he rubbed his chest.

"Oops, my bad. Ask away."

"I've never figured out how we got rescued in the first place. How did the feds know about the Golden Gate Bridge? In the ambulance, you told me Merkett's men destroyed the phone before anyone other than us saw it."

"*Your* phone," she said with that now familiar wink.

Suddenly, he remembered the last moments in the bank, when she had asked him to give her his phone with the dead battery. He frowned as he tried to figure the rest out for himself. "So, then, you got the real phone to the cops? But how?"

"Nope, not the cops. Way better. They're slow and bureaucratic until someone lights a fire under them. Even then, they can be as slow as molasses. There was no way I was going to trust that video to the cops, even after I was pretty sure that none of them were any part of Longmont's unit."

"Okay, not the cops. So who, then? And how?"

"Got a manila envelope from that sweet bank officer who let us into Box-22, the one who thought we'd just lost our dad, brother Blaine." He smiled at the shared memory. "Put the real phone in there and asked him if knew who Marguerite Goodman was. Figured that would be like asking someone in Massachusetts if they had ever heard of the Kennedys. He nodded that he did and I told him that if she didn't personally receive the envelope within the next two minutes, she'd buy the bank and fire his incompetent ass without hesitation. He complied, of course, hurrying out the front door of the bank even before I exited the back. Drove it to her house personally, Michael later told me. All we had to do at that point was serve as decoys."

Blaine was amazed. "But why Marguerite? You hadn't even met her and the only thing I told you about her was that she thought you were a fraud and a liar. Not exactly a shining endorsement."

"That wasn't the only thing you told me about her."

He cocked his head, trying to remember what else he'd said.

Kasey answered the unasked question: "You told me she was the most powerful woman in the state and would have given her last penny to punish the bastards responsible for her husband's murder. I figured no better ally at that precise moment than a woman who'd been wronged. A very powerful and wealthy woman who had been very grievously wronged. Whatever she may have initially thought of me, I knew that damned video would rectify in a heartbeat. I had little doubt, but also few viable options at that moment." She gave a wry smile. "Nothing like combining immense power and righteous indignation when you want something done hard and fast."

Again Blaine gave an expression of awe. Was there no end to this woman's resourcefulness and sheer audacity? "So we watched the video and the strikes were planned for late October or early

November. How did the feds know things were going down last Saturday? That's dumb luck if I ever saw it."

She rocked her head side to side to loosen muscles made stiff by days of sitting. She missed running, rowing, and being in the sun. She missed the river. "Not really. The video shook everyone up like the end of the world was coming. Immediately, they had the NSA, or somebody—I don't remember which agency—train a satellite on the ranch. It was easy to find the right one from the photos Marec Vanover had taken. When they saw four ambulances scurry from the place on Thursday afternoon, they called up everybody with a gun within a thousand miles. Only our ambulance had gotten away before the satellite got a view of the place. Seems it had left the day before, with Merkett onboard."

"Who's Marec Vanover?" Blaine asked, the name unfamiliar.

"He's the guy from the Unit who made the video, the one who started all this," she said.

"Actually," Blaine said sourly, "I think that person is General Clayton Longmont."

"Yeah, that's another thing," she said, sitting up smartly. "You know all this talk we had about the reasons people do things like this?"

"Sure, and just like I told you, these men were driven by blind patriotism, from Longmont on down. Money had nothing to do with it."

She shook her head adamantly. "Turns out Longmont had massive stock options with all of the major defense contractors. Everything totally under the table, of course. Worth hundreds of millions if the war continued for several more years. He was determined to see that it did—and longer—and used a bunch of brainwashed loyalists to help him pull it off."

Blaine sat dumfounded. It *was* all about the money, just like she said it would be. He apologized for having been wrong.

She took his hand and said sweetly, "You weren't wrong, Blaine. In the end, money may have been at the root of it all, but none of this would have been possible without blind, unquestioning loyalty by his men. We were both right."

"And it's a damned good thing for everyone," Marguerite Goodman said as she entered the room like a whirlwind. Kasey had left the door ajar when she'd arrived, though little things like doors never affected the powerhouse from Santa Barbara.

Kasey dropped her feet to the floor and stood. Blaine rose as well, though more slowly, but the older woman waved them both back into their chairs as soon as they did. The two large men behind her each carried more roses than either he or Kasey had seen in their lives outside a florist's shop. There must have been five dozen mixed-color, long-stem roses in each pair of massive arms. Every bud was the size of an orange.

"Over there, boys," Marguerite directed with a nonchalant wave of her hands, indicating the small table.

She smiled at Kasey. "Hello, young lady. I trust you're well."

"Yes, thank you."

The men set the Waterford crystal vases on a bedside table and the small dresser along the footboard wall and departed. The vases alone were worth hundreds. "You can never have too many roses when you're convalescing," Marguerite said, taking a seat on the corner of the bed closest to them. "How are you feeling, Blaine?"

He shook her outstretched hand. "Much better, thank you. I'm due to get out of here in a few days." His face showed his delight at the thought.

"So I hear. I've been checking on you every day."

"Really?" He was both amazed and pleased. This was a very busy woman, all the more so in recent days.

"Absolutely." She grew quite serious. "Blaine, do you have any idea how important you are to the entire Goodman family, but no one more than I?"

He shook his head.

"Well, you are. You've provided us a successful and satisfying resolution to Skipper's life, *and* his death, when nothing but closure could have helped begin the healing process. I will forever be grateful for the sacrifices you made to help that become a reality." She touched his arm with sincere affection, her eyes rimmed with tears.

All Blaine could do was put his hand on hers and say humbly, "It was my pleasure, Marguerite. I'm so glad I was able to help."

She took a tissue from her handbag and daubed her eyes, then said, "Here's a bit of news you will appreciate, I think." She had his undivided attention. "I called a few close friends in New York and got a little bidding war going over your book on Skipper. As of half an hour ago, your advance was up to six million if I remember the last call correctly." She seemed quite pleased with herself.

"Dollars!" Blaine practically shouted. He was on his feet again, and again she waved her hand to put him back in his seat.

She touched her chin for effect. "I don't think we were talking Rupees, but I could be wrong. If so, that's only about forty dollars, isn't it?" She gave him a devilish grin.

Blaine had fully expected to sell his book, considering the subject matter and the timing of its delivery, but the thought of an advance larger than fifty or a hundred thousand had never crossed his mind. Even his wildest dreams of total revenue from all sales and rights hadn't been a third of the number Marguerite had just thrown at him.

"I don't know what to say."

She gave him her warmest smile. "I'm assured it will be a Number-One New York Times bestseller for months, so the initial six is simply the start. Just see to it that I get the very first signed copy. That's all the thanks I want."

She then turned her attention to Kasey. They had met briefly Saturday evening, the day Blaine had been shot, when she'd come to the hospital to check on him, but because of the intense security surrounding everyone, had not been able to find the opportunity to speak privately.

"I cannot even begin to imagine what you've been through these last few weeks. How have you kept your sanity?"

Kasey smiled. "There are many who'd say I haven't, or that I didn't start out with all of it in the first place."

"Well, they're the crazy ones." She took Kasey's hand. "What can I do for you after all you've done for us?"

Kasey didn't know how to answer the question. The woman was a multi-billionaire. She could buy Kasey her own state. She considered the question with a puzzled expression, as one might ponder the theory of relativity or the infinity of space.

She could only shrug her shoulders and look helplessly at Blaine.

"Oh, come now, Kasey, this is an easy question. Surely there is something you want. Just name it and it's yours. The sky's the limit. I know money can't begin to repay you for your incredible heroism, and I'm not trying to diminish the importance of your sacrifice in any way. In time, I'm sure we'll come to know each other well enough for me to do much better, but for now, just tell me the one thing that would make your life perfect today and it's yours."

Blaine fully realized that the woman he'd had the privilege of knowing for nearly a decade wasn't kidding, but he also realized Kasey had no understanding at all of how to answer.

"Could you help get her old job back?" he asked.

Marguerite turned to him as did Kasey.

"Blaine!" Kasey said with a scowl of disapproval.

He held up a hand and pressed on. "She recently found out that she'd lost her job on the river. Her rafting company didn't take kindly to her being associated with the arson and deaths in Truman, despite a personal call from the FBI director Mullins exonerating her completely, even calling her a hero. They're a couple of old geezers who can't put the last few weeks behind them, and who apparently aren't the least bit interested in what's true or fair."

"They're actually really good people," Kasey said, defending her former employer and his wife. "Maybe a little old fashioned and narrow-minded, I suppose, but I can't blame them for what they did. Image is everything in that business."

"Well, I can sure as hell blame them," he said indignantly. "You didn't do anything but save half the known world, and we can't even tell them about it." He knew Marguerite was privy to everything that had happened, in regard to Longmont and his Unit, but she was not aware of their private 'deal' with Director Mullins or Secretary Chekhov. He curbed his tongue lest he become part of a federal highway or parking lot in D.C.

"Let me see what I can do to rectify the situation," Marguerite said as she stood. "I can be quite persuasive when push comes to shove. Besides, solutions can take on a myriad of forms. I'll be back with you in a few days."

With that, she bid them both farewell for the present, but not before commanding them to join her at the mansion for dinner the night Blaine was released from the hospital.

They agreed at once, thanked her for the flowers and her work on behalf of Blaine's book, and watched in wonder as she left.

"She's quite serious, you know," Blaine said when he was quite certain Marguerite could no longer hear his words. "You can have anything you want. Just ask for it and it's yours."

Kasey gave him a mischievous look. "Is she the only one who can grant me such a wish?"

Blaine saw something wonderfully impish in her eyes and it made him wish like hell he'd not been shot, or at the very least, was well enough to act on the feelings that were wreaking havoc with his mind and his body.

She leaned across and put her lips gently against his ear, then whispered her wish slowly, her soft breath caressing his skin like a warm summer breeze.

SIXTY-ONE

Saturday, 16 August—The Green River, Utah

THE NEARLY FLUORESCENT-ORANGE rafts bobbed and jostled in the caramel water like thoroughbreds in a paddock. Just as the anxious adventurers they would soon carry, they appeared impatient to begin the journey.

The small eddy where the boats were tied together, as well as to mooring boulders along the shore, sat at the base of an eight-hundred-foot mesa. Two hours earlier, with the guidance of a couple of boatmen—one guiding the group and one following—they had all made their way slowly and carefully down the narrow trail from the mesa's zenith to the river. Eight small planes, Cessna 182s and Piper Warriors, had flown all twenty-two guests the eighty miles from Grand Junction, Colorado, to the makeshift landing strip at the mesa's summit, formerly used by petrol-chemical companies when exploring the region for oil trapped for countless millennia in the loosely-packed shale.

Now, no longer in use by people seeking oil, it was a favorite launching point for river excursions through Utah's majestic Desolation Canyon.

For many, the breathtaking and frightening landing on the mesa top—about the size of a football field excluding both end zones—would be an indelible memory that would last a lifetime in and of itself. But it was far more than that for it had signaled the beginning of a seven-day voyage of discovery, both external and internal. A week filled with astonishing memories from the sublime to the intense, each creating a permanent place in the scrapbooks of their minds.

With a hand to her forehead to block the early morning sun, Kasey stared at the azure sky and felt the hot canyon breath against her skin. To her right, the river—*her* river—was calling to her as it had done for more than three years.

She was home.

Dressed in cutoff jeans and a yellow bikini top—though she'd lose the denim shorts by midday as the Utah sun raised the canyon temperature to three digits—she hurried the guests and other boatmen along.

"We're burning daylight, people," she called out pleasantly but with authority. "We need to be at our first campsite well before dusk or we'll all be eating dry bologna sandwiches in the dark."

It wasn't true, of course. Everyone would be fed three meals a day equal to the cuisine served on the finest sea cruise. But food, or rather the lack of food, was a benign threat that always did the trick. At the end of a hard day on the river, these "city slickers" would be as hungry as Olympic athletes and no one wanted to miss a meal if it could be avoided in any way.

At once, people who hadn't moved so quickly in years began to scurry toward their previously-indicated rendezvous points. Five boats to a tour; four or five guests per boat plus one boatman or boatwoman. Within three minutes, all were in life jackets and ready to board.

When the routine and mandatory safety lecture had been delivered by Alex Summers–now fully recovered from her encounter with the would-be assassin's bullet in early June–Kasey ordered everyone into the boats. The joyous glee from a throng of eager rafters sprang up in nearly perfect harmony, as it had on every trip she'd undertaken since her freshman voyage thirty-nine months before. It was a sound as close to her heart as a child's laughter is to its mother.

Alex stood at the bow of Boat-2 as Kasey approached, oars in hand. "Ready when you are, Skipper. You lead, I'll follow, just like always." She stopped beside her best friend at the edge of the mighty river, not only grateful to be alive, but also for the friendship she and Alex shared. All secrets had been revealed, all wounds, both emotional and physical, were healing nicely.

They were truly sisters.

"Not this time, Alex."

This earned Kasey a puzzling stare.

"This trip, you lead and I'll follow." She put her hands on Alex's shoulders and caressed them affectionately.

"You sure?" Alex said, excited but also apprehensive. She'd always followed Kasey, but she'd silently dreamed of leading a tour for more than two years.

"Oh, yeah, completely sure. You're more than ready, girl. Now, take *your* expedition downriver and let's have some fun."

Alex could not have grinned any wider, her rich, brown tan and long ebony hair a perfect backdrop to the expanse of pearly-white teeth that showed her unbridled excitement. "Try to keep up," she teased as she hurried to the first boat in line.

"Hey, buddy," Kasey called out to the lone straggler on the beach. "Move it or we're leaving you behind."

The man, dressed only in khaki cargo shorts and green and orange rubber Crocs, grabbed the last of his carefully-packed and waterproofed possessions and ran to her side.

"Easy, captain, this is my first trip, remember. Just because you own the business now, doesn't mean you have to let the power go to your head."

Kasey pulled Blaine to her, in front of the entire party, and kissed him like she hadn't seen him in a month. Whooping and whistling immediately erupted from all five rafts, accompanied by every imaginable joke about newlyweds and honeymoons—those that could be told with kids around, anyway.

Kasey raised her left hand and touched the end of his nose with the shiny gold band on her fourth finger. "Co-owner, Dr. McAllan, and since one of us has to be in charge, it might as well be the woman, right."

He gave her no argument, only a grin that was the bookend to Alex's.

"Now get your butt into your boat," Kasey ordered, "or you're in big trouble tonight."

She kissed him again before letting him go, to everyone's delight.

"Yes, ma'am. Anything you say." He gave a snappy salute before adding an exaggerated wink.

Terry Leigh and his wife, Shirley—in Boat-2—both gave Blaine "high-fives" as he stepped past them to take his designated place. Michael Anderson, his wife, and both children waved excitedly from Alex's boat, as did Doug Rozier. Since the hospital, he and Alex had been seeing each other regularly and it seemed apparent to all that there might be another wedding in the not too distant future. Kasey hoped so. She'd gotten to know Doug over the summer and considered him a really good guy, just the kind of man she would have picked for her best friend—had she been asked. As it stood, fate appeared to be playing a better matchmaker than she could have ever hoped to be.

The other three boats, piloted by longtime friends Mike, Brian, and Carolyn, now all enthusiastic employees of *her* rafting company, contained strangers at present, but by trip's end, each would be part of the extended "river family" they all enjoyed.

As she scanned the five rafts, with guests and boatmen busily chatting amongst themselves in anticipation of the days to come, Kasey reflected briefly on the past three months and realized with immense satisfaction that she'd been wrong about one thing: not all friendships faded away when the trauma of certain death no longer hung over your head like an executioner's axe. Some friends remained true friends. Some relationships lasted.

Everything was perfect, Kasey decided as she drew in a deep chest full of the warm summer air. She would ask nothing more from life than this river and this handful of immensely valuable friends. For the first time in her life she was confident that tomorrow—whatever its challenges—would take care of itself. The journey had been hard at times, to be sure, but the rewards that filled every one of her todays made all the pain and loss a bit more tolerable.

Both she and Alex would always miss her dad, and sweet old Will Cameron, but even those acute wounds had begun to heal.

Only time could do the rest, but after a lifetime of running, time finally appeared to be on her side.

Kasey joined Blaine in Boat-2 and took her seat on the center platform, oars in hand. She gave a warm nod to each of her friends in turn, then brought tear-rimmed eyes squarely in line with her husband's handsome face. His emerald gaze was alight with anticipation, and not just for the river that lay ahead.

"Prepare yourself for the ride of your lifetime," she said with a wink, and a smile that seemed to light up the entire canyon.

www.ingramcontent.com/pod-product-compliance
Lightning Source LLC
Chambersburg PA
CBHW051930020726
47501CB00001B/54